INFERENCE OF GUILT

by

Harris Greene

ROBERT HALE · LONDON

To Charlotte

GLOSSARY OF TERMS USED IN THIS BOOK

Bigot List: Term, of British intelligence origins, referring to a list of persons cleared for a specific activity or operation.

Box: Polygraph machine, or lie detector. This word is used by U.S. security people as a noun and as a verb, e.g., "to box" someone.

CI: Counter-intelligence; in effect, defensive intelligence gathered to protect one's own intelligence activities or government from hostile penetration or activity.

COS: Chief of Station, the commander of a CIA station abroad.

Cryptonym: In intelligence circles, a single random word assigned to protect the true identity of a specific clandestine source, agent, or operation. It is often preceded by a digraph, e.g., TTVELVET, SX-FORTUNE.

CT: Career Trainee, an Agency staff employee who undergoes lengthy training in clandestine tradecraft and operations prior to an initial assignment as a clandestine-service officer of the CIA.

Cut-out: An operational intermediary between two or more persons for whom direct contact is inadvisable.

DCI / DDCI: Respectively, the Director of Central Intelligence and his subordinate, the Deputy Director of Central Intelligence.

DDO: Deputy Director for Operations, one of the four top CIA officials; head of the Directorate for Operations.

DIA: Defense Intelligence Agency, the intelligence arm of the Department of Defense.

DS&T:	Directorate of Science and Technology, one of the four principal components of the CIA.
GRU:	The Soviet military intelligence service.
IG:	Inspector General.
INS:	Immigration and Naturalization Service of the U. S. Government.
KGB:	The Soviet security service, including espionage and counter-espionage inside and outside the USSR.
LP:	Listening Post, either a mobile or a fixed site from which clandestine electronic surveillances are monitored. LPs are usually located close to the target site.
MfS:	*Ministerium für Sicherheit*, the East German ministry engaged in espionage and counter-intelligence activity.
NFAC:	National Foreign Assessment Center, one of the four principal components of the CIA, primarily performing collation, analysis, and assessment of information and producing finished intelligence studies, estimates, and briefings for the President and other officials of the U. S. Government cleared to receive and read such material.
NSA:	National Security Agency, handling cryptographic intelligence for the U. S. Government.
OB:	Order of Battle.
OMB:	Office of Management and Budget, an agency under the direct aegis of the President.
OTS:	Office of Technical Services, a CIA component and part of the DS&T (see above). It handles technical support of all CIA operations.
PNG:	Persona non grata, an act by a government to get rid of a foreign diplomat by demanding his withdrawal.
Principal Agent:	A senior agent, usually non-American, with supervisory authority over other agents. Principal agents are *not* CIA staff officers and are usually directed by such staffers.

Pseudonym:	A fictitious name. In intelligence usage, pseudonyms, unlike cryptonyms, are full false names assigned for use in classified communications to protect true-name identification (e.g., an intelligence officer whose real name is John B. Simpson might be assigned by the CIA the pseudonym of Roscoe L. Polykarp for his entire Agency career, unless the pseudonym were somehow compromised at some point, in which case another pseudonym would be assigned).
Red Line:	CIA internal telephone circuit considered secure enough for discussion of most classified information. (There are other even more secure circuits in use.)
RIF:	Reduction in Force, one of the dread phrases in government bureaucracy. It refers to mass dismissals of government employees in a specific component or agency.
R&R:	Rest and Recuperation, usually an annual vacation, out of country, given to U.S. official personnel serving at hardship posts.
Safe House:	A carefully chosen room, apartment, or other enclosed area used to meet clandestine agents or sensitive collaborators, or to conduct clandestine business.
SAC:	Special Agent in Charge, the supervisor of an FBI field office.
SHAEF:	Supreme Headquarters, Allied Expeditionary Forces; wartime and postwar command. Located in France after World War II.
Spitzl:	A German police and intelligence slang word referring to an informer or informant.
SSCI:	U. S. Senate Select Committee for Intelligence.
SSU:	Strategic Services Unit, an interim organization between the termination of the OSS (1946) and the creation of the CIA (1948).
USFA:	United States Forces in Austria; an American military command that existed from 1945–55; its headquarters were located in Vienna.

INFERENCE OF GUILT

PROLOGUE

Radescu stood on the grimy railroad station platform, sniffing the late-morning air like a prairie dog standing atop its burrow. Something indefinable was wrong; he had learned to sense the presence of danger as surely as if it were a putrid odor hanging in the chill spring sunshine. Such a survival sense he had quickly acquired within days of his arrival at Mauthausen concentration camp four years—an eternity—ago. Unless you smelled danger and took steps to evade it, you wound up as another puff of smoke from the camp incinerator. And he smelled it now.

The slow-moving commuter train, a *Bummelzug* that seemed to stop every three kilometers, rolled out of the station toward Melk, its frantically chuffing engine belching black clouds of smoke into the still air. Around him scurried those passengers who had gotten off the train with him, most of them with rucksacks or cheap suitcases laden with food and drink, the imperatives of postwar life here in Sankt Pölten, now a garrison town in the Soviet Zone of Austria.

Radescu swiveled his head slowly from left to right, taking in everything: the self-important red-capped train dispatcher, his round white signal disk tucked under one arm, a pair of animated Red Army lieutenants, squat and stumpy in their military great-coats, a plump young peasant woman fearfully eyeing them as she clutched an infant to her bosom.

Everything had gone smoothly so far. He had sat silently in the chilly, jam-packed third-class compartment all the way from Vienna, the hard wooden seat numbing his bottom, wedged between two robust farm women returning from early-morning market in the capital. The Soviet military police sergeant who accompanied the Austrian conductor on his rounds had barely glanced at his stiff-backed identity card, its photo and impressive stamps identifying him as Michael Pokorny, carpenter, Austrian citizen, from Vienna, 13th Bezirk. This phony pass, one of twenty, had been bought by one of his displaced-person contacts from a corrupt *Meldeamt* clerk for six packs of American cigarettes and had been filled in by one of Browning's technical services lads.

The platform quickly cleared of people, and Radescu by instinct stepped into the shadow of the scarred stone station building. If "Anton" himself did not appear, someone would who must give the all-clear signal. He glanced at the station clock. He was three minutes early. With a shrug, he lowered his scuffed valise to the pavement, pulled his wide-brimmed felt hat closer over his forehead, and waited.

Once, during the long, uncomfortable ride on the train this morning, a sunken-faced old man sitting opposite him had been wakened from a doze by one of those bone-rattling station halts of the *Bummelzug* and had opened watery blue eyes with irritation. One frail old hand had briefly pointed out the dirty window at a senior Soviet officer with brightly shined boots and well-cut winter uniform climbing aboard a Soviet-requisitioned wagon-lit car opposite them.

"You see what happens when you lose a war?" he exclaimed in a piping voice with its Viennese accent. "*We* ride like swine"— and with another jab at the window—"and the *swine* ride like humans."

Three of the others in the compartment had fiercely admonished him, told him to shut up or he'd get them all sent to Siberia if he was overheard. They were all well aware that Soviet retribution in this, their occupation zone, was swift, summary and usually savage.

Yes, it was hard to lose a war, Radescu thought, as his eyes traversed the station platform, but he had resisted shouting at the entire compartment, "Austrian swine, you're only getting a little bit of what you deserve." The discipline of survival had stilled his tongue. He had survived Mauthausen. He had survived many missions for Browning. He would not now risk survival by telling these dispirited Austrians just what he really thought of them.

A short precise man, hatless, in a short leather coat which

gleamed as if it had been polished, paused on the opposite platform and tugged at dark leather gloves. Aha, there he is; "Anton"
himself. As Radescu's eyes caught his, he deliberately reached
into a pocket, came out with a white handkerchief, and blew his
nose vigorously: the all-clear signal. Had he not produced the
handkerchief, Radescu would not have budged from his shadowy
corner and would have taken the next train out of Sankt Pölten
station, whether east- or west-bound.

"Anton" sauntered slowly toward descending stairs which led to
a tunnel underneath the tracks into the station itself. After half a
minute, Radescu picked up his valise (which contained a volume
of Goethe, a half loaf of pumpernickel, a piece of local cheese,
and a small bottle of new raw Riesling) and made his way into
the stone-floored waiting room.

By now these clandestine meetings had become routine, but
this time there was a difference. On each previous occasion his
Fingerspitzengefühl, his seat-of-the-pants instinct, had told him
with growing intensity that something was not right. Today, *everything* in him cried out: it's wrong, it's bad, you should not
make the meeting: tell them in Vienna that you spotted hostile
surveillance and departed posthaste.

He had already made his fears known to all of them in Vienna:
to Browning, Silas, and even Mara. But Browning had reassured
him, had held him by both shoulders and looked straight into his
eyes.

"Mike," he had said gently but with a tone of command, "we
need the info, we really need it right away."

He stepped into the darkness of the waiting room. The contact point had already been described to him: the men's public toilet in Sankt Pölten station. He followed a white arrow on
the wall beneath the painted word *Toiletten,* and at the end of a
short corridor pushed his way into the room. An acrid smell of lye
and urine smote his nostrils and he peered around him for a moment to make certain that this was the right place.

No question about it. "Anton," clad in his elegantly gleaming
leather coat, was standing alone at a line of urinals, relieving himself. As Radescu entered, he turned his head, pointed to the
closed doors of the pay toilets, and mouthed the word in German,
"*Niemand,*" that no one occupied any of them.

Radescu placed his valise by the door and quickly walked up to a urinal adjacent to that of the other, who, in a single movement of his hand, reached into an inner pocket and produced an unsealed envelope which he extended without saying a word. Radescu seized it, opened the flap, withdrew four sheets of closely typed paper, briefly glanced at them, tucked them back into the envelope, which he then buried in an inner pocket. With the same gesture, he handed another envelope to the trim, clean-shaven man standing beside him. "Anton" pushed the envelope into his overcoat pocket.

"Don't you want to count it, Herr Anton?" Radescu asked him in a barely audible German.

"No," the other replied in a disdainful tone. "I know it's all there. If it isn't all there, there won't be anything to give you next time."

"And when will 'next time' be?"

"Same time, two P.M., same date a month from now, at Site Dora."

That would be the Vienna Woods meeting place.

"Good. I'm taking the two forty-two back to Vienna. Any problems?"

The other carefully buttoned his fly and turned to face him in the near-gloom of the room with an expression of displeasure.

"And why should there be any problems? Hasn't everything worked perfectly to date?"

"Yes, but . . ."

". . . But, nothing," the other said irritably. "That's the trouble with sending *Spitzls*. Why doesn't Browning come himself?"

Radescu said nothing for a moment. He stood facing the erect scar-faced man with a grimace of distaste.

"Shall I relay your complaint to Captain Browning?" he asked, now speaking in Romanian. "That he sends Romanian *Spitzls* instead of real Americans?"

"No need," answered the other after a long moment. "You'll find everything in that envelope I gave you, including a receipt in my code name for the ten thousand dollars."

Radescu said, in a slow deliberate voice, "You are very nervous about something. Have you noticed something wrong? You gave me an all-clear signal out there on the platform. Was there some reason . . . ?"

"No reason! No nervousness!" the other barked. He abruptly looked around him. "I'm leaving here first. Give me a good two minutes and then you leave. And when you go out this door, turn right. If you turn left you will find yourself at the main entrance to the *Bahnhof*; there are police and NKVD agents all over the place. Understood?"

"Understood."

Radescu stepped back one pace, and a bitter smile flitted across his face.

"You will excuse me, Herr Anton, if I don't salute. I know that under your real name, salutes were expected. And one more thing. Next time, I will not be your contact. Look for a man with a black briefcase and a walking stick. You know the recognition greeting. Approach him first."

The other stared at him thoughtfully for a moment. Radescu nodded.

"That's right. My presence is clearly not pleasing for you, and I have asked Captain Browning to ask another, more sympathetic soul to make the contact. As for the money"—and his lips turned up briefly at the corners—"the smell of it will be the same."

"Go to hell, you Jewish bastard," the other said, buttoning his leather coat, his tight features compressed. He turned on his heel and in two strides reached the door, flung it open, and was gone.

Radescu did not wait the requested two minutes. He counted to five, opened the door carefully, and turned left, not right. At the end of the short corridor, he pattered down a flight of stairs which led, as Anton had told him, to the main entrance of the Sankt Pölten station. Accelerating his pace, he strode past the ticket windows to the open door. All around him Soviet officers and soldiers, in their heavy-booted military uniforms and armed with holstered pistols, waited in clusters, puffing their *papirossi* with thumb and forefinger.

He marched onto the broad sidewalk where once taxicabs had waited for passengers and which now accommodated a wretched handful of requisitioned sedans and dusty Soviet trucks, and stopped in his tracks. Not twenty feet away stood his recent companion, back to him, in animated conversation with a bulky Soviet officer whose major's stars glittered on his epaulets. His blue-rimmed hat revealed to Radescu immediately who he was: NKVD.

Radescu whirled and, almost at a run, hastened to re-enter the station's confines. But a shout behind him told him that he had been detected. He broke into a sprint, but from both sides he was grabbed by grim-faced men in both civilian and military clothing. Anton and his Soviet military companion ran up to him as he panted in pain, his arms brutally pinioned behind him. All around him the Red Army soldiers in the waiting area had stopped all conversation, and some of them began to edge warily toward the nearest exit. This was an incident best not to witness.

"You Jewish swine!" snarled Anton in German, reaching for his overcoat lapels. "I told you not to leave the station! Now you know more than you ever should. And it will cost you dearly!"

Radescu answered, wincing with the pain of his arms twisted behind him.

"I knew all along that you were wrong. What else could you be with your background? Well, Commander Calinescu, alias Anton, if my little game is finished, so is yours."

The Soviet major, a great tree trunk of a man, barked to his captors, "Stop twisting his arm. He can't escape."

As swift hands groped for the contents of his pocket and patted his body for a weapon, the major said to him in a halting and ominous Slavic German, "You made a big mistake, Herr Radescu, in leaving the *Bahnhof*. A big mistake. Maybe the biggest one of your life."

"Bigger than this one, Herr Major?" Radescu asked, holding out his left arm, where six blue tattooed numbers defaced the pale, stretched skin. "These are my Mauthausen numbers. You will now tattoo six new numbers on the other arm?"

"You fool," Calinescu growled in Romanian. "There'll be no Mauthausens for you this time. We will do what Mauthausen didn't do."

The Soviet major, peering curiously down at the numbers on Radescu's arm, said in Russian, "Take him away. He's an American spy."

CHAPTER ONE

The Capitol policeman, standing with folded arms and an air of alert boredom, glanced at the identity badges of the two men, checked off their names on a clipboard, and opened the door to the congressional committee room just wide enough to let them slip through, one after the other. Powerful camera lights harshly illuminated the cavernous hall, filled with absorbed spectators and a platoon of the working press. The amplification of a caustic New York drawl, pitched low enough to have come from the throat of a man, boomed from the mouth of a woman sitting in the curved center of the inquisitorial dais. Two television cameras mounted on wooden platforms pointed at the speaker from opposite sides of the room.

"Jenny strikes again," the lean grizzled man muttered to his bulky companion. "You had it dead right the minute we got the notice to appear. She's made a bloody media event out of it."

A ferret of a woman scurried up to them, bent low as if to avoid whizzing bullets.

"Mr. Wendell of the CIA?" she whispered with a tense, worried urgency. "I'm Donna Rukeyser, clerk of the subcommittee."

Wendell nodded. "This is Marcus Adams, from our Legislative Liaison office."

He was certain she did not hear a word he had said and had caught only his nod.

"You're late," the ferret whispered reproachfully. "Congresswoman Pfitzner called your name to testify ten minutes ago, but you weren't here, so the committee called Mr. Lederer of Immigration and Naturalization. He's finishing his testimony now.

Will you follow me to your seats, over there just behind the witness, please."

Involuntarily, the two men emulated her infantryman crouch and moved in swift hunched steps to the empty chairs. The air was still filled with the voice of Congresswoman Pfitzner, who leaned into the microphone before her as if preparing to bite it if it did not amplify her words faithfully.

"Well, Mr. Lederer, for years I've been talking to you and your bosses at the Justice Department, and to all the other agencies in town, and with damned poor results, I can tell you that. In fact, I've been banging away on this topic since I came to Washington nine years ago. It's like knocking your head against a steel door. I'm talking about war criminals, Mr. Lederer, hundreds of them who have been living right here in the United States of America, in peace and prosperity, for years and years, despite the blood on their hands. And your agency hasn't lifted a finger to find them, arrest them, throw them out. How many war criminals have been deported? Just one, a German woman concentration camp guard. Only one in thirty-five years!" (Loud thump of hand near microphone.) "And that, Mr. Lederer, is a disgrace! A national scandal!" (Second bang of open hand on tabletop.)

She appeared more an avenging angel, Wendell thought, than the chairman of a House subcommittee. Her straight almost patrician nose sniffed the air for dangerous portents and scoundrels. She glowered at the witness over her reading glasses, an expression familiar to millions of television viewers, as was the accusing forefinger now aimed at the witness. Jenny Pfitzner put on quite a show.

But her witness, a feisty senior official of the Immigration and Naturalization Service, was not about to roll over and play dead. He pointed a long firm-fleshed finger like a pistol barrel, straight back at her.

"Now, hold on a second, Madam Chairman!" His voice cut like a saw, his quick blue eyes blazed in undisguised anger. "I can't remember how many times in the past four years or so you've beaten this same drum. Time and again, you make these extremely serious charges that imply that Immigration and the other agencies of the executive branch are somehow conspiring to cover up things or that we sit around on our hands, watching war criminals in this country thumbing their noses at us. But when it comes to details, the charges against these individuals can't be sustained."

He blinked his eyes against the intense camera lights, careful to keep his hands as steady as possible, and looked up at her a dozen feet away, ignoring the other two congressmen who sat, hands propping up their chins, flanking her on the dais.

"The charge of 'war criminal,' Mrs. Pfitzner, is an extremely serious one." Lederer slowed the speed of his words and deepened his voice to a magisterial bass. "You just can't come out, as you have, with sketchy information based on some second- or third-hand story, and ask us to arrest a citizen or a resident alien of this country and deport him back to his native country as a war criminal." Lederer paused and carefully reached for a glass of water. He sipped a mouthful, knowing that the delaying gesture irritated Jenny Pfitzner.

"The term 'war criminal,' " he went on, choosing his words carefully, "in this instance may not even be correct. Mr. Callin is accused of certain undefined acts against Romanian Jews in a situation of civil strife and turmoil. It is my understanding, Madam Chairman, that what was happening in Romania early in 1941, the time of these alleged acts, was internal agitation by extremist groups aimed at toppling the then-government of Romania headed by a General Antonescu. In this strife, Romanian Jews were tragically killed and injured; how many, we don't know, but the estimate is thousands. These outrages, however, were quickly stopped by the Romanian Army and large numbers of those murderers were, in fact, later tried and punished by the government. In some cases, the ringleaders were sentenced to life imprisonment."

Marcus Adams whispered in Wendell's ear, admiringly, "My God, Pat Lederer is giving a poli-sci course on contemporary Romanian history."

Jenny Pfitzner wriggled impatiently in her chair.

"Mr. Lederer, much as I appreciate hearing again what we already know, what's your point?"

"My point, Madam Chairman," Lederer resumed, "is simply that 'war criminals' are those whose outrages were performed in

wartime and who went unpunished. This was not the case in
Romania in the period we are discussing. . . ."

". . . All right, Mr. Lederer," Jenny's voice rose above his.
"Let's not split hairs. Let's call it 'mass murder,' OK? And let me
ask you: if someone like Mr. Callin, alias Calinescu, is proven to
have committed mass murder with his bare hands as a senior
officer of the fascist Iron Guard, and if he has lied on his application forms on these matters when he entered the United States in
1948, would that be cause for taking action against him?"

"Indeed that would, Madam Chairman," Lederer boomed back
at her, eyes hard under bushy brows. "But I repeat: our files do
not contain any substantial proof, and I want to underline three
or four times the words 'substantial proof,' that Callin or Calinescu committed these crimes or lied to the U. S. Government. To
the contrary: our files show that he was of considerable service to
our U.S. military intelligence people in Austria after the end of
World War II. We have affidavits to that effect on file. Further,
this man has become a classic American success story. Through
hard work, imagination, and an eye to the future, he is now the
owner of a number of highly successful commercial enterprises in
California and the Southwest. He has become a frequent contrib-
utor to charitable causes, to academic institutions, and to good
works in general. I am told he is indeed a pillar of his community
in California. Allegations against him for the terrible crimes you
say he committed in 1940 and 1941 must be proven. I am sure,
Madam Chairman, that you will agree with me that 'due process'
is not an idle term in this nation."

The room vibrated for a moment with his rejoinder. Nice
going, Pat Lederer, Wendell thought. One of the few men in this
town who would not be bullyragged by anyone, be he senator or
congressman. Pat would never make Commissioner, but he didn't
give a damn.

Jenny Pfitzner actually smiled, displaying small white teeth and
an incongruous dimple on one somber cheek. And that was bad,
for when she smiled, which was rare for her, it signaled a very
high card or two tucked up her sleeve.

"OK, put up or shut up, isn't that what you're saying, Mr.
Lederer?"

He bobbed his round shaved head.

"That's correct. That's exactly what I'm saying."

Down went her carefully coiffed head to read some notes before her. She nodded reflectively before peering up again over her half-moon glasses. Her erect seated figure reminded Wendell very much of his sixth-grade teacher so many decades ago. A tiny wraith of a woman, perhaps sixty years old, she slapped the largest moose-clumsy boys in her class when they stepped out of line. Her physical fragility was quite irrelevant to her unquestioned authority. Jenny Pfitzner was one of that kind. In her own (off-dais) words, she took no horseshit from anybody. And, he knew, she grudgingly respected those who took no horseshit from her. Could such a virago pick and choose, as he had heard, the men she wanted to take to bed, melt as a woman into a partner's arms? The rumor seemed incredible. . . .

"So what you're telling me now, Mr. Lederer, is that after years and years of complaints and accusations from me and others, you've never uncovered sufficient derogatory information against Dimitriu Calinescu, now known as James Callin, this paragon of virtue now living in California, a man frequently identified as a leader in the Romanian Iron Guard, which committed unspeakable crimes in his home country during World War II . . ."

Lederer held up a weary hand.

". . . We've already been down this road a half dozen times. We've investigated this man thoroughly. While he admits he was a member of Romanian nationalist groups before World War II, he denies any misdeeds in this capacity. He flatly denies membership in the Romanian Iron Guard. We have not been able to turn up hard facts or reliable witnesses to support any 'war crimes' or 'mass murder' charges against him."

Again that fleeting smile, belied by the intent glittering eyes, which animated Jenny Pfitzner's melancholy face.

Adams, sitting tensely beside him, knew that smile equally well.

"She must have the goods this time," he whispered in Wendell's ear, "or she wouldn't have convened this hearing. Something that's going to hook us, right here on camera, and we had better be ready to pick up some unexpected pieces."

Wendell nodded, without turning his head to his colleague.

Only two days earlier, the Director had phoned him on the Red Line and in his crisp now-hear-this manner told him to appear be-

fore the Pfitzner subcommittee in his stead. Representative
Pfitzner, the Director warned, would probably *not* be delighted
that the Director himself would not testify. She always wanted
top cabinet officers and federal agency chiefs at *her* hearings, especially the televised ones, but fortunately the Director had an
ironclad alibi: at the very hour of the scheduled hearing, he already
had a previous appointment to brief the President of the United
States. *That* had priority even over Mrs. Pfitzner's hearing. The
Director did not sound terribly distressed about his inability to appear at the Pfitzner committee. He did say, with that why-are-
they-bothering-us-busy-people tone of his, "I hope to hell, George,
that there aren't any spooky Agency shirttails flapping loose on
this one. We've taken enough static and grandstanding from the
Congress in the last five years to last us a lifetime."

Wendell remembered sighing as he realized what this task involved. His appointment book, opened next to his telephone with
its bank of internal connections, was crammed for the next ten
days ahead from 0900 to 1800 hours, all matters of pressing concern: a senior assignments panel; lunches and discussions on successive days with visiting chiefs of French, British, and Kenyan
services; and the annual operational review of all clandestine operations in Southeast Asia. This last was a tedious, if fascinating, insight into a submerged world of covert activity which resulted in a
kind of brutal report card he issued, noting successes, failures, and
gray areas in between. Not to mention the endless tsunamis of
highly classified paper he simply had to read every day, rolling in
from his own Directorate, from NFAC, DS&T, from the DIA,
NSA, State . . . Never time to think or ponder in such an impossible schedule. And now Jenny Pfitzner and her damned crusade
against elderly war criminals. But man proposes and the DCI
disposes: he told the Director he'd do the best he could and
wiped out his Monday appointments to permit his appearance at
the House subcommittee hearing.

His knowledge of the Calinescu case was a direct one. After all,
it was he, over thirty years previously, as Chief SSU Vienna, who
had given his approval to Calinescu's offer to assist the Americans
in collecting vital order-of-battle information concerning the Soviet armies in Central Europe. He had never met Calinescu, but

the responsibility to use him had been his. All this the Director knew and, Wendell was certain, that was precisely why the Director had lobbed the ball into his court. In effect, the Director was saying to him: you got us into this mess long ago; now you get us out of it without too much scraped skin.

Easier said than done, but he had survived larger and messier flaps before. He proceeded on this one in his usual deliberate manner. First, he had tasked his Special Assistant to search the Agency's computerized information-retrieval system, to locate any scrap of Agency information on Calinescu. He had requested any information in the files of the FBI, DIA, INS, and the Department of Justice, all on a top-priority basis.

Within an hour after his request that Agency files be searched, he was disquieted and irked to learn how little current information the Agency held on the man. Bits and pieces from the old OSS Vienna files were retrieved and confirmed in part that the Soviet order-of-battle information collected by Calinescu had been of sensational, if highly perishable, value at the time.

But the fat dossier on Calinescu? One which he himself had reviewed some six years earlier after he had learned of Calinescu's rising financial star on the West Coast from a clipping someone had sent him from the Los Angeles *Times?* Where was it?

After a day of silence, the chief of the documents-retrieval unit rang him up personally on the Red Line and with unfeigned embarrassment told him that it would, er, take a bit more time to retrieve the Calinescu dossier. But, for Christ's sake, he had shouted at the man (instantly regretting his discourtesy and disturbed that a now-familiar hypertensive pounding in his heart and temples had immediately appeared again), what in hell are we running here? Why can't the national intelligence service of the United States find a lousy OSS dossier in Archives within minutes?

"We *know* where it is, Mr. Wendell," the documents-retrieval man retorted, with a flash of temper of his own. "It's been charged out for months to a Mr. Silas Ruffing of your CI Staff. We tried to locate Ruffing. But he's not in today. We asked the Chief of the CI Staff to try to find the folder. They've gone through Ruffing's safe and holdings and they can't find it. Now they're trying to locate Ruffing. I'm damned sorry."

"My apologies," Wendell had finally breathed into the telephone. "Keep looking."

Silas Ruffing was another problem, but he had his priorities;
Ruffing would have to wait. Wendell had left his seventh-floor
office an hour earlier, to travel to his Canossa on the Hill, with
instructions to his Special Assistant: drop everything else and find
that damned Calinescu file.

As if through a thick filter, he heard Jenny Pfitzner dispose of
the Immigration and Naturalization assistant commissioner, after
wringing from him, one last time (" . . . and remember, you're
still under oath, Mr. Lederer . . ."), a promise that he would volunteer to the subcomittee any new information coming to his attention on the Calinescu case.

"Would you be kind enough, Mr. Lederer, to remain in the
room until the conclusion of this hearing?" This in a purring, very
un-Pfitzner tone.

She peered into the room, half blinded by the camera lights,
and growled, "Has Mr. Wendell of the Central Intelligence
Agency arrived yet?"

"Here, Madam Chairman," Wendell called from his chair.

"You're late." She made the statement as if he had betrayed the
national interest.

"My apologies, Madam Chairman," he boomed at her, project-
ing confidence and contriteness at the same time. "We were
delayed by . . ."

She waved his excuse aside impatiently.

"Never mind. Please come forward to be sworn."

He barely had time to shake Pat Lederer's hand and to mutter
to him, "Bloodied but unbowed," to which Lederer muttered
back, "That bitch scratches a lot of paint off the old chassis. And
watch it; I think she's got a sneak punch hidden up there. Good
luck."

It was a fact of survival that government professionals in this
city lengthened their antennae with each passing year of service.
Although she had organized such events in the past, Lederer and
he both knew that Jenny Pfitzner had not orchestrated this particular show simply to express periodic indignation, make a media
point, and withdraw. She had something more this time, of this

he was certain. He stood patiently, right hand raised, while the ritual oath swearing him in was rapidly read, wondering what she had prepared.

The seat of the witness chair was still warm when Wendell lowered himself into it. He touched the microphone which jutted up at him, glanced at the tight throbbing jaw of Marcus Adams seated at his left, folded his fingers before him, and waited.

"I thought," Jenny Pfitzner's voice metallically boomed through the room's amplifiers, "that if there was one thing spies and spy masters practiced, it was punctuality."

That got a predictable titter from the very youthful committee aides seated in chairs along the wall behind her, and a guffaw or two from the spectators.

Were they alone, he would have taken her on. He had no fear of this woman's hostile tongue and he did not enjoy gratuitous ridicule. But he had long ago learned not to lash back at each petty provocation. Always save up the riposte for the big one. It stung, however, and a sudden disturbing sweat suffused his forehead. He touched his beaded brow with a crisp linen handkerchief, knowing that his pulsebeat had accelerated to a brisk tympanic tempo. Easy does it, he told himself, taking two deep breaths. Doc Hocker would be very irritated at him that he had neglected to take his chlorthalidone pills this day.

"Touché, Madam Chairman," he said, bowing in mock apology to the straight-backed woman. This high dais upon which she sat had an inevitable effect of witness intimidation, the same sort of thing the late Benito Mussolini practiced in his office in the Palazzo Venezia. But he was no ingenue in such committee rooms and indeed had logged more than fifty hours sitting in witness chairs on the Hill in the previous year alone, precious time lost in the name of congressional oversight.

For a long moment, she stared down at him, slender ringed fingers holding and palpating each other, dark eyes peering intently out of a face devoid of cosmetics or color. Below her tightly restrained hair, bound by a severe pug in the back, soft molded cheeks hinted at some unexplained seething tension. What was it: wantonness, an arrogant sexuality? Whatever it was, he had to admit that this face in another woman he would have found appealing.

"Mr. Wendell, you hold the position of Deputy Director for Operations in the CIA—you are the DDO?"

It was the usual catechism, for the record, setting the stage for the onslaught. He and Lederer were bits of window dressing for whatever tableau she was going to unfold.

"Yes, I am the DDO. On this occasion I represent the Director of Central Intelligence, who, as you know, is unable to appear this morning."

"And the gentleman beside you . . ."

"Is Mr. Marcus Adams, from our Legislative Liaison Staff."

"And you are aware of the general reason you have been summoned as a witness this morning?"

"I am."

"And you are ready for questions?"

"I am."

"And would you like to make any remarks before we go to questions?"

He glanced at Adams, who nodded slightly. They had worked out the brief statement earlier that morning. He leaned earnestly toward the microphone and spoke in an assured voice which immediately betrayed him for what he was: New England, Ivy League, Old Boy of the CIA. His voice, dress, manner, and bearing, he knew, were not pleasing to her.

"Madam Chairman, as the Director's representative this morning, I would like to assure you and this subcommittee of our desire to cooperate with the purposes of the committee to the fullest extent."

In sonority and empty pomposity, he could never exceed that statement but protocol demanded that he utter it. He hunched his shoulders a bit, feeling the sweat sticky under his arms and shoulder blades, and mopped his brow yet again, listening with a certain fearful fascination to the thump-thump of his pulse before continuing.

"As for the particular personality of James Callin or Dimitriu Calinescu, his entrance into the United States occurred, as you well know, before the CIA was even created. We are examining at this moment all the OSS or other predecessor organization holdings in our archives, and we have initiated a full internal investigation to determine if . . ."

Jenny's rasp of a voice overrode his.

". . . Did your examination of the material in your archives or in your active files yield any information indicating who helped Calinescu migrate to this country?"

He knitted his brow at the question. The Agency did not have immigration records; this was one she should have hurled at Pat Lederer of INS. He shielded the microphone for a moment and leaned inquiringly toward Marcus Adams at his side.

"Punt," Adams advised him. "No sense making her mad by referring her back to INS. She's just fishing. Tell her: We don't have any info on that."

He turned back to the microphone and the steady stare of Jenny Pfitzner and the two congressmen flanking her.

"No, Madam Chairman, to the best of my knowledge we have no information indicating who helped him come to this country."

"But didn't Mr. Lederer just tell us that Calinescu helped American intelligence in Austria after the war?"

He nodded, deeply hoping that she would not ask him if he had any personal knowledge of the case. With congressmen, you answered questions and proffered nothing more. Any information gratuitously offered them was like voluntarily wandering off into an uncharted minefield.

"That is correct, Madam Chairman. Our old files clearly indicate that Mr. Calinescu collaborated briefly with our U.S. military intelligence people in Vienna after the war."

"And one would infer from that, would one not, Mr. Wendell, that these grateful American intelligence people would help this man to migrate to the United States?"

In the half dozen times he had sat in the witness chair before Jenny Pfitzner, he had come to admire, however grudgingly, the remorselessness of her logic even when it fairly reeked of hostility. Jenny understood cause and effect to a jesuitical degree and she was not failing him now. He nodded his head yet again, as if struck by her insight.

"One might well infer that, Madam Chairman. Our only problem is that we don't have any evidence of that. We're trying to find out more from our archives. If we uncover anything on that point, we'll inform you immediately."

But from a tightening of her lips and a clenching of her hands into little fists, he knew he was in for it.

"I want you to know, Mr. Wendell, that, as a given, I don't trust you and I don't trust your Agency. Not at all. I don't trust you to come up here on the Hill and to sit there in the witness chair and to level with me or my colleagues on this committee. You people are always holding back, always playing little games, always worried about need-to-know. You've had a full week"—she ignored his reproachful shake of his head at her exaggeration—"to look at your files and to talk to your people. You've already found out that he was working with your OSS people in Vienna after the war. Didn't OSS more or less become CIA in 1948? Didn't the OSS officers who used Calinescu's services become CIA people later? My God, doesn't that raise in your mind immediately some kind of quid pro quo, that you paid him off for services rendered by giving him a free ticket to come to the U.S? Yet here you are, with nothing but a pious statement that you're still looking at your files."

She again thumped the table, which amplified into a loud *crump* through the stilled chamber.

"You people out there in Langley don't seem to understand who's in charge in this country and that the People need to know. Yes, the People! And *we* are the People's surrogates!"

Her flanking colleagues exchanged uneasy glances, and one of them, a stern-faced older man from Illinois, reached out and discreetly touched her still-clenched fist.

"I am very much aware, Madam Chairman, who's in charge in the country," Wendell found himself saying, his pulse hammering with repressed fury. "Believe me, I don't need to be reminded of that."

He lowered his head toward the stippled surface of the black microphone and added, "And as a witness under oath, I can tell you and the subcommittee, Mrs. Pfitzner, that I would never countenance the use of any mass murderer as a collaborator in any way with my Agency, or anywhere else in the U. S. Government. It would be abhorrent to me. I have personally seen and smelled the massacred dead in the concentration camp of Mauthausen in 1945 awaiting burial, and I know what war crimes are all about. You may not trust me or my Agency, but there are ethical lines beyond which no U. S. Government agency can go. That's one of them. And if any individual in my Agency has gone beyond these lines in the past, he must answer to the Director and to myself."

He bit his lips to prevent himself from saying more. She had shaken him loose from his intention to appear imperturbable, damn her; a slight dizziness made the room reel for a moment. He swallowed virtually an entire glass of water in one convulsive gulp and, in the murmur of the crowded room behind him, he studied the quick, intelligent eyes of his tormentor. It was hard to believe that this woman was scarcely forty years old. Under the harsh camera lights she looked a full ten years older. But she would probably be around in the Congress a long time, a hell of a lot longer than *he* would be in government. The thought, for just a moment, depressed him.

"Very well, Mr. Wendell." Her voice was suddenly modulated, courteous, neutral. "Since you have nothing further to add to the committee's knowledge on this case, the committee releases you as a witness. But will you also please be good enough to remain in the committee room until the next witness has finished testifying?" A long pause and that fleeting smile again. "You just might learn something."

CHAPTER TWO

An anticipatory buzz filled the room, and press photographers, tipped that something unusual was in store, were already standing, their electronic flash packs glowing, ready to fire away. Wendell, now seated next to Lederer in a chair directly behind the witness table, watched the heads of the three congressmen bowed together in what appeared to be almost a moment of prayer. He could not prevent his thoughts from licking at the edge of the raw wound, now opened in him by his testimony and Jenny Pfitzner's questioning.

It was clear that she would go a hell of a long way to put the needle into the Agency's buttocks; she had already painfully pricked its pincushioned hide on many previous occasions when she could do so. But Jenny was hardly unique in this regard among congressmen and in fact was at least an open opponent, not like the ones who protested their understanding and sympathy with the Agency privately, and attacked it publicly.

Just how deeply in this case was the Agency involved? He remembered nothing of a sensational nature when he had reviewed the Calinescu file years before. What was most painful to him personally, he remembered, was the bitter remonstrations of Silas Ruffing against the use of the man. The whole thing stank, Ruffing had protested to him again and again; it sounded like a Soviet provocation operation, pure and simple. But Ruffing had no proof, nothing more than his seat-of-the-pants distrust, and had already begun to acquire his now-notorious paranoia and his reputation as "the Abominable No-Man of CI." The decision to play along with Calinescu had to be made, up or down, and he, Major George Wendell, Commander of SSU Vienna, had overruled Ruffing, his counter-espionage man. The operation had gone

forward, the OB information had rolled in, and the evaluations by
the USFA G-2 people had been ecstatic. The operation ended
with Calinescu's departure less than a year later. It was like so
many early hit-or-miss deals in that period.

Hanging like a thundercloud over the operation, he recalled,
had been the disappearance of the key cut-out to Calinescu. With
him disappeared ten thousand in green dollars, quid pro quo for
the incredibly detailed information. That event could be read in a
number of ways: Calinescu had taken the money and run; the cut-
out had taken the money and run . . . or betrayal somewhere.

Damn, he should have focused more on this matter from the
moment the Director had told him to appear. In the swirl of his
intense daily work routine, he had underestimated what this hearing could lead to. And here he sat waiting for Jenny Pfitzner to
drop the other shoe.

She leaned, body tense, into the microphone and announced in
grating, bitter tones, "The next witness is here almost by chance.
Two weeks ago I received a personal phone call from an Israeli
diplomat in Washington whom I will not identify. The Israeli
government is well aware of my . . . of this committee's strong interest in urging legal action against war criminals who are living in
this country.

"The Israeli diplomat told me that an Israeli tourist visiting in
the United States had spoken to him of an encounter she had on
the West Coast. It was so startling that I asked to see her. A week
ago I had that opportunity. The staff of this committee has inten-
sively interviewed this Israeli and finds her story of such com-
pelling interest that they convinced me that her testimony should
become part of this committee's ongoing inquiries into the war
criminals in this country."

"My God," Marcus Adams sighed in Wendell's ear. "This
woman has pulled an end run around Pat Lederer, INS, Justice,
and the whole damned executive branch! The next clatter you
hear . . ."

The clerk rose and announced in a high clear voice, "Will Mrs.
Klara Abramescu come forward to be sworn?"

A plump, short, pleasant-faced woman of indeterminate middle
age, puffy little hands nervously smoothing the sides of her shapeless navy blue dress, plodded hesitantly forward, steered firmly by

one arm by a young mustached committee aide. Her fearful black eyes flickered in all directions; she was clearly overwhelmed by the sight of so many strangers and the flashes and whirr of a half-dozen cameras not ten feet away from her.

"Swear the witness."

The young aide put his mouth to the ear of the confused woman. After brief urgent explanation, her right hand rose trembling in the air. She looked pleadingly at the congresswoman during the swearing-in and uttered a hardly audible "Yes, yes," to the request that she tell the truth, so help her God, after which she bowed her head as if asking forgiveness.

For once the grating voice was gentle as a mother's.

"You are Mrs. Klara Abramescu?"

The round head bobbed and nodded emphatically.

"And where do you live?"

A long pause and then, hesitantly, "Ramat Gan. Israel."

"How old are you?"

An embarrassed smile, and beseeching look at the young aide standing at her side, who nodded. The woman bit her lips as if she were about to reveal an atomic secret under duress.

"I have forty-seven years."

"Where were you born?"

"Bucureşti. Romanien."

"And how did you get to Israel?"

A pause while the woman thought out the answer in her sketchy English.

"Black. I go black to Palestina in 1947."

A brief huddle of the three congressmen.

"By 'black,' you mean you emigrated illegally to Palestine, which was then under British Mandate?"

Emphatic nodding of the head by the witness.

"Ya, illegal." (Accent on the last syllable.) "I go with 'Aliyah.' Many Romanian Jews go black to Palestina, to Israel."

"You went there alone?"

The witness stared at the microphone before answering, very softly. "Ya, alone. Nobody in my family alive to go with me."

Marcus Adams whispered, "Where the hell is this leading us?"

Wendell turned slowly to catch the other man's eyes. "Back to Romania."

And suddenly a huge black-and-white photograph of a man, fully a yard square, grainy and not too well defined, materialized in the hands of a committee aide, who now held it high so that it was visible to everyone in the room, and especially to the TV and press camera crews. Wendell peered at the photograph, seeking to find anything unusual in the tight-mouthed features, the smooth small chin, the carefully combed head. But, except for a curving scar on the chin, the face was curiously nondescript, banal, an Everyman visage. Such a face could appear and disappear in any crowd of Caucasian males without the slightest difficulty. It was not nondescript to Mrs. Abramescu, however, who sat straight in her chair as if the photo were a live person.

"Now, Mrs. Abramescu"—the rasp of authority had returned to Jenny Pfitzner's voice—"do you recognize this man?"

"Ya," the woman breathed. "Ya, it is Calinescu. Dimitriu Calinescu." Her voice, soft in its vowels, sang with an up-and-down lilt.

"From where do you know this man, Mrs. Abramescu?"

"From Bucureşti. From my childhood."

And suddenly the plump little woman lost her control. She half rose from the witness chair and pointed straight at the photo.

"This man is murderer!" Her voice was a shriek; it echoed chillingly throughout the high-ceilinged room. Wendell's hair bristled at the agonizing sound of it.

"You are sure?" Jenny Pfitzner's question clanged like a bell.

"Ya, sure, sure, sure! When I am child, many times I seen him in streets of Bucureşti in his green Eisene Garde shirt, leading those other . . . hooligans, shouting, 'Kill the Jews!' Things like that. . . ."

" 'Eisene Garde'; that means 'Iron Guard' in German." Jenny wanted everyone to understand everything. She addressed the highly agitated little woman before her with soothing tones.

"Please sit down, Mrs. Abramescu. I know how very painful it is for you to be here and to talk of such things, but it must be done. Please compose yourself." She pointed to the photo still held high. "Let it be noted for the record that this is a blow-up of the photo on Dimitriu Calinescu's immigration documents when he came to the U.S. in 1948," she announced to the room at large.

The aide handed the trembling witness a glass of water. After a convulsive swallow, she nodded; she was ready to continue.

"Did this man harm you in any way?"

Mrs. Abramescu took a long breath and spoke very carefully into the microphone. Her hesitant words bounced in melancholy echoes off the high-ceilinged room.

"In Januar 1941, Eisene Garde massacred my people, my family in Bucureşti. Eisene Garde trying to take power in Romanien. Making pogroms, slaughtering Jews."

"You're quite sure you recognize him as an Iron Guard person? This is very important, Mrs. Abramescu."

"Sure, sure, yes, I'm sure, sure." Her hands twisted each other as if wanting to tear her fingers loose.

"Now, Mrs. Abramescu, I don't want you to go through the harrowing account of that massacre again, but the man whose photograph is over there, was he definitely and personally involved?"

The round, soft, young-old face was convulsed.

"He . . . he . . . was commander. He was leader of many men, all in Eisene Garde green shirts, military bri . . . breech . . ."

"Military breeches, Mrs. Abramescu?"

"Ya, military breeches. They, they surround Choral Synagogue in Bucureşti, big synagogue, just after Shabat evening prayers, they beat, kick, smash Jews. Five, six young boys in synagogue run away, they see danger. The rest of us, maybe thirty, thirty-five Jews, many women, they throw in camions and drive us to municipal abattoir. Is dark when we get there. Everybody get off. Calinescu stand with big pistol in his hand and shout, 'Quick, quick, must prepare kosher food.'"

If Wendell had not known that the hearing room was full of people, he would have thought that he and this shapeless little woman speaking in her tremulous voice were alone. Only a slight electric buzz of fluorescent lights marred the silence.

"We . . . we not know why they take us to slaughterhouse for animals. We stand close together, very frightened, crying; old men saying the 'Shema Yisroel.' The old men, they know it is time to die. I am small girl and my mother whisper to me, 'Roll under camion, Klara, quick!' I do like that, quick. And from under camion, I see them taking Jews, one by one, to stone block. First one is the Rebbe, father of my mother. Rebbe Yakobescu. They pull his head back to show throat. 'Now we make you kosher!' they scream and they . . . they . . . they . . ." The congressmen leaned forward instinctively, seeking to catch her feeble voice before it vanished.

". . . Big Iron Guard man cut his throat with knife. Like . . . like . . . making kosher killing of chicken. Blood coming from throat like . . . like water from spigot. Calinescu stand with hands on hips and watch. Big smile on his face. Second is my uncle, Dr. Florescu, biggest *Chirurg* . . ."

"Surgeon." Jenny's translation mingled precisely with the witness's voice.

"Ya, surgeon. Calinescu hate Dr. Florescu, who very strong against Romanian fascists. Florescu say the 'Shema Yisroel' also, and . . ."

She stopped and pointed a quivering finger at the photograph propped on the dais.

"That man, Calinescu, he cut the throat of Dr. Florescu like you cut . . . a . . . a dog! Calinescu, he touch finger to blood from Dr. Florescu's neck and he put it in mouth, and he say, 'Ah, tastes like nectar!'"

The room crackled unbearably with her voice and Jenny's interruption was a blessing.

"That's enough, Mrs. Abramescu, you don't have to go into this much further. You are certain that the man who supervised that massacre, who participated himself, is the same person as in the photograph over there on the table?"

"Ya." It was no more than a sound of a slight wind. "Ya, Calinescu. Then, after Dr. Florescu, we hear sounds in distance, shots, noise. One Green Shirt say, 'The Army is coming. We must flee.' Calinescu stand calm, cold, nothing on his face. Like a man looking at cows. 'Line them up!' he shout. 'Kill the Yiddish swine, all of them. Quick!' So they fire with pistols, rifles on Jews standing against wall of the abattoir. I see all this from under camion. I see my mother and I run to her, shouting, 'Mama, mama, what do they do?' My mother push me behind her; she kneel in front of me and hold hands open to protect me with her body. Everybody fall down on top of me. Screams, screams . . ."

"That's enough, Mrs. Abramescu." Jenny Pfitzner's growl vibrated with pain. "That's quite enough."

"That's all. After screams and shooting, Romanian Army soldiers run up, Iron Guardists run away. Army men take out dead and wounded Jews. All dead, except four. I am only one without wounds. Nothing touch me, nothing. Not a scratch. But my mother, my father, grandfather, uncle, two sisters, all dead. Blood of my family on my dress, on my face, my hands, on wall of municipal abattoir."

Yet again, Wendell said to himself with the fervency of a curse. Yet another time. After thirty years and more, he thought he had heard the last of these nightmarish things. Why was it in his life's thread to have to hear these atrocities over and over? But they would be heard again, and again. As long as survivors were alive to tell them.

When the muted babble of spectators died, Jenny Pfitzner asked the still-trembling witness, "Did you ever see Mr. Calinescu again?"

The woman's smooth, olive face slowly regained its composure.

"Yes, I see him again in California." She held up two fingers. "Two months ago I see him. I am visiting Susza Patrascu, who is my dear friend from child years. She lives in Pacific Peli . . ."

"Pacific Palisades?"

A fleeting grateful smile.

"Ya, Pacific Palisades. I am in restaurant, very nice restaurant in Hollywood with Susza. And there at next table is Calinescu! So old now; old man with a cane. And fat! And beautiful clothes! Hair now gray. But mouth is same."

She made a grimace.

"That mouth, killer-mouth, like . . . like shark. I see him and I feel . . . dizzy. I say, 'Susza, that man! Is that man Calinescu?' She look, she grow pale. She . . . she tremble. She say, 'Ya, it is Calinescu, the Green Shirt leader.' Susza is Christian, not hurt in Romanian pogroms, but she also know Calinescu . . ."

"Are you *quite* sure this is the same man, Mrs. Abramescu?"

Mrs. Abramescu placed one hand on her ample bosom.

"I swear this, Madam Pfitzner. I swear by my dead mother and father. I wait until Calinescu finish his meal. Susza and I follow him outside restaurant. He walks slow, with cane. One foot drag a little. He is with beautiful young woman. I see him get into big Mercedes automobile with chauffeur. Susza write down license number. She work in Los Angeles County office and she find name of owner of auto. He has new name now: James"—she pronounced this "Yammes"—"Callin, who live in Beverly Hills."

She smiled timidly and quite unnecessarily added, "You see, he change name, Calinescu to Callin. But we no find name in telephone book. He have private number." She thought a moment. "Maybe he afraid someone phone him and remind him that he is murderer."

The older congressman on Pfitzner's left spoke up in the lull that floated into the room, clearing his throat of the long silence imposed on him.

"Mrs. Abramescu, what happened immediately after the . . . massacre in 1941?"

She turned her broad sad face toward him.

"After massacre, he disappear. I not know what happen to him. Some said Romanian Army catch him. Some say he fly away, outside Romania. I go live with mother of my friend Susza."

The soft lilting voice took on sudden strength.

"But I never forget him, never forget that face! Never!"

Jenny Pfitzner's voice, strident, brutal, announced, "This subcommittee has attempted to subpoena Mr. James Callin of Beverly Hills, California, as a witness. To date we have been unsuccessful in serving him. His doctors say he is too ill to appear. But we will persevere." The last four words were loud, remorseless.

She glanced perfunctorily at her two male colleagues.

"Are there any further questions of this witness?"

Both shook their heads. Jenny looked directly into a TV camera with a red on-the-air light gleaming on its head.

"The witness has kindly consented to remain in the United States at the disposition of the committee and other government agencies for a period of thirty more days. During this time, I trust that the various components of the executive branch understand that this committee means business. We hope to develop more eye-witness leads to confirm the status of many war criminals who have emigrated to this country since 1945. We will not permit this country to be a shelter for such monsters."

She held up the blow-up of Callin for a last time. "This man has heavy interests in a fast-food chain in California. He owns extensive real estate in Orange County there. He owns an import-export firm dealing with Far Eastern countries. He owns a luxurious home in Benedict Canyon in Beverly Hills, he has servants, fine cars, and has a reported gross income of a million dollars a year."

Quite a show, Wendell thought, shaking his head involuntarily. She really can lay it on. He could sense what her final words would be. She did not disappoint him.

"Some pickings!" Jenny Pfitzner grated. "Some pickings for a green-shirted fascist who slaughtered helpless Jews against a slaughterhouse wall over thirty-five years ago."

Legally, he knew, she would have been in deep trouble saying such things publicly. Callin's lawyers certainly knew the laws on slander. But she could not be touched uttering them in this room in her official congressional capacity. Callin knew that, as did Jenny and her colleagues.

The journalists and photographers began to flow out of the room in hasty Indian file. The hearing had indeed become a first-class media event.

"If there are no further questions, this hearing is adjourned."

There was a sharp *klop* of her gavel and the room dissolved quickly into clusters of reporters around the witness and at the dais around Jenny.

George Sheridan Wendell moved slowly through the thickened crowd toward the door, ignoring fingers plucking at his sleeve to stop him, blinking at the camera flashes in his face, with Marcus Adams pushing a path open ahead of him. He collided with Pat Lederer outside the committee room, pulled him aside, and asked the wizen-faced tough little man, "Pat, they asked me a question in there that I couldn't answer, but maybe you can: just who did sponsor the emigration of Dimmy Calinescu to the United States in 1948? Do you have that info at the top of your head?"

Lederer's grin was mischievous and regretful at the same time.

"George, you were lucky to have come to the hearing without that information, or you would have had to give it to Jenny, wouldn't you?"

"The truth, the whole truth, so help me God."

"Well, I'm glad she didn't ask it of *me*, at least this time around. Maybe we can sort this one out at your convenience."

"Stop playing games with me, Pat."

Lederer's flinty eyes reflected incredulity.

"No time for games, George. I'm absolutely stunned that you haven't seen the information. We sent it over to you some time ago. You mean you're not aware that Calinescu's principal sponsor was one of your Agency people? It's worse than that: your guy apparently took a small pot of money from Calinescu in the process."

He patted Wendell's arm in a gesture of grudging sympathy.

"You've got a really bad apple out there, George."

And suddenly a new problem had risen to the highest priority in the very busy life of George Sheridan Wendell.

CHAPTER THREE

Bill Regan, the CIA Inspector General's man, closed his black loose-leaf notebook and patted its nubby cover with a forced smile.

"This is about as good a place to break as any, Steve. We can pick it up from here tomorrow."

"No problem, Bill," Steve Browning said, uncrossing his legs. "Uncle Sam pays the freight from eight-thirty to five, and we've got almost a full hour to go."

"You're a real patriot." Regan's sarcasm was more a sigh than a reproach. "But picking my way through Austrian double-agent ops of three decades ago takes a hell of a lot of concentration. We've been at it all day now and we've barely scratched the surface." He pointed to the bulky operations files piled high at his elbow. "We never had anything quite like this in Tokyo or Jakarta."

That certainly didn't make it any easier to explain, Steve thought, studying the lean flinty-featured officer on the other side of the desk. Unless you were there in Europe during and after the Nazi defeat, with the Soviet and Western victors immediately circling each other like snarling dogs, it was damned hard to understand why things happened the way they did.

"Well, there was nothing quite like it," he said after an awkward second. You had to weigh your words carefully with Agency inspectors. "Places like Berlin and Vienna just after the war were just . . . jungles. No holds barred."

Regan, crisp and cool in a tan summer suit, leaned back, pulled out a pack of long cigarettes, and offered one with a hospitable air. Steve shook his head with a perfunctory smile.

"Mind if I smoke?"

Steve shrugged. Yes, he minded, but this was the IG man's pond. It would be best if he made no waves at this time.

"This woman, girl actually, the one you first met in Calinescu's place, sounds like quite a character." Regan clearly wanted to lighten the somber atmosphere of the interview, as he lighted up and leaned back. "Where did she get the nickname 'Cupcake'? Was it something about the way she was built or . . . ?"

"Not at all." Steve's voice was dry with impatience. "Her real name, as you can learn from that crypt list you have there, is Mara von Kueppke. Or Gräfin Mara von Kueppke, if you want the title as well. Her last name became corrupted by my replacement in Vienna, who was a smart-ass and whose German left a lot to be desired. 'Cupcake' became his unofficial crypt for her."

He folded his freckled hands tightly around his crossed knee.

"I always thought it was a goddamned silly nickname," he added, wondering why he was going to the trouble. "I always called her Mara myself."

The IG man shrugged and let a mouthful of smoke waft lazily into the still air of the room.

"Cupcake or Mara or . . . what's her crypt . . . TTVELVET-8, it's still a strange business. How old was she at the time: fifteen? sixteen? Must have been awfully young."

Steve tried to match Regan's assured jocularity. He knew, however, that it would take very little, after these hours of polite but barbed probing, to pull the pin, pound his fist on a corner of the Formica desk surface, and shout, "Stop fucking around, man, and come to the point!"

Instead, he leaned forward, braced both hands on his knees, and rose ponderously from the yielding armchair. He stretched his cramped arms with a sigh and straightened his rumpled seersucker jacket. The IG man did not rise with him. He studied Steve from behind the desk with slightly cocked head; his expression, at once quizzical and wary, seemed to say: screw you, Steve Browning; you may be an Old Boy around here and one of the original OSS hotshots, but I'm in charge of this inquiry and I speak for the Inspector General and for the Director.

Steve pursed his heavy lips for a moment.

"I'm a bit puzzled, Bill, about your line of questioning about Mara . . . about TTVELVET-8. Where does she fit in?"

Regan's reddish eyebrows formed quizzical inverted V's.

"Well, isn't she a direct link with Calinescu? Didn't she . . . ?"

"Didn't she shack up with him? Yes, she did. But it's always been my firm conviction, and except for Silas Ruffing I'm about the only guy left on active service around here who can comment on it with any firsthand authority, that her relationship with Dimmy Calinescu had no ops overtones. It was purely . . . personal."

"Just a lay, you're trying to say." Bill snorted. "Nothing else except a teen-age resident whore?"

"Look." Steve struggled to keep his tone neutral, professional. "She lived with him. She slept with him. She probably did any damned thing he wanted her to do. And in the quid pro quo of that period, he housed her, fed her, clothed her, protected her. If you had any idea what Vienna was like in that first winter after the war, you'll know that from a strictly material point of view, Mara had it good."

He leaned across the desk at the IG man and fixed him with a frown of dislike.

"If it's a matter of starving or not starving, being warm or freezing, being gang-raped by a bunch of Russian soldiers or not, sleeping in a stinking corner of a DP barrack or living more or less like a human being, yes, some women might peddle their ass. Mara did."

It was not wise to say more. From Bill's expression, he knew he should have kept his remarks to himself. But the whole business was being handled badly, in his view. He intended to play along with them as far as he could. Too much volunteering of his opinions, however, even in the name of accuracy, could only raise their suspicions. This he very much wanted to avoid.

"TTVELVET-8 *was* your agent, wasn't she?" It was an accusation, not a question, but he did not permit himself to be baited.

"Yes, for about a year. After Calinescu booted her out. Or she couldn't take it any more."

He paced heavily away from the desk before turning, and he held out a self-deprecatory hand.

"I know what you're thinking, Bill. And I'm not going to play games with you. If they want to put me on the Box and ask, 'Did *you* have sexual relations of any kind with Mara von Kueppke, also known as Cupcake, also known as TTVELVET-8?,' the needle would jump off the graph if I answered, 'No.'"

Bill studied his agitated eyes and compressed lips before answering carefully and soothingly.

"For Christ's sake, Steve, these aren't legal proceedings. While screwing your own agent is hardly playing the game by the rules, what happened over thirty years ago in Vienna between you and her isn't what we're sitting here talking about. The focus of my questioning is on Calinescu. Everything about him."

He unlimbered himself from his chair and perched on a corner of his desk, hands folded, craggy face cocked intently at Steve. As if by mutual agreement, they permitted a moment of silence to serve as air space in alleviating the tensions created by the long hours of question and answer.

"She and I used to talk about Calinescu," Steve finally said, pacing to a position directly behind the chair he had occupied. "I tried time and again to trap her into admitting that she had done some work for him of any kind: cut-out, courier, lookout. Anything involving his contacts. Nothing. She said he simply didn't trust her. He didn't trust any woman . . . especially one who was sixteen years old."

"Even a sixteen-year-old girl can . . ."

"Yeh, yeh, I know," he broke in, instantly regretting he had done so. "Even a sixteen-year-old can carry out all kinds of assignments. And a few months later, she sure as hell was useful to our unit in doing a lot of support chores as part of our surveillance team in Vienna. But if you knew Calinescu, you'd know first of all that he never used women in any of his businesses, black market or espionage. Women for him simply meant one thing: carnal knowledge."

He shook his heavy round head with finality.

"No, Bill, Mara doesn't figure with Calinescu, in the seven months she lived with him. She was just one of many women he took, abused—and looked after."

"Well, for now, that will have to be the authoritative word on Mara, of course," the IG man said after a moment of silence, a glint of mockery in his eyes.

He tapped the thick files with one long finger.

"Tomorrow, we have other info we'll have to discuss. And that

will include what happened to your principal agent, the one who
was your cut-out to Calinescu, what's his name . . . ?"

"Radescu. Mircea Radescu. TTVIGOR-4."

The two men exchanged challenging glances and Bill finally
looked down at the files.

"Sorry about this becoming an ordeal, Steve," he said, stubbing
out the cigarette with a nervous gesture. "I'm just carrying out instructions from the Director's office, you know that."

"Of course I know you're just doing your job," Steve assured
him, but the timbre of his voice intimated that he was not doing
it at all well.

He looked around at the soft gray tones of the modest room, its
muted wall-to-wall carpeting and crowded furnishings identical
with those in every other executive office in this enormous beehive
of a building: on the walls, blow-up color photographs of plains
and rivers of the American Far West. Two clinically severe chairs
shared the limited space of the room with a two-drawer safe, inevitably gray also, with a sign-out sheet on top, its navel of a three-
way combination lock half-obscured by a T-shaped OPEN sign.
There was precious little in this cold cube to reveal the inner personality of its inhabitant: a metal-framed triptych of family photographs perched at a corner of the desk, a small wooden plaque
declaiming "The buck does *not* stop here," a cheap coffee mug
with the golden decal on it reading "#1." On the wall behind the
IG man hung two framed black-and-white photographs of the last
two Directors, each autographed.

Here at Headquarters, he knew, grown men spent years, decades, in such rooms, laboring five, six, sometimes seven long days a
week. Bloody monastic cells they were. He, for one, had avoided
this place for almost twenty years except for occasional temporary-
duty visits from abroad, and between assignments. For him, he
had often told his colleagues, to serve permanently in this place
would be like dying a little bit each day. But now he was assigned
to Headquarters and dying a bit each day as he had foreseen.
Well, in two years and two months, he would have the maximum
thirty-five years in. He could get out with a full pension and kiss
these tiny offices and endless corridors goodbye.

He had intended to end this alternatingly tedious and tense afternoon on some sort of pleasant note, a banal reference, perhaps,

to the three half-grown children smiling vacuously out of the photographs on the desk, two of them with braces on their teeth. Instead, he found himself staring at the photograph on Bill's identity badge, which, like Steve's, was clamped to his lapel. The tanned angular face above the number on the blue plastic patch seemed far more worn and haggard than that of the man sitting opposite him, and its bushy mustache made for a peculiarly tough, rakish air.

"I'd never recognize you behind that hairy lip," he said, trying to inject the proper tone of jocular chiding. "How do you get past the building guards with that photo? And where did you get the hair on the upper lip? From the Techs disguise kits?"

Bill laughed embarrassedly.

"I'd just come back from Vietnam when this badge photo was taken." He peered down at it self-consciously. "The mustache was just a whim. I was up-country in II Corps. Man, that was rugged duty there! And it just got to be a chore keeping the chops trimmed. Had that *and* a full beard. I looked like some peacenik bastard. The beard came off the day I got back here, and the upper lip got it later when my kids told me I looked just like the bad guys in a TV cowboy film."

He glanced down at the badge photo again, brows momentarily knitted in concern. "You're right: I look like something out of the old RAF. I'd better go down there and get a new photo from Security."

"How was Vietnam?" Steve asked. He didn't particularly care, but as a decompression topic it was better than him trying to tell the man about post-World War II Vienna.

"Many things to many people," Bill said, lips tight with condemnation. "If you ask me, for years the Shop wasted the time and talents of hundreds of our best people out there in that miserable no-win war. And it hurt, getting your ass out of there at the end, on a Marine helicopter, with thousands of howling, weeping Vietnamese trying to scramble over the Embassy wall and fly out with you, including a lot of people we should have saved and didn't."

"That's a little bit what Vienna was like in '45," Steve said. "The people who wound up there wanted very much to get away, mostly from the Sovs. We had no helicopters to take them out,

however. It was the end of the line. A lot of them made it out
somehow, just like the people you left behind in Saigon."
He attempted to smooth his hopelessly crumpled jacket.
"Is that all for today, Bill?"
The IG man, with an apologetic expression, shoved a single
sheet of paper across his desk at him.
"Sorry about this, but I'd like you to sign this. It's purely routine but we've got to have some official record that we advised you
of your rights."
Steve pulled out heavy black-rimmed reading glasses and, with
an unfeigned glance of irritation, lowered his eyes to read the document.

I, Steven Browning, Jr., understand that the Central Intelligence Agency possesses information concerning certain issues which require clarification. I understand that I have the
constitutional right to remain silent.

Any information I provide will be furnished voluntarily on
my part, of my own free will and without any compulsion,
duress or a promise of reward or immunity. I understand that
I have the right to confer with an attorney prior to answering
any questions and to have an attorney present during the
questioning itself; if I cannot afford an attorney, one will be
appointed. I have read the foregoing and fully understand its
import.

IN WITNESS WHEREOF, I place my signature below
this date.

With a truculent sweep of his hand, he removed the glasses
from his nose.
"You make me feel like some goddamned Peeping Tom who's
just been booked at a precinct station, Bill. What the hell is
this?"
Bill said, "The Agency is under accusation in this Calinescu
case, Steve. The General Counsel people are making everyone involved in this case sign this kind of a statement. There's no infer-
ence of guilt, believe me."
"No," Steve said, "but they'll want somebody's ass before it's
over, right? And Uncle Stevie's ass is as available as anyone else's."
"Wrong," Bill said. "Totally wrong."

Steve extracted a black felt pen and wrote his name on the document in thick lines fully an inch high.

"There," he said, "to paraphrase another signer of another document, Old King George Wendell will be able to read that without his glasses."

"I'm sorry you feel that way."

Their eyes met, clashed, locked, and disengaged.

"See you tomorrow, Steve."

"*In'shallah.*"

Bill retrieved the document as Browning closed the door behind him and studied the bold, defiant signature thoughtfully. His telephone buzzed angrily and he turned to see the winking "hold" signal on the Secure Line. He punched the intercom button and asked his secretary, "Who is it?"

"Mr. Kobler's office," a tinkly woman's voice caroled in his ear. "He would like a word with you. Just a moment, please."

No gracious are-you-busy? with Kobler. Waiting for him to come on the line, he glanced down yet again at his badge. It was indeed a scruffy image.

"Kobler speaking. How did it go, Bill?" That high-pitched bark he could recognize anywhere. Old Super-Shark himself.

"Hi, Don. Well . . . he just left. I've spent a long hard day with him."

"Well?" It was an imperious question, voice rising and demanding full satisfaction.

"Well, I don't know what to make of it. This is a very difficult bag of worms to sort out, but one thing I know: he's holding back on me."

"Oh?"

"Yes, oh. No question about it. What it is, I don't know. He was especially uneasy about a woman in the case who apparently was an agent of his. She was living with Calinescu, left him, and then lived with Steve. But that's not what's wrong. Strange business. . . ."

After a pause Kobler said, "Well, you'll just have to keep chipping away at it. After all, it's Browning who was the first Agency officer to meet Calinescu. You've simply got to pull everything you can out of him. The Shop's reputation is on the line. Didn't he know he was dealing with a certified goddamn war criminal? If he did, why in hell did he?"

"We're going at it again tomorrow," Regan said, lips tight at being told how to handle this inquiry. "We'll keep boring in on everything he can remember."

"Call me at any time." Kobler's thin sharp voice brooked no rebuttal.

"Just keep in mind," Regan said uneasily, "*my* channel is to my boss, the IG, and through him to the Director. I'm not supposed to talk about it to you or anyone else in the DDO. This is strictly on the QT between me and you for old times' sake."

Kobler said evenly, "I know all that, Bill. But we'll stay in touch anyway, right?" He paused for a bare moment. "You are, after all, only on a two-year rotational tour with the IG and then you come back to us, to the DDO. The way you handle this might wind up making you look very good."

The son of a bitch made his point clear. Regan lowered the telephone carefully on its cradle. But it was indeed wise to stay on the right side of Don Kobler, a man whose star in the Agency was unmistakably on the ascendant.

The main corridor outside the IG offices was empty and it stretched into infinity. When Steve had entered and explored the enormous cement hulk of the then brand-new Headquarters building for the first time, these corridors, gleaming beige tunnels each fully a quarter of a mile long, had impressed, even excited him with their very dimensions. Somehow they exemplified by their yawning lengths the worldwide commitment of the Agency: behind every one of the hundreds of doors leading off from these brightly lit tunnels, intermeshing webs of operations, surreptitious contacts, double-agent plays, and political-action skulduggery were being spun, all in the cause of American national interest and dominance. The good guys of the Western world against insidious Soviet bad guys. The corridors led to points of action, points of decision; between the corridor floors, pneumatic missiles whirred through miles of tubes, each bearing urgent cables all over the building, telling of the rise and fall of governments, Soviet defections, recruitment approaches, hostile missile telemetry, successful or unsuccessful infiltrations, audio bugs in offices or bedrooms of Priority Targets half a world away . . .

Stretching so far into the distance that persons at the other end were but tiny puppets, these corridors had once blazed with recessed fluorescent lights, day and night, like the deck corridors of a mammoth liner. Now, energy directives dimmed the endless halls. One could not discern an approaching figure as friend, foe, or stranger until one had almost collided with the other. It was appropriate, he thought, that the corridor lighting had been dimmed. Within him the lights no longer blazed either.

He wheeled right, into a metal stairwell, and clattered down, his mind sifting through the interview, gnawing on the line of questioning and shaking his head in reluctant admiration at what now emerged as a pattern of clever and subtle elicitation by the IG man.

But it would take a far more clever interviewer than Regan to shake out of him what he knew. And even Regan, though much younger than he, knew what thirty-three years in this business did to you. It got to a point that on some matters he was scarcely able to tell himself the truth, much less reveal it to others. And on this matter, his guard was up. Regan would learn nothing. He would lie to Regan as convincingly as a parent assuring a very small child that, yes, the tooth fairy leaves money under your pillow.

The ground rules of operational schizophrenia permitted you to tell reassuring whoppers to agents, to developmental contacts, to foreigners of all kinds, to everyone in the Opposition. And the Opposition covered a far broader spectrum than the KGB or the GRU or their satellite comrades in East Germany, Czechoslovakia, Cuba, Bulgaria, and elsewhere. For him, the Opposition now included members of the media, foreign and domestic; he lied to his own Foreign Service and military colleagues, when he had to. He lied to people he met at cocktails, to those who happened to be sitting in airplane seats next to him. It was ingrained in him to lie, to conceal his Agency affiliation, to screen from others what he was up to, where he was going, and why.

But those same ground rules did not apply to the Team: to his colleagues and superiors in the Agency. He was not expected to lie to Regan, the IG man. That was what operational schizophrenia was all about: lie to the Opposition, tell the truth to the Team.

But he had crossed that schizophrenic Rubicon. He could no longer tell the truth to *anyone*. To do so would destroy him.

Regan had flung some razor-edged questions at him across that chasm of a desk between them. He had bobbed and weaved in his answers. But the same questions would probably be asked again when they eventually strapped him into that goddamned polygraph machine. He was confident that he could use enough body tensing, toe-wriggling exercises to produce equivocal responses on the jiggling lines of the polygraph sheets, but they would not clear him.

So far, he had answered Regan truthfully—but hardly fully. And the truth or a lie is also, damn them, what you don't say. He hated Regan at that moment for asking questions which cut too close. He dreaded the ones to come.

Two floors down, he swung through the access door of the stairwell and entered another main corridor, a duplicate of the one upstairs and equally dim, leaving him with a sense of *Götterdämmerung*. At least Harold Ickes used to turn the lights off in his Department *after* everybody went home. Allen Dulles, he was certain, would never have countenanced this sort of housekeeping bullshit. Such economies might be fine for the Department of the Interior but hardly for the Agency, for the elite. (He involuntarily grinned at his own outrage.) But Dulles was long dead and the bookkeepers and the watt-watchers were fast taking over here as thoroughly as they had done in the old-line departments downtown.

"Any calls?" he asked the languid secretary who sat in the outer office, serving four masters, none of whom was present. She was dressed in a silken pants suit which was enlivened, so help him God, by a motif of birds and bees. She put down a paperback novel without false embarrassment; he had given her nothing to do that entire day.

"A couple." She handed him two yellow memos.

"They said, no rush." Recently returned from a very swinging Latin-American assignment, she spoke with thinly concealed boredom. Two rotten telephone calls in three hours. Her desk was clean, dusted, empty. The electric typewriter already had its top popped up and its ribbon secured in a safe. For her, the end of the workday could not come a minute too soon.

He waited until he had closed the door to his own office before peering at the slips. The first one came from the Office of Training. They probably wanted him to give another bravura performance to new Career Trainees on "Tradecraft in Denied Areas." That could be answered tomorrow. The other slip read: "Mr. Ruffing of the CI Staff did not return your call. He cannot be reached." That meant Ruffing was gone for the day, and he knew exactly where Ruffing was and, by this time, how many vodka martinis he had drunk. Ruffing's very name gave him a pang, and much of this pain derived from what he knew Ruffing thought of him.

He slumped heavily into his desk chair and stared slowly around the room, a duplicate in size of Regan's but containing more of himself and his interests than Regan apparently cared to place on display: two watercolors of the Ring in Vienna, a good Piranesi print of Rome, a pair of valuable Dogon tribal masks, and a small Soviet military guidon stretched in a metal frame. The last had come off the whip antenna of a burning Soviet T-54 tank on the Andrassy Utca in Budapest during the 1956 uprising. Considering that he had no prior permission to take a single step outside the U. S. Embassy gates, he had been very foolish and very lucky in his impulse to leap on the tank's smoldering turret and pull the flag from its staff before slugs from the wildly directed small-arms fire all around him could hit him, and just before the tank exploded. He stared at the guidon for a moment. Could he have ever been so insane?

He reached into the inside pocket of his jacket for a scuffed address book remarkable for its impressive number of pages. Long schooled in an arcane craft, he ran his finger down a page behind the tab "V" and stopped at a neat inked notation, "Velvet 8." He rose and drew a deep breath as if he were a sponge diver about to plunge to the bottom of the sea. He reached for the phone, got an outside line, and carefully dialed in reverse sequence the telephone number written after the cryptonym. The phone at the other end burred twice and then a woman's contralto voice, unmistakably European, asked, "Hallo?" He again breathed deeply before answering. It would be the first time in over thirty years he had spoken with Mara von Kueppke.

CHAPTER FOUR

"I wonder," George Wendell intoned in a weary baritone, "if my worthy opposite number, head of the First Chief Directorate of the KGB, has spent as many hours as I have worrying about which of *his* low-five-percent officers should be canned."

He spoke, hands behind back, heavy body confronting the wall of green forest beyond the window. Behind him, one foot jiggling nervously, sat Don Kobler, his Special Assistant, leafing through an evaluation panel list of GS-14 operations officers which they had been discussing with growing acerbity for the past fifteen minutes.

"I would guess," his assistant commented in the flat nasal tones of the Midwest, "that somewhere on his great big desk in his office on Dzherzhinsky Square in Moscow, your KGB opposite number has installed a special button. When he has the names of a few low-performers to deal with, he presses that button. A KGB personnel officer pops in immediately. The chief hands him a slip of paper and says, 'Ivan Ivanovich, here's a list of ten of our losers who can't cut the *bliny*. I never want to see them again.' And he never does. That's all there is to it."

Wendell snorted involuntarily at the dark humor of which his quick-minded, impatient aide was capable.

"Damn, wouldn't that be something? Does my Soviet counterpart have to worry about chain-of-command grievance procedures, equal-employment-opportunity committees, Inspector General's people to tell him he's being beastly to some lunkhead? Does he have an Intelligence Oversight Board downtown to whom any Agency malcontent can turn? Or a bunch of congressmen only too willing to listen to laments which would confirm what a bunch of bastards the CIA leaders are? Does he have a Washington *Post* or a New York *Times*, or peephole journalists whose columns appear on the comic pages of newspapers, to whom any Agency sour-apple, on duty or retired, can whisper about classified snafus? No, the Director of KGB First Chief Directorate just presses a damned button, and *do svedanya*, his personnel problems vanish."

He trudged back to his desk and stretched mightily before settling into his swivel chair, like a zoo lion trapped for lack of exercise. It had been an absolute hell of a day, from his 8 A.M. arrival to this moment in late afternoon. He had been compelled to play catch-up ball after losing the previous morning and midday on Capitol Hill to Jenny Pfitzner and her one-ring war-crimes circus. Yesterday afternoon and today, the pace had accelerated to almost a blur.

His Special Assistant, reading glasses perched on nose, silently reviewed the list of names while Wendell peered at his Doomsday Book, as he called his huge scheduling agenda with its minute-by-minute boxes, to determine where he was in this pressure cooker of a day. He had trotted to three separate ad hoc meetings down the corridor with the DCI or DDCI, two of them fairly short and terse, on the topic of Jenny Pfitzner and the sudden media interest in the Agency as a result of the testimony of the day before. He had attended the senior staff meeting presided over by the Director, at which he had been nominated for the Most Boring Congressional Witness of the Year Award by the Agency's public relations officer. (He took the rather heavy-handed joshing ostensibly well but he seethed inwardly all the while. He abhorred public relations people in general and saw no reason for an Agency PR flack to be sitting in on meetings of senior U.S. intelligence officers and to be poking fun at him.) He had conducted at least four telephone calls on the Secure Line with two Assistant Secretaries in the Department of State who were most apprehensive about an impending Agency recruitment pitch to an Eastern European diplomat in New Delhi. (State's nervousness about recruitment approaches to foreign government officials, friendly or not, was wonderfully predictable and negative; such ventures rocked the tidy diplomatic boats of good relations and status quo.) He counted with his pencil the telephone calls:

eleven outgoing, twenty incoming this day alone thus far, many of
the latter from well-connected colleagues and acquaintances all
over Washington, congratulating him for his courage under fire
from Jenny. Two of the callers had asked him why he didn't tell
Jenny, plain and clear, to stuff it. (What did they think he was,
for God's sake, some kind of a bureaucratic kamikaze?)

He realized, guiltily, that he had again forgotten to take one of
those newer and more powerful diuretic pills which in the inele-
gant words of Dr. Angus Hocker, the Agency's director of medical
services, were supposed to squeeze the piss out of him at a much
more efficient rate. He reached in his desk drawer, took two of the
pills out of their bottle, sloshed water from an Executive Issue aluminum water pitcher into a glass, and downed the lumpy little
cylinders.

Don Kobler, he realized, had been sitting upright in his chair,
studying him coolly and carefully, as a Plains Indian looks for
smoke signals on the horizon.

His Special Assistant, for whom invidious service-versus-service
comparisons were by now familiar fare, took up the thread of the
lapsed conversation.

"What's not funny, George, is that we're boxing ourselves into
situations where the Sovs are running operational circles around
us while we futz around like some goddamned welfare-counseling
office. How the hell can you, as DDO, effectively manage a clandestine intelligence service and waste all of this precious time
squeezing your hands about these marginal guys? You have
enough pending top-priority sign-offs in those two 'in' boxes there
to last you right through next week even if they left you completely alone."

Wendell tightened his lips. While he understood and agreed
with his subordinate's exasperation, he didn't like the bitterness
with which it was uttered.

Rocking himself in his swivel chair, hands touching each other
under his chin as if in brief prayer, he was aware that his words
rang with a pomposity that he strove, in vain, to avoid.

"Futz around, Don, perhaps. And we *may* be overdoing it. But
I choose to believe that when the day arrives that we become
mirror images of the KGB and their miserable satellite services in
East Germany, Bulgaria, and Czechoslovakia, we may as well

close down the store right there. One of the enormous differences still remaining between Us and Them, I think, lies in a word which has also been steadily going out of style in Washington: compassion."

Kobler, half absorbed in reading yet again the findings and recommendations of the Directorate evaluation panel, tweaked a pale fleshy nose which gave a brutal strength to an otherwise uneventful face. When he finally looked up, his blue eyes were unrelenting.

"In this case, forgive me if I come on too strong, George, but I think you're showing misplaced compassion. For years, the Shop's been slowly squeezed to ever-lower manpower ceilings. You know that far better than I. Do more with less, they keep telling us. The OMB now says we've got to get rid of a hundred more bodies by the end of this fiscal year. The Agency has less than three weeks to identify them. My vote is: tie a can to all twelve of these GS-14s. The evaluation panels say they're the lowest five percent of their group. Why wait?"

Wendell's heavy cleft jaw jutted in disagreement. He intensely disliked the pandemic use of the bureaucratic term "bodies," a fact that Kobler knew very well. For almost a year Wendell had lived in uneasy daily collaboration with this high-tension, foot-jiggling senior assistant, one assigned to him by the Office of Personnel. Kobler had taken some getting used to. His predecessor, a grizzled old clandestine warrior named Martek, had an outlook and philosophy so much like Wendell's that one could start a sentence and the other would finish it. But retirement had taken Martek away. Kobler, fifteen years younger, had been touted as Top Drawer and got the job.

It was true that Kobler was the very model of a modern Special Assistant. He gobbled up problems and inquiries and spat out answers and solutions like some sort of a human Gatling gun. Wendell's office never ran more smoothly or professionally than with Kobler in the outer office.

He also knew that Kobler merited the nickname bandied about by the Old Boys in the executive dining room, where Kobler, not of sufficient rank, could not lunch save as a guest: Super-Shark. Kobler divided the world mercilessly into producers and non-producers. That Wendell's pointed remark to Kobler about com-

passion had bounced off the man like a BB shot off a tank was
predictable. And he was in no doubt about what Kobler, in effect, was telling him: "We're going to get rid of these old-timers
of yours, these elderly geezers going back to OSS and World War
II. And you, the DDO, have no choice but to go along because
they have been carefully evaluated and found wanting." He
wagged a forefinger at the list in Kobler's hand.

"All right, the last ten will have to go. We're agreed. But look at
those last two names, Don. Add up their combined years of service. Seventy-one years of intelligence experience between them, of
clandestine know-how, tradecraft, tribal memory, languages. Do
we have the luxury of throwing *that* kind of experience on the
junk heap of compulsory retirement? Both were fine officers at
one time, lots of fire in the belly. . . ."

"Not an ember in either one of their bellies now," Kobler broke
in.

"Maybe not. Maybe it's a case of professional tired blood. But
am I supposed to sit here as DDO and make a knee-jerk concur-
rence with senior evaluation panels and throw them out, like the
Eskimos do with their old people, to have them sit on an ice floe
and die? Maybe find jobs elsewhere in the Shop where their experience can really be useful, like Training. Heave them out, no."
He paused and added quite calmly, "Not while I'm running this
Directorate."

Kobler's eyes were flat and shielded. His left foot jiggled, and
again he tweaked his nose, a clear and familiar sign that Don
Kobler was swallowing his spit. He cleared his throat and his tone
was markedly more deferential.

"All right, sir, let's bite one bullet at a time. First one: Silas
Ruffing."

He's like a warden reading off the names of condemned men
readied to mount the gallows, Wendell thought.

"Silas Ruffing. One of the best counter-intelligence officers we
ever had," he said, half to himself. Then he remembered, and a
flame of anger leaped from his eyes. "Just where the hell is he? I
thought you were on his trail to find that Calinescu file, Don."

"I've done everything except stake out his office," Kobler
protested. "He left early for lunch today, and before that he simply disappeared somewhere in this building. Nobody knows where

he goes; as I've told you again and again, that's a pretty sloppy shop down there in Documents Review."

"Well, make damned sure that he is intercepted the minute he walks in from lunch and is told that I want to see him immediately!" Wendell knew that he must curb his choleric instincts but Ruffing's uncontrolled work habits offended his sense of work ethic. A breeze of remorse immediately cooled his ire: how far gone was poor old Silas, whose own concept of work and devotion to duty had fully equaled his, that he was now playing will-o'-the-wisp in an outer fringe of the Directorate's activity!

"How many commendations does Ruffing have, Don?" he asked. He wanted to make it clear to Kobler that Silas had not always been an aged corridor-wanderer with a pack-rat's penchant for collecting old files.

"A total of six." Kobler's remorseless eyes did not leave the page of the panel report on Ruffing. "One of them from you, dated 1946, when you were commanding SSU in Vienna."

He looked at Wendell with an expectant smile. Wendell knew exactly what was going on in his mind: here's the daddy of the Old Boys trying to save their asses.

"It's true that Ruffing was once considered one of the top CI officers in the Shop," Kobler went on. "But he's been in the low ten percent of his peer group for the last three years in a row. And any time after noon, he's usually out with that bunch of boozing losers at the Eagle, up on Connecticut Avenue. God alone knows how he even makes it back here alive in his car after lunch."

"That's the man who personally spotted and frustrated two separate efforts by the Soviets to penetrate this Agency!" Wendell exclaimed. Deep within him, he knew that he would also lose on this one. Ruffing would eventually have to go. A dignified retreat was the only resolution. But he could make no exceptions to his own iron rule that alcoholism for an intelligence officer had the same horrendous potential for operational disaster as it did for a motorist. The thought of the diminutive, intense, hunched-over man with a tangle of once-red hair and steady, canny eyes, made him pause. He looked out at the gently waving skyline of trees and back at Kobler, executioner's pencil raised.

"Silas Ruffing is a walking counter-espionage history book," he said, annoyed at the flush-and-queasiness that washed over him again. Perhaps these chlorthalidone medications were too damned strong.

Kobler had lowered his pencil with evident disappointment, and this secretly pleased Wendell.

"If we can get this damned matter of the Calinescu file cleared up, Silas has an awful lot of solid CI indoctrination to pass on to the new CTs. Look, drop around to the Director of Training on my behalf and find out whether he's not willing to take Silas on for a tour down on the Farm, teaching counter-intelligence doctrine. That will just about bring him to compulsory retirement age of sixty. He could bow out with dignity and without a can tied to his tail."

"And how about the drinking?" Kobler was, if nothing else, to the point.

Wendell rocked meditatively in his swivel chair for a moment.

"The assignment to the Farm will be contingent on Ruffing's agreement to seek medical advice for his alcoholism problem. I'll personally talk with Doc Hocker about him. I'm not sure just how far gone he is, even if he does hang around with that noontime bunch of tipplers at the Eagle. We've got to find out just how badly off he is."

He realized with a twinge of insight what was agitating him about Ruffing. It was his memory of Ruffing standing in the Vienna SSU office so long ago, a slight uniformed figure pacing around him and ticking off on the fingers of one hand the reasons why he, Wendell, should disapprove the Calinescu lead so forcefully advocated by Browning: first, the whole thing smacked of a Soviet provocation even if the preliminary information was excellent; second, Calinescu would not reveal the precise source of his information and that made it immediately suspect as a paper mill; third, Calinescu's money demands for the information were far too high; fourth, it simply sounded like some kind of an NKVD trap being carefully laid . . . But Wendell had overruled Silas. The sample of his information had been evaluated and was just too good, too valuable. He, Wendell, had decided that the risks were, in the end, acceptable. Silas had pointed a final prophetic finger at him and had said, "We'll live to regret this one, for a long time, George." And how appallingly right Ruffing was.

Kobler's foot jiggling accelerated and after a moment he straightened in his chair and smiled his bleak smile.

"You're the DDO. Ruffing is a loser, in my view, but if you want to try a training tour for him, subject to medical consultation, OK."

He scrawled the disposition of Ruffing's status beside his name, and looked up expectantly.

"Last but not least, Steven Browning, Jr."

Silence hung in the large sun-filled office like a black balloon. Kobler said, voice tinged with careful sarcasm, "A legend, I think you recently said, in our time."

Wendell placed three fingers of one hand reflectively in a vest pocket of his three-piece summer suit. He looked, Kobler reminded himself yet again, half mockingly, half admiringly, like a senior southern senator about to commence a filibuster. Goddamn, in a day as busy as this one, with a hundred things to do before close of business, the time Wendell consumed on such achingly trivial matters as getting rid of a few marginal personnel!

"When I came into OSS and got to Italy early in 1944," Wendell said, looking out at the green forest beyond the expanse of glass, "I was already a captain and Steve Browning was a first lieutenant."

He chuckled at the expression on Kobler's face.

"No, Don, we're not going to spend the rest of the afternoon telling war stories. But Browning was quite possibly the most audacious man I've ever worked with. He'd take chances where common sense said: you try that and you'll turn up dead. To give you an idea, he had two Purple Hearts, one of them serious, and three other decorations by the time the war ended. He probably deserved three more. One of the Purple Hearts, the serious one, he got on a quiet day in early summer 1944 when he and I went out to pick up a line-crosser who was returning from a mission into Florence, which was then still in German hands. I shouldn't have been up there in the jeep with Browning, but I was. I also shouldn't have been driving the jeep, but I was. I was curious to know just how you did those things up at the front. And it was I who took the wrong dirt road. The next thing I knew, bullets were ripping through the windshield and bouncing off the hood. We had inadvertently reached a German forward position."

Wendell stood up with ponderous grace. Kobler's eyes followed him attentively.

"I took a bullet here"—he pointed to a spot two inches below the lower pocket of his vest—"and another one in my right leg just above the knee, and a glancing one that made this neat little furrow just above my right eyebrow here. Luckily, the bullets didn't hit any bones or arteries, but blood was running into my eyes and I pitched clear out of the jeep into the road when I was hit."

Wendell walked slowly around his desk to Kobler, his florid features alive with the remembered scene.

"The jeep was still rolling down this dirt road, still under fire. I was watching it while lying in the road. 'Goodbye jeep,' I remembered saying to myself. Browning jumped from the passenger side into the driver's seat, with the thing still rolling along. I don't know how he did that. He shifted gears, made a tight U-turn off the road into an olive orchard, came steaming back up the road, with MG-42 slugs still whizzing at him from about a hundred yards away. He reached the spot where I lay, sprang out of the jeep, picked me up, all two hundred pounds of me, threw me into the back, and roared off, at which point I lost consciousness. When I woke up, I was in a U. S. Army field hospital near Orvieto. And guess who was in the next hospital cot? Steve Browning, with a bullet through his shoulder."

Wendell shook his head at the evocation of the incident.

"I still don't know why he didn't just leave me in the road, keep going, and save his own ass. That's a hell of a way to win a Purple Heart—and a Silver Star."

Kobler said, after a respectful moment, "A hell of a story."

Wendell plodded back to his desk, touching the wound spot with almost a sentimental affection.

"And two years after that," he said to Kobler, "he nagged and pushed and argued with me until he got us into this lousy Calinescu business."

"Do you know where he's been rated on the GS-14 promotion list for the last two years in a row?"

Wendell's steady eyes caught his.

"Pretty low on the list, by the happy sound in your voice, I'd say."

There, Kobler knew, he'd tipped his hand. With George Wendell, you had to be very careful. The man had almost feline reactions.

"It's nothing for me to be joyous about, George," he responded, injured innocence in every syllable. "He was last; out of a group of seventy-five or so GS-14 operations generalists. Last, for two years in a row."

Kobler was fully in command now. He had his facts marshaled precisely, and was happy to ram them home.

"And why? Because this 'legend in our time' can't hack it. Not any more. Listen to this, the most recent panel comment: 'This officer, after a genuinely brilliant and audacious career in intelligence, has outlived his usefulness to the Agency. He has performed only marginally in his staff operations-review assignment for the past two years. Because of his exposure to a number of foreign services, he cannot be assigned operationally to many areas overseas, except in an open liaison capacity. His managerial aptitudes are marginal. Regretfully, the panel recommends that he be urged to accept involuntary retirement after almost thirty-four years of service. . . .' "

Kobler did his homework very well, Wendell thought, watching the man's intent features as he read aloud the panel's assessment like a judge pronouncing a verdict to the accused. But would to God that "performed only marginally" were all there was to Steve Browning's status.

A month earlier, Matt McClure, his calm and composed Chief of Counter-Intelligence, had sat in the very chair now being occupied by the foot-jiggling Kobler and had addressed Wendell in his deceptively gentle, almost apologetic manner.

"I've got some troubling info to pass on to you, George," in a tone that priests use in telling next of kin that their loved ones are no more. "But first, I'm telling you that I've set up a Bigot List on this one, a very short list, as you can imagine. You're sixth on it. The others are Hank Nordholm, Chief of Security; Max Ingram, Chief of the Sov Div; Wally Trumbull, Max's man handling defector debriefing; my own secretary; and myself."

"Don't tell me you've uncovered a Soviet bug in our executive dining room!" Wendell said with a sigh as he plumped heavily into a chair close to McClure. But repartee was not Matt's strong suit. His light, almost transparent blue eyes held Wendell's reproachfully for a moment.

"Maybe something a hell of a lot more serious," he responded. "But I'll try to be as succinct as I can. You're busy and I have a lot to do."

Wendell waited. Matt could be depended on to report quickly and honestly. That was why Wendell had put him into the CI job.

"You know that we're still debriefing that junior Soviet diplomat who defected to us in East Africa about six weeks ago . . ."

"Encrypted source SLOWBOY," Wendell interrupted. He prided himself on keeping up with these cases.

"SLOWBOY it is," Matt acknowledged with a nod. "First tour abroad; he really seemed to have very little hot stuff to gladden our hearts. A few good insights into Soviet policy in East Africa and their assistance programs, training of nationalist blacks in Russia, but little else except his embassy's order of battle. We brought him to the States for resettlement mostly because we know that the word gets out that we accept *all* defectors."

Wendell nodded, struggling to keep his attention on McClure while his thoughts turned to a very busy day, with NSA and Defense meetings scheduled within the hour.

"Wally Trumbull, handling the current debriefing here, was chatting yesterday with SLOWBOY out at the holding area, about his assignment at his Foreign Ministry in Moscow, prior to assignment to Africa. You know: what was he doing at the office, who his friends were, what the Moscow gossip mill was turning out."

Matt bent his head to peer at his notes, every hair of his precisely combed silvery head in place.

"It turned out that SLOWBOY knew three or four young KGB types his age, with whom he had grown up in Moscow, all of them offspring of the top-banana crowd in Moscow: sons of KGB generals, Party big shots, senior government officials. SLOWBOY's crowd generally got fried on weekends and blabbed a lot of indiscreet inside stuff to each other when in that state.

Most of it was who was sleeping with whom, who was getting rake-offs from foreign contractors, the old *blat'* bit."

"I thought our Georgetown crowd had the monopoly on telling tales out of school," Wendell said abstractedly. For once, McClure was slow in getting to the point, almost as if he were reluctant to do so.

"Well, we're talking about *their* Georgetown crowd, George," Matt rejoined. "Even the Sovs blab to each other—if they know each other well. Remember, this is the junior 'in-crowd,' the golden set around the Kremlin. Anyway, SLOWBOY remembered something that he overheard one night, sitting in a big country dacha belonging to the father of one of them, drinking the best vodka. It was crowded and two of his buddies, both of them fairly new in the KGB, were talking louder than usual, given the noise and the booze."

Wendell found himself leaning toward McClure, his attention suddenly focusing totally on the CI Chief's narrative.

"KGB-One was bragging to KGB-Two about what their service was doing to the Main Enemy (that's us). KGB-Two says sarcastically, 'Well, *your* Directorate may be going great guns but I'll bet you haven't got anybody like Kim Philby, George Blake, or the German Felfe, have you?' To which KGB-One, sorely provoked, says to KGB-Two in a loud whisper, 'Listen, we have our hooks into the American service, one of their *stary*' (Old Boy, in Russian, George)."

"That might be pure bullshit." Wendell bit off the words acidly. "KGB-One simply trying to sound important."

Matt smiled pleasantly, his priestly features composed and understanding.

"KGB-Two said exactly the same thing, George. To which KGB-One answered, 'Listen, it's the truth. We've been dealing with this American, in New Delhi, in Amman . . .'"

Wendell pulled out a crisp white handkerchief and mopped his brow, suddenly damp as if with exertion. McClure shot him a glance full of sympathy.

"I can guess what you're thinking. Well, the minute I heard about SLOWBOY's recollections yesterday afternoon, I knew we were possibly on to something that was ticking like a time bomb: a Soviet termite in the Shop."

McClure, careful, methodical, turned again to his notebook.

"We immediately ran computer readouts of our personnel: who had served in New Delhi and Amman; who of those who had served there was an Old Boy, and still on duty at a time when KGB-One mentioned this."

Wendell leaned back in his chair and briefly closed his eyes.

"Let's have the good news, Matt."

McClure closed his notebook with a gesture of finality.

"The computer does not contain complete data"—his soft voice floated his words at Wendell—"and there may well be one or two others we'll have to look at carefully, but as of this moment, the man who fits the lead is none other than our old colleague, Steve Browning."

His words hung in the air for a moment and he watched Wendell instinctively shake his head, unable and unwilling to accept what he had heard.

"This is hardly hanging evidence, George," Matt said carefully. "As a matter of fact, it's almost mischievous. But as you can imagine, we're going to have to take immediate cauterizing action. We have no choice."

Wendell jumped to his feet, gnawing his lower lip. But he had not survived as DDO by vacillating.

"We've got to do two things immediately," he rumbled. "Sit down with Nordholm and put a twenty-four-hour surveillance on Steve, and don't take any flak from him that it will strip him of all his available men. This is top priority!"

McClure scribbled his instructions as Wendell paced around the room.

"Second, take Steve out of his present job and put him into something innocuous. Let's see: Steve's assigned to the Operational Review staff. I'll have him assigned to reviewing those old political-action projects we intend to declassify anyway."

McClure nodded and peered up at Wendell.

"And what about the Director? The Bureau? Intelligence Oversight Board? Department of Justice? . . ."

Wendell held up a peremptory hand.

"Not yet. Not yet. Look, Matt, I want you to clear one or two of your top CI analysts. Add them to the Bigot List and have them sift through every scrap of information from previous defectors, friendly services, anything that might authenticate or wash out this suspicion."

He marched to the broad window and stared at the waving line of trees in the distance.

"I won't go to the Director with this one yet; he'd simply go straight through the overcast. Remember, SLOWBOY is telling about a conversation he overheard a year ago. Whatever damage has been done is already irremediable. But we can't go off half cocked until we sort out just how bad this one is."

McClure rose to go, his lined, tranquil face thoughtful. He had many things to do.

"We'll scour all of our files, of course, George," he said. "But give Chief Near East Div a phone call, will you? We'll be wanting to read their chronos on what the Sovs were doing in Delhi and Amman during the periods of time when Steve was serving there. With special attention to the reasons Steve was PNGed from Amman."

"I'll do it as soon as we're finished here," Wendell assured him.

"And are you sure you don't want to clear anybody on your staff?" McClure's question was guarded. He knew that Wendell did not appreciate being told how to suck eggs.

"Look, as you know I've got a new Deputy coming on board who is taking an orientation trip to our Southeast Asia stations," Wendell replied. "I'm not going to lay this on him at the very outset."

He fingered a worn Phi Beta Kappa key chained to his vest, as if it were a talisman.

"How about your distinguished Special Assistant, Don Kobler?" McClure knew what the response would be. He was not wrong. Wendell shook his head once and wagged a forefinger.

"For the moment, Matt, just put my secretary, Clare Meehan, on your Bigot List. She can handle any info coming in from you or Hank in my absence and hold it for my return. I don't want anyone else on my staff witting; there's just too much blabbing in the cafeterias."

McClure's eyes crinkled appreciatively. Clare Meehan could be trusted with solutions to the riddle of the universe. He nodded and sidled toward the door.

"And, Matt"—Wendell's voice had sunk to a conspiratorial

bass—"don't put down anything in writing, for the moment. The minute you have an Eyes-Only memo, some smart-ass secretary or records clerk is going to get his mitts on it and run to a Xerox machine. We've paid dearly for things we've put into writing. As far as I'm concerned, Steve Browning is under suspicion but no one has proved anything against him. Are we agreed on that?"

McClure said, "You're the boss, George. We operate by word of mouth until you say otherwise."

At the door, he said softly, "I'm sorry as hell that it's Steve we have under the glass. He's got an incredible Agency record. And I happen to know what he did for you in Italy, George."

Wendell, biting his lip, responded, "That's nothing to what. he's doing *to* me today."

Kobler looked up at Wendell from under thin sandy brows. His superior was not taking this low-five business at all well. It was clearly bothering him deeply. But, damn him, this protectiveness toward old buddies who hadn't cut the mustard in years had to stop. If he, Kobler, let up now, Wendell would assign Browning as Special Assistant in Charge of Cold War Reminiscences.

"Then, as you said just a minute ago, there's this Calinescu thing . . ."

"I thought," Wendell said, looking quizzically at his assistant, "that the Director has assigned the Calinescu inquiry to the IG. I had promised him that we in the Operations Directorate would stay completely out of the IG investigation, especially since I happen to have been involved, back in 1946."

Kobler's expression was one Wendell had learned to recognize: aren't-you-lucky-to-have-me-around.

"Right, sir. And the IG is now going through the Calinescu operations files with Steve. But you may be interested to know that Steve's stonewalling them."

"Stonewalling?" Wendell's mobile face was cocked toward him, a curious interest flickering in his deep-set eyes.

"That's the honest opinion of the inspector who's handling the interviews with him." Kobler shrugged. "Steve hasn't been caught up in any specific fibs, but they sense he's holding back on them. Well, there's always the Box to put him on, at the end."

Too late, Kobler remembered that this was a word Wendell intensely disliked. The polygraph machine, he growled, should be referred to as such. "The Box" evoked an image of a coffin, just as did "bodies" when referring to personnel.

"And if he passes the Flutter, what then?" Wendell, in using the in-house term for the polygraph, administered the subtle rebuke. But there was something else in his tone, indefinable. "Is he then washed in the blood of the lamb?"

That was yet another of these old-timer quirks, Kobler felt, with annoyance: their dislike of the polygraph as a means of establishing truth or untruth. He was well aware that Wendell, who had personally undergone four routine polygraph interviews during his Agency career, made no bones about his personal antipathy to them while not denying their limited usefulness in certain situations.

Kobler himself thought that the polygraph wasn't being used nearly as frequently as it should be. It was uncomfortable being strapped into the thing, sure. Unpleasant, yes. But it invoked a definite residual fear, and you had to invoke fear in this business to keep everyone's nose clean. He decided to cut his losses.

"Well, George, we're getting a little bit ahead of the scenario, aren't we? By the end of next week, the IG should really have a fix on any lash-ups with our people past and present in this Calinescu case."

He jiggled his foot for another moment, rustled the personnel list in his hand, and stood to move his cramped legs.

"Well, that takes care of the low-five personnel situation for today, right?"

He scrawled a notation beside Browning's name.

"Maybe it'd be wiser to suspend any termination action on him until the Calinescu affair has been completely cleared up? Are you agreed to table it until then, and have a look at it? I'll put a 're-view in two weeks' note on my tickler list. The other ten are out and you'll talk to Hocker about Ruffing. OK?"

"Yes." Wendell's voice came after a pause and as if from a distant room. "Yes, that'll be fine. And I much appreciate the background work you've done on this one, Don. First-class staff work."

They were, Wendell thought, looking at Kobler gathering his precisely organized papers from the coffee table, men as different

as one could find in an Agency containing as diverse an assort-
ment of personalities and types as did the United Nations. He,
George Sheridan Wendell, Deputy Director for Operations of the
Central Intelligence Agency, in voice, dress, manner, and outlook,
represented a vanishing Agency species: Choate School, a Magna
and Phi Beta Kappa at Harvard, comfortably off (old money),
OSS in war and peace, one of the last of the original officers in the
Agency, a member of the Metropolitan and City Tavern clubs,
owner and resident of a Georgetown R Street town house—an assured Washington insider.

His Special Assistant, lanky, gaunt body seeming to cut through
the air even when standing still, was the Comer, vibrating with an
ambition chronically underfed and reaching out hungrily for more
sustenance. For Don Kobler, almost two decades younger than
his master, the difference in ages also meant one important thing:
Kobler was much too young to have participated in either World
War II or the Korean War. Out of the parochial school system in
Chicago, honor graduate of Notre Dame, a brief military participant in the early phases of the Vietnam War before joining the
Agency, he had made his way as a skilled halfback tears through
a tough opposing line: running hard, twisting past threatening
tackles, shifting his terrain when he saw new openings, capable of
making lightning feints when needed.

Kobler, he knew, had made his reputation early. His instructors
in the Junior Officer training courses were unanimous that while
he would hardly win popularity contests, Don Kobler would do
very well. And so he had in successive tours in Nairobi and Kuala
Lumpur, followed by a climactic two-tour (Agency people usually
fled the place after one *year*) stay in Vietnam, this time as an
Agency operative. There his formidable organizational abilities enabled him to create an interrogation center for Viet Cong prisoners which yielded precious information and high praise from
the station. In rapid succession, Kobler had served as Deputy
Chief of Station in two African countries where in each place he
converted a somnolent CIA presence into one of high productiv-
ity, including three excellent recruitments: one Soviet, one Yugoslav, and one black Foreign Minister. (Some inevitable cynics
muttered that other officers had done most of the spadework up to

the actual recruitment pitches, but the results were there in Kobler's personnel folder, unchallenged in writing by anyone.)

Prior to his present assignment, Kobler had completed a one-year tour at the Army War College in Carlisle Barracks, Pennsylvania, one of those prestigious military think tanks to which only those Agency officers tagged as possessing Senior Management Potential were detailed. When he was asked whether he cared to serve as Special Assistant to the DDO himself for a tour, Kobler did not hesitate for a moment: he was honored, he said.

Wendell remembered Don's first appearance as Special Assistant in this very room: had Kobler been a wild animal, his ears would have been quivering with alertness, his nose sniffing the wind. After using the word "criteria" twice as a singular noun, and two banalities ("That's the way the cookie crumbles" and "The bottom line is . . ."), all of which saddened Wendell's purist soul, Kobler had responded to his routinely courteous question "What sort of a position would you like to achieve in the Agency?" by pointing to Wendell's swivel chair and declaiming in that crisp, nasal voice, "Eventually, sir, I'd like *your* job—DDO."

That they coexisted these many months was simple testimony to the fact that they were both, in different ways, professionals, possessing complementary skills and work disciplines and an ability to cope with unexpected emergencies. Each was quite aware that the other, in a purely chemical sense, did not like him at all, and each disliked the other in turn. But Wendell ran the Directorate and he willingly used his assistant's pragmatic strength to get things done.

Kobler now rose, happy to have sealed the fate of the low-fives. Wendell was certain that he would gallop straight off with his news to the Career Management people and would pick up yet another brownie point for ramming the matter through the DDO. Well, if it made him feel good, why not?

"Oh, Don," he called, "I want to have Personnel prepare a separate letter for each of these ten low-fives, with thanks and appreciation for their long years of service, et cetera. For *my* signature."

"Will do, sir."

"And, Don?"

Kobler stopped in his tracks.

"Would you ask Clare to request Steve Browning's file from

Personnel. I want another look at it, the full one with all the Eyes-Alone stuff included."

A prescient grin creased Kobler's thin features.

"She won't have far to go. I had just borrowed it from the IG, who had it. The file is sitting on my desk."

"Oh, indeed! How fortuitous. Have you read it?"

Kobler's grin widened.

"Cover to cover. You certainly gave him some fancy fitness reports in the old days."

"He deserved them," Wendell snapped. With that word "fancy" Kobler had managed to place him on the defensive. "And since you say you have read the whole file, you'll note I was hardly alone in his cheering section."

"Seemed to rock the boat a lot." Kobler's even-toned demurrer signaled his failure to agree. "He did pull some impressive stunts. The info he got from Calinescu, the Yemen caper, the Greek thing, and that wild period during the Hungarian uprising in 1956. But he'd never get away with some of that stuff today. Under current Executive Orders and Agency ground rules, he'd have been fired in minutes."

"You're probably right," Wendell retorted. "But we weren't operating under *today's* ground rules in 1956. We can discuss that point another time, Don."

"Right. Another time."

Kobler closed the door carefully behind him. Wendell rose from his chair, rocked slightly on his feet for a moment or two, absently staring at the furled American flag on its stand.

With a tiny sigh, he reached for his reading glasses and peered at the half-foot-high stack of highly classified papers in his "in" box. Yes, he had been defensive and abrupt with Kobler when asked about Steve's fitness reports.

But when a man has literally saved your hide, your fitness reports could scarcely be objective, now, could they? (Deep within him, he knew that he should have focused more on Browning's personal conduct: his illegal "requisition" of the Vienna apartment he had occupied, the equally illegal "personal" jeep Steve had somehow acquired in wartime Italy and had driven into Austria, Steve's interminable end runs around the unit's finance and admin regulations.) In retrospect, Steve had constantly skirted the edge of permissible behavior. But in the postwar world of thirty-five years ago, Steve's peccadillos had seemed relatively minor compared to his successful operational deeds!

He studied the formidable "in" box, unseeing. There he was, rationalizing his conduct again. The odd thing was that he never really liked Steve. The war had thrown them together and it was fate that Browning had rescued him, but there had always been something . . . something *wrong* about Steve. At this moment, he hated feeling grateful to the man.

Then there was Kobler, increasingly assertive, his ambition almost a palpable force. Quick as a quarter horse was Kobler, very useful in certain situations but very dangerous as a Special Assistant with access to virtually everything in the Directorate. He was certain that Kobler smelled something about the Browning business. Being Kobler, he would go to great lengths to sniff his way to the source of the odor. But it was essential in this dicey investigation that the list of those witting be kept to a minimum. Kobler could not be brought into it, not yet.

As it was, the Bigot List on this one was growing. The Director now knew, as did his Deputy. And only God knew how many in their entourages had been alerted in one way or another. The vessel of need-to-know often sprang leaks at top levels. But he couldn't sit here and worry about the discretion of all of those in the know. That was on their heads.

"Seemed to rock the boat a lot," Kobler had said of Steve, in more truth than he knew.

Wendell reached for the top document in his "in" box, one with a bright red tag marked "Immediate Handling" stapled to its cover sheet. But he could not concentrate on its contents. The memory of the Director's expression, when Wendell had told him of the suspicions of Browning, burned like a branding iron.

"What's the need of all this pussyfooting around, George?" he had barked, fixing Wendell with an imperious flash of the eye that military commanders give to their subordinates. "Why shouldn't I fire him straightaway, get him out of this building, remove him from access to all the damned secrets we have in here? National security is at stake, George!"

"For two reasons, sir," Wendell had replied, hands folded before him in cool defiance. "First, nothing has been proven. We haven't spotted Steve meeting with or otherwise communicating with the Soviets. If we wrongly pin the donkey's tail of 'Soviet agent' on him, and he chooses to go public in protest, I'm sure you'd agree that the howl from Congress and the media would be . . . most unfortunate."

The Director had quickly cooled down; he understood Washington *Realpolitik* as well as anyone. Wendell had rumbled smoothly on, well aware what was going on in the mind of his superior: watch Wendell and his effort to put the best possible light on one of his Old Boys.

"Second, if Browning is really at present under Soviet control here in Washington, we and the FBI want to know all about it: who is handling him, how are they doing it, what do they want to learn from him, what are they getting from him? It's absolutely essential that we learn their MO. It would be most unfortunate if we tipped our hand prematurely."

His eyes on the fingers of the Director's right hand drumming the desk top impatiently, he added in a near-accusatory tone, "Counter-espionage involves an enormous amount of patience and vigilance."

To which the Director had replied testily, "Unfortunately, George, *I* don't happen to have a hell of a lot of patience. I'm the President's top intelligence adviser, remember, and I'm not a counter-espionage spook."

He pointed an unwavering right index finger across his tidy desk at Wendell.

"George, I'm giving you and Security thirty days to find out everything you can about this Browning case. After that, unless you've proven to your satisfaction and mine that Browning is innocent, I'm going to fire him without charges simply by invoking the national interest. That's my privilege as Director, and I have no hesitation about doing that. Then I intend to inform, on a need-to-know, the congressional committees and the Intelligence Oversight Board. Got it?"

That was three weeks ago. One more week from now Browning would be fired unless . . . unless SLOWBOY's little story was wrong.

As if on cue, the light on his telephone Secure Line began its urgent winking. Clare buzzed him on the intercom and said, "Matt McClure on Red, sir."

Matt came straight to the point.

"Daily sitrep on Our Hero."

"Shoot."

"Tonight he has a date to call on the wife of the Austrian Minister-Counselor at her home."

"Social?"

"I think not, although the Minister isn't home."

"And what does *that* mean, Matt?"

He thought he heard a barely suppressed snort.

"Don't know. Unless you want to make something of her maiden name."

"Which is?"

"Which is Mara von Kueppke, onetime member of your old SSU surveillance team in Vienna back in the forties."

Matt, hearing no reply, waited and cautiously asked, "George, are you still on line?"

Wendell finally said, as if talking to himself, "Mara, that East Prussian girl? The one who moved in with Steve?"

As he probed into the corners of his memory, his voice changed to a shout. "Good God, she was a playmate of Dimi Calinescu's! Vienna 1946!"

Matt's calm voice said, "Encrypted as TTVELVET-8. No one had a clue she was here until Steve made a phone call to her."

Wendell, his mind whirling, asked, "What are you doing about it?"

To which Matt answered quietly, "The only thing we can do, George. We've got two vehicles on Steve's tail all the time. Everywhere he goes."

CHAPTER FIVE

On the phone, Joanie's voice was, as always, calm, almost challengingly neutral.

"Evening work again, you say?" the soft-rounded words of her Carolina origins echoed his. "Well, that's OK with me, Stevie. I'm off to a PTA meeting at eight P.M. anyway. The parents of the kids in my class are comin' to chat with me about their little darlin's. I'll just leave some cold chicken in the fridge, with a tossed salad. Take anything else you can find when you get home."

And that was it. No perplexed rejoinders of "Just what the hell is this evening work all about?" Not a quiver of implied interest. Not that he expected any, not now, not after years and years of his making such calls. Not the way things were between them.

"Thanks," he said. "Appreciate the chicken and salad. Hope the parents aren't too much of a chore."

"I can take just about anything at this point, Steve," she answered, ever so evenly, the pointed needle of her voice barely pricking his skin.

"Yes, I believe that," he said after a moment to convey his awareness that her needle had been felt. "So long."

He trudged heavily from the phone booth along the carpeted corridor of the McLean restaurant, found an corner table near the front window where he could eat alone, and looked out into a clump of heavy-leafed oaks, basking in the dying shafts of sunlight.

There was so much in his career which he never mentioned to Joanie. Not a word about the postwar years in Austria, for example. She had asked about them in the first years of their marriage; in fact, in those early years together she had peppered him nightly, leaning across to him in bed, her modest breasts almost caressing his cheek, bubbling with questions about what he was doing, as excited as a child querying an ancient survivor of the Old West as he spun his yarns.

But she had learned that a wall of silence would fall over entire periods of time: what he did when he left their residence in Athens or Amman or New Delhi and did not return for days, a week.

Joanie was no fool. She knew he had much to hide. *How* much he had to hide, of course, she had no idea. She also knew that he was tormented by what he could not, would not, tell her. And so she stopped asking him. Whatever he said, at this juncture, was OK. She had her school kids or Timmy or PTA or some other damned thing to look after. He shook his head as if to fling all thoughts of his wife into the farthest corner of his mind.

Hunched over the tiny table, menu unopened, in the lone near-empty room, he stared at the bright, even flame of a candle burning inside its cylindrical glass sheath and tried to recall how brutally cold it was on that February morning in 1946 when most of Vienna shivered indoors.

The highly unpredictable telephone had buzzed in the flat he had contrived to requisition (a little friendly hanky-panky with a Viennese secretary in the USFA housing office, plus ten packs of cigarettes as a sweetener), conveniently located near his unit's office in the 1st Bezirk of Vienna. A banal code sentence uttered in the smooth undulating voice of Ernoe, one of his more slippery Hungarian informants, alerted him to proceed to an emergency meeting between them precisely six hours later. At that meeting, Ernoe wasted no time.

"One of my best contacts tells me that a Romanian named Calinescu wants to see you, Herr Chef. Very soon," Ernoe informed him in his lilting German, his frosted breath issuing with each word in the chill shabbiness of the safe-house room. Ernoe's black gypsy eyes glittered with an unquenchable excitement for life out of a face which resembled a slab of ruddy beef. The shock of graying hair and the deep lines around his eyes belied the fact that Ernoe was only twenty-seven years old. Two years of combat service on the Eastern Front with the hapless Hungarian Army, fighting with the Wehrmacht against the Soviets, drastically

speeded up the aging process, Steve reflected, as he handed his
agent a double shot of raw schnapps in a water glass. Ernoe immediately downed it in a gulp with an appreciative smack of his lips.

"Who is this Calinescu and why should I see him?"

Ernoe laid a finger along his nose, a gesture which signified: listen carefully, there's more to this than both of us know.

"Aha, Herr Chef, I have made my inquiries. This man was
once a big man in Romania. Very big man. I don't know much
about these Romanians. I don't like Romanians. But he ran into
much difficulty with the Germans, or so my *Spitzls* tell me. He
has been in a German internment camp. And now he's here in
Vienna. Don't ask why. This city is filled with people . . . like
him and me. DPs" (he pronounced it "Dippies"). "Flotsam." His
eyes danced with the intrigue of it all and he held out his glass
pleadingly until Browning, gloves still on chilled hands, poured
him another generous schnapps.

"But Calinescu isn't a little fish like me, buying and selling
black-market cigarettes, butter, nylons. Not him. I know that he
drives a good BMW Wanderer that must have belonged to a
Gauleiter or some other Nazi big shot in the old days." He rubbed
his thumb and fingers together. "That takes a lot of black-market
benzine. And he has a very nice apartment in a *Bezirk* in the British Zone. He has at least two bodyguards. A big shot. You see,
Ernoe knows everything."

Steve, rubbing two gloved hands together, held the gypsy's eyes
with his for a moment.

"And what do you think his game is? Why me?"

Ernoe, bulking out of a civilianized Wehrmacht officer's leather
greatcoat, shrugged his shoulders in a gesture of bemused ambiva-
lence.

"God only knows, Herr Chef. But I have done my duty in telling you of this man and his interest in you. Ernoe is useful to you,
yes?"

His beefy face lit up in a rapturous smile when Steve handed
him five packs of cigarettes, which in real value at that moment
exceeded a week's pay for a Viennese workingman.

But Ernoe's tip did not go over well at all with Silas Ruffing or
with Steve's supervisor, Major George Wendell, commander of
the Logistics Support Component of the United States Forces in

Austria, the cover name for the SSU in Vienna. And the reply from Washington was unencouraging.

"CALINESCU IS COMMON NAME IN ROMANIA. WITHOUT FURTHER BIO DATA, CANNOT GIVE MORE PRECISE TRACES," the decoded message read. "PERSON SEEKING CONTACT WITH DOLLOP [Browning's operational pseudonym] POSSIBLY IDEN WITH FORMER PROMINENT ROMANIAN YOUTH LEADER IN BUCHAREST WHO REPORTEDLY PARTICIPATED IN ATTEMPTED COUP AGAINST ANTONESCU REGIME IN 1941 AND ARRESTED BY THAT REGIME. RUMORED TO HAVE BEEN TAKEN TO GERMANY AND INTERNED THERE. HAS NOT BEEN HEARD FROM SINCE."

The last sentence made it clear how Washington felt about the matter.

"IF PERSON SEEKING OUT DOLLOP IS IDEN WITH ABOVE, GIVE HIM WIDE BERTH. IN ANY EVENT, RECOMMEND YOU HANDLE THIS LEAD WITH UTMOST CAUTION."

Ruffing, his laced paratroop boots resting on the corner of a battered desk in the dingy former premises of a Viennese insurance company, was even more emphatic. He stroked his newly grown bushy red mustache with some agitation.

"Steve, I wouldn't touch this guy with a ten-foot pole."

Browning, in civilian loden jacket and officer's pinks, pursed his lips in a frown he assumed when he was being denied his way. He knew well that Silas Ruffing recognized that expression. But their relationship had deepened and consolidated to a remarkable degree in the year they had been serving together in wartime Italy and now in Austria. Browning, for whom the old French military adage *"L'audace, l'audace, toujours l'audace"* had become a way of life, listened glumly to Silas' good sense and professional caution.

"Look, I know how you play long shots, Steve. But this funny little lead brought to you by that rat Ernoe should be in itself a red flag. I don't trust that gypsy bastard, as you know very well, even if he's useful in casing neighborhoods and spotting antique jewelry somebody's trying to sell. Ernoe would sell his father, assuming he knew who he was, for a carton of Philip Morris. I'll bet you that Calinescu has already bought into Ernoe and has drained every bit of information on you out of him."

Steve made a so-what motion with one hand.

"All right, Ruff. Let's assume you're correct. But what if Calinescu has something big, something important? Jesus, we aren't exactly burning up the track in this town these four months we've been here. You've got to keep rapping on doors, Ruff. Sooner or later one will open."

"Our priority task at this moment," Ruffing reminded him, "is collecting order-of-battle information on the Soviet armed forces in Austria, Hungary, and Czechoslovakia. Their whole goddamn show is run out of their headquarters in Baden bei Wien. We're still nibbling around the edges of it, copying down unit designations from Soviet trucks and tanks and milking a few dozen low-level Russian defectors back in our occupation zone in Salzburg and Linz. We need a real window into Soviet senior military staffs. So why waste our time with some shady Romanian DP?"

"Because," Steve answered him stubbornly, "it's another door to knock on. It won't take much time or money."

He remembered Ruffing's booted feet hitting the floor with exasperation.

"For Christ's sake, Steve, you've got Headquarters flashing red lights at you. And you know the conventional wisdom: being a Romanian isn't a nationality, it's a profession. This Calinescu is trying to hustle you. And he's probably been in the hustling business longer than you and me together. We're no match for these guys. Let's keep working on order of battle through Mike Radescu and his network, which at least has been tested out as OK, and through the CIC lads in Vienna and their contacts, and keep away from Ernoe's offerings."

Steve gave Silas Ruffing's cheek an affectionate pinch.

"You're in the hopeless business of trying to save me from myself, Ruff. I appreciate it. Any other suggestions?"

"Yes," Silas said dispiritedly. "At least check this out with Radescu. Every Romanian DP must know every other one."

Two days later, Mircea Radescu, chilled hands curled around a cup of weak tea for warmth, sat in an unlighted corner of a seedy gasthaus in Grinzing, across a small table from Browning, his gaunt cleanly shaven face a careful mask. When Steve stopped speaking, Radescu, in his precise, stilted English, got immediately down to business.

"It sounds to me, Captain Steve, that we are talking about Dimitriu Calinescu who until 1941 was one of the top leaders of the Iron Guard youth movement. I will not give you a long lecture on this group now, although you should know something about it before you get involved."

His wide liquid eyes held Steve's calmly but with an unnerving directness as if he could peer into his soul. What had happened to Mike Radescu had burned away any illusions or pretenses and enabled him to read these in others as one reads newspaper headlines.

"My family and my fellow Jews in Romania suffered so much under these Iron Guardists. For the ten years up to the beginning of the war we were like crops in the field being eaten by locusts," the quiet formal voice went on. "I am sure that the Western world knows little about what went on there in Romania even though it now knows the horrible things the Nazis did. A mystic lunatic named Corneliu Codreanu started this crazy group in 1927, under the name League of the Archangel Michael, and recruited a bunch of anti-foreign, anti-Semitic youths who wore green shirts and took vows of loyalty in each other's blood. The name was changed after some time to Garda de Fier, or Iron Guard."

"Nice crowd," Browning grunted.

"Nice crowd indeed. For years, they plotted to take power in Romania by violence and assassinations. By 1941, they had already killed in cold blood four Prime Ministers and hundreds of other top politicians and government people—and thousands of innocent Jews. They made one big mistake: they thought they had the Germans on their side when they tried to overthrow a very tough dictator, General Antonescu, in January 1941. He crushed them."

"Do you know Calinescu? Could you recognize him on sight?" Steve wriggled restlessly on the hard wooden chair.

Radescu turned large alert eyes on him.

"No, Captain Steve. I come from Cluj, and I don't ever remember meeting him. Oh, I heard about him all right. But at

that time, when the war was beginning, I was outside Romania,
studying here in Vienna at the university. And from here . . . you
know what happened to me."

Browning did indeed know what had happened to him, and he
bent his head over his glass of mulled wine to avoid those eyes
which had witnessed hell on earth: three years in Mauthausen.

It had actually been Major George Wendell, sitting in the front
seat of the open jeep, who had spotted what appeared to be a
gaunt striped bird kneeling exhaustedly in a grassy verge of the
road, not a quarter mile from the Ebensee Aussenlager, a grim
subcamp of Mauthausen, in the new zone of American occupation in Upper Austria. It was, Steve remembered well, the very
day that World War II officially came to an end. Wendell had
sprung from the jeep, followed closely by Silas Ruffing, to inspect
the apparition, too weak to hold its head upright.

Browning recalled picking Mike up; he could have weighed no
more than seventy-five pounds. And he had an indefinable smell
of death about him, an odor of decaying flesh. They had propped
him in the back seat braced by Ruffing's encircling arm and drove
him to the nearest U. S. Army field hospital. There Major Wendell made it clear that he completely rejected the argument of
the hospital's commander that they could not treat any non-
Americans, whether they be ex-concentration camp inmates or
not. The three of them peered incredulously and pityingly down
on the hospital cot where lay the naked collection of bones under
stretched skin and sunken pits of eyes staring out of a round
shaved skull, and made an informal pact that they would see to it
that this one, who was still alive on the day the killing stopped,
would survive. In the months that their OSS unit waited impatiently in Linz, denied by the Soviets from entering Vienna until
that city had been thoroughly sacked, looted, and raped by the armies of Marshal Konev, the three of them took turns driving
out to a bright whitewashed civilian hospital in Wels where
Mircea had been moved. They watched the daily miracle of life
flicker ever stronger back into the starved and wasted young body.
His eyes devoured their daily gifts of a bit of fruit, candy, pajamas, a safety razor, as if he were experiencing a joyous reverie
from which he feared he might wake.

When the day came that he could shakily take steps on his own, and the pipestem arms and legs showed flesh and muscle, George Wendell ordered that Mircea be brought to the billets of the unit and given a small dry room in the garret of one of the requisitioned houses. Within a week, he was already a dog robber for the unit, moving with a tottering speed to arrange for laundry, delivery of mail, and fresh dairy produce from the local farmers in exchange for nylons, chocolates, and cigarettes. Quick as lightning to learn, with the cunning of a survivor, he was clearly far too useful to serve as a military *tuttofare*. By the time the unit moved up to Vienna, he had absorbed English as a sponge does water. That, with his native Romanian, good university German, and great droplets of Magyar, made him first a unit interpreter, then an apprentice to Browning and Ruffing. Within three months after Wendell's unit had arrived in Vienna, Radescu had recruited a motley but effective network of informants and confidants: concierges, hotel employees, telephone repairmen, municipal workers. He slept and he worked. These Americans had given him back his life. His life was therefore devoted to them as long as they were there. He made that clear to them again and again.

"What do you think about this fishing expedition by Calinescu?"

"I would," Radescu answered without hesitation, "drop him in the Danube Canal with stone weights, just for being a bigshot Iron Guardist, a bastard. The only thing that puzzles me is why he is still alive. If you are asking me, Captain Steve, I answer you: Ignore him. Play it safe."

But playing it safe was simply not Browning's way.

"How do you think this Calinescu knew about me? After all, we've only been in Vienna for four months and we've pretty much kept out of sight. . . ."

Mike gave him a derisive glance.

"How does he know about you? In Vienna? A city filled with all conceivable kinds of spies, counterspies, informants, double agents? Come now, Captain Steve, everyone knows who is who in Vienna. Espionage is the major industry here. And, begging your pardon, yours is hardly the best-hidden unit in town."

The merest trace of a smile slitted across his fine-boned features.

"I don't know who you think you are fooling with that 'Logistics Support Component,' Captain Steve, but you are not fooling the Soviets or, for that matter, anyone else who makes it his business to know what is going on here. You and your American colleagues, including dear Lieutenant Silas, are—and please excuse me if you do not like to hear this—you are amateurs in a very dangerous business here. In Vienna, you are dealing with professionals, some of the best."

Steve, staring through an almost impenetrably dirty window at the sadness of winter slush, finally said, "OK, Mike. I appreciate the straight talk, but I want to know what Calinescu wants. I have a hunch that it's more than just a . . ."

"A provocation?" Radescu's eyes were somber over the teacup he brought to his lips.

Steve shrugged on his raincoat.

"You and Ruffing must be twins," he said with a wink. "You both think the same say. Well, I hope we're still . . . in business with each other. . . ."

Radescu seized him in a furious, if brief, embrace and Steve responded with an embarrassed pat of Mike's shoulders.

It was understandable that Mike Radescu embraced Browning in the gloomy gasthaus, inevitably with tears in his eyes.

"Captain Steve, forgive that I react so negative about Calinescu. But I promise myself I hide nothing from you, I speak to you the truth. You know how I feel about Iron Guard bastards. But if you want me to go to Calinescu for you, I do it. Captain Steve, from the minute you pick me up, mostly dead, by the road in Ebensee . . ."

"Come on, Mike, we had to pick you up. You were blocking traffic." Steve made the ritual response they had worked out to relieve the intensity of Mike's emotions. He gripped the slight shoulders, now gratifyingly wiry and firm.

"OK, Mike, this is an order. Find out where Calinescu lives and how he can be reached. Get word to him that I know he's looking for me and that I'll see him—when I'm damned good and ready."

Two days later, Mike Radescu stood in a remote and deserted corner of St. Stephen's Church, as prearranged. Carefully studying the altarpiece before him, he said quietly to Steve Browning, who walked up to his side:

"I've found him. He is a tough, very tough man, a real bastard, a killer. And yes, Ernoe was right—he wants to talk to you."

"Where does he live?"

"In an old apartment block in the British sector. About fifteen minutes by auto from here. He wants to see you soon, before the weekend. He says it is important enough to you that you should make the effort."

"No goddamned Iron Guard DP is going to dictate to me when I see him," Steve answered with enough bluster to warrant a reproachful sidelong glance from Radescu. "He's probably cooked up one of those paper mills with 'hot information' straight out of the Soviet officers' toilet in the Hotel Imperial."

Radescu listened impassively, peering up where a shaft of sunshine fought to enter the winter gloom of the church.

"When you do go to see him, Captain Steve," he said, buttoning the collar of his greatcoat more securely around him, "I will want to be there to keep everything . . . in order."

The final step in what Ruffing called "the Calinescu caper" had to be taken up with the commanding officer. Wendell looked up wearily from a staggering pile of papers, his youthful face reflecting his mingled emotions about Steve Browning, and said, "And what sort of unmitigated disaster are you going to try to con me into this gray Thursday afternoon?" Long ago, Steve had learned that with Wendell it was better to cut the preliminaries and move to the heart of the problem without apologies or circumventions.

"I'd like permission to contact Calinescu by the weekend." Wendell's forehead knitted and his lips closed in a tight disapproval. "George," Steve pleaded, "I just want to find out what he's up to and what he wants. I know that the home office doesn't like it and that you don't like it, Silas doesn't like it either, and Mike doesn't. But I have a hunch it may be something good. I promise you I'll simply meet him, hear him out, and come back. No promises or commitments whatsoever, and a full report to you the morning after I see him."

"You intend to do this alone?"

"No. Mike and two of his trusted people will surveill and cover. I hardly think it's a trap, but Silas will also be on standby."

Wendell, for a long disapproving moment, looked across his ugly, scantily furnished office, with its threadbare rug, peeling wallpaper, and a sad clump of much-read paperback books, and sighed, "Give it a try."

He turned quickly back to his paper work. Wendell still didn't like it at all, any part of it, but being Wendell, he either said yes or no. It was also implicit that if anything went wrong, it was Steve Browning's ass hanging out. Steve closed the door to Wendell's office carefully, grinning with pleasure. Taking risks made the adrenaline flow, made the blood tingle.

And so he set out the following night through the frozen and divided metropolis, his jeep crunching slowly down narrow icy tunnels of streets flanked by the battered hulks of buildings and mounds of masonry where the air bombings, street-by-street artillery and tank fire in the final days of the war had done their desecration.

Save for an occasional passing Military Police vehicle, the streets were completely deserted once they left the Ring and proceeded across the Danube Canal. Mircea Radescu sat silent and motionless beside him in the winterized jeep, sharply etched face in dark profile, eyes occasionally glinting against a wan streetlight. There was no need for conversation; they had already discussed who would do what and when.

He dropped Radescu off in the middle of a narrow street two blocks from the address they sought. He then circled the area slowly, grinding along in second gear until five minutes had passed, giving Radescu time to meet his agents, stride to the address, and stake it out. He parked a block away and carefully locked a robust anti-theft chain around the steering wheel and the gear shift, locked both doors with padlocks, and walked with careful steps in the gloomy stillness. Calinescu's address was an impressive if dilapidated apartment building five stories high, built in the pre-World War I days of the imperial capital. Its stucco façade had been nearly all shaken away by a near-miss from an air bomb during the wartime agony of the city, leaving the ugly wounds of exposed brick. Only here and there did a pale light appear in its cracked windows.

He ran his small flashlight up and down the dozen names listed under the door buzzers. At the name "P. Prohaska" he pressed the button. Before his thumb had released its pressure, a wooden door in the massive front gate swung open with a creak. He flashed his light briefly on a woman in ski pants and heavy sweater, a shawl pulled around her shoulders. In the large black hallway inside the door, it was fully as cold as outside.

"Please turn off the light," the woman told him in a clipped North German accent. "You are Herr Browning?"

"*Ja*, Browning."

She beckoned him to follow her. He peered back into the night, observed a slight movement in the doorway across the street, and remembered that if he did not emerge within thirty minutes, Radescu and his duo, pistols in hand, would come in to look for him. The heavy door swung shut behind him and he hastened after the figure disappearing up the broad marble staircase, their shuffling feet echoing weirdly as they climbed. Smells of dampness, unwashed grime, and sour cabbage assailed his half-frozen nose as he climbed. The woman stopped before a door at the end of a corridor, its once elegant frosted-glass panels cracked in three different directions. He fully expected to step into the usual shabby rooms teeming with strange and suspicious refugees.

He was quite unprepared for what he saw after walking through a dark foyer: a large chamber glowing with subdued light, a spacious and superbly furnished living room comfortably toasted by an enormous ornate porcelain stove in one corner, in which nothing had apparently been changed since 1918. Heavy mahogany furniture, a black monster of a grand piano, tasseled lamps, muted Persian rugs everywhere, velvet-covered sofa and chairs, colored pastoral prints, Bohemian cut-glass vases, a boarded-up fireplace, and a large photograph of a white-whiskered Kaiser Franz Josef. It was nothing short of a miracle that this flat and its furnishings had survived the air bombings, street fighting, official and unofficial looting, Allied requisitioning, and the panicked horde of refugees from all over Eastern Europe who crammed into these more or less intact buildings, sometimes five to a room. These luxurious premises seemed empty.

A man of middle height, assured and confident in his movements, marched through parted curtains opposite him, and ad-

vanced to the middle of the room, one hand still holding a long
Russian *papiross*, body straight as a spear. He bore a remarkable
resemblance to the late Field Marshal Erwin Rommel. It was his
mouth that Steve remembered with the clarity of a photograph: a
mouth of cruelty and decision. Radescu's assessment, that this
man could kill with dispassion, seemed an accurate one. A freshly
healed scar, starting from the corner of his mouth to the center of
his jaw, gave him all of the charm of an executioner.

He stepped forward with military precision, extended his right
hand, and shook Steve's hand formally, looking at him all the
while with shrewd appraising eyes whose lids fell across their outer
corners. Steve was surprised at the smallness of the hand.

"Good evening, Herr Browning, or rather Captain Browning. I
will not attempt to seduce you by referring to you as 'Colonel' as
the Viennese do." The man's German was almost accentless and
his thin, reedy voice betrayed no indication of his origin or nationality. "My name is Dimitriu Calinescu, formerly lieutenant colonel in the Romanian Army." The eyes seemed to be weighing.
"You appear much older than your age; you are twenty-five?" He
was making it clear, Steve knew, that he had done his homework
well.

For the first time, Steve was able to have a good look at the
woman who had led him to this room. She was but a girl, perhaps
sixteen years old, a square-faced attractive brunette with smooth
ruddy cheeks, whose shape was lost in bulky woolen clothing.
What riveted his stare was one of the most appalling black eyes
he had ever observed: her right eye had disappeared and its location was marked by a mere horizontal slit in the swollen blackened cheekbone. The other eye was a deep-set blue.

He turned away with a sudden surge of anger. That eye had
been deliberately struck. It was no accident.

"I didn't come here to play guessing games about my age," he
answered crisply. "I will simply tell you that I am an officer in
the U. S. Army, and I am in intelligence work. Both of these facts
you already know. You have urgently asked me to make contact
with you on matters which you believe to be of importance to us.
Well, here I am."

Without turning his head, Calinescu spoke curtly to the girl.
"Bring cognac, Mara."

She vanished. With no pretense at false camaraderie, he waved Steve to an ancient leather chair.

"Please sit down, Mr. Browning."

"First, if you don't mind, a couple of questions."

A shrug at his incivility. "*Bitte.*"

"May I see your documentation? What's your status here in Vienna?"

Another slight shrug and the man reached into an inner pocket of his well-cut green-lapeled Austrian jacket and handed two documents to Steve. A worn Romanian passport issued in 1938 identified its bearer as Dr. Phil. Dimitriu S. Calinescu, whose youthful photo smiled out at the world behind a bushy mustache that had since been removed. That photo bore no scar. The second, a displaced-person card, had been issued two months previously by the British occupation forces in Vienna. That one had the scar.

He handed them back to Calinescu without comment.

"And next, Captain Browning, you would like to know who Herr Prohaska is, whose apartment this clearly is, or was?"

The man was quick, intuitive, Steve realized. Every caution light in his brain turned on.

"I already know that. Mr. Prohaska was the last Nazi *Kreisleiter* of this district and is probably dead or in the hands of the Russians. Either way, he'll probably never appear."

The cunning eyes signaled that a point had been won.

"Quite correct, Herr Browning. I was . . . er . . . fortunate to find such a flat. No easy task to find such housing these days."

"This place is more luxurious than most assigned to U.S. generals," Steve said, looking admiringly around. "It's a miracle that you found it. A place like this could hold at least three entire families, Austrian or DPs."

The cruel mouth smiled, amused at his housing estimates.

"Life is better for some than for others. Myself, I have always felt that one must live as well as possible, even in brutal times, since one cannot change the misery of millions of others by small acts of self-abnegation."

There was a sense of ominousness about the room that was unnerving. Steve, settling into the leather chair with forced insouciance, asked himself what could be troubling him. His strong instinct was that he was being observed not by one but by several pairs of eyes. It was perfectly in order for Calinescu to have as many secret observers as he wanted; after all, Steve had come to his turf. But it was disturbing—and yet exhilarating. Radescu was right when he said in that clipped English of his, "Captain Steve, in you burns the excitement of danger. You would have been a fine *condottiere* in olden times." This was hardly a disputed barricade to assault but it *was* risky business. That made it interesting.

The girl with the terribly blackened eye returned, bearing a metal tray with two exquisite Venetian goblets and a musty, opened bottle of French cognac. She exchanged a long glance with him and he could have sworn that the expression in her good eye was that of a drowning person who briefly sees a life raft that is too far away to be reached. Steve watched her depart with soundless steps and reluctantly turned to the short, trim figure.

"All right, Herr Calinescu. I'll have a drop of your cognac and a brief idea of what's on your mind. I have . . . other appointments to keep this evening."

"Yes, yes, I'm sure you do," Calinescu responded, picking up the bottle and pouring each of them a generous shot.

"And those lookout men of yours across the street in those dark doorways, we don't want to let them freeze out there too long. Is one of them poor Radescu?"

Steve could not resist a bleak professional smile as he held out his glass in a silent toast to his host. The liquor had possibly the most exquisite bouquet he had ever inhaled, a superb aged cognac as rare in this city as self-confessed Nazis. He rubbed his lips appreciatively as the scented nectar burned slowly down inside him.

Calinescu downed the contents of his glass as if it were medicine and his eyes continued to assess and weigh the consistency of the young American lounging beside him. Steve was quite content to let Calinescu carry the conversational ball, and he did.

"Captain Browning, are you any relation to that ingenious inventor?"

At Steve's puzzled glance he explained, "You know, the one who devised firearms? The Browning automatic rifle? It has a slow rate of fire but is a very reliable weapon."

"No relation. Nor to the poet of the same name either. It's a common name in my country."

"Aha!" Then, after a pause, "Captain, I'll be as blunt as you would want me to be. You Americans have this directness I admire. I want to work for you. Or perhaps"—and his mouth twitched as if amused by an inner joke—"or perhaps we can work with each other."

Steve studied the remainder of the rich amber fluid in his glass before looking up directly into Calinescu's eyes. An inexplicable uneasiness came over him.

"In what way do you want to work for us, Herr Calinescu?"

"Not 'us,' Captain Browning. With *you* personally. I want to help you in your operations against the Soviets."

"Oh, indeed!" he answered, on his guard immediately. The offer was a familiar one, tendered by former Nazis and German collaborators, all professing to be bitterly anti-Communist. "And just what do you think you can do for us in that regard? After all, we're still hard at work trying to de-Nazify this country. Speaking of which, I'm frankly surprised that as a former Iron Guard member, you aren't in one Allied internment camp or other."

"Who said I was an Iron Guard officer?" The words came from clenched tight lips.

"I did, Herr Calinescu. You were one of Horia Sima's youth leaders. You know who *I* am. I know who *you* are." He smiled briefly, pleased at placing the man on the defensive, and held out his glass in a mock toast before drinking back the rest of its contents.

Calinescu's eyes had narrowed to slits.

"Bravo, Captain. Professional and well informed, just as I had been led to believe."

"Then answer my question," Steve said, the cognac warming his belly and stimulating his sense of bravado. "How is it that one of the Allies hasn't arrested you? You'd be behind barbed wire if I found you in the American Zone, and the Soviets would probably put a bullet through the back of your head."

"And why, Captain Browning, should I be interned by the Allies when I have already been persecuted and interned by the Germans for two and one-half years?"

The riposte was startling. He regretted he had not listened more carefully to Radescu's explanations of recent Romanian history.

"And why would they have wanted to do that to you? I thought you people got along splendidly with the Germans."

The tight lips relaxed in a half smile and reflected Calinescu's satisfaction: Steve did not know enough of what he should have known.

"You surprise me, Captain. I fear that your little Jewish agent, Radescu, has been, how shall we say, poisoning the well?"

"I'm not here to discuss Radescu or anyone else, Calinescu. Why did the Germans, to use your word, 'persecute' you?"

Calinescu uttered a faint sigh, signifying pain and distaste, before replying.

"You mentioned our great leader, Horia Sima, leader of our Movement, now . . . somewhere in the West, and alive and well."

Steve said, "You know damned well where he is."

Calinescu calmly replied, "Yes, and I'm not going to tell you. But you must know that after we attempted to rid our country of the youthful wretch of a king, Michael, and to gain true independence for our country, we were arrested by the Antonescu dictatorship."

Steve nodded.

"Then you must also know that Hitler and his minions arrested Horia Sima and the rest of us in early 1941 as a personal favor to General Antonescu, who had crushed our Movement and who aligned Romania's armies with those of Nazi Germany against the Red Army—to our everlasting tragedy. Sima and a few of his staff, of whom I was one, were bottled up in a wretched Nazi internment camp at Fichtenheim near Berlin. Sima escaped but the rest of us were released only in the last months of the war when the Germans were desperate for any anti-Bolshevik elements who would fight the Russians. And now you would stuff me into one of *your* internment camps? What irony!"

He leaned toward Steve with a derisive shake of his head.

"Come now, Captain, that doesn't make much sense now, does it?"

Steve, nonplussed, said, "We'll sort that out another time. You say you want to work with us against the Soviets. What could you do that would interest me in the slightest?"

Out of an inner pocket of his jacket came a sheaf of carbon-copy pages which Calinescu smoothed open and passed to Steve, who stared at the top sheet intently under the pale light of a table lamp.

"I know you read Russian, Captain," Calinescu said, almost soothingly. "At least well enough to understand what you are looking at."

He could indeed read enough Russian to know that the three sheets of paper contained, in single space, a typewritten order of battle of all the Soviet forces in Austria, including active troop strengths and locations, and the names of all commanding officers of all elements down to regimental levels.

The thin, precise voice said, "The American High Commissioner here in Vienna, General Mark Clark, would be very happy to have such information, would he not? Not to mention your Pentagon?"

"How do I know it isn't pure smoke?"

"Check it for yourself, unit by unit. It would take some time for your spies to do so, but they can do it and the validity of my information can be proved."

"And where did you get it?"

Calinescu's eyes clouded with exasperation.

"Come now, Mr. Browning, that's childish. You know I'm not going to tell you that. Certainly, not now."

"Is this a one-shot operation?"

The cold mouth parted and white crowded teeth appeared briefly in a confident smile.

"I can get you such an order-of-battle report, updated, every thirty days."

If Steve walked in with such a document, the entire senior staff of the United States Forces in Austria, its commanding general included, would collectively jump in the air with joy. And his commander, George Wendell, would be ecstatic. If this information were valid, the costly, risky efforts to recruit someone, even at a regimental level of the Soviet occupation forces, could be delayed or ended. The time-consuming scrutiny of casual Soviet trucks and sedans within the Soviet Zone of Austria simply to copy down their unit markings; the tangled and confusing mosaic of OB collection effort, with its inevitable contradictions, inaccuracies, and gaps, could be abandoned. This was something like

McClellan's scouts capturing the Confederate battle plan just *before* the battle of Antietam. To know exactly where the other guy was, and in what numbers, was half the fight.

He leaned back in the overstuffed leather chair, the order-of-battle papers still in his hand, already savoring the encomiums which would come his way.

"Rather impressive stuff, don't you think?" Calinescu's thin voice cut through his reflections. "Worth quite a bit, wouldn't you imagine?"

He looked up at the thin lips now contemptuously curling. Had he been hooked by a talented con man after all? He fixed Calinescu with a cold stare.

"Why didn't you bring this to the British? You are living in their district. They know you're here and probably know you're up to something."

Calinescu nodded.

"I thought you would ask that. The answer is simple: I don't want to work with the British or the French. My aim is to serve the Americans and to enter the United States. Europe is a cemetery. Once the dead have all been buried, it won't be a place I can live in. The United States is the country of the future, at least for my lifetime, and I want to emigrate there. I'm prepared to work my way. I've been on the lookout for a contact. You are young, but you have the reputation of being a clever, audacious, and ambitious intelligence officer, not like so many of your slothful colleagues in Vienna who live solely to eat, drink, sleep, and fornicate. You are involved in this laborious task of collecting Soviet order-of-battle information; you speak and read German and some Russian, and those who deal with you say that you are a man of your word. That's why I sought you out."

He sat on the corner of a sofa so close to Steve he could reach out and touch him, and for the first time, his words rang with a personal emotion.

"Mr. Browning, I am a man who plans his life. It is, of course, inevitable that unpleasant and unexpected events get in my way from time to time. But I, myself, have enormous ambition and I have all the energy to achieve my goals. Make no mistake of that. I wanted to achieve prominence in my own country. I was well on my way, but World War II tragically intervened. Now the Communists are in charge in Romania and there is nothing for me there. But I know I can achieve great things in a land which has great opportunities."

He grasped Steve's wrist in a vise-like grip, and the hooded eyes now burned like those of a man with fever.

"The costs of obtaining this information will be relatively modest for your people. Let me help you and, after a specific period, you can help me."

Steve rose uncertainly to his feet. The cognac had worked very quickly on him. Calinescu rose with him and, standing close, Steve noted that the man's ramrod posture made him seem deceptively tall; he was actually half a head shorter than Steve.

"Like all good salesmen, you leave out unpleasant pieces of information. You tell me that you were interned by the Germans as part of Horia Sima's group until the last months of the war. And just what did you do: join some SS unit and run around killing Jews?"

For the first time, the man's composure was ruffled, but only for a moment.

"I challenge anyone to prove that I was in the German SS at any time. I told you earlier that I was finally freed from internment when the Germans, on the defensive on the Eastern Front and desperate for those who were willing to fight Bolshevism, let me out of the camp. I briefly served as Romanian Army liaison officer, rank of lieutenant colonel, with the German forces in the Ukraine and in Romania fighting the Soviet hordes advancing westward. I can show you the Wehrmacht *Ausweis* which so identifies me, when next we meet."

His thin lips held a brief humorless smile for a moment.

"As for my attitudes toward Jews, we can talk about that some other time. Suffice it to say that my outlook was based on objective economic and ideological considerations; they, as a . . . a particular group, an alien group, represented a grave danger to a Christian Romania."

"No longer," Steve said softly. "That's been resolved, eh?"

"Please do not saddle me with Heinrich Himmler's sins."

"No, I think we all have plenty of our own."

A short insistent rapping on the door signified that Radescu had come to find his chief.

"Let me take a single page of this report to show my people," Steve said. "If the same stuff doesn't pop up from five other directions . . ."

"It will pop up nowhere," Calinescu said easily. "This is not a news-subscription service I am offering you, Captain Browning. I am deeply serious. I collect this information and I pass it to you at enormous risk to myself and those who collaborate with me. But I will work with you only if you guarantee to me that one day you will do everything possible to permit me to enter the United States."

"We can discuss that some other time," Steve rejoined with an impatient gesture.

The rapping on the door grew louder.

"I had better go," Steve said, "or my colleague will shoot the lock off the door."

"Radescu would know better than that," Calinescu commented dryly. "But before you go, Captain Browning, I would like to give you something to . . . commemorate our meeting and our future collaboration."

He reached in his jacket pocket and held out a flat rectangular object. Steve hesitantly took it in his hands. It was an exquisite silver cigarette case, worn with age and use, with the crest of the house of Habsburg, the long-necked double eagle, in bas-relief.

"I'm told that it belonged to one of the princes of the old regime," Calinescu said, voice sinking to a soft confidential tone as if he did not want to be overheard. "It came into my hands from . . . you know . . . the usual channels."

Steve studied the heirloom with heightened interest, and instinctively handed it back.

"No, no," Calinescu pleaded with him. "Take it. Look, consider it a signal between us. If you send anyone bearing this box to me, I'll know the authenticity of the bearer. A recognition signal, yes?"

He did not wait to observe Steve tuck the cigarette box in his pocket. In the dimly-lit foyer, he extended his hand. Steve, hesitating a moment, shook it.

"I have a feeling we will be working together," Calinescu said at the door, with utter confidence.

"We'll see," Steve responded, his voice unconvincing.

He looked behind him as Calinescu opened the door. Mara had padded in, in her slippered feet, to take away the cognac. He knew that Calinescu had inflicted that blow, and it was with a momentary pang that he knew he was dealing with a man who could strike a young girl as cruelly as that.

But then, feeling the hard metal object in his pocket, he knew something else—that Calinescu had his number.

CHAPTER SIX

An instinct, absurd but unyielding, whispered to Steve that he was being watched. But who would be tailing him here in the green affluence of Bethesda, Maryland? He peered right and left as he trudged up the flagstoned walk to the house entrance but saw nothing, no one in the still, hushed neighborhood. That, of course, meant nothing. A good stakeout team would be invisible. Was the strain beginning to play tricks with his nerves?

When he reached but three paces from the door stoop of the anonymous-looking brick rambler, an amber light suddenly flicked on over his head. One step later, the door itself swung open. He stepped through it, into the hallway, and the light flicked off. He closed the door quickly behind him, thinking: very professional; Ruffing and Radescu had taught Mara the tricks of the trade well.

And there she stood in the soft illumination of the hallway, composed and erect, her face and carriage little changed after thirty-two years. Her soft, straight hair, still russet by nature or artifice, was shorter than he remembered. The soft ruddy skin had lost its youthful vibrancy but had not creased or lined with the years. Under the beige summer dress, her figure seemed fuller than he recalled, but it was very hard for him to realize that she would now be in her late forties.

They stood a foot apart, wary and apprehensive of each other. In her deeply recessed blue eyes, suspicion vied with curiosity.

"The years have been very kind to you." He was first to speak although he barely trusted himself to get the words out. He wondered how he should greet her, but she resolved that by extending her right hand and shook his once, briskly, formally. There would be no pecks on the cheek or nostalgic embraces.

"I wish I could say the same for you, Steve." Her singsong Germanic English mocked him. "But you have gotten rather . . ." She switched to German to be precise. *"Du bist ziemlich dick geworden."* A ready smile appeared to take away the curse of the criticism, but he looked down at his belly pressing through the light summer suit.

"A price one pays for living the good life," he said, nodding his head in feigned agreement.

He studied her in the little hallway for an almost embarrassingly long moment. She had carefully applied cosmetics as if she were going out to a reception: a touch of black shadow to heighten the contrast with her eyes, a moist glistening red applied to the lips. It took very little to recall a firm-bodied young girl with tangled long hair the color of rich brown earth, red mouth open with love as she flung herself into his arms in the heavy mahogany dimness of his Vienna bedroom.

It was as if she knew exactly what his memory contained. She raised her head in a familiar imperious gesture, one which her East Prussian ancestors, the von Kueppkes, had passed along with their other qualities, good and bad, and held out her hand to show him into the living room. It was filled with the mélange of possessions acquired by any diplomatic family over the years: North African leather stools and puffs, an exquisite Chinese carved lacquered screen, a brass-studded Shirazi chest, a display of Burmese jade artifacts safely under glass, and two Buganda masks whose empty slitted eyes seemed to register a genuine dislike of him.

She seated herself at the edge of one chair at right angles to his and folded her hands in front of her, a gesture at once familiar and clearly calculated to place a barrier between them. He was aware of what she saw: a bulky, overweight American male in late middle age, straight thinning hair quite gray, heavy round face now resting on a sizable double chin, shaggy eyebrows above the hard brown eyes, striped tie hanging like a wet gonfalon from a sweated and rumpled shirt collar. She might well ask herself: My God, was it this man I once loved, obeyed?

She spoke without heat.

"You know, Stefi, I came very close to hanging up when you telephoned today. After all, what happened so many years ago is

all behind me. I have been more or less happily married to an
Austrian diplomat these past twenty-five years. Ernst is minister of
embassy here and has been ambassador to countries in Africa and
the Orient. Our twin daughters are now attending the university in
Vienna."

"You married well," he said, looking at the room's decor.

"All of this has nothing to do with you," she retorted. "In fact,
had my husband not been visiting our UN Mission in New York,
I would have said: No, Steve, don't come, ever. What happened
long ago is . . . between ourselves, and is over."

It was a particular, not always joyful, quality of Mara von
Kueppke to make everything clear. She hated equivocations, he
knew, and while the implicit sting of her words of unwelcome
were hardly balm to his ears, he was grateful that she had, in
effect, told him precisely where he stood with her.

A gentle rumble of the air-conditioning system was the only
sound in the room, and he stared at the attractive matron, wondering how to get on with the task that had brought him here in
the late hours of the night.

"It's not my intention to endanger your virtue or your reputation, Frau Minister," he said with a crooked smile. "But there are
a couple of things that you may or may not remember which
could help me out of what, in the American vernacular, is called a
jam."

He paused to hold her questioning glance and added, *"Auf
Deutsch gesagt, ich bin im Stich."*

She uttered a small peal of laughter, quickly stifled.

"A jam? *Im Stich?"* The moist lips curled with amusement.
"My dear Stefi, you have *always* been in jams. You used to thrive
on them."

He nodded almost contritely.

"That's right. And one of those jams concerned you and
Dimmy Calinescu. You probably saw the TV news tonight about
the congressional hearings?"

She nodded, eyes dropping with bitterness.

"Yes, I regret to say, I saw them."

"You remember when I met him for the first time, I saw that
black eye he had given you. I hated the bastard immediately. *You*
know that."

She struggled for a moment with an inner pain before she spoke, eyes now smoky with distaste and the memory of fear.

"Yes, you hated him, Stefi. Rightly so. A brutal man. But you and your service, you let him use you, and you used him. You paid him. Someone let this monster into this country."

He had known that in coming to her, he would have to pay a bitter price. He wondered now whether the price was not too high. But he could not remain silent to the accusations flung at him.

"No one knew then that he was a damned murderer. We had no information, no proof, that he was guilty of being anything except an Iron Guard type who wound up fighting with the Germans against the Russians. He had unique access to high-level information on Soviet troop strengths all over Central Europe. We were openly skeptical, unbelieving, at first. But the information proved to be true. Goddamnit, they were absolutely delighted with what we got, at the Pentagon, at USFA and EUCOM headquarters. Aren't we entitled to use a defeated enemy to build our defenses against a new enemy?"

Her smile was ironic and understanding at the same time.

"Fight fire with fire? An old philosophical argument, Stefi. Yes, you have used old Abwehr types like the Gehlen organization in Munich, the Ukrainian Bandera people whom you urged to fight the Soviets until they were wiped out. This I understand although I deplore it."

She pointed a small firm finger straight at him.

"But I cannot agree with you about Calinescu. Look, Stefi, you knew what *kind* of man he was. Didn't my battered face tell you anything? Silas Ruffing, that dear little man, how many times did he say: Dimmy Calinescu is just bad news. And you told me yourself that your own boss in Vienna, Major Wedd . . . Wand . . ."

"Wendell. George Wendell."

". . . Major Wendell. Did he enjoy the collaboration with Calinescu? No. But you went ahead. You wanted that information from Calinescu—oh, how badly you wanted it. And you were prepared to pay anything to get it. And how happy you were when they gave you commendations, medals . . ."

Her German accent became more pronounced as her agitation increased.

"And if there is one thing I cannot forgive you for, Stefi, it is that you let him into this country. This marvelous society which accepts all kinds of people. Pay him mountains of dollars, OK. But *that* one you should *not* have let in. That was . . . a . . . a shame, Stefi."

He closed his eyes for a moment and almost involuntarily mopped his damp brow. He had girded himself for such accusations but they hurt like hell all the same.

"And yet you . . ." he blurted.

Suddenly lightning flashed, and her voice deepened and darkened with indignation.

"No, Stefi, of all the people in this world, you are not going to finish what I know you intend to say: 'And what about you, Mara? You agreed to become the property of Dimmy Calinescu. You slept with him, did his bidding, served as his concubine, servant, his lapdog.' Is that not so? Strange how you've forgotten how Calinescu found me, unwashed, hungry, bitterly weeping in a miserable corner of the Ostbahnhof, dumped from the last civilian train arriving in Vienna just ahead of the Red Army, a train choked with East Prussians, all kinds of other Germans, fleeing the Russian hordes. I was a child of fifteen, Stefi, bundled aboard that wretched train in Breslau by my uncle, who was probably killed by the Russians. I never heard from him again. Eight terrible days on that train filled with hysterical and hungry people, together with my mother, who was determined we two were not going to be murdered and raped by the Russians. And I had to leave her poor bloody body on the train platform at Brno, lying in a row with the others who had been killed when some airplanes, Soviet or American I'll never know, strafed that train again and again. And I don't even know where she lies buried. . . ."

He remembered that whenever she wept in Vienna, she wept silently. Not a sound except for a slight shuddering of her shoulders. And so she wept now, covering her eyes with her hands while he sat in silence. Abruptly she wiped her tears away.

"I would have given a lot not to have brought that on," he told her.

"Never mind," she said. "When I see the old photos of those crowds of Jews going to their doom in Nazi concentration camps, perhaps in the same freight cars that we Germans fled in, I know that what happened to me was the last act of the tragedy, and that the riddled bodies of the German women and children lying on the platform at Brno were payments in blood for what the Germans did. But isn't it sad that the innocents pay the debt?"

"I'm sorry I mentioned . . ."

". . . No, Stefi." Her contralto voice was now clear and in control. "I haven't talked with anyone about this in years. Even my husband Ernst doesn't know about . . . Calinescu. . . ." She peered at him maliciously. "There, isn't that a wonderful blackmail opportunity for you: Ernst doesn't know about Calinescu."

"Does he know about me?"

She nodded matter-of-factly.

"I never mentioned your last name, but he knows that an American officer named Steve befriended me and that I lived in Vienna with Steve for a little more than a year before Steve departed for the U.S. He knows that Steve was generous with me when he left but that Steve certainly didn't consider me worth marrying. For Steve, I was a woman of . . . convenience."

"Mara," he began, but she waved him off.

"Ernst was very understanding of all this. He himself was lucky to survive in a Luftwaffe unit as an eighteen-year-old corporal, and when we met at the university in Vienna after you left, he was so wonderfully understanding and kind. But I don't think he'd have liked to hear about Calinescu."

She turned her lips down in a self-deprecatory frown.

"I only lasted five months with Calinescu. I wasn't *spritzig* enough for him. He liked young girls all right. He took me in, I'm sure, because he found out that I was Gräfin Mara von Kueppke, whose forebears went back to the Teutonic Knights. *That* appealed to him. But he had depraved tastes. He wanted his women more sexually imaginative, more *freigebig*. What did a fifteen-year-old *Pifke* like me, from East Prussia, raised with almost monastic Protestant strictness, know about sexual quirks? When the novelty wore off, out I went."

"To me."

"Yes, Stefi." Her smooth head was held high and unrepentant. "Yes, to you. But with you I thought it was something else. . . ."

"I never led you to believe it was something else."

"Yes, I know. But I, foolish girl that I was, *I* was convinced it could become something else. . . ."

Abruptly she clapped her hands with a gesture of consternation.

"For God's sake, I've lost completely my sense of hospitality. Stefi, please let me get you something: an iced tea, a drink . . ."

He shook his head slowly.

"No, Mara, nothing. Thank you. I've come on business, personal business, and I'll try to get it over with and get out of your life again."

She folded her hands once more.

"As you wish, Stefi."

There was a time when overcoming difficult and dicey moments came easily, when he could time the point of application sharply and precisely and perfectly, like a banderillero ramming home his sharp sticks. That was the way it was in recruiting a spy: you had to know precisely when and how to ask him and expect him to say yes. But his timing was gone. Here he was blundering about, unearthing old hurts and sorrows for this woman he had once held to his naked body, without accomplishing what he had come to do. He bit his upper lip and launched himself, an awkward diver plummeting from a high board to an uncertain landing.

"Mara, the Calinescu case will be big news in this town, and you'll see it all in the newspapers, on radio, and TV starting tomorrow. Congresswoman Pfitzner has made it a personal crusade to deport Calinescu and others she feels are illegally in this country and she has zeroed in on the Agency as one of the devils in the piece. In effect, she is saying that the Agency knew all about Dimmy's atrocities in Romania, that we've been covering up our knowledge, and that we willingly collaborated with this bloody-handed gent."

"But there *was* no Agency in 1946, no?"

"Correct. But what she is saying is that people who were involved with Dimmy later joined the Agency and are still in service, people like Wendell and me, and that our hands are not clean."

She looked at him as one on a high rooftop looks down on a street riot: it was somebody else's problem.

"What do you want of me, Stefi?" Her tone was patient as if he were a petulant child to be calmed. "Surely you don't want to involve me in this affair."

"No, the last person who's going to get involved is you, Mara. But my people, our Inspector General's staff, are conducting an investigation of this entire business and they're already questioning me about you: who you were, what role you played when you were living with Dimmy in Vienna, what kind of work you did for me before I left. I think I've convinced them that you were not involved in any meaningful way with our operational contact with Dimmy. In any event, I don't think they have a clue that you're here in Washington, married to an Austrian diplomat. I found *that* out just by chance a week ago from one of my State Department acquaintances who served in Vienna with me after the war. Believe me, I had no intention of ever coming near you again."

"But?"

"But I know that tomorrow they're going to start questioning me about Mike Radescu."

Her reaction was predictable. It was like an opaque curtain falling between him and her.

"What do you want of me, Stefi? He's on *your* conscience, not mine."

This interview was infinitely harder than he had imagined. All that kept him from leaving was the knowledge that the alternative, *not* having come and asked, was even worse.

"Yes." He nodded, looking away from her at the baleful Buganda masks. "Anybody who works for me and disappears without a trace is on my conscience."

"Come now, Stefi." She was not about to let it drop there. "It's more than that. *You* know, and Silas knows, and I know that he probably fell into a trap." She closed the shadowed eyes and shook her head in a gesture of grieving remembrance. "That dear, sweet man. When I think of kindness, I think of Mircea Radescu."

"Mara," he said, voice drained of energy, "when an agent with ten thousand in U.S. dollars disappears, any number of things could have happened to him, even to a guy like Mike whom I trusted. For all we know, he may be a merchant prince in Latin America somewhere, or doing well in Australia. . . ."

She threw him a caustic glance.

"Mike Radescu would cut his veins for you, Steve, you know that, despite all of his *schwarzhandel*, his black-market business. You of all people to say such things of him. . . ."

"You never know," he told her. "I know that Mike said he didn't want to take the money and meet Dimmy and that he felt going to the meeting was unsafe. But he didn't have any facts to support his fears. And we needed that monthly report on Soviet order of battle, and we needed it badly. Mike had gone three times before into the Soviet Zone and had safely returned with the information. Sure, it was a risky business, meeting people in the Soviet Zone. But espionage is a risky business. Mike knew the risks. And that last time was a milk run to Sankt Pölten, a routine meeting and pickup."

"No," she said. "You and I both know that it wasn't the usual thing. The usual thing was that two of Mike's network always went along to shadow him, to protect him. That last time, he went alone."

"He went alone because he *wanted* to go alone," Steve said, smashing his fist into the padded arm of his chair. "That could have meant that he was prepared to take off with the money and never return."

"He went alone," she retorted, voice implacable, "because he said that he didn't want to risk the lives of his comrades. My God, Stefi, you made your career on following hunches. Why didn't you listen to his?"

Steve lurched heavily to his feet. She rose smoothly, gracefully from her chair.

"To the best of your knowledge," he asked, voice hoarse with weariness, looking down on the smooth-molded face he had once touched, kissed, "did Mike Radescu know anything about Calinescu's crimes, murders, in Romania? I want to be able to tell the IG about that, at least."

She gazed somberly straight ahead for a long and reflective moment, arms folded before her, before responding.

"No, I never heard him say in so many words: Dimitriu Calinescu is a murderer. He did say what you have said and what I know: that Calinescu is a man of supreme opportunism, who would do anything if it served his purposes. But as for a specific massacre such as that little woman spoke of at the congressional hearing? No, Mike knew nothing of Calinescu's participation."

"Do you think that Calinescu betrayed him, that Dimmy was working for or doubling for the Soviets?"

"Doubling . . . ?"

"You know, *Doppelspiel*."

Again a long purposeful silence and she looked up, her features reflecting the pull of her emotions in differing directions.

"At the time Mike disappeared, I thought, as did Silas Ruffing, that it might have been an unlucky accident, a chance Soviet patrol in the Sankt Pölten railroad station which picked him up, or something like that. But how do I feel now, after so many years? I blame Calinescu. Yes, Dimmy betrayed him. Of that I'm certain. The only thing I don't know is just how it happened."

Her eyes were clouded with her memories and her bosom heaved with betrayed agitation, but her voice was calm.

"You know, before Mike left on that last meeting, the one you told him he must go on although he felt that something was not right, he took me for a glass of wine to a tiny café off the Ring and he said to me with a little smile on that tragic face of his, 'Gräfin Marushka, since this probably is the last meeting we shall have, I want to wish you all good things.' Then he reached into his pocket and handed me a little gold Star of David on a chain."

She reached into the top of her summer dress and pulled at a fine gold chain around her throat. The gleaming six-pointed star appeared and she held it in the palm of her hand for a moment.

"He said to me, 'It's good luck for you, Gräfin Marushka, and you certainly can use it.' Then he kissed my hand as if he were my servant and I was the lady of the *Schloss*."

Steve fixed his eyes on the shining little pendant cupped in her hand, as she added, "I never told you about it before. It was between him and me. But when you told me you were coming tonight, I decided to put it on. I wanted to show it to you."

Her eyes held his, curiously compassionate yet filled with righteous anger.

"You could have saved him, Stefi, but you threw him away."

He had had enough. It had gone much worse than he had imagined. Head down, he shambled toward the door.

"Wait," she called. "There's something else."

He stopped in his tracks. Mara's words had an imperial reson-
ance.

"I am sorry that I had to remind you about these unpleasant
matters," she said. "Seeing you again brought them all back in a
flood. But it's strange that you picked this particular week to seek
me out."

She extracted from a small pocket on her dress two carefully
folded sheets of paper.

"In a way, I wish it were all over," she continued with a small
sigh. "The past should stay where it belongs. God knows, Stefi, if
the years between 1940 and 1948 were wiped totally out of my
head, I would be very content. But here you are, standing in my
living room, such a large part of that painful past. And here is this
letter in my hand, mailed to me from Los Angeles only five days
ago."

There was something in her tone that quickened his heartbeat.

"It's from Mike Radescu."

Despite the coolness of the room, he felt sudden perspiration
spring onto his upper lip and forehead.

"Mike? From Los Angeles . . . ?"

She nodded.

"He wrote it on some motel stationery there . . ."

Steve reached out almost roughly to snatch the letter in her
hand, but she stepped back and protectively cupped her hands
with the letter to her bosom.

"Not so fast, Herr Hauptmann," she admonished him. "It's *my*
letter. Besides, I doubt you could read it. His handwriting is pathetic after so many years of prison, and it's written in German."

"Alive!" he breathed unbelievingly. "Is it possible?"

He perched himself shakily on the padded arm of a leather
chair as she reached for reading glasses and carefully smoothed
open the fragile pages.

"He writes, 'I'm back from Siberia, back from over twenty-five
years of GULAG hell. How I happen to be alive is a very interesting and almost unbelievable story I hope to tell you someday, if I
live to do so.'"

He watched her lips move with the intensity of a deaf-mute,
wagging his head slightly as if what he read there made no sense.

"'They released me at the Czech-Austrian border several

months ago. I was sent to an Austrian camp for refugees outside Vienna, and spent some weeks recovering my strength in a camp hospital there. Just imagine: I weighed only fifty kilos! Working for years in Soviet gas lines and railroad construction in the frozen tundra of eastern Siberia, with the kind of wretched food we got, is not recommended for your health. Unlike Mauthausen, they didn't pop you into a gas oven or shoot you in the back of the neck. But they work one to death. That happened to so many, many of my comrades.' " She paused and the silence in the room was painful for them both. Steve listened, eyes half closed, lips tightly closed, stifling a flood of questions which welled in his mouth. Mara, standing before him, head bent to read the crabbed and tremulous words, wiped a blurring tear from one eye and continued to read.

" 'But in Vienna, a stroke of luck occurred. As I wandered down the Mariahilfer Strasse in Vienna one day, who should I encounter but Ernoe, Captain Steve's old informant. And what happened to that Magyar, that rascal? He is owner of a very prosperous bar, the Café Rhapsody, around the corner from where you and Lieutenant Silas and Captain Steve used to meet, and I must say he was most generous, especially when he heard what had happened to me. But most important: he told me of your marriage to the Austrian diplomat, which he read in the Viennese papers years ago. For an old *Spitzl* like me, it was then easy to track you down, dear *Gräfin*.' "

"Ernoe!" Steve breathed. "A guy you couldn't trust as far as you could watch him!"

Mara's eyes flicked up from her reading and her lips drooped with dark humor.

"It depends, I suppose, on what one trusts another to do," she said. Her lips remained open as if to go on, but she decided not to and turned to the letter again.

" 'Ernoe was able to do many things; he developed many shadowy skills in the postwar years. One of the miracles he performed was procuring for me an Austrian passport. The real thing! And it cost but thirty thousand schillings under the counter! He gave me a job as a waiter so that I could repay him and save up enough money to buy a tourist round-trip air ticket to Los Angeles. And why am I here in Los Angeles?' "

Steve stood up, hands hanging loosely at his side. He knew what she was going to read to him.

"'I am here to find and kill Dimitriu Calinescu, the man who betrayed me to the NKVD, and the man who betrayed us all. I write, dear Gräfin Marushka, simply to tell you of this and to kiss your hand. I hope you find . . .'"

She could not go on, and swallowed convulsively several times before she trusted her voice again.

"'. . . I hope you find all the happiness that was denied to you as a child and as a young girl.

"'As for the Americans I once knew, it's best that I do not go near them. I don't want them involved. In any case, after I find Calinescu and do what I must do, who cares? I lived these terrible years for one thing only: revenge. Nothing else matters.'"

"For Christ's sake," Steve Browning breathed.

She folded the pages methodically into a small square again.

"I had thought," Mara said, "to send a brief and anonymous little letter to your FBI and to warn them that someone really wants to kill Calinescu. I don't care about him but I don't want Mike to suffer any more. First the Nazis, then the KGB, and now the Americans if he tries to kill!"

Her smile was contrived.

"Your good luck holds, Stefi. You came along just in the nick of time."

She extended a corner of an envelope to him and he automatically reached for it.

"Here's the motel address from his letter. *You* can inform your own people or the police. Do what you want. It's out of my hands."

In the darkened vehicle, within visual range of Mara's front door, the two Security men sprawled uncomfortably. As the heavy form of Steve Browning clumped down the steps of her home and tramped to his auto two blocks away, the younger one said softly from the rear seat, "That was either the shortest lay on record—or she's involved in a short snappy ops meet with old hotshot."

"Yours is not to reason why," the other retorted. "Come around to the front seat and we'll move out after him."

CHAPTER SEVEN

"If it were not for the fact that I love you far more than you deserve," George Wendell told his wife, holding her arm carefully in the Georgetown darkness as they navigated brick sidewalks made undulant by insistent tree roots, "and the other fact that the Curriers live exactly two blocks away from us, you'd never have gotten me out of the house tonight. I'm bone tired."

She gave him a sidelong glance filled with affectionate concern and squeezed his guiding arm. He was not exaggerating; his eyes drooped with fatigue. Not twenty minutes earlier, he had walked through the front door just when she was about to phone the Curriers and tell them that *force majeure* of some kind would prevent them from coming. He had plodded wearily to their bathroom, showered, run an electric razor across his face, and shrugged on the ensemble she had laid out for him.

"I wish," she said, "that you had come home half an hour later. By then, I would have canceled us out, given you a cup of hot bouillon, and put you to bed."

He gave her a thank-you squeeze.

"Damn, sometimes that place can be a zoo out there. As if it weren't bad enough under normal conditions, this Jenny Pfitzner hearing was incredible. Everybody wants to chat with me about it. I've talked three times with the DCI. The phone in my office rings off the hook with all kinds of people. I just had to stop taking calls. Clare logged a dozen of them between three and five P.M."

He tugged at his striped tie with a weary gesture. "Wouldn't you know," he went on, "just when I'm completely swamped, with my new Deputy visiting our stations in Southeast Asia for five weeks, with two annual division operations reviews, not to mention a Soviet defector who walked into our embassy in Tokyo a week ago and is now stashed away in the nearby countryside with all kinds of goodies for us—now we have Jenny Pfitzner and her congressional road show." He shook his head in wonderment. "And this Special Assistant of mine, Kobler, says he can't wait to get my job."

"Mr. Kobler will just have to be patient, at least ten more years of patience." The steel vibrated in her Bryn Mawr drawl. She was not an admirer of Don Kobler.

Around them, Georgetown was stirring for its nightly tribal rites—cocktails, dinners, get-togethers where the ephemeral power elite of the capital gathered to talk to, or to be listened to by, those whose keen pleasure it was to be with them. The narrow streets were filled with limousines and lesser vehicles seeking the one thing that is in the greatest demand in that storied neighborhood: a parking space.

"I was proud of you and how you did at the hearing," she said, looking up at him at a street intersection. "And all my friends are, too, so there. And we're going to present you with some kind of a civilian Purple Heart for suffering wounds and barbs from Jenny Pfitzner."

"I already have a Purple Heart, luv, thanks to an unthinking German machine-gunner in 1944," he said. "But I'll tell you something, Maudie."

He stopped in his tracks and his eyes were somber as he faced her for a moment in the darkness.

"It's true I was outraged at being there and given the Pfitzner treatment. But when she brought that frightened little woman in, that got to me. It was like talking to the survivors of Mauthausen all over again."

"But what should we do?" Maude had a no-nonsense attitude about the past. "That Romanian in this country, the one who is supposed to have committed those dreadful crimes, he must be, my goodness, almost eighty years old. What do you *do* with him?"

"There's no statute of limitations on murder," Wendell answered testily. "If he's guilty, he should pay. What much more concerns me is simply whether anyone or any files from the Agency or from the old OSS or SSU period reveal that we *knew* we were dealing with a war criminal or a murderer. *I* certainly remember very clearly that we used this man in Vienna after the war to get very valuable information on the Soviets. But I never dreamed that he was anything but a very sharp, if diabolical, DP who had managed to penetrate some Soviet military staff. And I don't think Steve Browning, who recruited him, knew any more than he told me."

Maude said as they walked slowly, "I'm sorry, George, but I don't trust Steve Browning."

"Yes," he answered, a brief edge to his voice. "I've heard from you on that before."

"I know he saved your life, George, but . . ."

He shook his head without responding, something he did more and more these days. She was right, of course, and he learned to his profit to listen carefully to her instincts. And, give her credit, she did not inflict them on him in a continuing tattoo. This woman whom he had married thirty-one years before, and by whom he had three children, all satisfyingly dispersed into their adult lives, was keenly aware of the pressures of his job and rarely burdened him with her insights or prejudices.

Decades in this strange craft had blunted his once sharply defined views on who was bad or good, who could be trusted or not trusted. There was x amount of bad or good in everyone. What counted much more in this clandestine intelligence business was a sense of trust which emerged from years and years of working together with colleagues against the frustrating and immensely difficult targets of the Service.

He could not, of course, tell Maude anything about the Browning case, now institutionalized as LZ-HERO, whose ironic cryptonym was known only to those on the Bigot List. To tell her anything violated his deepest convictions of need-to-know, although he was hardly naïve enough to think that others on that list could keep their mouths shut around their spouses and cronies. And he could not tell her how the suspicions about Steve had wounded his sense of pride in his colleagues. Even a suspicion of treason bruised the spirit and darkened his professional world.

He sighed as he walked arm in arm with her carefully down the uneven pavement. Although he trusted Maudie's discretion as much as his own, clandestine operations were not her affair. He hoped he was not becoming as paranoid as others of his colleagues were. Some weeks earlier, he had overheard the wife of one of his senior staff officers lamenting to Maude at a noisy Agency cocktail, "Every night I ask Ralph: What did you do today? And he holds his hands apart as if describing the length of a fish he had caught and he says, 'I've pushed that much paper today.' Now I ask you, Maude, what kind of pillow talk is *that?*"

He smiled at the memory of the woman's frustration. No, he wouldn't go *that* far, but he and Maude did not sit in bed nights talking about compromised Agency agents or triumphs of stolen codes. And, most definitely, not about Steve Browning. That one he would have to bear alone.

The habits of security had become so deeply ingrained in him that a repugnance came over him to talk shop with *anyone* after hours, from the moment that he steered his aging Mercedes out of the VIP basement parking area at Langley at day's end. Those who knew him well never attempted to chat him up at a cocktail on some clamorous intelligence item in the news, knowing how swiftly the urbane smile could vanish and a stinging rejoinder become their reward. He was fully aware that more genuine secrets were carelessly bruited about at social events in Washington, D.C., than anywhere else in the world; he, for one, would not play that game.

"Didn't mean to turn you off, Maudie," he said apologetically. "I've got a lot on my mind tonight, I guess."

"Well, perhaps it's a good idea we are going down to the Curriers'." She smiled reassuringly. "Take your mind off Langley and some of the things that bother you. Trudy says that a couple of old diplomatic friends of ours are coming. Peter and Ellen Wickham from Ankara, and Nate and Sue Ribbell, who've got their first embassy and are leaving for Malawi next week."

"Malawi!" he echoed in mock dismay. "What kind of an embassy is Nate going to run down there? *We* don't even have a station in Malawi!"

"Well, knowing Nate Ribbell, he'll insist on you opening a station there right away. He wouldn't be happy until he had a *full* embassy."

He shook his head vigorously.

"I wouldn't count on that, Maudie. Most U.S. ambassadors

would be very happy if we shut down our stations in their embassies and went home." He stopped her once again and flung at her, "Quick, what's the capital of Malawi?"

"Lilongwe," she answered demurely. "You can't catch me on these things, George Wendell."

"Damn, you're good!" he said admiringly. "Even the smart ones make a mistake and say Blantyre, assuming they even know where the country is. What an ambassador's wife you'd make, Maudie!"

And that, *au fond*, was the problem, he knew, as they reached the last short block to the Curriers': Maude Henshaw Wendell, descendant of physicians, lawyers, and a couple of governors, would much rather that he had chosen "something open": diplomacy or the law or even politics, rather than the shadowy eminence he had achieved in the shadowy trade he practiced. Had he gone the Foreign Service route, he would long ago have been an ambassador or an Assistant Secretary of State, appearing publicly under true colors. They would have been assigned to and traveled to all corners of the world, gathering mementos, friendships, memories of exotic places and incidents, forever to be addressed "Mr. Ambassador" or "Mr. Secretary." Instead, they had but one overseas post in their married life, a brief and troubled tour in Madrid twenty-five years previously, during the dour regime of Francisco Franco, in a situation of such awkwardness in terms of cover (he was nominally assigned to the Embassy Economic Section, whose head promptly exiled him to an isolated office and refused to have anything to do with the Spook) and in such wretched housing that they were happy to return to Washington. He had never been assigned overseas again, although he had traveled frequently on operational errands of increasing importance, never accompanied by Maude.

It was true that he now occupied a position of recondite power, and those of his non-Agency friends who knew the importance of the job he held were fascinated by it and were flattered when he accepted their invitations. (To any others, he described himself as "assigned to national security affairs" when asked just what he did in Washington.) Much of his "social life" consisted of entertainment of foreign intelligence and security officials who visited Washington on periodic liaison visits and briefings, from which Maude was again often excluded. Attendance with her at occasional intimate dinners given by, or for, the senior British SIS representative, or the German Bundesnachrichtendienst, or the French SDECE people in Washington was all very well but, except for rare evenings such as this one, with close personal friends (well, Maude's really), his was a discreet life. He was not often seen at the brilliant salons and sit-down dinners for thirty.. The Director and DDCI worked *that* circuit as befitted their rank.

George Wendell, as Maude only half-humorously put it, was "the man with the silent beeper." Carrying a paging device in Washington was actually prestigious, like having *two* telephones in your government car: evidence that you had a vital twenty-four-hour-a-day job. But while many Washington eminences carried beepers simply for show, Wendell's were constantly beeping. So much so that one night the device, left on the night table, had beeped disruptively on one of those now infrequent occasions when he was making love to Maude. He replaced it the next day with what the Technical Services people called a Thumper, a flat rectangular device some four inches long which vibrated silently against the skin when activated by Headquarters in an emergency.

The Thumper was attached this evening to the inside of his belt, flat against his body in the area of his appendix. He was not going to take the chance of carrying any noise-making device at Trudy and Bill Curriers', where you could expect to find anyone from a Soviet Embassy counselor to strange, flaky counterculture types with beards, bangles, buttons, and unconfined breasts.

He brushed his lips against her ear as they stood before the Curriers' elegant brick town house with its Italianate twin steps leading to the brightly lit front door, a house twice the width and depth of most houses in that prestigious neighborhood, including his own.

"I deeply do hope, Maudie, that the Curriers aren't going to have anyone who's going to hassle me. Did they swear by all that's holy . . . ?"

"Trudy swore by all that's unholy that tonight there would be no Bloc diplomats, no anti-Agency congressmen or staffers from the Hill, nor your own Director." She gave his arm a righteous squeeze. "Now there, wasn't that thoughtful of her?"

"Damn near saint-like. And do tell me again, speaking slowly and clearly, just what's this open-house thing all about?"

"It's her social 'catch-up,' Trudy says. Everybody they owe an invitation to whom they haven't seen in months and months. Plus a few out-of-towners. And I promised we'd put in at least an appearance. You know how fond Bill Currier is of you. After all, you went to Harvard together, you served in the military together . . ."

"Bill Currier," he said feelingly, "is a sympathetic, dumb, charming guy who got as far in the Foreign Service as charm and three million dollars of his wife's money could advance him. The cruel accident of fate which pushed him and me together in Dunster House and later dumped us into the same OSS unit in North Africa, is something I accept with resignation. But I've reached an age, dear Maudie, where soap bubbles do not replace real life, and I tire of coping with these strange and unpredictable birds the Curriers pick up and invite into their handsome home. 'Oh, so you're with the Agency, eh? And what do you do with the Agency, Mr. Wendell? Terminate people with extreme prejudice? Feed LSD to minority politicians? Sit around concocting harebrained schemes to kill Fidel Castro or Muammar Qaddafi? Run wire taps against the White House?' Just one peep tonight, Maudie . . ."

She stopped and faced him at the foot of the granite steps which led up through a thick matting of ground ivy to the noble entrance now illuminated by replicas of ships' lanterns. A distant babble of human voices within the house could already be heard.

"George Wendell," she told him in a quiet voice to which he knew he had to listen closely. "By now I can appreciate the fact that this day must have been a lulu for you. All right. I promise you this: within half an hour, you will feel a tug at your elbow. It will be me, urgently requesting you to take me home because I will feel a little faint. But you will have only one scotch and soda, and go *very* easy on the buffet. Eat nothing that's salted; you know your problem. By nine P.M. you will be home and will have drunk a hot cup of low-salt bouillon and, without glancing at any books, newspapers, reports, or memoranda, you will be in bed. Is that enough to get you up these steps?"

He kissed her lightly on the end of her long, fine nose.

"I count the minutes until I am tugged at the elbow. Now watch these damned stairs."

He suffered the kiss-kiss from Trudy and the overenthusiastic handshake and shoulder pats by Bill Currier, abstractedly noting that Trudy was dressed in what appeared to be loose-flowing brown pajamas, and that Bill in gray trousers, double-breasted blazer, and a predictable striped regimental tie, even in retirement, remained the quintessential embassy officer.

"You're lucky!" Bill honked, tanned round face filled with unrestrained hospitality. "They're just serving the hot dishes. God, feller, haven't seen you in weeks! Caught you on the TV news, though, at the hearings. Isn't that Jenny Pfitzner something? What are they doing to you out at the Puzzle Palace? You pulling night duty?"

"Day *and* night duty," Wendell answered, taking in the familiar grandeur of the foyer with its Venetian chandelier, fashionably peeling antique mirrors, and old oak floors gleaming with shy pride. "And what kind of schedule are *you* working these days, Bill?"

His host doubled over with a spasm of laughter. It didn't take much to convulse Bill Currier.

"Coupon clipping starts around here in midmorning," Bill told him. "But first, tennis."

"Ah promised Maudie," Trudy told him with a melting South Carolina smile, "that ah wouldn't have a soul in here who was going to fuss with you, Georgie, honey."

"Look me in the eye, Trudy," he commanded. "Are there any newspapermen in there?"

She winked one heavily lashed eye and her bow-shaped lips widened with ingenuous guilt.

"Yuh jus' got to have a *couple* of media people in, Georgie; there's somebody from the society page of the *Post* and a couple of magazine people down from New York." She touched his heavy chin playfully with a long-nailed finger.

"Now, Georgie, you jus' go in there and have a marvelous time, yuh hear?"

She turned to the next couple crossing the threshold.

The Curriers did these things up nobly, he commented to himself as he entered the high-ceilinged living room now pulsating with two dozen people, each apparently talking loudly to all the others at the same time. Fresh-cut flowers dazzled everywhere, a dozen long white candles lent warm light to all corners of the curtained room, and three servants moved through the animated guests bearing hors d'oeuvres and drinks; this was the way to do it. And in the next room, he knew, a long oval buffet table that was the envy of Georgetown had by now almost disappeared from sight with the crush of bodies circling it and gnawing away at its offerings. He caught the eye of one of the servants hired for the evening, bearing a tray of drinks, a young Cuban named Jorge whose olive face suddenly creased with a warm smile of recognition and deference. Jorge bore down on him and expertly handed him a glass he knew was scotch and water. To Maude at his side, the waiter presented a gin and tonic without being asked.

"Muchas gracias, Jorge. Hay mucha gente aquí esta noche."

"De nada, señor. Sí, tengo mucho trabajo."

Wendell had quietly run police, FBI, and Immigration and Naturalization traces as well as a check of Agency files prior to hiring this man for occasional dinners and cocktails of his own. Jorge was, he knew, in every way a solid, intuitive character, a younger brother of a man from the 2506 Brigade who had been taken prisoner at the Bay of Pigs and had been ransomed back from Castro in 1963. The lithe young waiter leaned gracefully toward him and whispered in his accented English,

"Atención, Señor Wendell. Watch out for the periodista, the large one in the next room with big mustache and long hair. He is from New York. He speaks poorly of your Agency. He is also drinking too much."

He glided away, tray balanced effortlessly in one hand, without looking back.

"What did he tell you, luv?" Maudie had not missed the muttered confidence. "Some femme fatale to look for in the next room with too much cleavage?"

He drank off half the contents of his glass before answering, feeling the cold bitter liquor on his palate.

"Didn't Trudy say that there wasn't a soul in here who was going to fuss with me? Well, someone apparently fell through the cracks because . . ."

"Mr. George Wendell, master spy, I presume." The thin, querulous New York voice, piped incongruously through a bushy downturned mustache, came from a burly, blunt-nosed man con-

fronting him. He was perhaps fifty years old, black hair now almost vanished from his crown but thick and curling in back and
on the sides. Glass in hand, quick perceptive eyes swimming behind thick-lensed spectacles, he looked like trouble.

Wendell wondered for a brief moment whether he should cut
his losses, turn on his heel, and depart without saying a word to
the man. He exchanged a fleeting glance with Maude. Her long,
softly lined face held an expression he well knew: don't make a
scene. He squared his shoulders and drew himself up to his most
forbidding stance, aware that he was emulating a puffed bullfrog.

"I *am* George Wendell. And I'm *not* a master spy, if you don't
mind. To get it right, I'm a spy *master*. It's a management role
and there's quite a lot of difference there," he replied with what
he hoped was a reasonable tone. He studied the flushed, large-
pored cheeks of the man and the way he had of drawing his brows
together to signal his bellicosity. "And who, sir, are you?"

"Barney Langer."

Perhaps it was arrogant of the man to presume that his name
alone identified him, but Wendell would not play "Barney
Who?" with him. He knew the name well. For the past six years,
Langer's feature stories about the Agency and its dirty linen had
been appearing in the written media: *Esquire, New York* magazine, the Sunday magazine supplement of the New York *Times,*
Penthouse. There was no question that Langer had steeped himself on the Agency to the fullest extent by attentive reading of voluminous and revealing congressional investigation reports and
other published materials, and (Security had told Wendell) from
the babblings of some retired Agency employees. Others in Washington and along the American journalistic circuit had done the
same; writing about the CIA had become a profitable free-lance
occupation. Unlike many of these others, however, personal malice persistently blurred Langer's words and tilted the balance of
his stories. Again and again he wrote about an Agency out of control, an Agency filled with amoral and stupid men who had done
amoral and stupid things, thumbing their noses at the law of the
land; an Agency whose wings should be amputated, not clipped.
(The sad fact was that there was just enough truth to some of his
stories to make it impossible to rebut them. They were not rebut-

ted; the Agency generally remained silent in the face of published truths or lies.)

Examining the hostile face before him, Wendell also knew what the other knew he knew: that eighteen years earlier, Bernard Langer had applied for Agency employment and had been rejected as "unsuitable" after the routine polygraph, which all applicants must take, revealed that he had lied about earlier homosexual experiences and a minor court record. It was probably sticking in the man's psyche like a poisoned arrow. As a matter of revenge, Langer would probably never stop writing his twisted stories on the Agency as long as someone was ready to publish them. Taking him on now, in the middle of this babbling crowd, and with a sharp-eyed woman reporter from the *Post* present, would be stupid and attention-drawing. Wendell decided to cope with Barney Langer as one copes with the bearer of an infectious disease: sympathetically, but carefully, keeping maximum distance between him and the other.

He was aware of Maude standing beside him, not touching him but close enough to do so. At Langer's side appeared a homely blonde with frizzy hair, excessively large round goggles, long looping silver earrings, a Mother Hubbard dress, and a full toothy smile. Langer introduced her as his "research assistant."

"Ah yes, Mr. Langer," Wendell said. "A writer. I've read your articles from time to time."

There, that was short and snappy. Now if only this aggressively hulking man in his rumpled cotton suit would go away, he might have a nibble of the superb giant shrimp the Curriers were serving, his first real food since morning. But Langer blocked his way. He seemed to be sizing him up, mentally photographing him, already writing the lines about his encounter with the Spy Master General of the United States.

They stood in a tight little group, the four of them, a momentary circle of silence in the little shrieks and braying sounds around them. Grim civilized smiles masked an immediate antipathy between the two couples. Damn Bill and Trudy Currier, he thought, lifting his glass deliberately to taste the remaining cold bite of scotch; damn them and their catch-up parties and, while he was at it, damn Maudie for dragging him here. He'd been nipped at and harried enough all this long day without having this hirsute Inquisition judge materialize, torch ablaze, to burn him and the Agency at the stake.

"I was present up on the Hill at the subcommittee hearing chaired by Representative Pfitzner." Langer finally spoke, peering at him through his thick lenses. "That wasn't much of a break-through, your testimony."

"Sorry I disappointed you," he answered, very tightly controlling his responses. "I was, as you probably noted, testifying under oath. At the risk of sounding trite, I told the truth. What I don't know, I don't know."

"That remains to be seen." The words emerged from a truculent mouth. His female companion nodded knowingly.

"You're calling me a liar, perhaps?" Wendell sensed the blood rushing into his cheeks.

"Nooo, Mr. Wendell, I wouldn't call you a liar. Maybe just uninformed about what your own people know. And they know a lot about the Calinescu case, I can tell you that, if you didn't already know it."

Maudie's fingers were like talons in his elbow. He heeded the painful reminder and asked in a civilized rumble, "Then you think me an incompetent, Mr. Langer?"

The other shrugged heavy shoulders and the corners of his mouth turned down with a you-said-it-I-didn't grimace.

"Let's just say that you probably can't be informed about everything your Agency is doing or did in the past, Mr. Wendell. But I'm telling you one thing: I'm on to this Calinescu story. I sense an enormous, important yarn down here. I sense that this hideous maze of a bureaucracy down here in Washington, D.C."—he spoke as if he arrived in the Inferno from cooler climes—"is again engaged in a fantastic cover-up to keep a bloodthirsty bunch of war criminals from being repatriated to face punishment in their home countries. I sense there's bribery of officials in high places. The Calinescu case is a superb illustration of all this. And *you* people"—he leveled a beefy forefinger at Wendell—"you brought him over here to the U.S.A. after he collaborated with you. He should have been tried and shot in Europe. A goddamn disgrace, if I do say so, Mr. Wendell."

There was a split second in which Wendell debated whether to hit him hard, just once but hard, on the open lips now flared, revealing an array of jagged irregular teeth. But in a blur, almost faster than eyes could register it, Jorge came straight at Bernard Langer from one side, tray filled with mixed drinks, looking sharply away as if heeding a call from a guest behind him. He collided heavily with Langer. A half-dozen glasses showered the man with liquids from forehead to waist as they cascaded from the tray, and the impetus of Jorge's movement from the side was enough to knock Langer to the floor, amid shards of broken glass.

"You crazy wop son of a bitch!" Langer shouted, struggling to his knees and flailing about for his dislodged spectacles, as an abject Jorge sought to pull him to his feet and to mop the liquor-soaked guest with a white linen towel. "Keep away from me, you sloppy bastard! Look what you've done to a brand-new suit!"

Maude said in his ear, "All right, George, just let's ease out of here. If Jorge hadn't done it, you probably would have."

And indeed Jorge, insisting on mopping his victim despite Langer's indignant gestures, winked just once discreetly at Wendell as he moved slowly away.

He scarcely had reached the main hall again, now still and empty, with his hosts at Langer's side, when he realized that his lower right side was receiving distinct pulsations. The Thumper was telling him he was being paged by Headquarters.

From a telephone behind the grand staircase of the Currier foyer, he quickly dialed the night duty officer's telephone number. After three rings, a male voice said, "Hello."

"This is Wendell, DDO," he said. "Badge number GG-1071. I've just been paged."

"Just a moment, sir," the voice said, now filled with deference toward the identified caller. Shuffling of paper could be heard.

"Yes, sir, an urgent telephone message for you from the congressional switchboard on Capitol Hill."

"From whom?"

"Just a second, sir. Oh, yes, from a woman congressman named Pfitzner, sir. Representative Jenny Pfitzner of New York. She says that she couldn't reach you at home and would like to talk with you at once, tonight if at all possible. Here's her home phone number and address."

He copied the number into a thick black address book and replaced the telephone on its cradle very gently.

Maudie, hovering behind him, studied the bemused expression on his fatigued face and said, standing very close to him, "I've said goodbye to the Curriers. You did get your one drink. Now it's home for that bouillon, maybe an omelet, and to bed."

"I wouldn't count on that," said George Wendell.

CHAPTER EIGHT

It was not difficult for Wendell to find the luxury apartment in southwest Washington where Jenny Pfitzner lived. He steered the old Mercedes carefully through the stream of nocturnal traffic, peering around him at the empty sidewalks, remembering with keen nostalgia the raffish waterfront along Maine Avenue, now vanished. And also vanished were the barracks-like rows of temporary buildings facing the Reflecting Pool, "I," "J," "K," and "L," which had once housed the Clandestine Services. Only a grassy picnic area remained of those hive-like buildings. The memory of highly classified deeds and blunders, and those who had performed them, hung like wraiths in the empty night air.

And he knew that he himself was coming closer and closer to becoming part of that past whose physical reminders were obliterated. Inevitably, the new people had arrived, the quick pragmatic ones, the Don Koblers, feet jiggling with ambition. For them he was a voice from the past, listened to impatiently, a kind of maddening roadblock.

He remembered this very morning the expression on Kobler's face when he realized that Wendell did not know the meaning of the computer term "spillage." That's what they had gotten on the computer run on Calinescu, Kobler said: spillage. "Mop it up yourself, Don," he had said. But Kobler was not amused.

Well, Kobler would have to wait a bit. Whether he liked it or not, George Wendell represented experience and continuity, commodities in short supply in the Agency. When they stopped paying people for experience he, George Wendell, would be fired. But for the moment it was his Directorate.

He gripped the wheel of the Mercedes with a sudden firmness, the surge of curiosity rippling through him. Events took strange bounces in this business. After his acrimonious clash with Jenny Pfitzner at her committee hearing, he would be, he thought, the last person in Washington to be summoned by her. And yet, here he was en route to a nocturnal rendezvous with her.

Why the urgency? Why him and not, say, the Director? From a corner of his cluttered accumulation of biographical snippets, he recalled Jenny's reputation as a woman who chose bedmates as a man would pick a tie: judiciously, and according to the mood. Was this what Jenny might have in mind? Impossible; he barely knew the woman.

He eased the Thumper, flat and hard against his lower abdomen, to a more comfortable position. What a weird way for a grown man to make a living!

"I'm here to visit Mrs. Pfitzner," he told the impassive guard at the gate leading to a cavernous underground parking area. The man consulted a list, nodded, and flipped a switch to raise the gate. Wendell eased the Mercedes down the unlit ramp into an empty parking space in the silent, echoing garage, locked it, and trudged up one floor to the building's main door. It was locked; like most such deluxe condominium residences adjoining a poor, crime-plagued district, this was run as if it were under siege. He dialed her apartment number from a house phone outside the building near the entrance.

"This is Wendell," he responded to a brief metallic query. A buzz opened the door to the lobby but he discovered, to his irritation, that once inside he could not summon the elevator without a special key. As he stared, nonplussed, at the elevator door, it suddenly opened. Jenny Pfitzner, in a low-cut rose-colored housecoat, waited inside and beckoned to him.

"Sorry about the security Mickey Mouse," she said, her strident New York intonation relieved by a crooked smile. "Can't be too careful around here. We've had some problems. Come in for a little ride."

They rode the short distance upward in silence, neither of them wanting to initiate a conversation and both of them self-consciously looking straight ahead as the elevator buttons flashed at the succeeding floors. But once inside her apartment she turned and grasped his extended right hand with both of hers. Standing close to her, he immediately perceived, was a much more agreeable experience than looking up at her from a witness chair. She was short in her slippered feet, shorter than he had imagined, and the top of her head came to the level of his chin.

She had gone to considerable effort to prepare for his appearance. Her hair had been liberated from its tight confines and cascaded to her shoulders in restrained ebullience, lustrous chestnut-brown shot through with a few gray threads. Her face, apart from a pair of shallow pockmarks, was smooth and shiny, with generously applied color to the long cheeks and the wide lips, and she exuded a fragrance he much enjoyed—that of a woman who has just bathed. And he could not prevent his eyes from peering briefly downward where full round breasts welled out of the housecoat. They had been quite unapparent to him from the witness table. Tonight she looked young enough to be the daughter of the fierce female who had hectored him from her congressional dais. He was no fool: Jenny had not dressed like this to sift through draft legislation with him.

Without the half-moon reading glasses, her button eyes were a curious amalgam: the tough, almost brutal directness in them contained a vulnerability he had not noticed before. Perhaps he had not looked hard enough; perhaps she was a Dr. Jekyll/Mrs. Hyde. These eyes now looked penitently up at him and she held his hand as she said, "Mr. Wendell, please forgive me for doing this. I know you've probably had enough of Jenny Pfitzner to last you a lifetime, but I *had* to see you. It's important and it's . . . deeply troubling to me, what I want to talk with you about."

As she escorted him along a carpeted corridor past a closet mirror he glanced at himself. His facial appearance shocked him: above the unwelcome wattles sagging from his jaw, vertical lines of (one had to face it) age had deepened with fatigue. He was almost old enough to be Jenny Pfitzner's father, and his vanity was not strong enough to prevent the truth from filtering through: tonight he looked it. The mirror also revealed a strand of his lank, iron-gray hair drooping over his forehead. With a wipe of his hand, he disciplined the errant lock and walked by her side into her living room.

He looked around him with pleased surprise. Jenny's furnishings were in exquisite taste. Modern unobtrusive sofa and chairs modestly introduced walls enriched with signed lithographs of Miró, Tobey, and Appel. Two abstract iron sculptures faced each other harmoniously from opposite sides of the room, and an intricate tan Qashqai rug covered nearly all of the living-room floor. It was an uncluttered place with softened lights, a refuge from a harsh world, with each piece of furniture and artifact acquired and sited to soothe the spirit.

A glance at an almost solid wall of books also gave him quick confirmation that Jenny had done her homework on her *idée fixe*. Row upon row of volumes in English, French, and German, all on the war-crimes theme, including an entire set on the Nuremberg War Crimes Tribunal. It would be typical of Jenny that she prepared herself to the point of overflowing on matters important to her intensely partisan spirit.

The glass door to a tiny balcony was open and he stepped out for a moment to take in the view, a spectacular night scene of the downriver Potomac, with blinking lights of aircraft taking off and landing at National Airport across the black waters.

"I would have been much happier if you had held the hearings up here, Mrs. Pfitzner," he said to her, stepping back inside. "This is a little Shangri-La."

Jenny Pfitzner held out her hands in supplication.

"Please, what can I get you? I think I've got about any kind of a drink—as long as it's scotch or bourbon."

He smiled at her candor.

"A light scotch, if you don't mind."

She was back in a moment with two drinks on a silver tray with napkins. She had also activated a tape deck and the precise etched forms of a Bach toccata and fugue clanged discreetly from the far corners of the room. He sank into one of the soft beige chairs with a sigh and noted again with a pleased attentiveness the tops of her breasts, which quivered slightly as she bent over him with the tray. In a silent toast of thanks to her he held out his glass as she perched on a footstool close by him. Jenny Pfitzner, he noted, was not much of a drinker: she was sipping a glass of white wine. As middle-aged foreplay, it was pretty tame stuff.

"I congratulate you on your apartment, Mrs. Pfitzner." He bowed his head slightly at her. "Superbly done. I want the name and address of your decorator immediately."

She flushed slightly with pride.

"Her name is Jenny Pfitzner and she's unfortunately busy on other jobs. But thank you. I live my private life here, alone. It's my sanctuary. The time I spend here, little as it is, is *my* time and I don't conduct any work here—unless it's an emergency."

He watched slow-moving points of flashing aircraft lights in the night sky beyond the window.

"And I assume that my being here—is an emergency?"

She knitted her forehead for a moment before replying.

"Well, yes and no. But before I get into it, and it's troubling me more than I can tell you, I've got to make an apology to you first, Mr. Wendell."

He permitted his eyebrows to raise barely perceptibly before responding with an amused smile.

"I am at an age where I accept apologies from anybody about anything, Mrs. Pfitzner."

She leaned toward him like an eager child but the eyes burned with a steely intensity.

"I really laid into you, Mr. Wendell, at the hearing. But you've got to understand a little about me. That's the way I grew up and that's the way I am."

Her truculence contrasted strangely with the femininity of her moist, brightly reddened lips so close to him.

"Look, I've been a fighter ever since I lived over a candy store in the Bronx and watched my sweet old dad get pushed around by everybody, like a large rubber ball."

Her voice, low and almost menacing, crackled with emotion.

"*Nobody*, I promised myself, would ever push Jenny around!"

"We both share that feeling," Wendell said uneasily. "None of us wants to be pushed around."

"You're not a woman," she retorted bitterly. "You don't have to take the crap a woman has to take, and that goes tenfold in the halls of Congress. Oh, they're full of superficial courtesy, especially those mush-mouthed Southerners with all that ol' southern charm. And I know damned well that they're thinking: there's that Yankee Jew girl shootin' off her big New York mouth. Well, screw them! I'm twice as smart and twice as tough as most of them. I play rough and I don't give a damn whether they like it or not."

"What can I tell you?" Wendell said, sipping his cold scotch. "After four terms in the House, you seem to be a success story on the Hill."

She shook her locks in a decisive negative.

"No, I haven't been able to budge them on things that *I* really believe in: ERA, national health insurance. Take this business of war criminals in the United States. Look at that wall over there. See those eleven green volumes on the left? Those are the minutes of congressional hearings held over the last five years on how the U.S. has not only let these bastards in, but the government won't try to round them up and throw them out. Damn it, it's a maddening matter of thwarted justice. Those monsters, fat and happy, running around this country! You know something? When my late husband, Henry, died in office, one of the main reasons I decided to run to take his seat was my indignation at this mindless attitude we have in this country. The one that says: those poor old war criminals; they're getting old and feeble. Let 'em die here in peace."

Bach's prisms of sound marched joyously up and down the room, a counterpoint to the dark, smoldering sound from this woman.

This was an appalling imposition on him, he thought, slumped in her chair, his long workday and the unpleasantness at the Curriers' still swirling around in his tired head. It was actually outrageous that she had summoned him to her apartment as if a matter of national emergency were involved, only to pour out this defensive rationale of her personal obsession, her deep hurts. An unreal moment. And, something told him, not an auspicious one.

"When I give witnesses the rough side of my tongue," Jenny continued, one hand extended in atonement, "I usually do it to stop them from shilly-shallying around, from fibbing, to provoke them into telling me the truth—or more of the truth than they're prepared to tell me. *You* people: you Agency types, INS, Justice Department people, you come before the committee under oath and you try to tell me the absolute minimum you can get away with. *I* understand that game, but that's why I bite back. At times I'm terribly unfair and I know damned well what the media and my own colleagues say about me, but I really don't care. I represent the people of my district and they seem happy with Jenny

Pfitzner, happy enough to send her to the House four times in a row, and a fifth time coming up. That's the main thing."

"I hear you, Mrs. Pfitzner," he said without enthusiasm. It was all defensive as hell but it didn't sound like much of an apology so far.

"You've been up four or five times testifying before me in the last couple of years." Her eyes were now hard and resentful. "Not only before my subcommittee but also before the House Intelligence Committee, where I also sit. I don't know: maybe it was that go-to-hell way you have, your assurance when you sit in the witness chair, dressed like some . . . some British banker with that goddamn Phi Beta Kappa key hanging from that chain on your vest." (She *noticed* it, he realized with astonishment.) "*I* have a Phi Beta Kappa key from Barnard, for God's sake, but I don't flaunt it on a damned chain."

He bit back the temptation to tell her that minor conceits were no excuse for badgering witnesses, but she was hurrying on, aware that he was becoming restless.

"In general, I *don't* trust Agency people to level with us. But I decided, at that last hearing, that I *do* trust *you*. I guess it was your response to me about how you would never countenance the use of any kind of a mass murderer or war criminal by your Agency or by the government in any way. *That* got through to me. I just *knew* you meant it. I said to myself: that's a thoroughly decent, responsible statement to make and the only kind of a person who would make it is a thoroughly decent, responsible human being."

He inclined his head gracefully in her direction.

"I appreciate hearing that, Mrs. Pfitzner . . ."

She held out imploring hands.

"Look." Her singsong intonation took on an almost comic quality. "Let's cut out the 'Mr.' and 'Mrs.' business. I'm Jenny to about a million people. Can you bring yourself to call me Jenny?"

Bach's toccata trills sang softly on her behalf. He yielded gracefully.

". . . Very well, Jenny, I thank you for your kind words. I'm sorry that I've appeared to you to be an arrogant witness. Sometimes it's just a reaction to my inner turmoil: I know that for every minute I'm sitting in that witness chair, I'll have to work *two* extra minutes to catch up when I get back to my office."

It was as if she had not heard him. Her eyes were now intent with concern.

"Listen, I've got to tell you what's happening in this Calinescu case."

A warning buzzer sounded in his brain and he straightened with interest.

"And why me?"

"Because I trust you, as I just told you," she said, "and because for once, we're both on the same side of the fence." She held the gleaming glass of pale wine briefly to her lips, and her expression had changed to that of an uncertain child peering down a dark alley at night. "You heard Klara Abramescu's testimony, George. What did you think?"

He placed his drink precisely on its coaster and meditatively held the arms of his chair. The Agency's Legal Counsel would tell him: don't express any opinions; fudge whatever you do say. Jenny had no right to ask him, a recent witness before her committee, what he thought of the sworn testimony of others. But her troubled eyes and the gently heaving bosom under the satiny housecoat told him it was not a setup or a provocation, whatever else it was.

"What I thought? I believe she was telling a story as truthfully as she could remember it. Calinescu should be investigated fully and if the evidence is there, the Justice Department should take him to court and try to get him deported."

She pursed her lips in satisfaction, but a gleam of malice forecast her next words, uttered with the rasp of the real Jenny.

"But you know, and I know, George, that at least one of your Agency guys got him into the country in 1948, sponsored his immigration request. We've really got him cold. We have a copy of the report that Justice sent to you."

His pulse rate accelerated in a surge of anger and alarm. He felt like an absolute fool sitting there: *she* and her committee had the report and he, the DDO, didn't. What do you say when you're blind-sided?

"You'll have to take my word that I'm leveling with you, Jenny," he said awkwardly, looking straight at her. "I'm embarrassed to tell you that I still haven't gotten that wretched report. I don't know who's responsible. But when I do, someone will pay—in full." He slapped his hands against the chair arms with each of the last two words.

She held out both pale hands placatingly.

"George, I believe you. You'll notice that I didn't use that in the testimony the other day. I could have really socked it to you. Don't ask me why I didn't."

Long lashes fell briefly. "Maybe I didn't *want* to sock it to you just then." She paused and her glance was bold, revealing. "You really appeal to me, y'know."

"All right then," he said, picking up his glass again as she pulled her footstool closer to him, so close that he could perceive a tiny glistening of excitement on the soft down below the long sensitive nose. "You resisted making a public fool out of a private one. My deepest thanks. But let me ask two quick questions, Jenny: first, what's your obsession with Calinescu, and just why am I here?"

"Fair enough. Answer to question one: I'm Jewish, and more than that, I'm of Romanian Jewish origin. I've known since the end of World War II that my grandmother in Bucharest was killed in one of these Iron Guard slaughters. If Klara is right, maybe, just maybe, it was Calinescu or one of his buddies who shot her, or cut her throat, or whatever those bastards did to her. Is that reason enough to go after him?"

He averted his eyes from hers, and stared out the window at the slowly circling dots of light.

"As good an answer as I'll get, I think," he said.

"Answer number two: you're here because I . . . I need someone to talk to . . . and I'm a little bit lonely and upset."

It would really take something to upset Jenny Pfitzner, he thought.

"About what?"

She had inched the footstool closer. One long, sensitive hand touched his wrist. It was warm, almost feverish to the touch.

"Give me some advice, George. What do you think is going on?"

He waited. This day was one of the longest ones for him in years, and his body yearned to rest. But his interest was piqued to a razor-like alertness. Her face was no more than a foot from his.

"George, in the two days since that testimony, I've got—now listen to this—no less than a half-dozen different telephone calls or visits from my colleagues. To be exact, from two senators and five from the House. And the one I got this afternoon takes the cake."

She jumped agitatedly to her feet and prowled nervously before him.

"The goddamned White House, I swear. Some flunky who says, now look, this isn't an official call in any sense of the word, see, but this . . . er . . . um . . . Mr. Callin has been . . . er . . . ah . . . very generous to the campaign fund of the President in the past and, besides, the matter is in the hands of the Immigration and Naturalization people. In effect, lay off."

She clenched tiny fists with rage.

"That's what they all want me to do: stop the hearings, stop the publicity—lay off Dimitriu Calinescu alias Jimmy Callin."

"Lay off?" his mouth made an incredulous inverted U. "Why lay off?"

"Exactly. Why lay off? And the reasons they gave were pretty much the same, and equally unconvincing."

She ticked them off on the fingers of a tiny hand.

"Here's what they say: One, Calinescu or Callin is a decent law-abiding American citizen with a great success story, rags to riches, in California, the Never-Never Land. Two, I'm paranoid in year after year chasing these alleged war criminals in the United States, all of whom are now elderly and ailing people who should be left alone. Three, Mrs. Abramescu was a hysterical and unreliable witness who is relating an incident that happened when she was an eight-year-old child and in effect is making up the whole story."

"Interesting," Wendell said. "I wouldn't dream that Calinescu had such a cheering section."

Jenny said, contempt curling her wide mouth, "In the Middle East, you buy a mob. In Italy, you buy a claque, if you're an opera singer. In the United States, you buy congressmen. And it's as clear to me as it is to you, George, that Calinescu has really bought himself a bunch of corruptible *shtunks*. And not all of them from California either."

Her eyes briefly changed again, diamond-hard with anger, the old Jenny, and her voice rasped like a hacksaw.

"Goddamn them, George, I'm so goddamned ashamed of them."

A slight dizziness descended on him, a tight giddy gust in his brain. That was the third time that day; something really to talk about with Doc Hocker tomorrow. He found himself mopping his brow with his handkerchief. Surely, Hocker could give him something better to cope with these . . . what did Hocker call them . . . these events.

She was watching him intently as a cat, a mixture of concern, passion, and curiosity now fleeting across her mobile face.

"Strong drinks you serve, Jenny," he said, tucking the handkerchief into his jacket breast pocket with a flourish.

He thought for a moment.

"Have you taken this up with the Speaker or your party whip? It doesn't sound like something they'd be delighted to know about, but on the other hand, shouldn't they . . . ?"

But Jenny paced the carpeting restlessly for a minute. Clearly there was more.

"No," she spoke abstractedly. "I haven't gone to anybody yet. Damn, I know I've gotta. But there may be even more to this lousy business, and I'm sick at heart about it. . . ."

She returned to her footstool and again pulled it close to him.

"George, a couple of hours ago, Klara Abramescu was here. I cooked supper for her and talked. You know, that sweet little woman is almost like family to me. And we talked and we talked about all kinds of things. . . ."

The New York singsong in her voice had reached a quickening tempo. He could have sworn that she was embarrassed. She fidgeted briefly with the zipper fastener on her housecoat, face cast down. This is how you get into the housecoat, the gesture plainly told him, but not right now. Finally, she tossed her head in a gesture of decision and looked him straight in the eye.

"Klara's testimony at the hearing was not complete," she announced. "She got flustered under all those lights and the crowd and the photographers, and she omitted something in her sworn testimony."

"So?"

"So. She had literally forgotten the incident but tonight I was drawing her out about her life in Romania from the time of the massacre, which was in 1941, to the time she illegally shipped out to Palestine, which was sometime in 1947."

"She stayed there during the entire war?"

"The whole time. The family of her school chum, Susza, a Christian kid, took her in, told the authorities that she was a relative from the country. The neighbors knew damned well what was going on, but didn't squeal. They were deeply ashamed of what had happened to Klara's family. So, all during the German period of the war, she stayed there illegally. The stories she tells . . . !"

Jenny's eyes glittered at the recollection.

"So the big day comes. The Germans pull out of Romania and in come the conquering Russian troops. For the first time, it was safe for Jews to come out on the streets of Bucharest. So one day, late in autumn 1944, Klara and Susza are wheeling Susza's little brother in a pram down a main street of Bucharest, past the Ministry of Interior building. Lots of Russian and Romanian soldiers and civilians rushing in and out. A Russian military auto rolls up to the main entrance of the building just as they are passing by. And who is in the backseat of that automobile? Calinescu, in civilian clothing. She swears it. Unmistakably him."

He felt his hair crawl on the back of his neck.

"Was Calinescu alone?"

"No. Klara remembers this clearly, a mental photograph. She recalls Calinescu stepping out of the backseat right behind a big Russian officer who's wearing one of those long military overcoats. And get this: he's wearing an officer's hat, what you call a garrison hat, with a visor—and made of blue cloth. A blue top! Even that early in the Russian occupation, Klara tells me, the Romanians warned each other to watch out for the Russkies wearing the blue hats: NKVD, secret police. And that's the bunch *you* worry about, right?"

Wendell said, "When in uniform, the KGB and its predecessor organizations, like the NKVD, wear blue hats and shoulderboards. Yes. That's the bunch we worry about."

The spiraling Bach contrapuntal rhythms achieved an apogee, resolved themselves, and ended.

"Does she remember anything else?" His question was simply a pole to fend her off while his mind, whirling like a centrifuge, sought to sort out a variety of consequences and repercussions, none of them pleasant.

"She says she remembers standing there, a twelve-year-old kid, almost close enough to touch the man who organized the massacre of her family. She says she just stared at him while he jabbered in Russian with the officer. At one point, Calinescu looked straight at her. But of course he didn't know her from Adam's off ox. All he saw were two small girls pushing an infant in a pram. Finally, the Russian gave him a big bear hug, said 'Do svedanya,' and marched into the building, and Calinescu got back in the military car and the chauffeur drove off. The whole thing took, maybe, two minutes."

He pushed his body out of the chair and she rose with him.

"What do you think, George? Does that make any sense?"

He looked down at her, lips tightened.

"It makes entirely too much sense, Jenny. I wish to hell we'd heard that story thirty-four years ago."

"So this is news to you? It's something you didn't know before?"

He nodded twice before speaking.

"If we had known that, Jenny, we would have played him for what he was: a Soviet provocation agent. I strongly doubt that he would have ever reached the United States either as a visitor or as an immigrant."

Jenny, eyes narrowed with speculation, groaned.

"God, it isn't enough that these lunkhead colleagues of mine have been bought by Calinescu! But if they're playing footsie with some damned Soviet spy . . ."

"I'd go very slowly on that one, Jenny," he warned her. "You're on thin legal ice there. Suppose what Mrs. Abramescu saw was a man playing a dangerous game with the Soviets to facilitate his move to Vienna and from there to the States? It certainly sounds ominous, but we don't know the whole story by a long shot."

She had reached for both his hands in a gesture at once ingenuous and calculating. They felt soft and warm in his, and she looked up at him, the soft, long cheeks diffused with expectancy and anticipation. He knew precisely what was occurring but he suffered his hands to be held.

"Look, Jenny." He smiled at her, secretly amused at the tigress of two days ago now turned pussycat. "I urge you to call in the Department of Justice people tomorrow morning and tell them what you told me. I know it'll be hard for you to do because you and they aren't exactly a mutual-admiration society, but this little story of Mrs. Abramescu is something quite important, and they'll be grateful for your information. And don't talk to your staffers about it. There's enough loose talk up on the Hill as it is. The FBI will be most interested. After all, they're the people in charge of internal security in this country. Let Mrs. Abramescu talk to them herself, if they like."

He smiled his most winning smile.

"Voilà. Your troubles are over, although for some of your colleagues they may just be beginning."

She stood looking up at him for a moment, lips parted, eyes shining with what he thought was satisfaction. She suddenly reached up, arms around his neck, pulled his head down toward hers, and kissed him, mouth softly moist and pliant.

"I want you to stay, George," she whispered in his ear. "Stay tonight . . . as long as you like. You know what I said to myself after you left the witness chair? I thought: he'll be a gentle lover. He'll remind me that I'm a woman, an honest-to-God loving woman, and we'll be good for each other. . . ."

So what he had heard about her was true: "Whatever Jenny wants, Jenny gets." And it was he she wanted. Well, it would be a matter of utter simplicity and minimum fuss to suffer himself to be led into her darkened bedroom and to make love to her. She clearly yearned to unwind, clearly had designated him as the unwinder. All that remained was for him to agree and to drive home some hours later with one more friend on Capitol Hill. She clung to him almost desperately.

He took her clinging hands from around him with reluctance and stepped back a pace, a small sad smile hovering on his face.

"I'm flattered at the invitation, Jenny," he said, still holding both her hands. "And it's almost an offer I can't refuse. But it puts me in a difficult situation: I've got to keep looking at myself in the mirror in the morning and, if I go to bed with you, I won't be able to do that—or to look at Maude Henshaw Wendell, my wife. And I'm really not that good as a stud."

And—poof—there stood Representative Jenny Pfitzner, eyes flashing with scorned pride.

"Get the hell out of here, you son of a bitch!" she screamed at him. "Maybe I'm not good enough for you! You come on strong with all that Ivy League rumble to your voice, but it's all a put-on, just like your Agency buddies. I don't know, maybe you just haven't got what it takes to be with a real woman! OK, OK, you've made it clear what you think of me. Now go, for God's sake. . . ."

"I'll find my way out," he said, and closed the door behind him. He wondered, as he walked slowly down the long corridor to the elevator, whether it was the menopause that could do such things to a woman. Of one thing he was certain: Jenny Pfitzner would make him pay.

CHAPTER NINE

"Ruffing, there are few people in this Agency or else-where in our government who can, or ever will, qualify as professional CI officers. To be a good one takes a mind almost incapable of trusting his brother or his mother or his wife; a mind with an almost photographic recall of dates, names, places, incidents; constantly fascinated with putting these and other bits of information together to make meaningful patterns or mosaics."

The then Chief of the CI Staff, pipe wedged into a corner of his mouth, had spoken these words long ago, staring past Ruffing at the winter-stripped skyline beyond the window, and his precisely spoken words were deceptive in their silky softness.

"But a first-class CI officer must have one more attribute: a deep and abiding ideology, in which there is an Enemy, a Black Hat, a visible and palpable villain who must be detected, engaged, and foiled. Counter-intelligence is nothing more or less than a continuing war, a struggle to intercept and negate that enemy's efforts to penetrate our camp. The struggle never stops. It goes on and on, it permeates your dreams, your free moments, your in-nermost life."

His craggy saturnine face did not change expression when he added, "And during my adult lifetime and yours, that enemy is the Soviet Union or, more correctly, the Soviet empire."

He touched Silas lightly on one shoulder as if conferring knight-hood on him, and a wintery smile appeared, disclosing teeth grimed and ragged with years of clenching a pipe.

"By my criteria, Silas, you're on your way to becoming a first-class CI officer."

Eyes crinkling at the corners, he then shook Ruffing's hand, proffered an official certificate of commendation, and offered a final warning.

"If they start saying, 'Silas Ruffing is paranoid, a schizoid, a real fanatic,' you'll know you've arrived."

Silas had cherished that accolade of twenty years ago. It had occurred during a discreet, almost mystic, ceremony held in the large and disordered office of the Chief of the Counter-intelligence Staff, amid a tangle of files and books on intelligence and espionage. The ceremony, including paper cups of white wine, was attended only by Ruffing's own immediate supervisor and by the Deputy Chief of the Staff, an urbane and affable man whose *raison d'être* consisted of keeping his distinguished boss out of trouble with Agency finance, personnel, and administrative natterers.

Ruffing had also been awarded on that same occasion a Quality Step Increase, an incentive to reward government employees for unusually high performance over a sustained period. While the QSI comported no ribbon, medal, or rosette, it did add an extra five hundred dollars annually to his pay, far more welcome to him than the certificate. And for Ruffing it meant much more: recognition by his peers and supervisors that he was good at his job.

Both certificate and QSI had been well earned. Silas had been assigned the task of sifting through voluminous operational files of the German Station, to determine if they could provide clues as to what had gone wrong with the activities of a hitherto highly successful Agency surveillance team working out of Frankfurt. One by one, the team's human targets, a variety of Europeans engaged in espionage assignments for Communist countries in West Germany, seemed to learn immediately of the team's presence and its interest in them. The targets had either disappeared or took unusual evasive actions to shake their "tails."

Silas, hunched in his tiny pillbox of an office, peered intently at every piece of paper for over two weeks. At last he spotted what he set out to find: a routine cable originating from one of the team members requesting Headquarters information on an "acquaintance," and the equally routine Headquarters reply: "No traces." But the team member in this instance, Silas noted, was a divorced middle-aged German woman, originally from Breslau in East Germany. The "acquaintance," as described by her, was from her old home city, a man five years older than she, tall, slender, with a full head of hair, and "well educated." Silas also noted that the team's operations began to go sour two months after the man had appeared in Frankfurt and sought her out.

Despite resistance from an embarrassed German Station, Silas had insisted that the "acquaintance" be carefully checked out, and that he be polygraphed, in conjunction with the West German security service. This eventually came to pass. The acquaintance flunked the test, confessed that he had indeed been sent by the East Germans to seduce the team member and to wheedle out of her an idea of the team's assignments, a task which he had most successfully achieved.

The man was turned over to the West German service for disposition (one of over two hundred such East German agents caught red-handed in West Germany that year). The hapless surveillance team was dissolved, its American supervisor returned to Headquarters under a cloud, and 60 percent of the station's operations against East Germany had to be abandoned or placed on ice. That, Silas' boss said, was what the CI business was all about. (But they hated him on the German desk for years thereafter.)

He labored in the vineyards of counter-intelligence, year in, year out. And the prediction of his Chief, long turned out to pasture, was fulfilled. Silas Ruffing became a man obsessed, paranoid in his pursuit of penetrations, real or imagined, of the Directorate's activities, a gadfly in exposing the professional sloppiness of his colleagues, a nag in urging them to abandon collaborators and agents who showed clear signs of unreliability or suspicious behavior. He peppered Agency field stations the world over with memos exhorting them to pull up their socks and show more tradecraft in their handling of specific operations.

Once, when he had just passed his forty-second birthday, he received a stinging rebuke from a station chief for refusing to grant a clearance on that official's Croat maid, one who had to be fired some weeks later as a penetration agent of the Yugoslav service. In a fit of anger at such an unjustified lament, he had vigorously attempted to transfer out of the Staff and to take an assignment in the field. Certainly, he could serve as a valuable counter-espionage watchdog in some large station; after all, he was a charter member of the Agency, coming out of OSS and SSU, and possessed enough tribal memory to be of great use. But his efforts came to nothing. Not a single station wanted a Savonarola of his notoriety in its midst. And the new Chief of the CI Staff assured him that he could not be spared. He stayed on.

His marriage failed. His wife, who he had predictably found among the clerical employees of the Staff, could not endure Silas' increasing obsession with possible penetrations of the Agency, or his days at his desk, surrounded with files and dispatches, which often ended late in the evening. She sought to serve as a safety valve: wouldn't Silas want to talk out his concerns with her? He looked at her with his small yellow-green eyes as if she were uttering blasphemies.

"Jesus, Betty. I *can't* talk about these things—even to you!"

So she left him, moved out, and in time gained a divorce, remarried, and went back to work on another Agency staff, and Silas lived alone in the small house on a quiet middle-class street in Vienna, Virginia, and which he maintained with the same compulsive tidiness that he applied to his work. One of the bedrooms became an intelligence library, filled with books on the lore of espionage and counter-espionage going back to Elizabethan England and to George Washington's networks run by Tallmadge and Caleb Brewster. At his desk in that library, where he kept letters and correspondence, he had glued hairs across each of the drawers so that any surreptitious entry would be immediately revealed to him. (Not once over the years had he detected any such disturbance, but he went on the premise that there would always be a first time.)

His intense focus narrowed and deepened: how to detect and expose penetrations of the Agency. He did not doubt for a moment that such penetrations existed. Uncovering them, he was convinced, was simply a matter of endless research, alert perusal of the mounds of highly classified reports which washed into the Staff, assiduous checking and cross-checking of names and suspects, their backgrounds, and any inconsistencies in their lives— and a modicum of good luck.

His passion for seeking out the viper in the nest was shared with Manley ("Manny") Mulcahy, his professional clone at the Federal Bureau of Investigation's counter-intelligence staff. Happiness was spending long hours with Manny, sifting through the now cold ashes of previous penetration cases—the Rosenbergs, Alger Hiss, Burgess-McLean, Kim Philby, and George Blake—to determine where background checks had failed or indicators ignored. Together with a pair of kindred spirits from the Agency's Office of Security, they occasionally combined their forces at their watering hole, the Eagle, where their caustic insights and hypotheses on the defensive shortcomings of the Western world's intelligence services would have caused consternation had they been overheard by the directors of those services.

But the solitude and the intensity of his search for penetrations brought him another inevitable companion: alcohol. Only in recent years had he come to enjoy a hard drink at lunchtime when he and the Old Guard met as a group. Initially, one vodka on the rocks sufficed. Then it became one double vodka, then two doubles. . . . Alcohol also ruined his relationship with another companion, a cheerful, heavy-bosomed forty-year-old divorcée who worked in Technical Services. Their semi-monthly assignations, which were characterized by a surprising amount of sexual energy and stamina on both sides, came to an end after he arrived at her apartment drunk enough to fall down several times and smash two of her favorite majolica plates from Italy, following which he botched his sexual performance and snored noisily through the night.

Now he sat in a tiny cubbyhole in the basement of the massive Headquarters building, or as one Director (a Navy man) once called it, the engine room. (In Silas' view, he sat below the engine room; this was the bilge.) His offices over the years reflected a curious parallel to his career: a slow downward spiral through floors and components.

He peered at a modest rectangle of a window high up on the wall. It was covered with a heavy security mesh of metal which confounded the few feeble rays of sunshine seeking for a few minutes every morning to penetrate his underground cell. The room was barely large enough to contain a battered and scarred wooden desk whose inspection stickers identified it as a survivor from OSS days, a black telephone with two internal extension numbers listed on it, two plastic chairs, and a gray hulk of a safe with a three-way combination lock. Not a single item decorated the beige walls except for a government calendar affixed to one wall by Scotch tape. He had no intention of identifying himself with this place of ignominy in any way.

He kept the door to this grim box of an office closed at all times. Were it open, he could not help but overhear the endless chatter of the stenos and secretaries who gathered to use the nearby copier machine. He had quite enough of listening to menstruation difficulties, birth-control measures, boyfriend problems, and how much annual leave remained to be used that year.

He glanced at the dusty folders from the OSS archives. Four months ago, the latest crisis in his career occurred when he had returned from what had become a daily liquid lunch. His new supervisor, a man twelve years his junior, had found him sound asleep with his head on the desk, had wakened him rather briskly, and after telling him in no uncertain terms what the office hours were, had taken him to task on the draft of a lengthy memo he had completed.

Actually, he thought it was one of the better papers he had written, one which pulled together a number of field-inspection reports and focused on the incredible carelessness which U.S. operatives overseas displayed in their use of office and home telephones to discuss sensitive business. He had not taken kindly to suggestions from the DDO staffs that he modify his language and draconian recommendations (reprimands, dismissals) and he had wound up telling his supervisor to stuff the report, sideways.

That had apparently been the last straw. He was then assigned to Documents Review, a tiny unit that did nothing but read OSS wartime reports, to determine whether they could, or could not, be declassified. Documents Review was where old Agency elephants went to die.

It was, he knew, a sinecure. They didn't want to fire him outright, not just then at any rate, because of his impressive service record and his status as an Old Boy. He had a strong hunch that George Wendell, the DDO, had arranged this assignment out of old times' sake. Wendell, after all, had been his OSS boss and the boss of that son of a bitch Steve Browning in Austria, in those wild postwar months. Wendell, one of the few good ones left, had a very strong sense of noblesse oblige. . . .

His throat felt parched, his tongue dry. Each working day he was expected by his supervisor to read or review approximately three good-sized OSS folders. (The Soviets would take care to acquire, by indirect means, any such declassified documents under the Freedom of Information Act. This he well knew. Goddamn them!)

He also knew full well that he could complete this daily norm within three hours, after which he had developed what he called his escape-and-evasion routine until lunch. He would lock his safe, spin the combination lock shut, and with an air of a man with high purpose, he would stride into the large outer office where sat three women stenographers, and hand the folders to one of them with his little red strips sticking to the papers, flagging those which were to remain SECRET or CONFIDENTIAL. Then, without a word, he would march out into the quiet, usually deserted corridor to the chosen safe haven within Headquarters where he would stay secreted for the rest of the morning.

He glanced at the calendar. Today his safe haven was a specific remote basement corner in the library stacks, a little cranny so unused that most of the library people themselves didn't know about it. There he would sit in utter silence, reading the New York *Times* or a good book on the Sorge network from the Historical Intelligence library until noon. He would then stride briskly back through the now teeming corridors, peer briefly at the headlines of the *Wall Street Journal* at the concession stand, and reappear at his basement cubicle long enough to pick up his overcoat or umbrella, as needed. He would check for telephone calls or inquiries, and walk out of the south entrance of Headquarters, flashing his badge at the bored building guard, march a quarter mile to the furthermost parking lane, start up his geriatric Mustang, and drive to the Eagle. There he would meet with a number of the Old Guard, sitting in the relaxed intimacy of a back room for two hours of gossip on the Agency's latest death rattles and possibly a virtuoso analysis by one of those present on an intelligence coup of yesteryear. At something past 2:30 P.M. he would wobble unsteadily but purposefully to his parked car, and drive equally unsteadily but purposefully back to the outermost parking lane at the Agency.

By 3:15 P.M. he would march past the mocking and reproachful glances of the three harpies into his cubicle, close the door, and fall sound asleep, head resting on the scarred desk top. At 4 P.M. he would waken, mouth tasting like sour cotton, reach for his "in" basket, carefully read the Credit Union announcements, the entire list of GSA cafeteria menus for the week ahead, an exhortation or two from someone in the Leadership asking him to be more secure or more cost-conscious, to buy U. S. Savings Bonds, or to give blood to the Red Cross.

Then he would re-emerge from his cubicle, walk past the harpies to a large and well-appointed office where sat his supervisor, the branch chief of the Documents Review activity. If this worthy were in, Silas would poke his head in, ask if all was well. If he were not there, and Silas deeply hoped the man would not be, he would scratch a note on a yellow buck slip: "Ruffing called," with the exact hour and minute, and impale it on the man's executive pen. After that, it would be but a moment or two to return to his cubicle, twirl the safe lock shut, initial the security check sheet, and depart. And that would be one day less to the moment thirteen months hence when he would be compelled to retire, a moment toward which he looked as a stricken man looks to the day of his death: with anticipation at the release from pain, with infinite sadness that there would be no tomorrows.

He glanced tentatively at the folders to be reviewed this day and hunched himself into his chair for the intensive reading. An intermittent buzzing and a flashing light on one of the internal Red Line numbers told him that there was an incoming phone call for him. He punched "hold."

"Who is it, Emmy?"

"Mr. Browning. Didn't you answer his phone call from yesterday?"

He reflected for a brief second. It would not do for him to tell her: (a) none of your goddamned business whose phone calls I answer or don't answer, and (b) I'm not about to answer Steve Browning on anything.

"Tell him I'm busy, Emmy."

Irritatedly: "I can't do that, Mr. Ruffing. He says it's important."

He studied the calendar on the wall to find any occult signs there. None appeared. He said, very carefully, "Thank you, I'll take it."

He punched the internal extension button.

"Ruffing speaking."

"Still pissed off, are you?" Browning's tough voice had a curious defensive tone.

"Yes, still pissed off," he answered, attempting to sound a little jocular about it. "Where I come from, a grudge is a lifetime career."

"Too bad," Steve said. "I wish I could be pissed off in return. Then we could have a real feud. Hatfield and McCoy. Montague and Capulet. But I can't reciprocate. And it's time we buried the hatchet."

"What do you want, Steve?" He had little stomach for telephonic fencings any more. And he knew it was going to be a long morning this day until he tasted that first double vodka on the rocks.

"I've got to talk to you. It's about the Calinescu case. You've seen the morning papers."

"I also saw Wendell's testimony on TV. And what that Romanian survivor had to say about watching her grandfather's throat cut. I'm pissed off about that too, if you really want to know."

"Same old Ruff. The Agency's conscience. Well, you know damned well that neither of us back there in Vienna knew Dimmy Calinescu was somebody's mass murderer."

"We also knew he wasn't somebody's cherub, either. But you bought him hook, line, and sinker."

Browning's voice took on a strained quality. He was struggling to retain his composure.

"Look, remember the stuff he was giving us? Didn't USFA G-2 tell us that was the best Soviet order-of-battle information available to them in the whole theater?"

"Was it worth Mike Radescu's life?"

"You can't pin that on me," Browning shouted. "And I sure as hell didn't turn him in to the NKVD."

"You sent him off on a mission he didn't want to go on, and one from which he never returned."

For a long moment Browning did not reply. Then he said,

choosing his words, "We've been over that terrain a dozen times. I'm not going to get into that. Listen, Ruff, the IG is baying on my trail about the Calinescu case, and I've got to level with them or else. . . ."

"Or else, what? What else is there to do with them? Are you going to tell them how thoroughly Calinescu had you conned? Or that Mircea Radescu is probably lying dead and buried out there in some goddamned Siberian snowdrift?"

Browning whispered, "Suppose I told you that Mike Radescu is alive? Would that make you relent in the slightest about talking with me?"

Silas felt the hair rising along the back of his neck. Radescu alive! After, migod, half a lifetime!

"I don't want to talk to you here in the building," he said huskily. "Meet me at the Eagle at one o'clock. And if you're shitting me, Steve Browning, I'll . . ."

"You'll do nothing," Steve said, "because I'm in no position to play games. See you at one."

Silas Ruffing sat for a long time looking up at the pale shafts of late-summer sunshine shooting through the grilled half-window on the opposite wall. He rose, walked around his desk to the safe with its OPEN sign above the combination lock. With a sigh, he knelt and rolled open the bottom safe drawer, from the rear of which he withdrew a bulky manila envelope marked "MISC ADMIN." He rose, carrying the envelope with both hands, and slowly tore open its flap, heavily sealed with Scotch tape, and extracted a file two inches thick with yellowed pages and a ragged and musty cardboard cover.

A firm hand of long ago had identified its contents with bold inked words: "TTVIGOR Operation," underneath which another hand had printed in parentheses: "CALINESCU, Dimitriu, aka CALLIN, James D." On the file's cover, words twice underlined bore the sentence: "EYES ONLY to persons on TTVIGOR Bigot List, By Request of the DDO."

He would run and hide in the library stacks this morning. But this time, he would take this file with him and read it again in uninterrupted silence, and would attempt to fathom, yet again, what had happened. And the TTVIGOR file already revealed one thing with painful clarity: Steve Browning was in far more trouble than Steve himself realized.

Matt McClure held his hands together in a prayerful pose, and stared past the overdressed person of the Director of Security agitatedly leaning at him from the other side of the careful clutter of his desk.

"From that transcript, I'd say that Ruff is clean, wouldn't you?"

Nordholm's eyes glanced down at the sheaves of telephone transcripts in his hand.

"Why 'clean'?" he rejoined. "They could both be collaborators for the Sovs, or were in the past, couldn't they? Maybe they've had a falling out of some kind but . . ."

"But nothing," McClure interrupted with a kindly wave of one hand. "Steve may be in it up to his belly button, but Silas? Not for my money. As a matter of fact, all this telephoning from Steve on his own office telephone to Mara, to Ruffing . . . there's something about this that doesn't come together. . . ."

"Steve's on the make," Nordholm insisted, thumping McClure's desk with the flat of his hand. "The Sovs got to him years ago. It's just a matter of watching—and pouncing when we've got the goods."

"Well, Hank," McClure murmured, studying a duplicate of the transcript Nordholm held in his hand. "*You* keep watching—and *we*, the DCI, Wendell, and myself, will tell you when to pounce."

He did something rare for him: he reached in a desk drawer, came out with a long thin cigarillo, and lit it quickly. For Nordholm the gesture was a signal that Matt McClure was extremely exercised, deeply moved.

"You know, Hank," he said in the silky undertone that could scarcely be heard two yards away, "we don't have a single blip of confirmation that Steve is actually under KGB control. Mind you, I have a gut feeling that the story was not in itself a provocation to take our attention away from some other, more important Soviet penetration inside the Shop. It sounds like the casual lead that's usually authentic."

"But . . ." Nordholm said helpfully.

"No 'buts' really. But damn, Steve is either one of the more inspired actors in this fudge factory or he's totally relaxed and confident no one is on to him. The first premise doesn't fit. And knowing Steve, he's got a sense of smell that would hardly permit him to behave as openly as he is."

He took a deep puff of his cigarillo and promptly went into a paroxysm of coughing that alarmed Nordholm, who rose solicitously to his feet. Matt waved him off.

"Pure poison, these damned weeds. But they make me think better, for some damned reason."

He glanced at a wall clock.

"OK. I'll phone Wendell and fill him in on this. Send one of your people to the Eagle, just to watch how the meeting goes."

Nordholm said, "There'll be somebody else there. Manny Mulcahy of the Bureau's counter-intelligence crowd. He's one of the Bureau people on our Bigot List."

"Quite a lot of folks getting on your little Bigot List."

McClure's reproach nettled Nordholm, who responded with some heat. "Look, Matt, an espionage case inside the U.S. is the Bureau's competency even if a CIA employee is involved. *You* know that."

"Right. No offense. It's just a little bit ironic that we've told Manny and friends and yet our own guy who has been one of my staff's standing and sitting experts on counter-espionage, Silas Ruffing, is kept in the dark."

"Boss's orders, Matt. Ruffing used to be very close to Steve."

"Bullshit." The vulgarity issued incongruously from the priestly mouth. "Read the transcript again. To me it proves that Ruffing has had it in for Steve since Vienna days."

He looked reproachfully at the smoldering cigarillo.

"Well, maybe it's great that Ruff isn't in on this. If he was, he might try to strangle Steve in a moment of drunken patriotism."

He crushed the cigarillo with sudden irritation.

"Damn. I only wish I knew when and where they got their hooks into Steve. What was the bait? When was it sprung? They had dozens of occasions to pitch him."

"A slick customer," Nordholm offered, busily stowing his papers into his attaché case.

"A sad goddamned case," Matt retorted.

CHAPTER TEN

Unless you were looking for it, or stumbled on it by chance, the odds are that you would never find the Eagle restaurant. It is one of dozens of cafés, bars, and little eating places littering the broad avenues and shady side streets of northwest Washington, often occupying the premises of failed art galleries, mom-and-pop grocery stores, and dry-cleaning emporia.

To those who knew, it was as much a hobby as a business, a full-time whim indulged in by two former Central Intelligence Agency employees who, after early retirement, decided to open the place to keep busy. Both men, gregarious, blasphemous Irish-Americans from Rhode Island, referred to by their steady customers only as Mac-I and Mac-II, sank half of their life savings into the place and put up their homes as collateral to renovate the innards of an expired bar named Morry's. They retained the bar's precious liquor license and the word quickly spread that at the Eagle you could get a cocktail and an excellent lunch of onion soup, quiche lorraine, omelets, a chop, or fresh fish for modest prices.

Inevitably their Agency colleagues heard that you could also hang around there from noon into the evening, purchasing only minimum amounts of booze and beer and chatting it up with the proprietors. It was easy for the latter to identify Shop people. A quiet query or two established the bona fides.

Mac-I waited on customers (Mac-II ran the kitchen with a phlegmatic Vietnamese "boat people" couple) and became a human central reference point, keeping his Agency customers *au courant* with what was going with one another and events at what Mac-I dryly referred to as the Puzzle Palace, the Fudge Factory, and other pejorative euphemisms for the CIA Headquarters. Mac-I apparently learned more quickly of high-level personnel changes at the CIA than did senior executives in the Agency itself, often before such changes were officially announced.

"The tendency to blab, an ancient American curse, makes this goddamned place a goddamned security hazard, you know that," Ruffing scolded an unabashed Mac-I, looking up from the heavy round oaken table where he sat with the others, a half-consumed vodka on the rocks held in one hand.

"Then stop listening," Mac-I advised him with a disarming smile. "Actually, I like it when you get upset, Ruff, because you drink more, but we don't want you to get upset thinking of the secrets you hear in this place."

Mac-I, if the truth were known, was not as insouciant as he sounded. Whenever customers drifted in at lunch or dinner who were not among his identified regulars, he gave a discreet finger-across-lips warning to any of his regulars who were talking too audibly about matters best not overheard. And with the help of Manny Mulcahy, of the FBI Washington Field Office, Mac-I, an old Office of Security man himself, kept an eye on employees of the Soviet and other Communist embassies in Washington who occasionally appeared at the Eagle in obvious attempts to ingratiate themselves with Mac-I or to become regular patrons. To one none too subtle Russian, already identified by the regulars as Probable KGB, Mac-I had been overheard to bark, "Look, Ivan, I really don't want your patronage or your money. So just get the hell out of here, and don't come back." Ivan went and didn't come back.

To ensure more privacy for the regulars, a small inner dining room was created, adjacent to the kitchen and far more informal than the outer one. Two circular wooden tables, bereft of table-cloths, their ancient surfaces defaced with glass rings and scars, occupied much of the space, flanking a bar which ran along one wall. Here in this room, the wall decor was partisan and irreverent, dominated by a huge hand-painted replica of the official seal of the Central Intelligence Agency, with but one significant alteration: the eagle's eye had been blinded; only a white blank instead of the fierce pupil, at once a silent reproach and a gesture of concern by the proprietors that a combination of political events in recent years had so damaged the Agency's ability to function that it could not perceive its enemies.

Beside the great seal hung a large two-word sign in Cyrillic, "*Chto Kovo,*" the KGB motto for "Who is doing what to whom?" Three bumper stickers of varying vintage affixed at intervals on the wall read: "Frank Church Uses Russian Dressing," "Free the Teheran Fifty," and "Swap Philip Agee for Andrei Sakharov."

Ruffing, peering from time to time at the swinging door leading to the outer room, sat hunched in his usual place, only half listening to an earnest and authoritative disquisition on the Rote Kapelle, a Soviet espionage network in World War II, by a wistful-eyed CI specialist who had retired from the Agency two years earlier and who showed up like an eager child at the Eagle every weekday at noon to savor the company of his old comrades. (The burden of his analysis, to which Silas listened with only intermittent attention, was that the Soviets to this very day were running good penetration agents inside West Germany stemming from the old Rote Kapelle network, and that no one in the Shop seemed to give a damn.)

He regretted having agreed to meet Steve here. Not that the others would suspect anything unusual about it; they were all aware that he and Steve had served together in the OSS at the dawn of time and although Browning rarely came here, he would attract little attention. But Steve's thunderbolt news that Mike was alive had so unnerved him that he had mentioned the Eagle as the first place that came to mind. And it was, so to speak, his own home turf.

Radescu's disappearance had been the beginning of the end of his intense wartime and, he had to face it, symbiotic friendship with Steve that began in Officer's Training School at Camp Ritchie and arched across the North African and Italian campaigns of World War II. Steve Browning's zest for living and his ebullient camaraderie lingered in Silas' memory like a golden whirlwind across desert sands. Being with him in those wartime years was watching a man determined to seize life by the throat and to shake it vigorously. And Steve had offered him companionship on total terms: pulling him along through Vatican museums on a dead run; lying next to him on the earthen floor of an abandoned *podère* in Tuscany drinking raw Chianti from a bunged cask on hands and knees until they collapsed in drunken laughter; shouting to Silas to hold on to his seat as Steve hurled his jeep through columns of dust-covered guns and men to be one of the first to reach the center of liberated Bologna; a tableau of fornication with him and Steve in adjacent beds in a Milan hotel room banging two young Italian whores Steve had whistled up on ten minutes' notice.

But there was the other, darker side: Steve the scrounger, Steve with a quick hand to reach out and take what was really not his. "Liberating things," as Steve smilingly retorted in defense of his actions.

The jeep, for one thing. Not one jeep but several, all of them simply stolen from military car parks or depots. The last such acquisition came from the motor pool of the hapless if magnificently equipped Brazilian division which arrived on the Italian front late in the war and simply did not understand that up there an unlocked jeep was a lost jeep.

In Bologna, it was the department store. They had driven into the city as part of the advance guard of the victorious Allied army that day in late April 1945, and while Ruffing sat across the street from the store in Steve's latest jeep, uncomfortably aware of the contempt on the faces of the Bolognese watching with him as Steve and a dozen other looters, all in Allied uniforms, rampaged through the place. Steve had finally emerged with two bulging suitcases and had flung his booty in the back seat of the jeep with a triumphant grunt.

"Got enough perfume, lingerie, and gewgaws to buy up every *putana* from here to the Brenner Pass," he explained to a silently reproachful Ruffing. "Aw, come on, Ruff, you know the rules of war: *Vae Victis!*"

"Where I come from, it's just plain stealing," Ruffing had burst at him disgustedly.

"In wartime, baby," Steve had crowed, "the rules get bent a lot, Ruff old crock. These Bennies don't deserve any sympathy."

"It wasn't Italian Army property you took," Ruffing had responded. "That was a private store."

"Belonged to some big Fascist." Steve was unrepentant. "Besides, the place was up for grabs. Did you see those guys from British 13 Corps in there?"

But the rules got bent in postwar as well, Silas observed. In Vienna, Steve swapped his illegal jeep to a Military Government major for an equally illegal BMW Wanderer, a great powerful monster of a vehicle which had once been used by the head of the German Gestapo for Lower Austria. Steve scrounged documentation attesting to the vehicle's status as a Captured Enemy Vehicle.

And there was his furnished two-bedroom apartment in the American sector of Vienna, close by the Ring, at a time when U.S. colonels were happy to have a bleak single room in the Hotel Bristol as lodgings. From Ernoe, his *Spitzl*, Steve had learned of the flat and the fact that it was owned and occupied by an elderly Austrian Nazi. Through the American de-Nazification authorities, Steve had contrived to have the man arrested the next time he visited relatives in the American occupation zone of Upper Austria and had moved into the place, armed with a requisition order he had filled in and had stamped himself. *Vae Victis*.

Ruffing had struggled to rationalize Steve's actions. During three years of war, Steve's companionship had been exhilarating. With him, life was lived at its highest bearable decibel, enhanced by the constant whiff of danger as they plotted agent penetration operations, supervised line-crossers, dashed up and down the fighting fronts on errands of real or feigned spookiness.

Looking back on it, the corroding element of corruption in Steve seemed almost predictable. In the ultimate obscenity of war, killing and being killed, what were a few baubles taken from a looted Bologna store, a few "liberated" jeeps and illegally scrounged supplies, an illegally requisitioned flat in the anarchy of postwar Vienna?

But what had appeared glamorous, macho, high adventure in wartime became foolhardiness, needless risk-taking in times of peace. It was more than Browning's hair-raising stunt of jumping from the rear of one moving Vienna trolley to another moving in the opposite direction to shake a suspected Soviet surveillance. It was Steve's recklessness in his operational use of an eternally grateful Radescu that had brought Silas to bitter words with him.

The struggle over the Calinescu business had widened the cracks of their diverging outlooks on such matters.

What finally broke it irretrievably between them, after Radescu disappeared, was Steve's abrupt abandonment of Mara, whose woman-child adoration of him was total. For Steve to leave Vienna for the United States without so much as a word of farewell to her was, in Silas' eyes, contemptible. The letter and the thick wad of U.S. dollars Steve left behind for Mara simply underlined, at last, the man's essential insensitivity and his ability to betray.

Today Silas recognized that much of his rage at that time was jealousy and was permeated with his own longing for the fresh-faced Mara. But it was a rotten show. As for Radescu, Silas had never forgiven Steve in all these years. He had spoken to him on operational matters perhaps a dozen times in the intervening decades, but only coldly, correctly. With Steve's wife, Joan, whom he had met early in their marriage, it was something else, an instinctive warmth shared by two victims of the same disaster, a gladness at seeing each other at occasional social events attended by Shop people. But for Steve Browning himself, he had nothing but thoroughly tarnished memories—and over the years a welling suspicion that something was wrong.

Now he knew precisely what was wrong and he sat waiting in the back room of the Eagle, planning, as he always did, what he would say, how he would say it. He and Steve Browning were now a couple of ancient leaking hulks, each shipping water, each sinking steadily. It would have been far better that they had sunk separately, but what lay in the Calinescu file had suddenly placed in focus all of his blurred doubts, his nagging what-ifs.

He took another swallow of his iced vodka and looked leadenly at the far wall, where an enormously enlarged air photo of bombs whistling down on a hapless city bore the legend: "Visit Picturesque Hanoi." And high on the wall, two crossed American flags hung, begrimed with cigarette smoke and kitchen fumes. Mac-I promised everyone that he would have the flags laundered or replaced by "the next Fourth of July." He had been promising this for the last three years in a row.

Silas' listless eyes watched the swinging door and his ears quickened at the sound of approaching feet. But instead of Steve, a gaunt gray man, albeit jaunty in movement, strode through the

doors and stopped to look quickly around the room as if to memo-
rize every detail in it. Manny Mulcahy, resident tribal memory of
the FBI's Washington Field Office, had materialized. It was
Manny's invariable routine to show up for Saturday lunch and to
sit, drink, and listen well into the afternoon to the operational
yarns and maunderings of others. But this was the first time he
could remember that Manny had come here on a weekday.

He knew little of Manny's personal life (what little there was of
it since Manny's wife had died), but for years he and this dour,
forbidding man had been close professional colleagues. What
linked them closely was their mutual consuming passion for
counter-espionage, the entire submerged world of spies and agents,
and the tactics used to uncover them and use against them. For
Manny, like himself, counter-espionage was more than a job; it
was a passion, a consuming obsession. And for Manny, like himself, the frightening prospect of compulsory retirement loomed
ever closer. Manny was already sixty-three and he was kept on in
the Bureau primarily because he knew the answers quicker and
better than the Bureau's own files.

Manny walked up to him with the wariness of a cop moving up
a slum alley in the dark.

"If you had a bowl of that stuff, you could drown in it," Manny
commented, his harsh Boston Irish accent lending a cutting edge
to his statement. Manny himself was a beer man, and two glasses
lasted him an entire afternoon.

"Piss off, Manny," Silas retorted, attempting to pronounce his
words without slurring them. "I've got some business to attend to
here."

"Oh?" Manny said with unusual politeness. "What kind of
business? Stealing a hot stove while nobody's looking?"

He looked blearily up at Manny. Did he detect something more
than the usual barbed but permissible repartee? This slight, pasty-
faced man had a disconcerting, extrasensory manner.

"The real trick, Manny, is to steal a hot stove while *everybody's*
looking."

"Well," Manny said, looking at the occupants of the other
round table, "why don't I sit down over there and watch you do it
while I have lunch. I'm not too old to learn things."

He sauntered over to the other table, seated himself in an

empty chair, nodded to the other three occupants in turn, and from across the room he gave Silas a clenched-fist gesture: the old Fight sign. Silas gave him a perfunctory thumbs-up gesture in return and resumed staring at the swinging door.

It would not be an easy thing to sit and talk with Silas Ruffing again, Steve Browning knew as he pulled open the heavy front door of the Eagle and tramped into the outer restaurant area. Silas' grudges, as he had admitted, lasted a lifetime. It had been repeatedly painful for him to meet Silas in the endless corridors at Headquarters, greet him with a smile and a "Hi there, Ruff," and be answered only with a blank stare or a head turned away in disdain. On several occasions, Silas had quickly turned into an office doorway or another corridor to avoid any encounter with him at all.

In years past, it would have been a challenge to take on an embittered Silas and to win him back again, carefully, steadily, with minimum pressure. Manipulation of others came easily to him; indeed it had been a cornerstone of his career. But like so many other artificialities, the manipulation technique gradually palled. It tired him to be an operational Sisyphus, pushing that stone of personality massage up the steep hill to achieve acquiescence of the other, only to repeat the process with the next candidate for such treatment. "Mental fatigue" was a descriptive phrase the Agency psychologists liked to throw around. With Silas it had connoted booze and morose silences. As for himself, he listened to persistent sounds of inner breaking.

He had not set foot in the Eagle for months but nothing had changed. In the outer room, a half-dozen customers, most of them conservatively dressed men from nearby shops and offices, were quietly chewing on Mac-II's lunch specials for the day: Chinese omelet and what Mac-I described as lasagna Cholonese.

He strode quickly through the muted light, eyeing the patrons, but he recognized none of them. With a deliberate swagger, he pushed through the swinging door into the inner room, where one of the two round tables was fully occupied. Silas Ruffing sat alone at the other table directly facing the door. As Steve entered, Silas raised his glass in a silent signal before pushing back his heavy chair and rising a bit unsteadily.

At the other table sat three of the Agency's lunchtime regulars; all of their faces were more or less familiar to him. A fourth face he also recognized: Manny Mulcahy of the Bureau, Ruffing's CI chum. He had met Manny no more than a half-dozen times in his entire Agency career, and was happy that it was not necessary to deal with him more often. The man had that slitted-eye, guilty-until-proven-innocent expression, a mind that looked at his job as one which enabled him to hang a rap on someone. Manny now peered up at him, his hands cradling a mug of beer, with unmistakable malevolence. Did he just happen to be sitting there? Had Ruff put him there? Was this some sort of an entrapment meeting? For the past four months, he had been expecting anything, everything.

Mac-I, from his position behind the bar, announced to those present, "For the love of Richard Milhous Nixon, look what the evil wind blew in!"

"Hello, Mac," he responded with a forced smile. "Still watering the drinks, I see."

Mac-I, waddling from around the bar, handed Steve a filled glass of amber liquor.

"Here, the first bourbon is on the house, to tempt you into buying the next five." He peered up into Steve's heavy features. "Why the hell aren't you out destabilizing some half-ass third-world nation instead of sneaking into a place like this?"

Steve extended a friendly hand of greeting. Francis Xavier McLowery, now Mac-I, had served as regional security officer in New Delhi Station a dozen years earlier and had come to Amman to investigate one of the three occasions when Steve had been PNGed. McLowery had not pulled his punches in his report on the incident; Steve was to blame. But Mac-I had been scrupulously fair and neither of them bore the other any ill will.

"*All* of the third-world nations are already destabilized, Mac," he answered, aware that all of the others were listening carefully. "I've written up a project outline offering to go around and *re*stabilize them all if they just sign sworn statements of allegiance to the United States." They all smiled vaguely; two of the younger ones, he noted with concealed contempt, were already the worse for alcoholic wear and tear.

Steve walked with his drink slowly to Ruffing's table, pulled out a solid wooden armchair, and slid into it, next to Silas, whose chair was wedged in a corner where he could observe everything going on in the room.

"Are you holding office hours?" he asked, feigning camaraderie. "Or is this an R and R day?"

Silas Ruffing looked up from his drink and stared at him with an unfocused distaste.

"You wanted to see me." It was a flat statement devoid of emotion.

"Yes, and I told you on the phone why."

It was a shock for him to observe this once alert little man, laconic and retiring but with a dry and crackling wit, in such a condition. He had heard of Silas' downward slide these last months but seeing it was something else. A rush of sadness, a brief ache for the long-lost friendship, came over him as he watched two beads of vodka hang from Silas' untended, once russet mustache, now shot with gray, until his hand came up to brush them away. The slight body now bulged in its middle as Silas slumped in his chair, not looking at him, and twitched his lips to frame his reply.

"Yes, I know why. You said that Mike Radescu is alive and well, right?" A needle point of fire flashed in his dulled eyes and he reached over with his right hand to grasp Steve fiercely by his jacket lapel.

"Alive, for Christ's sake!" He bit the words, keeping his voice low but vibrant. "And I thought you had sent him to his death, you son of a bitch!"

Steve was big and strong enough to trample Silas underfoot, especially in his present sodden condition, but he suffered his jacket to remain seized and looked at Ruffing's wet gasping lips before responding.

"He's not dead. He's in Los Angeles, of all places."

"L-los Angeles?" Silas' voice lost its stridency and he looked wonderingly at Steve.

They both watched the heads turn at the next table and Steve leaned forward into Silas' ear.

"Keep your goddamned voice down, even if those characters over there belong to your lost platoon of CI stragglers. This is strictly between you and me, *comprende?*" he hissed. Still talking into Ruffing's ear, he went on, "Now blow the cobwebs out of your head for a moment, Ruff, and listen to me: Radescu has made it alive out of Soviet imprisonment. I don't know how he did it. I don't know anything except that I have a motel address in the Manhattan Beach area of Los Angeles."

"Mike Radescu, old TTVIGOR-4, alive?" Silas spoke as does one who has revived a dead beloved in his dreams and fears to waken. "What the hell is he doing in Los Angeles?"

The years of professional instincts kept his voice to a hoarse whisper now and Steve watched with wonderment as the old Ruffing burned out of the alcoholic figure beside him, to grasp the new situation.

With his face no more than two inches from Ruffing's, observing the dilated pupils and the growing intensity of his interest, Steve said, barely moving his lips, "Dimmy Calinescu's there, isn't he?"

Steve took a long swig from his glass. Ruffing slumped back in his chair for a long moment, and when he sat up and moved close to Steve again, there was no more of the despairing boozer.

"And what are you going to do about all this, Steve, old hotshot? Ring up Dimmy on the phone and tell him to order a bulletproof jacket for himself?"

Steve's thick lips parted in a forced smile.

"Not a bad idea. But why should I do that for him?"

"Because," Silas said to him, thin voice now acidly precise, "you sold out to the bastard years ago."

"What the hell do you mean by that?" Steve asked, but the elevator had started to drop. Silas knew, then. Somehow, it seemed inevitable that he would know.

He turned to Silas, his jowled heavy face drained of color.

"Where . . . what's your source of information for all this?"

Silas waved an impatient hand at him, looking past him at the cloud of cigarette smoke curling sinuously over the other table.

"Come off it, Steve. You're talking to Silas Ruffing, the old CI pro, scourge of a dozen stations. I don't make up these things. For years now, off and on, I've been working with the Department of Justice and its FBI guys on Dimmy's case. And you know damned well that Jenny Pfitzner has been on his trail, as well as going after the fifty other Nazi shits living in the United States she's

convinced are war criminals. So one day, six weeks ago, I'm downtown at the FBI office and my flatfoot Feebee friend sitting over
there"—he nodded his head at the other table—"Manny Mulcahy,
salt of the earth, says to me, 'Here's something that'll raise your
blood pressure.' And he pulls out a photocopy of a canceled
check, dated 1948 and made out to one Steven J. Browning, Jr.,
from a law office in California, for twenty thousand dollars.
Twenty big ones. That law firm was handling, and is still handling, legal matters for one James D. Callin, also known as Dimitriu Calinescu."

He smiled grimly at Steve.

"I'm looking past you, at Manny's face. He's really getting a
bang out of seeing in person one of our very few true-blue Agency
types who sold his soul for twenty big ones."

Silas drained his vodka glass, wiped his lips and mustache with
the back of one hand, and leaned confidentially toward Steve, as
if he were telling him a particularly salacious yarn.

"Then Manny lays the emigration file of Calinescu on the desk
in front of me, and lo and behold, there's your name on the bottom line as the noble sponsor of Dimmy for emigration to the
U.S. It was all handled through the American Consulate in
Athens at the same time you were there. Strange coincidence, isn't
it? The date of the check is six weeks after the date you signed the
affidavit as sponsor for Dimmy into the Home of the Free and the
Brave, complete with a letter of recommendation from you calling
attention to his patriotic services to the U.S. fighting Bolshevism."

He patted Steve on the sleeve.

"Maybe, I'm just speculating now, maybe with the twenty grand
he was also trying to pay you a little blood money for your dear
old lost agent, old TTVIGOR-4. He knew how badly you felt.
Whatever the reason, he also knew that everybody's got his price.
After all, for that kind of money you didn't even have to steal
Uncle Sam's secrets and pass them to the Russians. And I honestly
don't think you could ever be made to do that." He squinted his
eyes at Steve. "Or could you?"

On the other side of the room, the voice of the Rote Kapelle
specialist droned on, hand occasionally flapping in the air to emphasize a point, and Steve's ashen face turned to watch him as
one watches animals at a zoo through thick plate glass. He

avoided a fixed hypnotic stare from Manny Mulcahy of the FBI.

Silas said, his voice now stripped of bitterness, tinged with sorrow, "I know how badly you were under the gun to get your hands on twenty thousand dollars. Joanie made it clear to me a number of times that she had put a lot of pressure on you to buy that nice house in Kensington. The place must be worth five or six times what you originally paid for it back in '48, the way the real estate market in Washington is going. But getting bought out by Dimmy is just bad news, Steve. You got snookered by him in Vienna and you got snookered by him later in this immigration thing. He *owns* you, Steve."

"I think"—Steve struggled to push the words out of his throat—"that I've heard enough for one day." He placed both hands on the tabletop to rise, but Silas held him by the arm.

"No, Steve, it's got to be said and it's all going to hang out sooner or later. Right now I'm one of the few people who've really got your number, together with Manny sitting over there. Maybe Mara has it, too, and probably Joanie. And I don't claim that you deliberately betrayed Mike Radescu. But Dimmy corrupted you. The big con man, Steve Browning, master of the operational scam, was conned by an even bigger artist. It's true, you were pretty young at the time, but you didn't stand a chance, did you? Anyway, I'm convinced you lack that missing chromosome, the one that's got 'integrity' locked into it. Dimmy promised you in Vienna that he'd make you look good, didn't he? That you would light up the sky with his information. And you did, by God, you did. You soared like a rocket and that got you into the Agency at the beginning, with a fat GS-12, landing on both feet and running."

Steve said nothing.

"You're in the wrong business if you want to cover things up, Steve," Silas said, sloshing the melting ice in his glass, keeping his voice at a level where the ears on the other side of the room could not hear. "We pick each other's pockets in the Agency, don't we? I knew something was up when you came back from that caper in Greece. Remember the one in 1948 when you and that Athens Station guy conned that skipper of a U.S. heavy cruiser (and how you did it, I'll never know) to steam up and down the Attic coast with his ship's direction-finding gear doing sweeps until he got a fix on that Greek Communist clandestine radio transmitter operating near Glyfada? Nice deal; the Greek service rolled up the whole net. You got your first big Agency medal, didn't you? *And* a promotion! But I also noticed at the time that you were able to put down twenty thousand dollars on that house in Kensington you had been pissing and moaning about because you couldn't afford to buy it. Joanie told me that and it stuck in my mind for years. CI people are terrible about such things. The Greeks didn't give you the money. You didn't get it from old Uncle Sugar. No rich relatives. No Irish Sweepstakes. Where did you get it? So that photocopy of the check Manny Mulcahy showed me, that moved the tumblers. All of a sudden it all came together."

Mac-I lumbered over to them, a glass in his hand, chortling, "One last drink on the house for Steve Browning, the PNG kid himself."

His round, slightly piggish eyes semaphored his good intentions. "Maybe it'll encourage you to come in here and spend some money. We have Happy Hour here from five to seven. Half price on all drinks."

Something in Silas' eyes made him put the drink down and walk heavily back to the bar.

Steve said evenly, "Why haven't you turned me in?"

Silas, head slightly cocked, answered as if surprised by the question.

"I really don't know. Maybe I thought at the time: Jesus, this is just what the Agency doesn't need—a big fat scandal on conflict of interests, subornation of an Agency officer by a sleazy Romanian ex-spy. And one of those buzzards who write Washington newspaper columns would get hold of it and howl it to the winds. Oh, how the Director would like that! But I really don't know exactly why I didn't, Steve. Anyway, the statute of limitations has expired long since, I think. So you can't go to jail."

"You could have gotten me fired," Steve said.

"In a flash. George Sheridan Wendell, our old CO, would be in the Director's office and have your ass in five minutes. Make it three. Considering what encomiums he used to write about you, he'd be doubly eager to give you the heave-ho. But I didn't do anything. And I'll tell you why I won't do it now."

Steve held the glass of bourbon in his hand, as if estimating its weight, and drank it back with a brief shudder. He was not certain which emotion had the upper hand in him, but shame seemed to lead the pack. Silas twisted his empty glass in its wet ring on the table.

"Here goes my last remaining secret, which I wangled without much trouble from an old buddy on the Career Management Staff: you and me, Steve Browning, are on the low-five list. The two of us and ten others, bearers of the flame, watchdogs of the Republic, superannuated GS-14s, are to be canned, involuntarily retired, 'surplus to the needs of the Service.' So why should I go to George Wendell and get you fired for what you did thirty years ago when you'll shortly get fired anyway for being a poor performer?"

He pounded one fist against the hard oaken surface of the table with a futile thump that for a moment turned the eyes of the others in the room in their direction.

"Shit, imagine it! They're firing *me* along with *you* as a poor performer! *I've* forgotten more about counter-espionage operations and tradecraft than nine-tenths of the fatheads out in that building will ever learn!"

Steve asked, in the detached tone of a scientist describing potentially lethal bacteria seen through his microscope, "If the Bureau has that information on me, why haven't they sent it over to the Agency? That would tear it . . ."

The gleam in Silas' eyes was that of a small boy who has hidden Grandfather's favorite pipe.

"Aha, but they did! Justice sent over info copies of the whole ball of wax on Calinescu. The Agency's CI Staff got it and guess whose hands it came through? Mine, Stevie boy! Oh, it was logged in all right with the Staff, but no one got to see it. They sent it to me. *I* took the Justice report, *I* sealed it in a separate envelope which *I* stapled into the inside of Dimmy's file and marked it in big red letters: 'Eyes-Only. Bigot List Information.' Before I sent it back to Archives, I put a flag on Dimmy's file so that before it's released to anybody, *I* get phoned first. Pretty slick, eh? It worked fine up to now. Nobody expressed any interest in it. But, as you know, the DDO, our old buddy, was called to testify before Jenny Pfitzner. He wanted to review the Calinescu file last weekend. So quick like a bunny, I got to it before he did and pulled it out of Archives again. He never got to see it. Knowing Wendell, he must have been thoroughly browned off that the Document Retrieval people couldn't find it."

Steve followed Silas' eyes and lips with a near-hypnotized stare.

"The file's still in my safe," Silas said, peering down at the melted ice in his glass. "No one will find it because I've got it buried in an envelope marked 'MISC ADMIN.' And it will stay missing until you and I are out on our keesters, surplus to the needs of the Service. Then the Justice report and the Calinescu file will surface—and if I know those legal eagles in the General Counsel's Office, they'll say good riddance to bad rubbish and they won't take any further action against me—or you."

Steve laboriously pushed back the oak chair and, with an effort, rose to his feet. He swayed there for a moment, pulled out a handkerchief, and mopped his forehead and eyes.

"What now?" Silas asked him, standing beside him. With a pained effort, Steve turned to him and looked into the familiar pinched face as if he wanted to remember forever every feature in minute detail.

"Strange as it may sound to you, Ruff," he finally said after clearing his throat, "thanks for leveling with me. I don't know whether to laugh or cry. I may wind up doing both."

Silas said, "I've been carrying this Calinescu business around like a stone in my gut for years. I knew I'd have to square off with you someday. But believe me, Steve, I'm . . ."

". . . No, no, don't start back-pedaling now, Ruff. Thanks, real thanks."

He placed a heavy, slightly trembling hand on Silas' shoulder.

"You always were a smart little bastard. And that business of hiding the evidence on the twenty thousand in the most obvious place, in 'MISC ADMIN'—pure Ruffing. But it won't work. You're holding back the tide with a sieve."

Silas gnawed his ragged mustache.

"Just for a little bit longer, Steve. Just until they lower the boom and boot us out under compulsory retirement. . . ."

Steve shook his head impatiently.

"Yes, OK, but there are other things to think about."

He squeezed Silas' shoulder in a familiar gesture and attempted a roguish wink.

"And now, cher colleague, so long. I've got fish to fry."

"Where?"

"On the West Coast. That's what I wanted to tell you, before you dropped this . . . this cheery little A-bomb about times gone by."

Bleary eyes peering up at him, Silas shook his head.

"Don't do it, Steve. That's just running away from the problem. Stay close to the ranch here until all this is cleared up. Look, I'll go to Wendell and . . ."

Steve turned his broad back to the other table, whose occupants, feigning nonchalance, were striving to overhear their conversation.

"Listen, Ruff," he said, voice hoarsened with emotion, "it's too late to clear things up. I know I'm cooked but I'm going out there to try to find Mike and stop him from doing something that will simply get him thrown into the local slammer. He's already done enough time in Nazi concentration camps and Soviet GULAGs to last him two or three lifetimes."

"And you're also going to protect Dimmy, the guy with your twenty thousand . . . ?" Silas could not prevent the old wound from reopening.

For a brief moment, Steve grasped Silas' jacket with both hands, bodily lifting him off the ground. The others at the next table half rose from their chairs at the spectacle but Steve, after a terrifying moment, released Silas and smoothed his jacket lapels contritely.

"Sorry I did that, Ruff," he muttered. "But, God, you know how to stick the needle a long way in."

Perspiration started from his forehead in glistening irregular beads.

"I know I've got a hell of a lot of explaining to do, but right now, Mike Radescu is my top priority."

He patted Silas on the sleeve in a patronizing gesture.

"See you around, Ruff. Maybe we can sit down and talk about the war. Great times, no?"

"Wait," Silas pleaded with him. "Wait out on the sidewalk for a minute. I've got a couple of ideas . . ."

Steve, without another word, whirled and strode through the door. Manny Mulcahy was at Silas' side before the doors had ceased their swinging motion.

"What the hell was all that about?" he demanded in a voice Silas had never heard before.

"None of your damned business," he responded sullenly.

"But it definitely *is* my damned business, you rum-soaked little twit," Manny retorted, eyes burning into his. "And I may be getting my ass into a fatal sling by telling you something you don't know: your large buddy has been named as a Soviet penetration, and we're on his tail."

As Silas' eyes widened with the shock of his words, Manny added, much more gently, "So tell me quickly, Ruff: do you know where he's headed?"

"To Los Angeles," Silas said dazedly. "If you want any more info, why don't you ask *him?* He's waiting for me out on the street."

A young intense man, with one hand in the pocket of his beige raincoat, loped through the swinging door and ran up to Mulcahy.

"He's heading up Connecticut Avenue in his own car, Manny. Sam and Gerty are in the two tail cars, right behind him."

"Stay with me, Lee," Mulcahy barked. "We're going to have to alert the LA Field Office that he's heading their way."

"Steve a Soviet penetration!" Silas breathed, hunched in his chair. "And I had him pegged as just a no-good, hustling Dimmy for twenty thousand."

"You're a disappointment to me, Ruff," Mulcahy said, sinking into the chair vacated by Steve. "You let your loyalty to that bastard blind you to the fact that the twenty big ones was Soviet money, entrapment money; bait. And he snapped it up, hook, line, and sinker."

Mac-I approached them, his slow steps reflecting his uneasiness and puzzlement at the comings and goings.

"I don't know what you guys are up to, running in and out of this place like it was a French whorehouse," he said to them, "but does anybody want to order another drink?"

Mulcahy looked up at him with feigned annoyance.

"Listen, you County Mayo bandit, bring the bill. And let me use your phone in that cubbyhole of an office back there, will you?"

"Only if it's in the national interest," Mac-I intoned. "And don't call long-distance."

"Sit here and finish your drink, Ruff." Mulcahy's voice contained a gravelly kindness. "I'm going to make a couple of calls. And don't be surprised if your people send you off to Los Angeles . . . afterwards."

"After what?"

"After you take a polygraph and you run clean on your knowledge about Steve and the KGB," Mulcahy answered with a wintery smile. He picked himself out of the chair and headed toward Mac-I's telephone.

CHAPTER ELEVEN

"We've got to stop meeting each other like this," Dr. Angus Hocker announced in an exaggerated stage whisper to Wendell as he groped for a blood-pressure kit in the bottom drawer of his gleaming executive desk. He squinted his eyes at Wendell in a familiar expression of world-weary humor, and brushed the wispy remains of his hair into some temporary semblance of order. "The gals in my front office out there honest to God think that the DDO and I are sitting behind closed doors at nine o'clock in the morning, plotting how to destabilize the North Vietnamese politburo by smuggling fish sauce laced with LSD into their kitchens. Little do they know that I'm just taking your damned blood pressure."

George Wendell smiled perfunctorily at the physician's effort to lighten his mood.

"It's as good a cover story as any I could make up, Angus. Just as long as they don't find out what we're really up to."

He braced his hands on his knees and pulled himself with an effort to his feet, a gesture that did not escape the small quick eyes of the physician. Wendell shed his jacket and vest, rolled up the shirt sleeve of his left arm, seated himself again and extended the arm, palm up, to Hocker, who had bounded from behind his memento-laden desk to reach his side. Hocker adjusted the blood-pressure cuff on Wendell's arm just above the elbow and deftly pumped constricting air into the device, stethoscope in his ears, peering intently down through his steel-rimmed bifocal glasses at the pressure gauge as air escaped from the cuff with a polite sigh.

Wendell studied the physician's face. Hocker could be as impassive as any man he had known but his lips betrayed him. If the news was not good, they twitched. Wendell was dispirited, although not surprised, to observe Hocker's lips twitch once, then twice.

"Goddamnit, George." Hocker's voice was thin and strained. "Are you taking the medication I prescribed? Are you watching your sodium intake?"

"Never mind the nattering, Angus." Wendell's voice was almost soothing, as if telling Mother that, hey, he was all right despite the sandlot welt on the head. "What's the reading this morning?"

"One hundred and eighty-five over one hundred and fifteen. Ungood. *Very* ungood!" Hocker ripped the blood-pressure sleeve from Wendell's arm with a disappointed yank. He reached for a scratch pad on his desk and jotted down the reading.

"That's not the direction I want you to be going. Three days ago, I thought we had you heading right. Today you're up ten points diastolic, ten points systolic."

He bounced to his feet and did a quick turn around his desk while Wendell carefully rolled down the shirt sleeve, fastened it with a delicately wrought gold cuff link, shrugged on vest and jacket, and stood at parade rest, braced for the inevitable scolding.

"Look, George." Hocker held out his hands in supplication. "We can't help you if you won't help yourself. I'm going to give it to you straight. I've already told you what hypertension is. You've got it, my friend, and you've got it good, and that connotes all kinds of other things we are going to have to look into. If you haven't been following my instructions with the medication, following a salt-free diet, and reducing your weight by at least twenty pounds—and I strongly think you've paid little or no attention to much of what I've prescribed for you—you're in real trouble. One hundred eighty-five over one hundred goddamn fifteen is bad news. I repeat: Bad News."

"You've made your point, Angus," Wendell said. "I'm sorry I'm not flourishing under your care. I *am* taking the medication even though they're giving me the side effects you warned me about. And I *am* trying to watch the salt intake, although it seems that everything I eat or drink has some sodium cleverly hidden in it."

"And how much exercise are you getting these days?" Hocker's eyes snapped with professional impatience. "Apart from swiveling back and forth in your chair, I mean?"

Wendell rubbed his cleft chin ruefully.

"There was a time when I was playing early-morning squash four times a week. But I cannot tell you lies, Angus. I just can't find the time any more. The flaps are coming in almost on the hour. They must be dealt with. Apart from the usual cliché of jumping to conclusions, I'm not getting a hell of a lot of exercise these last six months."

Hocker lowered his head and peered with despair at him, hands folded over a noisy checked tie, strands of his sparse silver hair forming a rear-halo from the morning sunshine streaming through the window directly behind him. A good medic, Wendell knew. A compassionate medic, doing the best he could in an Agency where you sometimes had to conceal illnesses and medical problems as if they were atomic secrets. This was precisely why he was consulting the Director of Medical Services himself, behind closed doors, instead of dealing with any one of a half dozen of Hocker's staff physicians: both he and Hocker were quite aware what would happen if the word got out that the Deputy Director for Operations had developed a serious hypertensive condition. There were would-be heirs apparent within the Agency hungry for his job. A number of highly placed officials in Washington would react with varying interest to news of his health. And in the offices of powerful, if unpublicized, intelligence and security chiefs all over the world, from Moscow to Peking, to London, Bonn, Tel Aviv, and Cairo, the condition of the CIA's Deputy Director for Operations would more than raise eyebrows. . . .

He knew what was troubling Hocker and he moved to him, lightly touching the physician on one shoulder.

"I'm sorry, Angus, that I'm putting you in a hell of a box by refusing to let you inform the DCI or the DDCI about my condition, but I'm going to have to presume on our friendship to hold off doing that."

They were of the same height, although Hocker was a thin restless wraith next to Wendell's ponderous form. Hocker's brief eye contact with him revealed his unwillingness to go along.

"But I'll make a deal with you, Angus," Wendell continued, speaking slowly. "If my condition doesn't improve in the next sixty days, I'll release you from the bind I've put you in. I'll even tell the boss myself, and we'll see where we go from there."

The physician's monkey-wise eyes widened for a moment and Hocker permitted himself a fleeting smile of gratification.

"That's the first sensible thing you've said to me in weeks, George," he said. "But I'm not going to let you off that easily. You've also got to agree to undergo a full executive physical, top to bottom, immediately. I'll lay it on with my staff for a week from today. You'll have to tear yourself away from problems of Palestine terrorists, botched recruitments, Soviets in Afghanistan, the whole ball of wax, for about two maybe three half-days. That will include the stress test and anything else the examination indicates we should do."

He shook his head disapprovingly.

"Look, George, you've already had two separate . . . events in the past six months. You passed out cold in your own office not five weeks ago. Lucky your secretary Clare was still around. I put the word out that it was momentary fatigue from overwork. But you're under an unremitting pressure all the time. Now, from the way the old BP is spurting, it's gotten worse. Something new gnawing at you?"

He chuckled at Wendell's instinctive frown.

"Don't worry, I'll not attempt to elicit any top-secret stuff out of you. Jesus, I've been playing this need-to-know game for years. That's one of your main problems: you can't or won't talk about your damned business to anybody."

He briefly patted Wendell's hand still resting lightly on his shoulder, and shook his head once again.

"You know, old friend, even sixty days is too long to wait before you tell the DCI."

"And what can happen to me in sixty days? Won't the medication carry me along until then?"

Hocker wagged a finger at him.

"The answer to that one is a big fat categorical 'maybe.' George, for Christ's sake, can't you understand what you're doing to yourself? You've overloaded your system. You're working under intolerable stresses and strains for a physically inactive fifty-nine-year-old Caucasian male who is at least twenty pounds over-weight and with a family history of hypertension. This clandestine intelligence game exacts a terrible toll. Time is not on your side. . . ."

"All right, all right, Angus!" Hocker knew that metallic boom. He had gone just a bit too far in his compassionate concern and Wendell had had enough of it for this session. The moment passed. They smiled broadly at each other and instinctively patted each other's upper arms in a near-*abrazo*.

Wendell had suffered this scolding a half-dozen times before from Hocker, but on behalf of others. Usually the indictment was uttered when Wendell sought him out to ask for a medical waiver for one of his DDO operatives with a dangerous ulcer, or one kidney, or an arrhythmic heart, who was needed for a mission or a tour of duty overseas. Hocker had repeatedly tilted lances in such sessions with Wendell and the division chiefs in the Operations Directorate. The statistics were against them, Hocker pointed out: six out of every ten such waivers he had granted had ended badly, with medical evacuations from the field, and even death. But the Agency operatives involved had themselves bitterly demanded, insisted on signing the waivers despite their realization that any subsequent medical problems would be exclusively their responsibility. They reminded Hocker of the professional football players whose egos made them play when hurt, filling themselves with pain-killers and numbing injections.

It was fortunate for the Agency people that he, Angus Hocker, M.D., had also paid his dues and had served on the regional medic beats throughout Africa and the Middle East. He had seen them on the job, reeling with fever or injuries, determined to finish the assignment at hand, trying to carry on despite mutinous and neglected wives and children on their consciences. He had seen them carried out of tropical posts, bodies a-tremble with fever, looked into faces haggard with fear and sleeplessness after meeting with agents under the nose of hard-eyed and hostile secret police.

He would never understand why they persisted in such careers. After he had grasped and discarded many theories, Hocker thought he had it right: they were just a different, rather special breed of cat. Clandestine operations were in their blood. They were risk junkies, delighting in operating where the dangers were palpable and constant. But that breed of cat had to pay the price in emotional and physical wear and tear. George Sheridan Wen-

dell was such a cat. And after thirty years of such a career, the precise price was becoming clear. And it had to be paid now.

"Angus, I'm going to be a good little boy," Wendell rumbled
placatingly.

"Stop agreeing with me," Hocker retorted. "And start taking
those pills twice a day instead of once. And take yourself in
hand right away and get rid of at least ten pounds in the next
couple of months. I've already given you enough salt-free diets to
last you a year."

"How about an apple a day, Angus?"

"Screw you, George. It won't keep me away. And besides,
that's eighty-five calories an apple. Try a carrot instead. And start
getting some exercise: take a nice brisk two-mile walk every day instead of pacing around your office like a trapped tiger."

He flipped the pages ahead in his schedule book.

"The executive physical exam starts exactly one week from
now, right here, same time, same place."

Wendell walked to the window and peered for a long moment
out at the green leaves of late summer fitfully waving in the forest
beyond the perimeter fence of the Headquarters area.

"New subject, Angus," he said, not turning. "Silas Ruffing . . ."

". . . A predictable tragedy," Hocker said, perched on a corner
of his desk, smoothing his white smock. "But he needs care in his
way just as you do. He's well en route to becoming an alcoholic."

"I'd like to save him," Wendell said. "FYI only, he's on a low-
five list of officers of his grade who are going to be booted out. I'm
thinking of sending him to the Farm as a training instructor if I
can swing it."

He walked toward Hocker, who held one reflective hand to his
jaw.

"It won't work, George. He needs to be close to Headquarters
for medical consultations and tests. It won't just do to assign him
another job someplace else. You've got to get at the reasons that
make him drink—and I don't think that's going to be easy, or perhaps even possible."

"Would it be better," Wendell said softly, "for us to fire him
and let him drink himself to death as a pensioner in some lonely
room?"

"You're playing God again, George," Hocker replied. "Look, I know and I deeply commend you for your . . . your damned paternalistic attitude toward your Old Boys. But it won't help, George. *He* has to come to *us* for help, realize what his problem is, and be prepared to work himself out of it. Otherwise, sending him to the Farm merely transfers the boozing to the Farm. Do you want the young kids, the trainees, to see some sloshed fifty-five-year-old instructor staggering around, giving them the idea that that's what an Agency career eventually amounts to?"

He withstood one of Wendell's most intimidating hard-eyed stares, and shook his head. Wendell abruptly turned on his heel and marched to the door. There he turned and nodded.

"So be it."

His heavy face softened and he gave Hocker a thumbs-up salute.

"I appreciate your keeping my own condition quiet, Angus."

Hocker leaned forward, arms folded over his smock.

"Only as long as I'm not asked, George. But if the Director should ring me up ten minutes from now and ask point-blank: 'Angus, what the hell's wrong with George Wendell?' I can't plead doctor-patient relationship. I'll have to level with him. *You* know that."

Hocker's bony face turned to him almost pleadingly.

"And, George . . ."

"Yes, Angus."

"If an . . . anything really starts to bother you again, you know, a splitting headache, a fainting spell, nausea, funny pressure in the chest, anything like that, see to it, if you can, that I'm called immediately. You carry a Thumper around, outside the building. So do I. Page me. They can reach me anywhere in the District."

Wendell cocked his head appreciatively.

"You'll never learn how to behave like a good medical bureaucrat, will you? At heart, you're still back there in the emergency room. The bell rings and off you go in an ambulance."

"That's where I started," Hocker said. "And I think I was happiest back there in Emergency. At least I didn't have to take a lot of crap from DDOs."

Thirty minutes later, Wendell sat heavily in his swivel chair, his Doomsday Book schedule for the day already coming apart, and the morning not yet over. Matt McClure, Chief of his Counter-intelligence Staff, lounged in a chair to his left, alert eyes wide with a deceptive expression of astonishment, seemingly unaware that his tattered tweed jacket and unpressed slacks were not the usual dress of those visiting the DDO. To Wendell's right, Henry Nordholm perched on the arm of a modern ochre-colored divan, cigarette in mouth, wearing a frown of perpetual anxiety. This morning, he appeared almost on the verge of bursting out of his tight-fitting suit, and he peered down at a tiny notebook in the palm of his hand as if in it was written the future of mankind.

He turnéd inquiringly to each of them in turn. Their voices, gestures, the way their minds worked, were quite familiar to him and the fact that both of them had come to see him together (Matt had phoned on the Secure Line only a few minutes earlier and had asked for a brief audience—urgently) meant only one thing: something important had transpired which required an im-mediate decision. There were several unsavory flaps bubbling on back burners at the moment but his instinct told him that this time it had something to do with Steve Browning. And within seconds, he knew that his instincts had not played him false.

"Is this some kind of a joke?" He could not restrain his irrita-tion, directing the question to McClure. He had known this steady, highly secretive man with a face like a Dürer saint for more than thirty years. They had served in the European Division two decades earlier in that brief abortive tour of his in Madrid. He had been happy to assign Matt to the CI Staff after McClure had been placed on a permanent medical hold (ulcers), thus bar-ring him from further overseas assignment. McClure was hardly the classic Byzantine master of his arcane responsibilities, as some of his predecessors had been, but he possessed qualities Wendell cherished: a careful, legalistic mind which refused to accept or as-sume anything at first glance, an insistence on making worst-case premises for any operations that had failed and preparing fall-back solutions swiftly and remorselessly, and he was a good hater. McClure did not view foreign espionage and counter-espionage as Great Games. He hated the Soviets with a personal vindictiveness, thoroughly enjoyed exposing them and frustrating them in their intelligence activity abroad. And he had a deep loyalty to George Wendell.

As for Nordholm, with permanent creases of worry stamped on his forehead, life for him, he once confided to Wendell, seemed to consist of dodging endless little balls of shit flung in his direction.

"No joke, George." McClure could not restrain a slight smile at Wendell's blustering query. "Like so many things in this world, this one is getting complicated."

"But Silas Ruffing?" It was as much exasperation as a question. "Why get him involved in this?"

"It's the Bureau's idea." Nordholm's thin voice was apologetic. "After all, Ruff is probably the only officer in Headquarters who's close to Steve. Whatever happens out there, they'd like to have Ruff as our man on the scene. They'd rather not cut in our people out on the West Coast."

"How do you know that Ruffing isn't mixed up in this Soviet business with Steve?"

"The evidence is completely against that." McClure spoke effortlessly. "And to make sure, we've just had him polygraphed. He passed with flying colors. And now we've got to have your permission to use him."

Wendell's mobile, ruddy face reflected his perturbation.

"Let me get this straight," he said, pointing to Nordholm. "You're telling me that Steve Browning is heading out to the West Coast on his own, and that he just may be en route to some kind of rendezvous with his Soviet control out there?"

McClure nodded.

"It's a possibility. As I told you, he told Ruff that he had word that an old agent of his has apparently gotten out of a Soviet prison and is somehow in the U.S. A funny story at best . . ."

". . . Mike Radescu," Wendell murmured.

McClure shrugged.

"A Romanian. This entire Romanian lash-up is quite unclear."

Nordholm, straight smooth hair glistening in the room's illumination, broke in with his high-pitched intensity.

"Look, George, the Bureau wants us to send Ruff out there as liaison between us and them until this business of Steve is cleared up. They've alerted their Los Angeles Field Office. The problem out there seems to be that the LA Field Office has also organized some kind of super-duper audio operation against Calinescu or . . . what's his name now? . . . Jimmy Callin, and they're terribly

afraid that either Steve or this former agent, Radescu, is going to
screw it up in some way. Since Ruffing is persona grata to the Bureau for a lot of things you and Matt already know, they'd like
Ruff out there as a little insurance premium. He knows all the
parties involved."

Wendell pried himself from his chair and padded heavily
around to them, resting his posterior on the corner of his desk.

"Now look, both of you," he growled. "*You* know, Matt, and I
think you know as well, Hank, that Silas Ruffing has become a
lush, thoroughly smashed by two P.M. every day. How in God's
name can we send an officer in that condition to help anybody?
He can't even help himself."

McClure, words floating gently but precisely from barely moving lips, said, "Manny Mulcahy of the Bureau, who's apparently
behind their request, says he knows Ruff's problem very well. Just
talked with him half an hour ago. He says that if we brace him
with the seriousness of the situation, Ruff will go cold turkey
every minute he's out there. And, as Manny puts it, there's no
substitute."

"Is this Manny freewheeling?"

"I confirmed the whole thing with Assistant Director Cran-
ahan of the Bureau. His precise words were: 'Will you please get
Ruffing's ass out to LA?' He's willing to talk to you if you
want . . .'"

"Not necessary," Wendell said, after giving McClure a long
probing glance. He shook his head involuntarily. "I hope you're
right and I'm wrong. I sense this entire business is on some kind
of collision course. I don't feel good about it."

"None of us feels good about it, George," Matt said quietly.
"Ruffing least of all."

Wendell clapped his hands once, as if summoning a genie to do
his bidding.

"Very well, full speed ahead and damn the torpedoes, as some
of our previous Directors would have said. Matt, have your secretary cut orders sending Ruffing on TDY to the West Coast for
the purpose of consulting with our security people out there. And
remember, both of you, there's a Bigot List hold-down on all of
this. I don't want to hear this business being whispered about in
the executive dining room or downstairs in the cafeterias."

The intercom buzzer rasped through his words and McClure jumped to his feet as if this were an awaited signal.

"Your weekly staff meeting, Mr. Wendell," Clare Meehan's voice announced, with just the right nuance to warn him that he was already running eight minutes late.

"Where's Browning?" he asked Nordholm as he gathered up his worn black plastic notebook containing minutes of all recent meetings and conferences for use in briefing his staff.

"Poised for flight. He's got an air reservation this afternoon for a nonstop to Los Angeles International."

"And just what kind of a tail do we have on him?"

"It's the Bureau that's tailing him," Nordholm replied. "This *is* an espionage case within the United States, after all. And I'm secretly pleased; believe me when I tell you that my Security shop doesn't have anywhere near enough people to mount any kind of massive twenty-four-hours-a-day surveillance operation for any length of time."

"I hope they're not under any illusion that Steve's not on to them," Wendell said with a sad pride in his voice. "He used to spend days shaking tails in Vienna."

"Knowing Steve," Matt said, "he's on to them all right and is taking the whole thing as a challenge. But we can't tell the Bureau how to butter bread."

"This business," Wendell muttered, "is taking years off my life."

McClure and Nordholm stood to one side as Wendell, with a mechanical thumbs-up farewell, strode for the door to his outer office.

"I've told them that you were delayed by an urgent phone call for a few minutes," Clare called, looking up as Wendell marched past her, his face a fixed stony mask.

"Good. Thanks," he responded, not slackening his pace. Clare Meehan had been his secretary for eleven years, moving with him as he progressed up the Directorate's management ladder from Deputy Division Chief to Division Chief to Chief of the Foreign Intelligence Staff to Associate Deputy Director and now to DDO.

She was seven years his junior, a homely little sharp-eyed woman with wispy hair, no-nonsense plaid skirts and jackets, a passion for Italian opera, home cooking, and Roman Catholic charities. He had discovered her in a dreary division typing pool, depressed and on the verge of resigning after a disastrous first tour in Istanbul, where two overenthusiastic Turks had totally misinterpreted her shy and innocently American smile for a come-on and had attempted, without success, to rape her. Within a week, Wendell knew he had a find in Clare Meehan.

The relationship had pleased them both, and she had developed an enormous diplomatic capacity for mothering him and sheltering him from those who would waste his precious work minutes. She was dedicated to him and to the Archdiocese of Washington in about equal measure. He and she both knew that, like Indian widows who must perform the act of suttee, she would probably have to go also when he retired. Senior executive secretaries to Deputy Directors were not easily transferable bodies (ugh) in the Agency.

He held out one hairy hand to Clare as he passed.

From a smaller office behind her, Don Kobler emerged, lumpy nose alert as a fox's, and wearing a brimming expression Wendell had learned to decipher. It meant: I know something you don't know and I'm going to startle you with it as soon as possible.

Well, the day had a long way to go, and Kobler would have to wait. Patience was not one of Kobler's stronger virtues but he would have to acquire it. And, give him credit, if it helped his career, Kobler would probably learn it well.

CHAPTER TWELVE

He had driven his old sedan slowly, at times at almost
stalling speed, from the Eagle to his Maryland home.
His spirits, if anything, sagged even more when he saw
Joanie's battered Volkswagen in the driveway. He had
deeply hoped this one time that she would still be away on her
teaching chores, but apparently she had finished her school duties
early. There was no help for it; he had to pack, pull out five hundred dollars from a much-diminished nest egg at the Credit
Union, get out to Dulles to purchase his ticket, and depart.

Joanie had looked up brightly from a bridge table she had put
up in the cozy corner sun room she had staked out as her all-pur-
pose sanctuary: sewing room, reading room, watercolor studio,
and her care and feeding of a number of useless and unattractive
green plants, some of them coaxed out of rotted potatoes.

"Workdays are getting shorter and shorter out at the Puzzle
Palace," she called at him, lifting her head from a stack of fifth-
grade compositions. She had, he knew, a quixotic and wildly unre-
alistic notion that fifth-grade students should be taught to write
grammatically correct English prose before they went on to
greater things.

"No," he answered, continuing up the stairs to their bedroom.
"Got to pack. A flap came up. Got to go to the West Coast."

He performed the chore automatically. How many dozens of
times had he filled his suitcases with careful attention to items
needed, these last thirty years, his brain turning all the while, as if
on ball bearings, assessing the possibilities, the risks, the fall-back
positions, the limits to which he could go. Each time in the past,
the curious admixture of euphoria, queasiness, the sweaty thrill of
it had buoyed him on his way. This time he packed almost haphaz-

ardly, discarding his newer shirts, underclothes, socks, shoes, and taking only those that were worn, scuffed, comfortable. As if everything chosen was to be abandoned.

Last of all, he reached high in the closet to where the pistol was secreted, removed it from its soft protective wrapping, and gingerly examined the deadly metal. He worked the bolt action, peered into the barrel and chamber, both lightly oiled and in top working condition, activated the safety mechanism, and rewrapped it together with an extra clip. He had never been able to work up a passion for handguns. They were used against people and fell into the category of whips: perhaps useful but unlovable objects. He creaked heavily down the stairs, one suitcase and the carry-on bag, and briefly laid them at his feet at the entrance to the sun room.

"Something must have come up fast." Joanie smiled mechanically at him. Her smile was predictable, unrelenting. Long ago he had ceased mentioning it to her after she had responded, "Steve, smiling is the only alternative in living with you. Now which do you want: a mechanical smile or real tears?"

He knew that his bulky frame filling the doorway was hardly a cue for her to jump to her feet and run to him with joy, although this day, unlike the others, he wished she would. As it was, she peered at him abstractedly through thick reading glasses, her once blond hair attractively coiled on the top of her head, piquant ears in full view, each with a pearl earring he had bought for her long ago in Hong Kong. Her pale attractiveness had faded and an intricate symmetry of wrinkles had gradually invaded the smooth cheeks and throat. Joanie remained what she was: unsinkable, indomitable. She knew him better than anyone else alive. But there were some things even she did not know. One was the matter of the twenty thousand dollars from Dimitriu Calinescu. *That* she would undoubtedly learn about, with all of its ramifications. She certainly knew enough about him to sit and talk to him from her bridge table instead of running to embrace him or to say goodbye to him. He had earned her indifference and her contempt, he knew, but as he stood in the doorway, they stuck in him like Bushman spears.

"Something *did* come up fast," he answered. "Do you remember me talking about an agent of mine in Austria, a fellow who disappeared on a mission and has never been heard of again?"

She took a sip of the glass of tea at her side and said politely, "Well, yes, I *do* remember something about that. You mentioned him in passing every now and again. That was before we met each other. Just after the war in Vienna?"

"That's the one. We never did know just what had happened. It was almost certain that the Soviets got their hands on him, but damned if he hasn't turned up in the U.S., out on the West Coast."

"Well, how nice!" her pleasure was unfeigned. "And they're sending you out to talk to him?"

"Correct," he lied. It would not be safe to tell her more. "I'll probably be a couple of days or so. I've got a five P.M. nonstop to Los Angeles. I'll leave my car out at Dulles in the parking area."

Her eyes briefly studied his as if a routine count of her silverware had revealed one piece missing. Joanie had all the instincts of a first-class counter-intelligence officer, including the instincts that wives develop anyway. I know there's more to this than you're telling me, her glance informed him. But it had been this way now for decades: he telling her the minimum possible about an assignment, she at first accepting with indignation, then resignation, that he was not telling her more. And now, disinterest; go where you will, Stevie.

He lingered in the doorway. She was not about to rise to bid him farewell. A dead marriage is a dead marriage, after all, and with no one else present, there was no need to go through a fond-farewell charade.

"I hear your niece is doing well down at the Farm," he said, trying to reach a more personal level of rapport, of communion with her, realizing that he was like a brush salesman with his foot in the door of an inhospitable home. "They tell me she's tops in her class." This was not altogether true, but close enough.

"Yes," Joan said, looking at him a bit owlishly. "Maryanne is doing just fine."

She paused in her reading of essay papers and as if an afterthought occurred to her, added, "I've told Maryanne *not* to mention that she has an uncle in the Shop. We'll see whether she can make it on her own."

Her words were reasoned and dispassionate but there was no mistaking her meaning: Steve Browning wasn't exactly the sort of relative a new Career Trainee should brag about. He bit his lip for a moment.

"How's Timmy?" he asked, instinctively checking his inside pockets for wallet, reading glasses, address book. "He was limping this morning."

"So you noticed?" Pure malignity on her part. "Well, he's perfectly OK," she assured him from her chair. "He's playing doubles this afternoon out in Potomac with a couple of rich friends of his. I hope you'll be back in time for his birthday next week. It's impossible for me to believe that he's eighteen years old, and leaving for college."

She shook her head incredulously without looking at him. Timmy was an accidental result of their final round of trying to find their way back to each other during a brief vacation in Crete. He had tried yet again to brake his ingrained obsession with operational challenges and to redress himself to a greater interest in his wife, his family, his children, his home.

That effort had failed as had all the previous ones. The obsession was simply overwhelming to get out on the street, to recruit agents for the sheer challenge of it, to operate slickly at the fringes of foreign laws and regulations, to pull off clandestine coups, some of which, he knew, were still discussed (in sanitized form) in the Agency's training classes.

Their two older boys, now sober-minded businessmen, one in New England, the other in Florida, had simply grown up, grown away, married, and moved off. He had always been the vanishing parent, at home and abroad, a blurred figure to them, heartily masculine, sporadically interested in sports, climbing, swimming, a sustainer of the household, but too often absent. Timmy once said that the part of his father he recognized easiest was the back of Steve's head.

"I'll try especially hard to be back for Timmy's birthday," he said to Joan.

"That would be nice," she answered, taking another sip. "Especially since you've missed twelve out of the last seventeen of them."

Since that was the way things were, he did not mention to her that he was on a list of those who were to be soon fired as surplus to the needs of the Agency. It would have startled her for a moment, perhaps, but hardly surprised her. And she might easily have rejoined, "Oh, so *they've* got your number, too."

Steve lay inert in his seat, staring at the darkened ceiling of the aircraft. That surveillance team he had left behind at Dulles wasn't bad, even by his critical standards. Good tactics in switching bags, hats, coats, and suitcases, and using at least one woman on their team, to keep him, the rabbit, from spotting them. How many of them were targeted on him, he did not know, but one of them, a young man wearing tinted glasses, made the mistake of looking away too quickly when Steve abruptly doubled back on his tracks at the men's room.

How long had they been on his tail? Days, weeks? Had they been present at that last encounter at the Tyson's Corner parking lot, one that still made his hands shake to think of it? One thing certain: these were Bureau people. The Agency simply didn't have the manpower or the expertise to orchestrate a show like that.

Were he in a less depressed state, he would have chuckled at the memory of his surveillants unknowingly watching him smuggle his gun into the security monitor where carry-on luggage passed through an X-ray machine. As his carry-on bag, with the pistol inside, moved on the conveyor belt, he had waited until the precise moment before pointing with sudden alarm at the bored female security guard, calling, "Miss, there's something crawling on the back of your head!"

The woman had almost jumped out of her shoes, swatting frantically at her hair with both hands until he assured her, "You got it! It's gone! It fell to the floor—some kind of big bug or insect. Must have come from the ceiling or something."

The carry-on bag had moved through the X-ray monitor unexamined, and the guard had thanked him profusely for his concern.

That was slick, performed under the eyes of some of the best surveillance people in the country. Of course Silas would not have liked it at all. "That was a crazy, risky, thoroughly dumb thing to do," he would have scolded. "You could have gotten arrested. You know the airlines' rules on smuggling arms aboard aircraft. Think of the notoriety for the Shop if the media ever got hold of such a story."

Good old Ruff. A real company man. Thirty years before the mast, loyal and true blue, and what would be his reward? A free goose as he walked out the door for the last time? An empty box of a house in Vienna, Virginia, with a commanding view of the funeral-parlor parking lot next door? And with the pink slip in his hand, no less. Sacked, found wanting, just as was Steve Browning.

He closed his eyes for a moment. Old Ruff at least had salvaged a certain dignity out of a career now ending in ignominy and booze. A dignified loser.

The cool blue eyes of his wife, swimming large behind her reading goggles, appeared, looking at him as neutrally as one regards beasts grazing in the field. Silas and Joanie. A loser and the wife of a loser. A real pair.

At his feet lay the carry-on bag, his loaded pistol inside it, carefully wrapped in an old T-shirt. He wondered now why he had brought it along, why he had risked so much to bring it on the plane with him. It was as if he were tempting fate to bring him down.

And did it make sense at all to embark on this trip, now that he knew the FBI had him under surveillance? Would it not have been better to seek out George Wendell and say, "Look, I don't know precisely who has what kind of goods on me but let's sit down and sort things out." But he would have to look into those deep hooded eyes, the mobile lips barely concealing contempt, the whole humiliating running of the gauntlet: polygraph, endless further interviews/interrogations, the whispers in the corridors as he passed. . . .

No, it was better this way, hunting and being hunted. It was a long time since his nerves tingled with such anticipation. It might well be a caper he couldn't possibly win but one well worth playing. First, there was the Bureau surveillance team to give the slip to, the moment they landed in Los Angeles. Then there was the needle, Mircea Radescu, to find in the haystack that was Los Angeles. And that was just for openers. . . .

He peered through half-closed eyes at a firm-jawed young man walking slowly down the plane aisle. The man looked hard at him without stopping. Now, *that* one gave himself away completely. A good tail shouldn't ever try to come that close, or give the rabbit that good a look at him.

Half smiling, he wondered what sort of a chewing-out this one, and the others waiting to take up the chase at the airport, would receive from their supervisor when they all realized that Steve Browning, no rabbit but a quickly moving fox, had given them the slip.

He curled his bulky body sideways in the reclined seat and dozed until the huge jet circled down for landing.

CHAPTER THIRTEEN

The distance between Wendell's swivel chair and the Directorate conference room was no more than two dozen strides. By the time he had covered that short distance and had reached the closed door with a sign affixed: "DDO Staff Meeting. Do Not Enter," he was leading a small parade consisting of McClure, Kobler, and Clare.

He flung open the door with cheery energy and boomed, "Good morning, sorry I'm late," as he strode purposefully into the brightly lit conference room to his chair. The hubbub abruptly died. Wendell's eyes darted around the room. Although there were chairs for twenty persons at the shining oval expanse of conference table, only half of them were occupied, all by his division and senior staff chiefs. Around the fringes of the windowless room, whose paneled walls bore intimidating photographs of previous DCIs and DDOs, sat another half-dozen men and women, the need-to-know special assistants, joined by Kobler. Clare Meehan, shorthand pad in hand, took her place at an empty chair slightly away from the table, at his right hand. She would record the gist of this meeting, as she had done for years—For the Record.

Wendell, with a flourish, extracted his heavy reading glasses from the breast pocket of his jacket and opened his ringed notebook, aware that he looked, as Clare was not hesitant to tell him, like the chairman of Chase Manhattan. Even to the Phi Beta Kappa key (curious how Jenny Pfitzner resented him wearing it!). Superficially he was very much that: an executive talking to subordinate executives.

He had over the years bitterly resisted the facile comparison. Clandestine intelligence was *not* a business, he protested loudly to those who sought to institutionalize the analogy; no, it was not an art either, nor was it a science. It defied being jammed into a neat little descriptive box. It was a strange, esoteric human activity, a way of life understandable only to those who had engaged in it. Just as only a nun can describe how a nunnery functions, so only a clandestine intelligence operative can know how it really feels, smells, *sounds* to be inside an organization devoted to espionage and clandestine intelligence. It was so easy to make up sensational, marvelously fantastic, and quite untrue stories about it if you didn't know. And if you *did* know, you didn't tell stories, virtually all of which were classified anyway.

His eyes took in the room's occupants. He knew every one of them, some of them intimately, all of them cordially enough to call them by first name. Many had served with him in the old days at branch and division assignments. He knew a good deal about them, just as they knew a good deal about him: their foibles, problems at home, their strengths and their predictable lapses from grace. All of them had been, more or less, tempered by years and decades in the Shop: the many enormous disappointments, the very few shining successes, the gut-turning flaps, some of which had been flung on the front pages and TV screens of the world. They were, all of them, survivors, including the two graying women along the wall who had entered the upper reaches of this hitherto white male domain. They, too, had paid their dues, at Headquarters and abroad. And, like himself, they were the generation who had joined the Agency at its beginnings. The last of the Old Boys—and Girls.

Wendell recited the litany from his notebook: kudos to the East Asia Division from the President's National Security Adviser for the reporting of its Hong Kong Station on the developments along the troubled South China–Vietnam border; irritation and hard feelings at State that an Agency operative in an African country (Wendell would not tell them which one) had been declared persona non grata. . . .

At which point, Connor, an irrepressible wag from the Planning Staff who knew where all the old bones in the Directorate were buried, asked, "Steve Browning again?" which elicited muffled chuckles from those who knew his checkered record but which brought a rare rebuke from Wendell ("Not very funny, Ed").

Looking down the table at McClure, Wendell said, "The Director was most complimentary about our debriefing of the Soviet defector who walked into Tokyo Station. We've now moved him to the United States, and interrogation is going on at maximum speed. That right, Matt?"

"As much as he can stand," Matt replied. He did not add what he and Wendell both knew: that Matt would be questioning the Soviet personally.

Wendell then sighed and rattled off a series of obligatory announcements which had as much to do with the clandestine services as a discussion of diaper rash at a senior citizens' dance.

"I am asked to plead with you all, and with your people, yet again, for full participation in the United Fund. Our Directorate has pledged only fifty-four percent of our quota, way behind last year. And our Blood Bank contributions are dropping off. Since the media have us exposed as a band of bloody assassins, couldn't we sluice off a few gallons for the Red Cross?" (Smiles, no laughter.) "Finally, keep your spookier people out of Headquarters for the next two or three days. Italian television crews, so help me God, have been given permission to make some interior shots of the ground floor of this building . . ."

Pressure on his kidneys, from his medication, made him suddenly uncomfortable.

"I'm running a bit late today," he said. "Let's make a quick run around the table for any comments, ruminations, or offers to retire."

A decade ago that would have been like an opening gun for a verbal free-for-all, when the chiefs of the geographical divisions had been barons with autonomous fiefdoms and direct lines to the Director's office. He knew all that. He had been a baron himself.

But the old barons were gone now, fishing in Florida or collecting consultant's fees—or had died. The heady covert-action projects that had pleased and perplexed the Powers downtown and those on the Hill for twenty years had one by one been terminated, and the bright, often willfully arrogant and audacious operators who had run them had departed or were about to depart, like Steve Browning.

Now the men around this sleek-surfaced conference table were middle-aged division chiefs, firmly under his hand and that of the Director. Money and personnel were mercilessly controlled and doled out by comptrollers, systems analysts, the Office of Management and Budget, the Congress. And the name of the DDO's game now was the collection of clandestine intelligence, serving as the government's eyes and ears abroad. This was fine with Wendell, whose distaste for political-action schemes he had never concealed from anyone. He and the others in this room had been through it all. A rare pang of pride in them stirred in him as he looked at them, his peers, bound to each other willy-nilly in a closed fraternity of shared experiences, most of which would never achieve their valid niches as footnotes in history books.

But, he had to admit, the two terrible "R's"—routine and regulations—had grown up like proliferating tropical vines, twisting their tough tendrils around the people sitting in this room and what they did every day here. Five bloody loose-leaf folders, the Pentateuch of Agency regulations, containing more "don'ts" than the Talmud, had made them all prudent, cautious bureaucrats. Perhaps it was true that organizations, like people, were organic: from fresh, chaotic, brimming origins and sense of mission, they developed symptoms of age: arteriosclerosis of regulations, a dimming of managerial eyes to innovations and audacity. There, along the wall, sat Don Kobler, right foot vibrating for his chance to become a senior bureaucrat. And *he* knew the regs.

"My schedule this week calls for our annual operations review of Near East Division operations: 1330 to 1630 hours tomorrow and Friday in this conference room. Saturday morning, I fly down to the Farm to talk to the graduating CT class, including informal bull sessions, and I'll be back Sunday night."

He did not mention the half-days of medical examinations. That would simply create an apprehensive murmur. He held up his hand in his traditional meeting's-over gesture. "Peace!" he intoned, and headed for the large washroom nearby. Don Kobler trod at his heels and shared the act of urinating with him, side by side.

"Got to talk to you, George, for a couple of minutes," Kobler breathed, after craning his head to ensure that no one occupied the toilets behind them.

"Can it wait until I finish pissing?" Wendell tried to keep the edge out of his response as he looked straight ahead at the white squares of tiles. Kobler, he reflected wearily, had so much damned energy and so little damned style.

"It's about that Calinescu file you wanted me to find." Kobler would not be denied. He shook his organ vigorously and zipped his trousers with the air of a knight on horseback preparing to charge into the lists.

"You've found it and you're glad," Wendell said.

"More." Kobler's animation had become agitation. "I've found it all right, but *where* I found it and what's in it are far more important."

Wendell glanced at his watch and washed his hands mechanically. He had managed to clip a full five minutes from the time allotted to the weekly meeting and had planned to spend the next quarter hour reading one of NFAC's better analysis papers on the readiness level of the Warsaw Pact armies; one simply had to keep up with such things.

"I guess, from your tone, that it won't wait."

"It *won't* wait, George." He could not decide as they paced together back to his office whether Kobler's tone was that of genuine concern or secret gloating. He decided, as he slid back into his swivel chair, that it was both.

"Here it is," Kobler said, and handed him a heavy manila envelope, its flap opened. "It took some looking to find it."

Wendell, reaching for his reading glasses, pointed to the heavy black admonition on the envelope cover: "EYES ONLY." A flame of anger kindled in his eyes and tightened his lips.

"Did you open this envelope, Don?"

The alert fleshy nose scented something in the air.

"Yes, I did. Why?"

"This is a highly restricted file, Don. And that means that only those who are specifically cleared can read it. Now, Hank Nordholm has the list of people vetted to look at the Calinescu file. Your name is *not* on it."

Kobler's expression was akin to that of a patriot who has suddenly been accused of treason.

"B-but, George, as your Special Assistant, I've always assumed that I had the right to read *anything* you asked for. . . ."

"The Israelis *assumed* the Egyptians wouldn't attack in 1973.

We *assumed* the Japanese wouldn't attack us at Pearl Harbor."
His voice was implacable. "In this business, one *assumes* nothing,
Don, except, perhaps, the worst. Now this happens to be a lim-
ited-access file. Couldn't you at least have had the grace to *ask*
me before you opened it?"

A good deal of the gloat had vanished from Kobler's bearing,
which was precisely Wendell's aim.

He waved a priest-like hand of forgiveness.

"All right, I've made my point. But it's an important one, Don.
Need-to-know is way of life around here. Damn, I don't have to
tell *you* that. And we're not talking about twenty lashes or time in
the stocks. Just remember, next time. . . ."

Kobler sank into one of the curved modern chairs before Wendell's desk, stared at the carpeting for a moment as if seeking to
regain air in his lungs. Finally he nodded, without looking up.

"The point's well taken, George."

"Fine. And that's the end of that. Now, then, just where did
they find this damned thing?"

"In the bottom drawer of Silas Ruffing's safe."

Wendell shook his head in involuntary surprise.

"Everyone had already scoured the contents of the safe. But
Ruffing had put the file inside another folder marked 'MISC
ADMIN' and no one thought to look inside it the first time
around."

Wendell smiled inwardly. When an old pro like Silas wanted to
hide a file, he certainly knew how to do it: in the most obvious
place. The thick folder emitted a musty smell when he opened it
to examine its yellowing memos and badly blurred Thermofax
pages. How many thousands of such files he had held in his hands
over the decades! The name "CALINESCU, Dimitriu, aka CAL-
LIN, James D." followed by an Agency dossier number appeared
in the little plastic-covered file tab, printed in ink by a precise
hand. He wondered if there was anything still sensitive in this file
that would still warrant its "Eyes Only" designation.

Peering over his reading glasses at Kobler, he asked, "How did
you happen to look there?"

Kobler's briefly wounded amour propre had healed instantly.
He issued a triumphant shark smile.

"Just a hunch. After all, Ruffing had the file signed out to him.

And while there was a chance he might have taken the file out of the building or hidden it somewhere, I didn't think he'd do anything like that, Ruffing being a pro and all. Incidentally, George, I'll say it yet again: that Document Retrieval shop is in such a mess, you wouldn't believe. They really need somebody to take them in hand and get a handle on precise location of documents from one day to the next. There's no tickler system at all down there to warn them that a document's been charged out for weeks and weeks and is overdue. Really, somebody ought to bite their ass. . . ."

Wendell nodded wearily.

"The point has been thoroughly made, Don."

He tapped the file cover under his hand.

"So, Ruffing hadn't done anything with it. He just hid it under 'MISC ADMIN'? Incidentally, who found it there?"

Kobler's eyes behind the round glasses sparkled.

"I did. I told the people in the CI Staff that you had to read the file soonest, given the going-over you got from Jenny Pfitzner, and I got their permission to search his safe personally. . . ."

"Pulled *my* rank on them, did you?" Wendell was genuinely amused. He remembered the words of one of Kobler's recent fitness reports, written by a supervisor without illusions or grudges: "This man gets things done! And when he does, get out of his way."

"Look, George," Kobler said uneasily. "I seem to be on your shit list today and if I've done something just over the edge . . ."

"Enough!" Wendell told him sternly. "No self-flagellation around here, please. You found the file, and I'm grateful you did."

Absolved, Kobler sprang to his feet, leaned across the desk, and tapped a smaller envelope stapled to the inside cover of the Calinescu dossier. Its most recent seal also had been broken open.

"Now read what's in that, please!"

Wendell did. He read slowly and carefully, folding back the official stapled pages of the Department of Justice report, one after another. When he finished, he turned back the pages and read them all over again. The minutes of silence were almost unbearable for Kobler, who jiggled his foot, picked nervously at his nose, reviewed his checkbook entries, and studied his address book distractedly.

Wendell reached over for his executive water pitcher, poured a glass of water from it with a steady hand, extracted a green-and-yellow pill the size of a minié ball from a bottle in his desk, and downed the object with a grimace. He tucked his glasses into his jacket pocket and lumbered around his desk to the window, where he examined the cloud-heavy sky with the interest of a rainmaker.

"I hate to read things like that," he finally said. "It's a little bit like finding out that Mom is a junkie."

He faced Kobler with a pained grin.

"I guess that solves one low-five-percent problem for this year, doesn't it?"

"More than that, I'm afraid," Kobler answered. "We've got to inform the IG, Director of Security, General Counsel's Office, and the Director. We've also got to write a memo for the Director to send to the Intelligence Oversight Board on this. We may even have to brief the SSCI if the Director says we must. Those are Agency procedures in the cases of improper conduct, or indications of commission of a crime, by an Agency employee."

"Really did your homework quickly! Splendid!" Wendell complimented him. He looked at him, voice bland with solicitude. "How's your German, Don?"

"Pretty rusty, I'm afraid," Kobler answered, perplexity narrowing his eyes. "Why do you ask?"

"Too bad, because if you did, you'd know what *Schadenfreude* means." Wendell smiled. "Look it up sometime."

Kobler pursed his lips. He was being given the idiot treatment again.

"Look, George, believe me when I say that I know how you feel about Steve Browning . . ." Kobler began.

". . . No, you don't, Don." Wendell's interruption was pitched to a controlled conversational timbre but his heavy-jowled face was suffused with something approaching a choleric rage. "You don't and you never can. So don't, for Christ's sake, tell me that you do!"

He wheeled at the noise of the intercom buzzer, stabbed the blinking "hold" button on the telephone, and asked with a mustered calm, "What is it, Clare?"

"It's Mr. Chambers, on a Secure Line. He's downtown with the Director, sir."

"And what does our distinguished Press Relations Officer want
with me?"

"He says it's terribly urgent."

"Put him on."

"Mr. Chambers? Go ahead, sir."

Larry Chambers' voice, never an instrument of *sotto voce*
nuances, could be heard through the telephone across the room
and, as in cases where indignation got the better of him, it sput-
tered like a row of ignited Chinese firecrackers.

"George, damn it to hell, did you meet a free-lance journalist
named Barney Langer the other night? Did you have some kind
of a run-in with him?"

"In the order of your questions, Larry, the answers are 'yes,' and
'no.' Yes, I met him. No, I did not have a run-in with him, although he seemed to be spoiling for a fight. He did have a run-in,
literally, with a waiter at the party I was attending and got several
dollars' worth of good scotch spilled on him."

"Well, he's going to spill several million dollars of good horseshit all over us, did you know that?"

Kobler was still standing there, very much aware that a new flap
of unforeseen dimensions was materializing. Wendell sat slowly
down, half turned away from Kobler, and studied his daily schedule book.

"No, Larry, I don't know anything about Mr. Langer except
that he is a most unattractive man. Now, what's he going to do to
us that hasn't already been done ten times over by every newspaper in the country?"

"I'll tell you what he's going to do: he's going to print, in tomorrow's *Times*, a documented feature story about a CIA senior
officer, whose true name he will reveal, who was paid twenty thousand dollars some years ago by that goddamned Romanian war
criminal Jenny Pfitzner's been after. The CIA officer got the
money as a bribe to sponsor and assist the immigration of that
character . . . what's his name . . ."

"Calinescu, Larry. The name is Dimitriu Calinescu."

"Yeh, yeh, that's the name. George, this is absolutely dreadful,
awful! Just when the media and Congress were finally starting to
lay off us and to show a little sympathy and confidence in the

Agency! I told the Director about it ten minutes ago and he's fit
to be tied! George, we're in deep *kimshi*. . . ."

Wendell uttered a silent prayer of thanks that the DCI had not
seen fit to add Larry Chambers to the Bigot List on the Steve
Browning case. Had he done so, Chambers would have keeled
over with apoplexy of the lower media.

"Now hold on, Larry, just a goddamned minute!" he bayed in
his best command voice. For a moment the room eerily tilted at a
fifteen-degree angle and he was aware of Kobler's intent eyes taking in his every gesture.

"All of this took place over thirty years ago. The Agency was
barely in being. We can take appropriate action without pressing
the panic button."

"How do you know," Chambers shouted at him, "that this
wasn't part of some nutty covert-action caper the Agency was involved in?"

"I'll stake my job on it." Wendell's voice was cold and unyielding.

"So you know about this?" Chambers shouted. "You've known
about it all along and you've kept it under wraps?" Wendell wondered whether Chambers was reaching what the nuclear scientists
called a critical mass.

"Yes, I've known about it for some time, Larry. It's a dreadful
and unhappy thing. But the world is full of dreadful and unhappy
things and there's no sense coming unglued about it. . . ."

But Chambers was inconsolable.

"Look, George, you had better line up your drakes pretty
damned quick. The Director will be back out there after lunch
and he's going to want to have some pretty cogent reasons from
you and everyone else concerned why he was caught out on this
one. You'd better do your homework, feller. . . ."

Wendell said, "One more thing. Where did the leak come
from? Which agency in town did Langer get the story from?"

"As near as we can figure, it must have come from some component in Justice. Maybe Immigration and Naturalization."

"How about Congress? Wasn't an info copy of Justice's report
on the CIA bribery sent to the Hill? I'm certain that Jenny Pfitzner's subcommittee got its hands on it."

Chambers said, "I don't have a clue, but it's something we'll have to sort out. I'm going to call Legislative Liaison and ask them to get on it. Good point. . . ."

He remembered that he had inadvertently dropped his indignation for a moment and hastened to revive it.

"George, I repeat: this couldn't have come at a worse time. Our Agency budget is moving through OMB; we've got closed-session hearings on it next week in the House. Jesus. . . ."

Wendell held the phone away from his ear. It rested in his right hand as if it were a grenade about to have its pin pulled, and thrown.

". . . George, are you still on the line?" Chambers called. "George, anything the matter?"

"Nothing," Wendell replied, "that a good old-fashioned cry couldn't cure."

Kobler was perched on the arm of the chair facing him, eyes appraising, faintly mocking. Get yourself out of this one, Wendell, the expression told him, you and your sad-ass old-timers.

CHAPTER FOURTEEN

"Please fasten your seat belts, adjust your seat backs to the upright position, and extinguish all cigarettes," the air attendant's flat, bored voice advised. "We are making our final approach to Los Angeles International Airport."

Peering past the passenger seated at the window, Silas Ruffing had a brief glimpse at a power company's paradise: a billion lights, blue and white and yellow, thick as a carpet, filled the horizon as the huge bird dipped its wing and floated ever lower over the endless sprawl of Los Angeles.

He knew the place well enough. Several times he had come here on Agency trips to consult with his colleagues assigned permanently on the West Coast and twice in the distant past he had accompanied his now divorced wife on her dutiful visits to her parents in the Valley. Los Angeles was not a city of particularly happy memories.

With the greatest reluctance he had been prevailed upon to accede to the Bureau's request that he come out here and help them out with Steve Browning in particular and the Calinescu/Callin case in general. It had taken the combined persuasions of Manny Mulcahy, Matt McClure, and that Nervous Nelly, Nordholm, to convince him that he had to go, and they had to wrap it in the tired old mantle of the National Interest. For just a brief moment, he was about to tell them where they could stuff the National Interest; what goddamned nerve they had, when they were about to tie a can to his tail! Suddenly old Ruff was needed to keep the books straight on that pathetic self-destruct, Steve Browning.

But in the end it was Manny Mulcahy who carried the day. Fixing him with those ageless, suspicious hawk eyes, Manny had

barked at him in that indefinable Long Island intonation,
"You've spent your entire damned career looking for Soviet penetrations, right? A watchdog of the goddamned Republic? OK,
OK, we're treated like watchdogs: a daily bone to gnaw on, an occasional kick in the ribs. But here we have something, Ruff—an
honest-to-God CI case with a hell of a lot riding on it. How badly
have we been had? What can we learn about it? Look, you
shrewd, pissed-off little bastard, you have no choice this time. We
need you."

He tramped along the endless corridor leading from the aircraft
to the baggage-claim area. The hours of the flight had served as a
cocoon, secure if temporary insulation between problems left behind and those to come. But now, in this long tunnel leading to
nowhere, he felt a sense of loss, loneliness, an immense sadness for
himself, Steve, the whole business of betrayal and uncovering
those who betrayed. There was much to be said about the brutal
KGB motto: Who is doing what to whom? And a further question: Why?

A husky Latin-looking man, with a wary weathered face, dressed
in the casual Californian uniform of light slacks, open sports shirt,
and cotton jacket, stepped forward from a public telephone booth
where he had been scanning all passengers leaving the Washington plane, and held up a warning hand.

"Would you, by chance, be a man named Ruffing?"

"Right the first time," Silas said.

"Could you give me your first name and middle initial?" the
other asked, smiling professionally.

"Silas L. You'd better call me Ruff. Here's a Virginia driver's license."

A black leather rectangle appeared in the man's hand, which he
flipped open with one expert finger.

"Special Agent Angelo Fusco, Los Angeles Field Office. Call
me anything. Welcome to Paradise, U.S.A."

They shook hands briskly.

Fusco, hard black eyes taking in Silas' appearance with a cool
and initially unenthusiastic professionalism, said, "We got the
TWX on you just a couple of hours ago. But Manny Mulcahy

phoned earlier and said you were coming. Anybody Manny vouches for is good enough for me. He was my boss when we were both in the New York office, rinky-dink squad, a dozen years ago. I'd cut my throat for that little mick."

He had already rented a baggage cart, and as he pushed it toward the baggage-claim area, he suddenly nudged Silas with a flash of recognition.

"Hey, I've heard of you! Aren't you the Agency guy who put us on to the Russky on the UN staff in New York who was shacking up with a typist right in our New York office? Weren't you commended in person by Mr. Hoover himself?"

The tough alert face was now all smiles.

"Boy, I'll bet you're the only Agency guy he ever did *that* to. God, he was down on you guys at the end!"

"All that was a hell of a long time ago," Silas answered with a thin smile. "And I'd keep it quiet out here if I were you. In some places out here, like Berkeley, a commendation from Mr. Hoover is a little bit like receiving the Iron Cross from the Nazis."

"Screw those Berkeley bastards," Fusco retorted with much feeling. "Doing a good job out here despite those creeps takes a lot of patriotism."

"Amen to that," Silas said.

A black dented Ford sedan stood at the curb outside the terminal building. As they emerged, a youthful colleague of Fusco, in the same nondescript dress as he, jumped from the driver's seat. Without a word, he nodded at Silas, opened the car's trunk, flung Silas' suitcase in it, resumed his place at the wheel, and plunged them into the thick nocturnal molasses of airport traffic.

"Bill Wherry, one of my squad," Fusco introduced the man, who briefly turned and said, "Hi."

"Now first of all, the bad news." Fusco, sitting beside Wherry, turned to address Silas slumped in the rear seat. His frown combined embarrassment with irritation. "Your bad penny, Browning, has given our tail the slip. We had a guy from the Washington office on the same plane with him and, in addition, we had a six-man team waiting to take up the tail at this damned terminal. Seven goddamned people! But he shook them all."

"How did he get away with anything like that?" Silas asked, bringing a handkerchief to his lips to cover his involuntary grin.

He recalled those endless "shake the tail" games he and Steve had played in Vienna. Steve had gotten very good at it. Apparently he was still good at it.

"He caught them all flat-footed," Fusco confessed. "He was standing around the baggage carousel at the terminal as if he was waiting for his stuff he had checked through from Washington. And since the damned carousel hadn't even started moving, they all relaxed for a minute. Our guy on the plane was talking out in the corridor with two guys from our team. But it turned out that Browning didn't have any baggage on the plane, just his carry-on bag. He drifted around toward the exit and kept looking at the carousel to start up. Before we knew what happened, he was gone. Either he grabbed a passing empty taxi, or someone signaled him from outside to make a run for it. But he got away, clean."

Fusco shook his head in grudging praise.

"Got to hand it to him. And boy, did the team catch screaming hell from our SAC!"

The Ford reached the freeway and merged into the metallic river of vehicles flowing north, a thousand angry red taillights ahead of them.

Silas sat in the rear seat in silence. It was so like Steve to do something as harebrained as that. Shaking an FBI surveillance team was, after all, an arrogant stunt and it only confirmed in their minds that he had substantial and nefarious reasons for doing so. A suspicion darted into his thoughts that at this point Steve Browning didn't give a damn about the consequences of any of his acts. He was, in a very real sense, out of control.

"That certainly complicates the ball game," he finally said from the darkness of the rear seat. "Now what do you have on the former agent of ours, the Romanian named Radescu, who's reportedly come out here to nail Calinescu?"

"Zilch. We got the lead in the TWX and we checked out the motel address in Manhattan Beach that you apparently got from Browning. But nobody by that name was registered there. The motel people remember a weird old bird with a wispy white beard and a wild look in his eye, traveling with an Austrian passport, who checked in a week or so ago and checked out again after staying for three days. He's the only foreigner there in weeks. Either your pigeon used the motel stationery and is somewhere else, or he's traveling under a passport with a different name. Anyway, no further info on him, although we're watching for that Austrian passport and name to pop up again."

He lit a cigarette with a nervous gesture.

"Goddamn, that's not such a good sitrep, is it?"

Silas said, "Don't tell *me* what bad days are like, er . . ."

"Angelo."

"Angelo. I know what it's like to have odd-ball situations come up like this. That's why I came out here. Manny seems to think I can help."

Fusco, smoke tendrils issuing from his mouth, shook his head perplexedly.

"Look, Ruff, I don't really know precisely what the hell is going on here. All I know is that my SAC has instructed me to take you by the hand. I'm your point of contact for the LA office. But I'm busy as a buck in rutting season. And I can tell you, buddy, that I don't want you to knock down any blocks in my playpen."

Noting Silas' puzzlement, he added testily, "I can see that I've got to draw pictures for you. OK, let's wait until we get to the Place. That's *my* playpen."

They had long turned off the crowded freeway traffic, wound through the dips and turns of Sunset Boulevard, and climbed slowly and steadily through narrow, tortuous residential streets, past theatrically floodlighted house façades. At a solid-metal gate, the car came to a halt. Wherry pressed the button on an electronic panel he held in his hand and the gate slid ponderously open. The Ford moved through the entrance and slowly crunched up a dark curved gravel allée flanked with alternating palm and eucalyptus tree sentinels, purring on smooth asphalt to a main entrance.

The Place, even in the brief illumination of the Ford's headlights, was an estate of quintessential Beverly Hills opulence. It sat like a ship's prow on a crag, with a view of Los Angeles sprawled below them that was fully as breathtaking as that from the aircraft window. A one-level hacienda-style mansion, it was built in an L. Its sloping red tile roofs, intricately curved iron grillwork on its windows, and the stuccoed elegance of its broad open patios identified it as a residence of the Very Rich Indeed. Incongruously, the lighted courtyard contained but two modest workaday American sedans. A curious air of abandonment eddied around them in the clear night air.

They stood in a silent huddle for a moment at the foot of several broad ceramic steps leading up to a main patio and front door.

Fusco, his tough intense face half in shadow, nudged Silas and jerked his head in a peremptory manner.

"Ruff, I wanna talk to you for just a minute, the two of us, OK?"

Silas moved away with Fusco, their feet soundless on the thick tufted grass.

"Look, Ruff, I haven't got a good fix on what's happening to this rotten apple of yours, and you haven't got a clue what I'm up to here." Fusco spoke with intensity, eyes glittering in the reflection of the parking-area floodlights. "But I'm telling you loud and clear. I'm involved in a high-risk, high-stakes need-to-know special. There's a hell of a lot riding on it, for me, for the Bureau, and for the government."

"You don't have to tell me anything you don't want to," Silas replied. "As for what I'm doing here, all I know is that Steve Browning has been identified as a *possible*, not a *probable*, KGB collaborator. Since it's domestic espionage, the Agency has passed the case to the Bureau. Steve's been under close surveillance in Washington from the moment the info on him came to light. The fact that he shook that surveillance at LAX clearly proves that he has been on to that tail, maybe for some time."

Fusco frowned in his perplexity.

"But if that's the case, why the hell did he come out here? He's an old pro. Once he knows that he's under suspicion, he's a Typhoid Mary; he'd lead us to anybody he contacts."

"I can't answer that." Silas' tone was bitter. "And the fact that you lost him at the airport doesn't help. The one thing I do know is that Steve's trip here has something to do with finding Radescu. Why, I don't know entirely. Certainly a bad conscience."

"Or maybe all these bad pennies come together to rattle: Browning, Radescu, and Jimmy C."

Silas tapped Fusco's shoulder for emphasis.

"Listen, Angelo, you've got to understand one thing clearly. Jimmy C., or Dimitriu Calinescu, was run as an agent by Steve in

Vienna over thirty years ago. We now know that Calinescu corrupted him, bought into him for twenty thousand dollars. Where that leaves us, I don't know. Is Jimmy C. on the Soviet payroll? Does he still deal with Steve in some way? Maybe *you* can tell *me!*"

Fusco cocked his head as if listening for sounds in the still night air, narrowing his eyes with concentration.

"Well, if Jimmy C. is involved with anybody, you sure as hell are standing in the right line," he finally blurted, with the air of a magician about to produce a pair of pigeons from a top hat. "Silas, I'm going to level with you about this whole operation. What Manny says about you, and what you did for the Bureau, makes you an OK guy as far as I'm concerned, even if you are an edgy little bastard."

They walked back to Wherry standing quietly in the darkness.

"The owner of this hovel, believe it or not, is an Iranian," Fusco explained with an expansive wave of his hand. "I guess he must have smelled bad news in Iran long before the Shah bugged out. He bought this place, I'm told, almost three years ago for a million dollars *in cash*. It's worth over three times as much now. The view alone is worth the admission fee."

He pointed to where the driveway dipped down and out of sight.

"He's got a five-car garage underneath, over there. These jalopies you see here belong to my guys on shift duty inside. Down below in the garage there's a black Rolls, a blue Rolls, a Mercedes 450 SL, a Cadillac, and a dune buggy."

He shook his head wistfully.

"On my salary, I couldn't even afford to keep those babies in gasoline."

Silas, taking in the cultivated jungle of cactus, rubber plants, and shrubbery, said, "I don't want to get ahead of your story, but this looks like more than an FBI house-sitting chore, Angelo."

Fusco winked conspiratorially.

"It's more than house-sitting, Ruff. As for the Iranians, we found out that they were going off for a three-month visit to Europe. It was just what we were looking for and when we approached the owner, being the good instant patriot he suddenly became, he was delighted to have us house-sit for him while he's away as long as we don't break anything. After all, he's right: if the FBI can't protect a house from break-ins, who can?"

They ascended the stairway in silence, traversed the broad tiled patio, and Fusco pushed against the huge wooden door, slightly ajar. The dimly lit foyer, a ballroom expanse of tile covered with what appeared to be an acre of outsized Persian carpets, was empty. White ghost-like protective sheets covered all the furniture and lamps. The glitter from extinguished twin wheel-shaped chandeliers caught and refracted the solitary light from a floor lamp in one corner.

"We had to tell him to pay off all the servants, except for the gardener, who comes in from the outside anyway, and to give them a long holiday," Fusco said as they followed him down a long carpeted corridor, feet soundless in the thick piling, "and so the place is starting to get a little dusty. We're ostensibly doing extensive electrical repairs as a private company. When we're through here, we put everything back in place, fold our tents in the night, and call in some local cleaning service to get it ready for the owner again."

At the end of the corridor, he paused at a door and turned to them.

"And now," he announced, "this is where we earn our union wages."

They entered the brightly lit chamber, with heavy wooden shutters closed, blocking the entrance to the terrace outside. A large guest bedroom, it had been emptied of its original furniture and ornaments. One wall was lined with tables pushed together to form a rough but serviceable workbench, now covered with tape recorders, headsets, video screens, typewriters, and an impressive bank of wires leading to three telephone earpieces. Through a half-opened door leading into a huge marble bathroom, they glimpsed black streamers of drying film negatives hanging from wires: an improvised photographic darkroom. Two middle-aged men in T-shirts and slacks, each with earpieces fastened to his head and with yellow lined pads before them, sat at two of the tape recorders and waved nonchalantly at Fusco and his companions.

Silas took in the scene with expert eyes.

"Quite an LP," he finally said.

Fusco pointed with pride to the darkened video screen.

"*Live* closed-circuit TV, I'll have you know. Not as sharp as cable TV but then we're not that fussy." He pushed through a connecting door into what was still a handsome study, its one large window also covered by wooden shutters, its walls solid with impressive legal volumes and richly bound books-you-buy-but-don't-read. In one corner, at an executive angle, a massive desk supported loose files, typed reports, a battered portable typewriter, and stacks of photographs.

"This is my command post," Fusco announced, waving Silas into a leather chair. He doffed his jacket, threw it on a couch, and extricated himself from a shoulder holster with its snub-nosed revolver. Then with a sigh he lowered himself into a straight-backed chair behind the desk. He smoothed his thinning curly black hair and made an expansive gesture around him.

"And this is the locus for Operation Scorpion. The scorpion has a fatal sting and that's what I hope this one's gonna be. This may not be the tidiest listening post you've ever seen, but I'll bet you that it's certainly one of the fanciest places we've ever put an LP into. Goddamn, finding it was just a stroke of luck."

His dark Italian face lit up with pride and conspiracy.

"And why is the FBI sitting in splendor in this Taj Mahal high in the million-dollar neighborhood of Beverly Hills? Or more precisely, in this particular pad? Since you're an old pro, you probably know the answer: this place is ideally suited to surveill another house close by."

He strode to the shuttered door, beckoned Silas to follow him, unfolded one vertical panel of the wooden shutter, and led him out to the edge of the broad, tiled terrace and pointed downhill in the darkness. About two hundred feet away, on a separate rock outcropping but lower than the terrace on which they stood, and separated from it by a steep chasm of the canyon, sat a large squat square house, wide terraces facing them, its expanse of flat roof barely outlined in the darkness. Two lights gleamed on one of the terraces and the faint voices of a small group of people drifted up to them. Beyond, invisible because of a high fence around it but floodlighted from above, was a swimming pool. An occasional splash or two indicated that it was being used.

"That's it," said Fusco softly. "That's my baby down there."

He led Silas back into the library, carefully replaced the shutter panel, and returned to his desk, again running one hand nervously through his black locks.

"That's the residence of Mr. James D. Callin, also known as Jimmy C., also known as Dimitriu Calinescu. Big-time Southern Cal businessman, influence peddler, the politician's best friend. Manny tells me that Jenny Pfitzner, the Joan of Arc of the congressional civil-rights crowd and no friend of the Bureau or of your bunch, is on his tail as some kind of war criminal. Well, we don't know about this war-criminal business at all, and that's not our affair. As far as this operation is concerned, it just doesn't feature. What we *are* on to, and we stumbled on it by chance, is that Jimmy is a bad boy. Specifically we've got him cold in the act of bribing public officials, politicians, you name it. Jimmy C. buys anybody he needs. And he seems to enjoy doing it. Everybody, he keeps saying over and over, has his price and all Jimmy has to do is to find out what that price is. If he wants that person bad enough, eventually he pays."

Fusco reached into the breast pocket of his sweat-rimmed white shirt, pulled out a long cigarette from a pack bulging there, and lit up with a euphoric puff Silas recognized and could well appreciate.

"This is one beautiful plant. We've got a hidden TV camera with a telephoto lens covering those two terraces down there, perfect line of sight. With them, we take pictures of all of the good people who come up to eat, drink, and get paid off in Jimmy C.'s lovely place down there. We've borrowed some infrared binoculars and I can sit here and see their happy faces nice and clear even in the middle of the night."

He took a deep breath.

"And the beauty part is that we've got that house bugged. I mean *bugged*. Best penetration I've ever seen, done by the best techs in the Bureau. We piggybacked on an emergency call for an electrician Jimmy made two months ago. We put an audio transmitter, with a battery pack, in the game room, right under a wet bar there. We managed to install *three* mike-and-wire jobs on that big terrace facing us; they're embedded in that concrete wall just where everybody down there stands and looks at the view of LA. The wires on that one go down into that gully there and back up to here, nicely buried in the dirt. Great job, and we did it in two nights when Jimmy was away."

He jumped to his feet with the joy of his success.

". . . But the real take comes from the closed-circuit TV we installed in his library. Turns out that's where most of the intimate chatter and the payoffs happen. Clever as hell; the camera is concealed in an air-conditioning duct facing the desk. That's where we've picked up the best stuff to date: between the bug under his desk and that camera, it's just beautiful video and sound, ten by ten clarity, all of it being recorded. We've got reels of 'Jimmy in the Library' and it's going to get top ratings with the grand jury."

Fusco leaned toward Silas triumphantly.

"How's that for coverage?"

"Absolutely first-class," Silas assured him. Then with piqued curiosity he asked, "What sort of goings-on are you watching? Is it quiet drinking, swinging on chandeliers, running around the pool?"

Fusco reached for a stack of blown-up black-and-white photographs and shuffled quickly through them, choosing a handful, which he passed over to Silas. Each was a clear, if somewhat grainy shot of one or more men, most of them middle-aged, some in swimming trunks, some well dressed in a Southern California manner, men with an assured air, men who possessed power. Silas recognized two of them immediately: a congressman from California and a senator from another western state.

"What sort of goings-on?" Fusco echoed. "Mostly the quiet, almost noiseless sound of envelopes filled with money exchanging hands."

And suddenly Silas was staring at a square-faced figure standing in the background of one of the photographs. Elegantly dressed, white-haired head meticulously combed, eyes calculating and narrowed against the sun, the man had the face of a tiger, thin lips drooping as if with contempt. A scar was faintly visible on the suntanned jaw, like a scrawl from a white-inked pen.

Silas held the glossy print for a long moment and studied the tough, jowled figure minutely. Then he raised it up to Fusco with sudden emotion, and his trembling hand betrayed his excitement.

"And that's . . . ?"

Fusco nodded, after a cursory glance at the photo.

"You know'm, right? That's our pigeon, Jimmy C. himself. And he's not really smiling although it looks it. He had a stroke about two years ago. He limps a little, his mouth droops a little, and he's gotten awfully fat, but he gets around and he's running his businesses and making his payoffs just like before."

Silas sat back in his chair, grasping the photo, seeking to find in it something he had missed. Reluctantly, he lifted his eyes to Fusco, who sat with an air of triumph in his chair.

"What are you getting for results, Angelo? Has it been worth the caper, the expense, the time?"

Fusco tapped the pile of papers in a wooden box. "These are transcripts of what we've been picking up down there. It's all coordinated: dates, times, and who said what to whom; the photographs and video are dated by hour and day. When visitors are due, we site a van, with a commercial-sewage-company logo on it, on the road below Jimmy's house, with two of my guys photographing the cars and license plates as they go in and out of his gate. The phone taps tell us when they're due to visit. The way things are going, another two weeks should be more than plenty. We've been in business up here for five weeks and the evidence from the bugs and photography is almost too much to handle."

"It's legal?" Silas asked with arched eyebrows.

"Legal as hell!" Fusco assured him heatedly. "Look, we started here in LA with an informer, a little INS file clerk who's been on the take for peanuts, from Jimmy. His divorced wife squealed on him, said he was being bribed by some big-time California big shot. It didn't take much. He put the finger on Jimmy. All Jimmy wanted from him was a copy of any new piece of paper added to Jimmy's INS file, or any time the file was looked at, and by whom. We got a court order to tap Jimmy's phone for a week. Right away, strange calls and funny business, leading to the first of our illustrious congressmen. It started to snowball. It finally got to the point where our SAC got to Washington on it and the word came back: go at it with a task force. So they gave me a squad."

He patted his chest with one determined hairy hand.

"This is my first big case of this kind. I'm a field supervisor now. And nuthin' is going to screw it up for me, Ruff. Nuthin'! This one can really make me. My SAC here in LA, the U.S. attorney in LA, and my Director in Washington are all watching it like hawks. We send Washington a daily teletype report. The Attorney General is being briefed and Justice is almost ready to throw the whole thing at a grand jury. I've got my buddies in the Beverly Hills Police Department backstopping us up here and they're not asking questions like: What's that sewage-company van doing on the road every week or so? We've got the goods on Jimmy C.—and on all of the guys he's bribed. He may be a clever, ruthless son of a bitch, Ruff, but Operation Scorpion is going to get him. Bribery of public officials, acceptance of bribes by public officials, obstruction of justice, subornation of witnesses, intimidation, willful evasion of federal and state income taxes . . . we can throw the entire U. S. Criminal Code at him, and at them."

Fusco threw an ebullient right-hand punch at the missing malefactors.

Silas, rubbing the stubble of reddish-gray beard, said, "Angelo, I hope you throw the entire cast of characters in the slammer. But just what has Jimmy Callin been doing out here? We certainly don't hear much of him back East but he seems to be a pretty large tuna out in these waters."

Fusco, leaning at him across the desk, snorted.

"Pretty large tuna? Listen, this guy came to the U.S. from Europe as a political refugee, right? Barely spoke English. Never stops claiming that he fought against the Russians in World War II, that he helped the Americans, helped *you* guys, after the war. By early '49 he'd arrived in Southern Cal. He joins up in a partnership with another Romanian, a strange character who apparently was able to get lots of money out of the old country just after the war. Don't ask me how he did it, but he did. The two of them got involved in real estate here at a time when you could buy up whole orchards and farm country up and down the Valley for what's now peanuts. When the first big housing booms started in the Valley, they doubled, quadrupled earnings on their investments. Then his partner died and Jimmy got into all kinds of things: tract housing, import-export of technology, supermarket plazas, a fast-food chain, a car-wash chain. Eight years ago, Jimmy C. was worth over two million. Today it must be easily ten times that."

He scrabbled about the organized confusion on the desk and

pounced on a paper which he unfolded and held up. On it, in large felt-pen printing, was a list of twelve companies and firms.

"That's where it all comes from. Estimated annual gross income, over a million a year, before all the tax shelters, charitable claims, and other write-offs. And this guy has really sweetened the water all around him. You name a charity, a raffle, a benefit concert, a church bazaar, a Girl Scout troop money-raiser anywhere in a twenty-five-mile radius of here, and nine times out of ten, Jimmy Callin has contributed to it. Ten bucks, a hundred bucks, even a thousand, he comes across. You know, when we got in there to put the quick-fix transmitter in his library, we saw a whole wall covered with scrolls, plaques, testimonials, telling the world what a saint and a benefactor to mankind Jimmy C. is."

Silas said, "Did you see the testimony before Congress three days ago? The little Romanian witness describing how Jimmy, as Dimitriu Calinescu, slaughtered a bunch of Jews at the city slaughterhouse in Bucharest?"

Fusco nodded, alert black eyes narrowed with cynicism.

"Yes, I caught it on an evening TV news show. Imagine, our local saint and benefactor doing anything like that! It's enough to make you doubt your fellow man! And you should hear Jimmy's friends talking about Pfitzner! The language they use!"

He held up with a flourish another square of paper, with approximately twenty names printed on it.

"And here are the cast of characters playing footsie with Jimmy C. Look at them: the first six are congressmen from the state of California. Then these two senators, neither of them from California but who enjoy getting campaign contributions and baksheesh from Jimmy, such as birthday gifts of a little stack of hundred-dollar bills. Here are the state legislators in on the take. These five are from the Valley or Los Angeles County. Lots of money crossing palms. And it's all in cash, cold cash.

"And why? Well, for one thing, it's this war-crimes thing. He's scared blue that Jenny Pfitzner will try to nail him on something that will lead to deportation, and by God, he's determined to head that off even if he has to buy off a majority of the House of Representatives. He even wants to put money up to help somebody defeat Jenny Pfitzner in November. And you know something? At ten thousand bucks a congressman, say (and there were

535 of them when I last looked), buying the votes of half of them
would set him back something like two and a half million bucks.
If they stayed bought, what an investment!"

Fusco laughed at his own cynical arithmetic, a choked high-
pitched sound betraying his deep-felt emotions about the man.

"You should see who he's got for legal assistance! A former INS
examiner who knows that agency inside and out, and a lawyer
who had to resign from Internal Revenue suddenly. Jimmy helped
them start their own firm right here on dear old Wilshire Boulevard. Talk about fighting fire with fire. . . ."

A brief high-pitched squeal pierced the room, and Fusco
opened the top right desk drawer, picked up a walkie-talkie, and
spoke into it.

"Canyon One to Canyon Six, can you read me? Over."

A rush of babbling sounds followed. Fusco listened attentively.

"I read you, Canyon Six, I read you. Now, listen: don't disturb
him, or scare him off. But if he tries to get over Scorpion's main
gate or onto his property, nab him. I'm on my way down for a
look at 'im. I'll be there in"—he glanced at his watch—"about two
minutes. Over and out."

He replaced the transceiver inside the desk drawer, reached for
his holster, strapped it back on in quick familiar movements, patted the revolver under his arm, and shrugged on his jacket.

"Sorry, Ruff, first things first. And you better come along."

With Silas at his heels, Fusco barked at him as he strode rapidly along the corridor, "There's a strange character Wherry spotted as he drove back down the canyon road to town; a man,
crouching off the road just opposite Jimmy's house. He's got no
reason to be up here. Wherry passed the word to our guys in the
van and they've picked him up with the infrared glasses. We're
gonna have a look."

Clearly Fusco left nothing to chance, Silas realized, as he trotted to keep up with him across the ghost-like salon, out the main
door, and down the broad stairway, where Wherry, hunched at
the wheel of the Ford, was waiting.

Fusco, pointing at the rear seat for Silas, flung himself in beside
Wherry. The Ford hurtled from the darkened driveway through
the opened gate and turned downhill on the narrow high-crowned
road.

"This may be nuthin'," Fusco said, flinging his words back to Silas. "But whoever he is, he could louse up our act. If Jimmy or any of his friends or staff spot him, they may all tighten their sphincters. And I don't want *any*thing or *any*body pissing on Angelo Fusco's operation. Come on, Bill, let's have a look at him."

Wherry slowed the car's speed expertly as it rounded hairpin turns, to avoid squealing of tires, as the unlit road twisted and bent its way downward.

"Once we have a look," Fusco muttered to Silas, "I'll have Bill drop you off at a motel where I've got you booked, in Hollywood just north of Santa Monica Boulevard. But first we've got to look over this guy, identify him, and find out why he's up here."

His white teeth gleamed in the dark.

"Maybe he's a Hollywood producer who got lost jogging. All kinds of funny folks out here. But I've got too much invested in Scorpion to risk anything. . . ."

Wherry applied the brakes very gently and extinguished the headlights of the car. Then he cut the engine, and the Ford rolled downhill without a sound, the road barely visible before them.

"See him?" Fusco whispered. "On the left-hand side. He's kneeling beside that tree, looking away from us at the wall of Jimmy's estate across the road."

"I see him," Silas said.

"Look, Bill, roll right up to him and put this flashlight on him. Be ready to flash your credentials and ask him to identify himself."

"Right," said Wherry as Fusco pulled out his revolver and held it in his lap.

The Ford glided up to the figure and stopped. Wherry extended a small pencil-sized flashlight out the window and abruptly shone it on the man's face. Startled eyes stared out of a long, haggard, thin-bearded face crowned with loose strands of dead-white hair. With a choked cry, the man sprang off the road down into a steeply angled hillside thickly carpeted with bushes and underbrush. They briefly heard him crashing his way in the dark, tripping and tearing through the obstacles in his path. Then silence.

"Shit!" Fusco fumed. "We'll never find him down there in the dark. That's open ground down for half a mile, all the way to the bottom."

He turned to Silas sitting behind Wherry.

"Did you get a look at him?"

Silas nodded and closed his eyes.

"Yes, I got a good look."

"Anybody we know?"

"Yes, he's one of your two missing persons. That was Mircea Radescu—or what's left of him."

CHAPTER FIFTEEN

George Wendell, head unnaturally high, swinging his arms as though passing in review, marched past his secretary and nodded his head at her in a slight, virtually imperceptible gesture which told her to take up her shorthand pad and to follow him to his office. She closed the door, plumped herself into her favored chair near the window, flipped open the pad, and looked up, poised to take dictation. She was appalled at his appearance: his handsome old face mottled and haggard, drops of sweat stippling his forehead from hairline to eyebrows, lips paled to a grayish white. Even when he had briefly collapsed at his desk some weeks earlier, she had not seen him in such a state.

"Mr. Wendell!" The words burst from her as she jumped from her chair to reach his side. (He had always been "Mr. Wendell" from the day she had become his secretary; she wanted it that way and so did he.) "What in dear God's name has happened . . . ?"

"Pour me a glass of water," he told her thickly. "I'll be perfectly all right."

He accepted the glass with a half-clenched but steady right hand, but his left hand clutched his chest as if to pull away an intolerable weight lying there. He had shaken two pills from one of the tinted bottles cached away in a bottom drawer of his desk and he swallowed them together with the water in two convulsive swallows.

She had served long enough with him to know how to behave in these situations. Since he did not wave her out of the room, she did not budge and sat immobile as Wendell mopped his wet brow with a soggy handkerchief. He panted audibly as a runner gasps for air after completing his competitive dash. Three minutes passed in silence. Beyond the broad window, the tops of the distant trees danced and swayed to a minstrel wind.

She often had seen Wendell look out at the woods with delight in the occasional moment between appointments. Once, when he realized she was watching him at the doorway of his office, he had grinned like a small boy caught in some mischief and said to her, "You know, Clare, there's freedom out there, pure freedom beyond that fence. Damn, if I could only walk out of this building this minute into those woods and sit under them and smell the outdoors; just for half an hour."

To which she had retorted, "There aren't any bars on the windows or the door of this office, Mr. Wendell. Why don't you get out of here, walk out the front door, and take a stroll?"

He had pointed to his head with a wry grin. "The bars are in here, Clare."

Now his face recovered its composure. Into the firm lips, color crept back. A more uniform floridity tinged his cheeks and his broad forehead no longer gleamed with moisture. Only his long, meticulously combed steel-gray hair was a reminder of the brief seizure: ruffled locks of it had broken ranks from a careful uniformity. He caught her glance, removed a small comb from his desk, ran it through his hair, restoring order, and rubbed his hands with feigned briskness.

"Well, to market, to market . . ."

"Mr. Wendell"—she knew she would be ruled out of order but she had to say it—"won't you please either see Dr. Hocker immediately or go home to rest? You've been under some terrible kind of . . ."

He held up both hands, smiling his thanks at her concern.

"'A touch of the sun, a touch of the sun, the colour-serjeant said.' Thank you, Clare. Everything's under control. Besides, the Doomsday Book here tells me that I've got to see two station chiefs just back from Central America; then there's the promotion list of GS-13s to discuss with Career Management; a courtesy call from the new Deputy Director of DIA; another round with the Comptroller on our personnel ceilings for the next fiscal year . . ."

"Mr. Wendell," she said, squeezing her courage to a point of no return. "You are *not* well. I *know* you're not well, and perhaps it's only Dr. Hocker and I who really know just how . . . how *not* well you are." She tried to control the quaver in her words. "All of those appointments can be either postponed or canceled. . . ."

Grasping both arms of his swivel chair, he pulled himself upright, stood uncertainly for a moment and walked around behind her to his favorite dictation spot, at the window, and fingered the plastic blue-and-white identity badge pinned to his lapel.

"Memorandum for the Record," he began, as if she had said nothing. "Subject: Conference with the DCI, this date.

"Participants: The DCI, the DDCI, the Inspector General, the Deputy Director for Administration, the Director of Personnel, the General Counsel, the Chief of Legislative Liaison, the Director of the Office of Security, the Special Assistant for Public Relations, and yours truly. Present, but not participating in the discussion, was an aide from the office of the DCI, Commander (USN, Retired) Theodore Dominick."

He snorted with the remembrance of the scene.

"Also present were six members of a firing-squad detail from the Third Infantry Regiment at Fort Myer."

He chuckled at the expression on her face as she wrote before realizing his last words were gallows humor.

"Strike that last sentence, Clare."

He stood with his broad back to her, his eyes following the freshening wind outside as it careened and buffeted the compliant wall of green.

"Paragraph one. This emergency meeting, convened by the Director, opened with a statement from him that he was immensely distressed and irritated to learn that a Department of Justice report, originating with the Department's Immigration and Naturalization Service, classified SECRET SENSITIVE, would be appearing in tomorrow's New York *Times* under the by-line of a free-lance journalist named Barney Langer. This story alleges that in 1948 a Romanian displaced person, born Dimitriu Calinescu and now legally changed to James D. Callin of Beverly Hills, California, bribed Mr. Steven Browning, an employee of the Agency, to sponsor his immigration to the United States and to assist him in other, unspecified ways, in exchange for twenty thousand dollars allegedly paid by a cashier's check to Mr. Browning, drawn on a California bank."

He briefly turned to her and said, reflectively, "Ugh, what a bureaucratic sentence, Clare! See if you can break it down into two or three little ones."

"Don't worry about it, Mr. Wendell."

"Very well. Where were we? Oh, yes. New paragraph: The DCI was especially agitated, he said, by two egregious factors: First, that this story, casting grave disrepute on a veteran CIA operations officer, could not have come at a worse time, given the Agency's and his personal strenuous efforts to convince the media, the Congress, and the public that any Agency misdeeds and excesses were long since behind us. He, the DCI, must now face sharp congressional and White House questioning on this matter just when future Agency budgetary and manpower requirements are being considered by the Administration. Second, the DCI understood that the Justice Department report on Browning had already been received some time ago by the Agency but that its contents had been suppressed within the Directorate of Operations, which, if true, was, in his words, 'unconscionable.' "

Clare's mouth had tightened to a compressed slit as she wrote.

"New paragraph, Clare. Speaking in response to the above, I expressed my own dismay that the INS report, which had been classified SECRET SENSITIVE, had been leaked to Mr. Langer and the media, a matter which I felt warranted an immediate strong CIA protest to the Department of Justice and an urgent request that the Department investigate just how this leak occurred. I also expressed deep personal regret that the Justice Department report on Browning had indeed been suppressed within the Agency. I had learned of this fact only this forenoon, minutes before I was informed that the New York *Times* would be printing the story. While I had no role whatsoever in suppressing knowledge of the INS report and indeed knew nothing of the report's existence until this very day, I was prepared to assume full responsibility for it and its consequences, as DDO."

Wendell bit his tongue and paced heavily right and left, head bowed, eyes unseeing.

"Questioned by the Deputy Director for Administration concerning the identity of the person or persons within the Agency responsible for suppressing the INS report on Browning, I identified him as Mr. Silas Ruffing, a veteran CI officer who, as a long-time associate of Browning, saw to it that the report was

buried in a file and was not seen or acted on by anyone else in the
Agency. This act, I agreed with the Director, was 'unconscion-
able.' The Director of Personnel interjected that both officers,
Browning and Ruffing, had appeared on a list of low performers
slated for involuntary separation from the Agency, but that I as
DDO had offered some objection to their dismissals."

Wendell was facing Clare now and his preoccupation with his
dictation was suddenly shot through with a gleam of pure amusement.

"And just how quickly could the Director of Personnel have
learned *that!*" he said to Clare. "Our Mr. Kobler moves with
wingèd feet his errands to perform."

"Our Mr. Kobler!" she echoed, pronouncing each word like a
curse.

"No, give him credit, Clare. I did have my objections and he
passed them on. I do wish occasionally, however, that he didn't
move with such lightning speed."

Wendell paused, absently fingering the metallic outline of his
Phi Beta Kappa key, and then looked down as if surprised to find
it still there, before resuming his restless prowl.

"By the by, is there any word about Ruffing or Browning?" he
asked, tearing his eyes reluctantly from the window.

"No, sir."

"If we get anything from the Bureau, let me know immediately,
wherever I am."

"Yes, Mr. Wendell."

Hands now akimbo, he pursed his lips and squinted his eyes to
recall with verbatim accuracy who had said what to whom.

"The Director, who was well aware that several of those present
had not been Bigot-Listed on the Browning espionage case, made
no reference to that sensitive matter. Instead he asked why low
performers like Browning and Ruffing had not been immediately
declared surplus to the needs of the Service and involuntarily retired. The Director of Personnel, who is as yet unwitting of the
Browning case, pointed out that Agency regulations stipulate that
a staff employee had to be rated in the lowest five percent of his
peer group for two consecutive years before involuntary separation
action could be taken. He mentioned that Browning's previous in-

telligence career had been one marked by significant contributions and commendations.

"I then noted that Ruffing had an equally impressive record and that, at one time, he was considered one of the outstanding counter-intelligence officers in the federal service. I added that I knew both of these officers personally since World War II, that both had in the past performed with unusual distinction, and that I was deeply saddened and disappointed by their current acts and conduct."

He was now standing almost directly before Clare, watching her swift, sure shorthand squiggles almost with fascination. He sighed once and continued.

"The DCI responded that while he appreciated our comments and the previous excellent record of both men, he was guided by the concept that the Agency and its employees had to emulate Caesar's wife and to be above reproach."

His eyes met Clare's as she flipped a page of her shorthand pad.

"You know, Clare, they were all sitting around that conference table like a hanging jury. Half of them knew Steve and Silas very well but they sat on their hands like gutless bureaucrats the world over. I guess that the three of them who were Bigot-Listed and knew the kind of trouble Steve was in, couldn't say a hell of a lot to the boss about that sad-assed pair. But you've got to stand up for your people, good or bad. That's what leadership's all about."

Clare dabbed at her eyes. An unbidden image of Steve Browning swam into her memory: big and bulky, shrewd, quick eyes taking her in as she sat in the front office of the African Division. He had produced a modest cup-shaped malachite ashtray, presented it to her with a flourish, and told her, "I hereby bribe you to announce my arrival to your venerable boss, George Wendell. Tell him that Steve Browning has returned from TDY in Zaïre with the left ears of five senior KGB officers and desires to collect the bounty on them." That was vintage Browning.

"New paragraph, Clare: The Public Relations officer stated that he intended to answer any media inquiries by stating that the Agency has no comment except to say that the story is under intensive internal investigation. The Director then asked the Director of Security to prepare a thorough damage-assessment report for him on the *Times* story and, as he put it, 'all other pertinent aspects.' Appropriate memos will be prepared for the Intelligence Oversight Board, for the Senate and House Select Committees on Intelligence, and for the Department of Justice, given the strong possibility that Browning may face criminal action if current charges against him are confirmed."

He stared for a long moment out the window.

"Ambushed," he finally said softly. "No warning to me, not even a premonition. That pair really let me down. I deserved better from them."

As he trudged to his desk, he passed behind Clare and gave her shoulder a brief squeeze. She reached up to touch his hand but he had already moved on to his desk.

"OK, Clare. That will be one memo. Type it up in two copies: one for me and one for the IG. Hand-carry the IG's copy to him, once I sign off."

He breathed deeply.

"And now, a second memo, for the record. No subject. Stamp this one 'Eyes Alone' and make one copy only, to be kept in my own personal file, together with the copy of the memo I just dictated."

Her eyes were wide with worried curiosity. Eleven years with George Wendell had sharpened her sense of prescience about the tone and timbre of his voice.

"After the meeting of this date, principal points of which have been noted in a separate memo, the DCI asked to have a word with me once the others had departed. In the ensuing tête-à-tête, the DCI again expressed his anger and disappointment with the two officers, Ruffing and Browning. These were the very kind of people, he said, he had been trying to clean out of the Agency and the clandestine services, and yet I as DDO had apparently been trying to keep them on. Without mincing words, he said that this smacked to him of blatant cronyism."

Clare stopped writing and her eyes were widened with disbelief. Wendell nodded at her gently.

"That's what the man said: blatant cronyism."

"Cronyism! You?" she exclaimed, unbelieving. "A man who wouldn't lift a finger to get his own daughter into Agency service?"

He winked at her, a clumsy effort to gloss the hurt in him.

"New paragraph: I told the DCI that he was, in effect, questioning my integrity and my judgment. I had served the Agency for thirty years and the U. S. Government for a total of thirty-five, and that this was the first time in all those years that I had been charged, formally or otherwise, with cronyism. I readily admitted to occasional poor judgment in my career. I am not infallible and I have, like others, made my share of mistakes, but I deeply resented his charge. Compassion, in my view, is not the same thing as cronyism. Both men in this instance had served their government and the Agency with distinction in the past. Both had now clearly committed serious offenses and deserved appropriate punishment. In Browning's case, he may even be tried for espionage and treason. Nevertheless, I wanted to be scrupulously fair to them and to give them the full benefit of any doubt or inconclusive evidence. If that be 'cronyism,' I plead *nolo contendere.*"

Clare continued her methodical shorthand scrawl despite the tears on the lined pages dripping from her eyes and cheeks. One droplet clung to her identity badge hanging from an aluminum chain at her bosom. Wendell, seated at his desk, observed the tear attentively until it dropped out of sight.

"New paragraph," he announced, voice descending to its gloomiest baritone. "I told the DCI that I had long ago decided that should I ever incur the distrust or dissatisfaction of my superiors inside or outside the Agency, I would not hesitate for a moment to step aside. I therefore informed the Director of my intention of retiring within sixty days of this date . . ."

He looked across at her, made a that's-the-way-it-is gesture with both hands, and paused as she covered her face with both hands.

"It couldn't go on forever, Clare." His voice was fatherly, soothing and apologetic at the same time. "I'm fifty-nine, and not in such hot physical shape anyway. I know the boss felt undermined in this Browning affair. And I have no sense of having handled this one that well. So the way to go out is with the bands playing, all the flags flying, and a thousand hypocritical hands reaching out to wish me Godspeed."

Just as she had earlier waited for him to pull himself together, so he now sat quietly until she composed herself. Then he said, "Read me back the last sentence, please."

She snuffled once and read to him: ". . . I therefore informed

the Director of my intention of retiring within sixty days of this
date . . ."

". . . because of a number of factors, not the least of which is a
recent deterioration in my health. In the interim, my Deputy,
now returning from a field trip, can carry on until a new DDO is
selected. The DCI very graciously expressed his regret at my decision and said that perhaps he had overstated himself concerning
cronyism. He asked if I, at the least, would consider postponing
my retirement for several months. On learning that I would not
consider this, he expressed his immediate intention to set a date
when the Distinguished Intelligence Medal could be presented to
me. I thanked him but reminded him that I had already received
the DIM from his predecessor three years ago and did not feel I
had done anything since to deserve another one. I did ask him, as
a personal favor, if my executive secretary, Clare Meehan, could
be reassigned after my departure to a job equal to or better than
her present one. The DCI said he would take this under consid-
eration . . ."

"You should *not* have done that!" Clare's pug-nosed face was
aflame. "Do you honestly think I'd stay? Look, Mr. Wendell, I
have twenty-six years of government service. For the last twelve
years of them, I've had the best boss of anyone in this building.
Do you think I'm going to sit in some empty office, after you
leave, with make-work chores, just because the Director feels sorry
for me? The day you walk out that door for the last time, I do
too."

"Clare, I . . ."

Now, for once, she waved him off without waiting to hear him
out.

"Please don't worry. Once I retire, I've got enough things to do
to last me a lifetime. Just doing charity work in the Archdiocese is
a full-time job. And I'll be able to tell everybody exactly what I
do, for a change. Not like now. No, Mr. Wendell, when you
leave, *I* leave."

George Wendell rose once more from his chair and did something he had never done in their years together: he embraced her
short stubby figure and held her close to him for a long minute as
her silent tears plashed unheeding on his jacket. Behind her, he

watched the lights of incoming calls flash soundlessly on his telephone console.

"See to it," he said to her, "that my eminent Special Assistant,
Mr. Kobler, gets both memos. Need-to-know. I'm certain that
he'll get a real charge out of it, one way or another. And just
where is that eventual DDO?"

"He's down at the CI staff," Clare said. "He's hand-carrying
your questions for Mr. McClure to ask the KGB defector from
Tokyo this afternoon. The defector is now at a holding area near
Middleburg. Don said to tell you that there's still a lot of hot stuff
being revealed by the KGB man."

Wendell nodded.

"Hot stuff, indeed. Well, I'm delighted there's *some* good news
around here."

He turned to his "in" box with a sigh. There would be another
eight weeks or so of this, another forty-odd working days, each
carefully divided into little fudge squares of appointments and
things to do. And then it would all cease. He could sit, think,
sleep, wake, walk, without giving a care to minutes or days. A
slight chill, like a premonition of fever, rippled through his body:
he hated the idea that it all had to end.

CHAPTER SIXTEEN

Silas Ruffing walked along the north sidewalk of Sunset
Boulevard, alternatingly peering at the cloud-heavy sky
and the ostentatious splendor of the closely packed
mansions and their incredibly manicured lawns. He
had stepped out of the taxicab two blocks before his destination
to scout this completely unfamiliar terrain. Casing a strange meeting spot was instinctive with him even if the rendezvous point
had been selected by FBI Special Agent Fusco, who presumably
knew what he was doing.

The sickly salmon-and-green eminence of the Beverly Hills
Hotel reared before him and he trudged up the motor ramp leading to its main entrance, shaking his head in disbelief at the auto-
mobiles parked along it: four Rolls-Royces, two Mercedes 450s,
and a stretched-out Cadillac long enough to hold the full passenger complement of a school bus. He self-consciously pulled his
jacket straight and ran his hand across his freshly shaven chin. At
the entrance he paused to watch taxi doors being flung open by
the doorman (the man looked like an unemployed airlines pilot,
with stripes on his sleeve and a 2000-hours angle to his hat) with a
theatrical flourish, and he grinned sympathetically at the man's
sour frown of disappointment when the tokens of appreciation
from departing guests were deemed inadequate. Silas glanced once
more up at the clouds, now menacingly low and heavy-bellied as
they trundled northeast. Whatever might happen to him this day,
rain appeared to be included, a phenomenon as rare for Beverly
Hills as a long marriage.

He moved with seeming casualness through the hotel's carpeted
lobby, examining the goods in the windows of the promenade
boutiques as if their impossible prices were actually within his

reach. Five minutes before the hour, he sauntered into the Polo
Lounge, its pink-tableclothed expanse virtually deserted save for a
couple in identical blue jeans and velour shirts who alternated between sipping coffee and nibbling each other's lips. The man, he
noted, was fully as old as himself, the remains of his hairline
smoothed sleekly back to his neck, and an obligatory pendant of
gold dangled from his throat as he embraced a slim young brunette with a conventionally pretty face and breasts that strained
through her thin shirt.

It would be so pleasant, he thought, to have nothing better to
do on a midmorning in September than to sit with a sensual
young woman in a lounge of a Beverly Hills hotel, working with
deliberateness at the foreplay requisite to bring her to some soft
bed upstairs. He thought with a brief wave of *tristesse* of Betty
Ann, the divorcée, who had made his weekends so worthwhile
until his boozing had broken her crockery and her patience.

He realized to his surprise, as he cupped his hands around the
mug of coffee before him, that he had not had a single drink since
he had left Washington, D.C., two days before. He was about to
congratulate himself when Special Agent Angelo Fusco entered
the room. He brushed aside the broad-smiled greeting of the
woman hostess and walked over to Silas' table with the strut of an
angry rooster.

"Good morning." Silas waved to a chair on his left. "What do
you want for what appears to be a fevered spirit?"

Fusco, again wearing a jacket to conceal his holstered weapon,
pulled the chair out, and plumped down in it with an unmistakable gesture: he was hopping mad.

"I never dreamed," he said, struggling to keep his voice under
control, "that you Agency guys might be bad news to me, but son
of a bitch, you really are!"

He could not bring himself to say more. From a side pocket of
his jacket, he pulled a tightly rolled front-page section of a New
York *Times*, opened it, and laid it before Silas, covering coffee
mug and saucer. Reaching under the paper, Silas retrieved his
coffee, and with an inquiring glance at Fusco, read the front-page
article in silence, turning to the inside page to finish it, after
which he carefully refolded it and pushed it back to Fusco. The

FBI man sat momentarily like a stone image. Only the glittering hostility in his eyes betrayed his volcanic anger.

"What's to say, Angelo?" Silas said, taking another sip of his coffee and now beginning to develop an enormous interest in ordering a double vodka, perhaps two, even at this early hour.

"What's to say?" Fusco echoed, incredulity straining his words. "Do you know what this story is doing to Scorpion? In the few hours since this New York Times story appeared, all our audio and wire taps are picking up telephone calls zipping in and out of Jimmy C.'s house like it was some kind of a numbers joint. You should see what we're picking up on the closed-circuit TV in his library: like a command post under enemy attack. Lawyers and his house goons running all over the place. And it's frightened all the mice away from the cheese."

"Look, Angelo." Silas spoke with a practiced assurance that concealed his inner dismay that the Justice Department memo was now in the public domain. "You're a big boy. You've just been handed a grenade with the pin pulled. I can only tell you I'm sorry as hell about it. And I'll bet that a lot of people in high places in Washington are, as well."

"Easy for you to say," Fusco retorted, lighting and taking a deep drag on a cigarette. "Jesus, why didn't somebody warn me that Browning was on the take for twenty grand from Jimmy C.?"

He leaned wearily back in his chair and his mobile lips curled in disgust.

"No wonder Manny Mulcahy was so edgy about Browning when he phoned me. Some pal you've got there, Ruff. A crooked federal officer, a guy the Soviets apparently have got in their pocket. God, he's up for everything except incest."

Silas studied the calm black surface of coffee in his cup before looking up at Fusco from under shaggy brows.

"What do you want me to do, Angelo?" He rapped out his words with unconcealed bitterness. "I'm out here to help you with your investigation of Steve. You've lost him. So we're all out here having a fun time, aren't we? You, me, Steve, Radescu, and even Jimmy C. and his crowd. And now some son of a bitch in Washington has broken security and has slipped a highly classified Justice memo on Steve to the New York Times. Look, you can sit here and beat on my back all you want. If it makes you feel better, fine."

Thinking of Wendell and Matt McClure and what was probably transpiring at Headquarters made Silas more ravenous for a strong belt of vodka. He abstractedly lifted the cup of coffee to his lips. It was already cool.

Fusco pointed a finger of sudden realization across the table at him.

"You little bastard! I'll bet you knew all about this twenty-thousand bribe before you even came out here, didn't you?"

Silas nodded, eyes cast down.

"Right, Angelo, I did."

"Then why in hell didn't your people tie a can to Browning's tail a long time ago?"

Silas leaned toward Fusco with a bitter smile and answered evenly, "Because, until this leaked story hit the papers, my Agency didn't know about the bribe either. And you know why not? Because I, Silas Ruffing, the grand old man of the Counter-intelligence Staff, withheld the Justice report from my own superiors. I covered up for him. If you think Steve is in trouble, guess who else's ass is in a sling."

Fusco shook his head unbelievingly.

"You crazy little son of a bitch. You've screwed this up as thoroughly as if you were a Cub Scout. A guy with your track record, your reputation . . ."

"Stuff it, Angelo. Yeh, I screwed it up. That's not the first time but it's quite probably the last."

Fusco absorbed the admission in silence. He took in the slight figure, puffed face, pale defeated eyes, and the straggling, once auburn hair and mustache. He cleared his throat to screen his discomfort.

"Well, that at least explains the urgent TWX I just got this morning. It's a relay message from your Agency for you through us. I'll read it to you."

From his wallet he extracted a half sheet of paper.

" 'Attention Ruffing. I request that you return to Headquarters immediately. Report directly to me or to the Director of Security within twenty-four hours.' It's signed 'Wendell, DDO.' "

Ruffing nodded, sipped his cold coffee, and said, "Thanks, Angelo."

"That's all? 'Thanks, Angelo'? What do you want me to reply?" Silas hoped that his anguish was not too apparent.

"Just send word that Ruffing will get in touch with Wendell directly."

Fusco looked at the empty expanse of the elegant coffee room and then at Silas' hunched figure opposite him. When he spoke, his voice was hoarse with an unaccustomed if grudging sympathy.

"They say that sometimes we stay on too long in this business. That's why Bureau people like to get out early when they can; leave the rat race before it gets to them. Twenty years is usually plenty. Too damned much wear and tear. How many years you got in, Ruff?"

"Thirty-four."

"Thirty-four! My God, that's incredible. Maybe that's what's happened, Ruff. You should have quit when you were still ahead."

Ruffing's contorted expression briefly relaxed and he essayed a brief grin, patting Fusco on the sleeve with appreciation.

"You're right, Angelo. In my case, you're dead right. But in Steve's case . . ." He shook his head with bitterness. "In Steve's case, we should have weeded him out at the very beginning, back in 1948. For pure gall, a willingness to gamble, a sense of operational hunches that paid off, he really had it. He might have made a million dollars betting on horses. Or commodity futures. He was quick and he was lucky and he loved the business. But in here"— he tapped his left breast—"he had it all wrong."

He peered into his empty cup of coffee.

"Remember the old story about the baseball player who could never steal second base because while his heart was filled with larceny, his feet were honest? With Steve, no matter how hard he tried, that larceny was in his heart. A great guy in many ways, Angelo, but not for our business. Too many wiggles in what's got to be a straight line."

His pale eyes glinted like razors.

"I can tell you, Angelo, it's worse than even you might imagine. And the tragedy is that *he* knows how bad it is."

Fusco's glance flickered away to examine the unsmiling face of the waitress who arrived with his coffee, moved to the booth across the room where the goat-eyed male had insinuated his right hand around the waist and under the tight shirt of his female companion. The slow rotation of his palm on her firm breast had now aroused her to the point of slow writhing desire. Ruffing followed his glance. It was a scene of complete incongruity: their foreplay and his hindsight.

"If we stick around for another ten minutes, he's going to screw her right there in the booth," Fusco said, his voice coarse with disgust. "Christ, you wouldn't believe the things that go on in public in this town."

He drained his coffee, reached in his inside jacket pocket, extracted three one-dollar bills, and dropped them on the table.

"Coffee's on me, Ruff," he said. "Gotta go. I'm in a sweat to learn what Jimmy C. is going to do now. He's nervous as a cat, from all the pacing up and down his terraces and the phone calls he's making."

Silas said, studying the blunt tough face, "He's got more right to be worried than he knows."

"What do you mean by that, Ruff?"

Ruffing said, hands still cupped around his empty coffee mug, "Just remember that Mike Radescu is out there somewhere. Your people haven't spotted him in the area since last evening, but I'm certain as hell that he's here to kill your friend, Jimmy C.—if he can get close enough to do it."

"If Jimmy stays where he is, he's all right," Fusco assured him. "His house is built like a fort. And between Jimmy's household artillery and my own Scorpion squad, I don't think Radescu is going to get even close. I've given my men his description and told them to pick him up immediately and hold him for questioning if they spot him anywhere in LA. Don't worry about him."

"All right. How about Steve?"

Fusco's swarthy face mirrored his concern.

"OK, I'm worrying about him. Got any ideas?"

"No, except for this: Steve Browning, even pushing sixty and over the hill for years now, is still about twice as inventive and street-smart as most of our case officers in their prime. You'd better find him quick or . . . or he may turn up on the same Moscow park bench with Kim Philby."

Fusco stared at the sinuous amatory wrigglings across the room with fierce hostility for a moment before he spoke.

"Why would a guy trying to leave the country take a gun along with him?"

Silas could not conceal his surprise.

"Steve? A gun? You're putting me on, Angelo. Steve hates the damned things. He used to tell me that he had enough of guns in World War II to last him a lifetime."

"Well, he's got one. A nine-millimeter automatic, I'm told. The crazy bastard actually smuggled it right through the passenger control counter at Dulles in Washington. He distracted the woman monitoring the carry-on stuff for a moment. But one of our woman agents assigned to the Washington office who was on his tail got a look at the screen as his bag went through. Unmistakably an automatic."

"You could have arrested him right then and there."

Fusco's bony features registered a knowing grimace.

"Come on, Ruff—that would have blown the caper. He's the rabbit. We wanted him to lead us to his West Coast contacts. But now he's running around out here with that heater in his possession. You don't think an old spook like Steve is going to shoot his way out of the country, do you?"

He crushed his cigarette in an ashtray with the gesture of a climber who has decided to have a go at the north face of the Eiger.

"Look, Ruff, when are you leaving for Washington?"

"As soon as I can book a seat on a flight. Probably on a red-eye tonight. Why?"

Fusco beckoned to him.

"I'll have one of my people arrange that. Why don't you come up to the Place and hang around for the rest of the day up there?"

The two men exchanged glances.

"You're telling me that that's where the honey is, Angelo?"

"I'm telling you that there are a couple of pissed-off bees buzzing around. Neither of them has gone near the Soviet Consulate people in Frisco or their little mother's helpers here. So you come up with me and house-sit. It's worth the price of admission to watch the closed-circuit TV action in Jimmy's library anyway. Whaddyasay?"

"Lead on, Mr. Scorpion."

CHAPTER SEVENTEEN

The defector, Matt McClure decided, was a dead ringer for one of his neighbors long ago in a working-class district of Bethlehem, Pennsylvania, a Slavic steelworker who used to drink bottle after bottle of beer on Saturday nights at the Ukrainian Club. Unlike the steelworker, whose lips were usually creased in a cherubic grin, however, the man sitting opposite him had what the Soviets might call a "Chekist face": stern, seamed, granite-textured cheeks framing an inquisitive beak of a nose. Above the square tough jaw, shrewd and calculating peasant eyes took in every movement, every nuance around him. Fleshy ears flanked a head of long white-blond wavy hair that somehow looked like a wig. And when the Russian opened his mouth, two gold-capped eyeteeth glittered cheerlessly at his interlocutor. A rock-hard countenance, one which engendered respect if not fear. He must have been a terrifying interrogator, Matt thought.

Yet, incongruous as a Masai warrior at a Texas cookout, here the Russian sat in a country house in rural Virginia, clad in beige American slacks, a blue Lacoste sports shirt, sandals, holding his long *papiross* between thumb and forefinger, Russian style, a man who had deliberately chosen to destroy his career and abandon his life among his own kind, forever. Matt had handled, in his career, over a dozen such defectors and had developed a profound sympathy with those who had stepped, as it were, out of a well-lighted and cozy home into permanent darkness. Such a decision took an enormous act of will, no matter what the motive.

A small glass, half filled, perched on an end table at the defector's elbow, and judging from the depleted contents of the bottle of Stolichnaya next to it, the glass was not filled with water. Matt had been warned of heavy drinking by the defector but the man apparently had an enormous capacity. Certainly the dark, almost opaque eyes were not the slightest glazed, nor his alertness noticeably affected. Most Soviet defectors drank heavily, Matt knew. Whether it was a continuation of their previous habits or because of the traumatic nature of their new situation had never been analyzed as far as he knew. This one was consuming a bottle a day, according to his keepers, in a steady sip-sip-sip that seemed to fuel his ability to cope with his new status.

The defector in turn studied Matt with cool expert eyes as if he, the Russian, were in charge here. But his fleshy body hulked in the chintz-covered chair in an attitude of resignation. He knew full well that he was in for yet another round of questions in the endless series of interrogations these Americans had arranged, wave after wave, since he had, so to speak, pulled the chain.

Peter Danoff, one of the better middle-level Soviet Division case officers, fidgeted self-consciously in his chair at one side facing them both. It was 4 P.M. and this session with Matt McClure, Chief of the Agency's Counter-intelligence Staff, was the last scheduled Q&A of the day. Peter looked expectantly and deferentially at Matt: the delicate case of Steve Browning and Dimitriu Calinescu was to be Topic A.

Matt peered around the sunny interior of this informal old living room with its rustic furniture, hooked rugs, worn leather chairs and sofa, and dark oak floor. The gentle stillness of the place appealed to him, although the open yard beyond the windows reminded him that it had been carefully selected for its present purpose. Because Rogov had arrived here by helicopter at dusk, he was unaware that this comfortable old house sat safely in a corner of a rambling U.S. military facility and that beyond the far clump of trees ran a fifteen-foot-high chain-steel perimeter fence, patrolled by MP sedans night and day. Rogov was also unaware that a half-dozen security officers were guarding him around the clock outside the house, using the nearby garage as their dormitory and communications post.

Peter, clad in a much-rumpled wash-and-wear suit, tie loosened for comfort, said to Matt, "Mr. Rogov understands English quite well and is actually getting pretty good at it, but he's shy about speaking. He's really been swatting the English-language tapes every day. But for these sessions, he usually speaks in Russian to make sure he's not being misunderstood."

Matt's long, bony, almost ascetic face bore a deliberate expression of non-urgency and calm. He actually understood more Russian than Rogov did English but, as was his habit, he did not reveal this ability either to Peter or to Rogov. It was always interesting and sometimes essential to hear what others were saying to each other in that language, unaware that he could follow.

Peter, swinging to face Rogov, spoke in a clear slow Russian.

"Vladimir Sergeyevich, this gentleman is an important official of our Counter-intelligence Staff whom we shall call Mr. Brown."

Rogov, almost sniffing at Matt, nodded and bowed his head slightly in greeting. He understood the reasons why he would not hear the true names or exact ranks or jobs of any of his American interrogators. There *was*, after all, a phenomenon of *redefection*, of returning where you came from. No one took any chances.

Following Matt's eyes as he took in the handsome old room, Rogov smiled thinly and said in a heavily accented but understandable English, "Is good safe house, no? Very . . . uh . . . capitalist, very big." He held out expansive arms. "*Very* big bedroom. Biggest bedroom for me in my life. And food is . . . is"—he smiled broadly—"*ochin khorosho*, very good."

Matt nodded and smiled mechanically at the Russian.

"Happy to hear that you like this place."

"Volodya told me earlier," the young officer said, with a deferential nod to the powerfully built Russian, "that it reminds him of a deluxe dacha, the kind that the Politburo bosses have outside Moscow and in the Crimea. He won't believe me when I tell him that ordinary Americans own places much better than this one, and that for us it's just another comfortable old house with leaky plumbing and poor insulation."

"Petya makes big American propaganda," the Russian said with a basso chuckle. "He will make good CIA officer." He clearly felt comfortable with his younger, eager-faced American watchdog.

He pointed to the vodka bottle in an unmistakable gesture of hospitality, but Matt smilingly refused, pointing to his stomach in a pantomime signifying medical problems. With a shrug, the defector stubbed out his cigarette, picked up the glass in a great paw of a hand, and drank back half its contents. A double shot at least, Matt estimated with grudging admiration.

"Colonel Rogov," Matt began, speaking slowly and distinctly, holding the Russian's eyes with his own. "I know that some of the questions I will ask you have been asked before, but you will understand that I am deeply concerned here with the internal security of our own Agency. You understand my English, is that correct?"

Rogov nodded and smiled shrewdly at Matt.

"*Konyechno*, of course," he answered. "If you speak slowly English, I understand everything." He threw a wry grin at the young American beside him and held up one self-deprecatory hand. "Well, *almost* everything."

He lifted the glass once again to his lips, slurped the potent liquid, and pursed his fleshy lips. He was waiting.

In his long career, Matt had personally handled over a dozen defectors of varying rank and importance: Soviets, East Germans from the Ministerium für Sicherheit, Polish UB officers, and even a Cuban DGI man who came bounding out of Angola. This one, KGB Colonel Vladimir Sergeyevich Rogov, was not only the highest-ranking defector he had ever encountered but certainly one of the most assured and poised.

And his bona fides had been thoroughly established even to those surviving psychotics on the CI Staff who were convinced that *every* KGB defector was really dispatched by Moscow to spread misinformation and confusion in the West. No KGB plant would have identified the names and tasks of four separate penetrations of the U. S. Embassy in Tokyo and the sprawling U.S. military offices and installations in Japan. (Three of them were previously unsuspected, including a Japanese whore who was easily extracting information from a trio of teen-aged Marine security guards. Also revealed by Rogov as a KGB agent was a veteran Japanese employee of the Embassy finance office, and a highly trusted analyst with the Economics Section, also Japanese.)

No phony defector would have also identified two KGB espionage networks active in Southeast Asian countries. These had already been pounced upon and rolled up by the services in those nations. And finally, the KGB would hardly have sent a ringer to the Americans who was giving verifiable biographical information on dozens of his former KGB colleagues.

Rogov had taken not one, but two grueling polygraph tests. The results were unequivocal each time: no deception involved. He was, to use a tired Security Office cliché, the real Mikoyan.

Unquestionably Rogov had already seriously harmed his old service and torn as much of its fabric of subversion and penetrations as he knew. His motives, while initially unbelievable, came also to be accepted as genuine. He had defected purely for personal, family reasons, for revenge. Ideology played no role in it at all. An enormous bitterness, a growing rage at the unfairness with which he felt he had been treated: these were the motors which had driven him to his irrevocable act.

All this Matt McClure knew and had pondered on the long drive out to question this defector. It was a banal story of an aging KGB career officer increasingly in the doghouse as a result of the activities of his only child, who had grown up to become an open dissident. When the son was sentenced to three years for "hooliganism," a catchall for a public protest in which he had participated at a trial of yet another opponent of the system, Rogov's career was doomed.

There was more, the final straw. Rogov, stationed in Tokyo, had been refused permission by his *Rezident* to return to Moscow to be with his dying wife.

As Tokyo Station had elatedly announced, Rogov had brought with him "a lot of goodies." He knew he had to pay his way.

"Tell me," Matt said, speaking directly to Rogov, "what do you know of Dimitriu Calinescu, in this country known as James Callin, a former Romanian Iron Guard official, now living in California?"

The Russian lit a fresh *papiross* and scratched his hairy throat for a moment. Wrinkling his forehead, he looked away from Matt and commenced to speak in a mellifluous Russian, stopping with each two or three sentences to give Peter time to translate. Matt courteously waited for the unnecessary translation.

"Strange that you people should ask me about this so frequently." Peter parroted Rogov's exact tone. "Strange because Calinescu was the first agent I handled after I was taken into the NKVD in wartime, in 1944, selected from my Guards unit."

Matt looked at him questioningly. This was simply too much coincidence. But Rogov nodded repeatedly, his full lips pulled down in ironic humor at the corners.

"It's true. Mind you, I didn't recruit him. Someone had done that long before the Great Fatherland War began. As early as 1937 he was our penetration of the Iron Guard movement in Bucharest. What you probably don't know is that Calinescu's father had been a pioneer Romanian Communist from the time of the Bolshevik Revolution. The father, a socialist labor agitator, was shot by Romanian police during a violent strike in Craiova in 1934. The son was then taken to the Soviet Union by other Romanian comrades fleeing the Romanian authorities and was placed in a Soviet state school for some years. When he was of university age, Calinescu was sent back by the NKVD to his relatives in Bucharest, with the mission of joining the Iron Guard and keeping us informed about them."

Rogov's lips curled with contempt at the memory.

"We didn't encourage him to get so completely involved with the Iron Guard, that fascist rabble who wore the green shirts. That was *his* idea. But once he did so, our operatives had an excellent window into that wretched band of cutthroats."

He puffed his *papiross* reflectively.

"Calinescu was always quite undisciplined, especially in his early years. Didn't like to follow our orders at first. And as an Iron Guardist, he did some terrible things to the Jews."

He shook his head.

"Had I been his control at that time, I would have found some way to have him shot. Not for what he did but because he was disobedient. As it was, one of our major concerns was to track the activities of the crazy leaders of that movement, Horia Sima and the others. And, give him credit, Calinescu gave us excellent information up until the Iron Guard was crushed. He and Sima and that crowd were sent off as prisoners from Romania to Germany for temporary internment, under the friendly eyes of Heinrich Himmler."

That was the recurring thing about the intelligence business, Matt thought. Truth outran fiction. Coincidence overleaped convoluted plots.

"We lost track of him for about three years, in Germany. But

when he got out of the German internment camp, late in 1943, I
think it was, he came back into our hands. Our illegal network inside German-occupied Romania picked up contact with him. He
was ordered by us to join the Romanian Army fighting with the
Nazis in the Odessa area against our Red Army, and to report on
their tactical military situation. This he did, very well, and being
the enterprising type he was, he rose to the rank of, I believe,
major or lieutenant colonel in the Romanian Army. But when our
armies overran Romania and took up direct contact with him in
Bucharest (he ostensibly a prisoner of war), he became very . . .
very undisciplined. Wanted to receive all sorts of benefits and unusual privileges."

The glittering gold teeth came mirthlessly into view.

"It was there in Bucharest in late 1944 that I took over the handling of him, after we had liberated the country from the fascists.
I had heard about his arrogant ways. So, in my first session with
him, I had to show him who was boss. I hit him as hard as I could
with my pistol butt. Opened up his face from lip to the point of
his chin. He bled like a wounded pig."

Matt peered down the list of questions prepared by Wendell,
and checked off one which read: "Ask him if he knows where
Calinescu got the scar on his chin."

Rogov's eyes seemed turned in on themselves. Wispy smoke
from the *papiross* in his hand curled upward unnoticed.

"He was a *very* good lad after that, at least under my control.
And it was in Bucharest in 1944 that he suggested a long-range
plan in which he would emigrate to the United States, with our
help, as a normal displaced person. Not only that, but he would
go there as someone recommended by the American intelligence
people . . ."

He made a near-contemptuous gesture to Matt with his *papiross*.

". . . By *you* people. His bona fides would therefore be ir-
reproachable and would more than compensate for his Iron
Guard past."

Matt shook his head involuntarily. It was hard to swallow, but
the Soviets had taken them. And not for the first time. Wendell
would *not* be pleased.

"By the time the Center in Moscow had initially received this

plan, the war was almost over. The Center had become most en-
thusiastic about sending reliable new collaborators to the land of
the Main Enemy: the United States. So Calinescu and I drew up
the scenario, the cover legend, how the trap would be baited.
Calinescu was ideal for the part. He was tough, ambitious—and
he knew how to exploit venality. After all, it takes a thief to know
another."

Rogov's somber face for a moment lit up with a smile of accom-
plishment.

"So," Matt said after a pause, "Calinescu was set up as a future
Illegal."

"No! *Nyet!*" Rogov shouted. "*Only* Soviet citizens, trustworthy
Russians trained by the Organs, are Illegals. We would *never* trust
a Romanian to be an Illegal. Even the son of a martyred Communist comrade. Never!"

He calmed quickly, and held up a forefinger like a lecturer
explaining an obscure point to a class.

"But he *could* be useful, very useful. A man who could meet
many influential people, do many useful chores for us."

"A support agent," Matt said. "That's our term."

Rogov nodded vigorously.

"*Da*, a support agent."

He looked longingly at the empty vodka glass but did not reach
for the bottle to refill it. Instead, he scratched his hairy throat
again and shifted his body restlessly.

"And it worked," he went on. "All the way through, to this very
day. The trap was sprung in Vienna, with the approach to your
man . . . Browning. Those were good informations Calinescu
gave to Browning in Vienna, the order-of-battle information on
the Soviet armies. But you must know by now that the information we gave you in them was always about three to six months
out of date. The reports could do us no real harm—unless the
Americans were preparing to attack the Red Army in Europe.
And we knew beyond a doubt that the Americans would not attack. By 1947 you were far too weak and you had no stomach to
fight anyone."

Rogov, briefly agitated, subsided and looked at Matt with a
weary shake of the head. "And, if anything, you are even weaker

today. *Then*, at least, you had the exclusivity of the Bomb. Now . . ."

Matt interrupted briskly. "We can discuss that point another time, Mr. Rogov."

He cocked his head in a calculating gesture. What came next was a fishing expedition. He had to find out what Rogov knew and did not know before he could ask him more about Browning. That was what the CI game was all about: giving the minimum, taking the maximum, and fitting lots of little pieces together.

Rogov's hard unblinking glance caught his. Steel on steel.

"The bribe to Browning: that's what you want to ask next?" Danoff translated, using the same inflection of near-disdain with which Rogov flung the words at him.

Matt said carefully, "Tell me what you know of it."

Rogov again turned to the Stolichnaya with a longing glance and then, with a wry smile, said, *"Dienst ist Dienst, Schnapps ist Schnapps.* I'll drink later."

He licked his lips as if that would refresh his memory.

"By the time Browning took the bribe, and that must have been 1948, Calinescu was no longer my agent to run. I was transferred from Austria late in 1947 back to the Center in Moscow. Calinescu had been sent to cool off a bit in Italy with excellent false papers and I passed him to the control of the *Rezidentura* in Rome. But the bribe had always been in our plan. Browning had shown us in little ways that he was venal, he could perhaps be bought. He had accepted some gifts from Calinescu in Vienna without much reluctance. Some years later when I met the colleague who took over Calinescu in Rome, he told me that Browning had been offered twenty thousand dollars to sign an affidavit for Calinescu's immigration application. We found out Browning was serving in Greece and we sent Calinescu to Athens. He literally stationed himself near the entrance of the American Embassy there and within two days had spotted Browning entering the building. It was easy for him to take up the contact, as if by accident, to convince Browning he had become very wealthy, and that he needed Browning's personal affidavit. Browning did not see the trap we had sprung for him. He must have thought Calinescu an utter fool for giving that much money for a perfectly bona fide testimonial. After all, he wrote that Calinescu had helped the

Americans. That was true. Our agent reported that Browning was enraptured. He apparently needed the money badly."

A silence descended on the room. Danoff looked embarrassedly away from the two men. This airing of soiled linen, he sensed, was somehow repugnant to both men. Rogov's heavy lids drooped over his eyes, waiting for Matt to speak.

"And so you had Browning. What did you get out of him?" Matt rapped at him, his words ruffling the calm air of the room.

Rogov lit a new *papiross* from the burning stub of the earlier one. Matt recalled Danoff's words to him earlier when they had chatted alone at the entrance of the house: Rogov seemed to live on cigarettes, vodka, and a burning desire to tell all he could about the system that had failed him.

"It was true that we had accurately assessed, through Calinescu, this weakness of Browning's. He *was* very vulnerable. But . . ."

The mirthless smile appeared briefly.

". . . But we were wrong on just how difficult Browning would be. My understanding is that he was approached by us on three separate occasions, in three different parts of the world. And on all three occasions he parried us. Oh, he pretended to collaborate with us on the first two occasions, but the material he passed to us was clearly worthless and he wriggled out of our grasp, once by being declared persona non grata. He was playing games with us. A desperate game for him. But like small trapped animals do, he fought back in every way he knew. He must have known it was a losing battle. The KGB is not famed for its mercy or humanity."

Gray smoke trickled out of his nose and mouth and he stared beyond Matt for a moment with a ferocity that was startling.

"KGB isn't merciful even to its own," he said. "That's why I sit before you this moment."

Matt, fighting to conceal the growing excitement in him, leaned to Rogov and asked, "Are you telling me, Mr. Rogov, that Browning did not become your agent? He did not pass you information or documents of value?"

Rogov nodded slowly twice, heavy face a mask.

"That's what I was told by Rudenko of the North American Directorate, about two years ago. They determined that he was not recruitable, that he had played games with them and possibly had alerted your service to his situation. This caused considerable anger at the Center. And *I* was held responsible. Calinescu's assessment was wrong, but *I* was blamed."

His mouth clamped tight with remembered bitterness.

"The determination was made by Andropov himself that Browning should be exposed and his career destroyed."

He reached over to Danoff, and patted him on the arm in an avuncular manner.

"Remember *that*, Petr Ivanovich, in your career: when you use blackmail, you must *not* bluff. It is an ultimate weapon and you must be prepared to use it."

He turned to Matt.

"And so the proof of the bribe of Browning by Calinescu was propelled into the hands of the proper American authorities, to the best of my understanding."

His eyes kindled with interest.

"And now, Gospodin Brown, *you* tell *me*: was this done? You must have the information on the bribe. What have you done with him? This for me is simply a matter of intense *personal* curiosity. In a similar situation, KGB would shoot such an officer, without hesitation. Did you kick him out?"

Matt shook his head. "No, Mr. Rogov, we didn't kick him out. But I must be absolutely sure of all this, and I ask you to answer me carefully once again: Did he at any time meaningfully collaborate with you? Did he ever give you information of any value to your service at any time?"

"No," Rogov answered in English. "*Nichevo*. Nothing of value. Was Browning venal? Yes. But a traitor, like Philby or Blake or the German Felfe? No."

"One final question in this matter, Mr. Rogov," Matt said, "and I'm finished. What happened to the Romanian agent whom Browning was using in Vienna as his cut-out to Calinescu? A man by the name of Mircea Radescu. He disappeared in the Soviet Zone of Austria while making clandestine contact with Calinescu, and we've never heard from him again."

"Ah, the Romanian!" Rogov exclaimed, peering up at the ceiling with the air of a man who is trying to remember the maiden name of an old boyhood flame. "Let me see . . . ah, yes, I recall. It was a genuine case of bad luck for that agent of Browning's . . ."

". . . Radescu."

"Yes, Radescu. We were on to him like cats watching a mouse, you know, from the outset. After all, Calinescu had put out the bait. The big mouse—Browning—bit at it, and the little mouse—Radescu—came to collect the cheese. Our surveillance teams had him under constant observation the moment he arrived for his meetings with Calinescu in our zone of Austria."

Rogov could not restrain his satisfaction.

"It was a classic operation. It was *I* who wrote out the receipts for the ten thousand dollars which Radescu brought on each occasion, you know, the ones with Calinescu's signature on them." He closed his eyes for a moment, savoring the success of the operation of long ago, and as he did so, Matt shot a veiled inquiring glance at Danoff, who understood and nodded: the entire interview was being covertly taped.

"Radescu was arrested by your people on that final occasion," Matt prompted him. "Why didn't you do so earlier?"

Rogov shot him a look of contempt.

"We had to build up the bona fides of Calinescu," he retorted. "So of course Radescu made his 'clandestine' meetings with Calinescu and brought back the treasured information to the American high command."

He scratched his stubbled jaw, and his expression darkened.

"As a matter of fact, it was not at all in my plan that Radescu be caught by us. After all, if he were arrested, it could only cast suspicion on Calinescu in the eyes of the Americans. But there was bad blood there. Calinescu feared Radescu. He loathed him as a Jew. He told me many times that he had an instinct that Radescu already knew of his collaboration with . . . with us. And on that last time, Calinescu, I am convinced, deliberately walked over to me in my NKVD uniform after he had met Radescu in the Sankt Pölten railroad station and had passed the latest information to him. He *knew* that Radescu would try to follow him for a brief period and when he marched up to me, standing there just outside the train platform, he whirled and pointed to Radescu, who was observing him a few meters away, and said, 'You must arrest him, Comrade Major. You see, he has spotted us together.'"

Rogov stopped for a moment and compressed his lips. He lifted his hard eyes to Matt's and held out an apologetic hand.

"As a veteran officer, Mr. Brown, you understand what I had to do. On the one hand, I knew Calinescu had forced my hand. So I pulled out my pistol and arrested Radescu at gunpoint. On the other hand, I was furious at Calinescu for doing what he did, in order to seal Radescu's doom. But at that moment, Radescu could destroy the entire operational plan if he were permitted to return safely to his American control in Vienna."

Matt said evenly, "So you sent him off to Siberia."

Rogov, strangely agitated, said, "In that period, I could easily have one of my men put a bullet in Radescu's head. In Stalin's time, such things were completely in order. To protect our activities, killing was common. The prisoner was always shot while trying to escape."

"But you didn't."

Rogov, puffing his cigarette furiously, stared past Matt into a fury of memories.

"I interrogated the man. One thing alone saved him from a bullet: on his forearm were those tattooed numbers from Mauthausen."

He closed his eyes and shook his head through the swirl of smoke.

"I could not order a survivor of a Nazi death camp to be killed."

"What did you do with him?"

"I had no choice. We sent him back to Moscow on a prison train, a convoy. There, he was sentenced under Article 58/6 of the Soviet Criminal Code. Espionage. Twenty-five years in the GULAG."

"A little bit like a death warrant. The bullet in the head might have been more merciful," Matt said.

Something gave way in Rogov. He whirled to the bottle next to him, filled the water glass almost to the brim with vodka, and drank off a third of it in one convulsive gulp. His hard flat eyes shot anger as they met Matt's.

"It was not all sentimentality, *Mister* Brown."

He pointed a stubby forefinger at Matt.

"I wrote to the Center and told them that Radescu, if at all possible, must remain alive. He should not be sent to any camp where he would surely die. And why did I want this? Because"— and he reached forward to tap Matt heavily on his knee—"one day we might need Radescu."

Matt said quietly, "I think I follow you. Radescu would be your instrument of revenge, or for exchange, if needed."

"Exactly! Precisely! And I urged the Center to do just that!"

Rogov leaned back in his chair again, emotion draining from him. The liquor was finally getting to him. He had difficulty finding his mouth to insert his cigarette. Danoff glanced meaningfully at Matt: wrap it up as quickly as possible. Matt nodded.

"Colonel Rogov, I am most grateful for your candor in clarifying this episode. But one last question: why would you want to unleash Radescu against Calinescu?"

Clearly in another five minutes Rogov would be *hors de combat* for that day, but he slitted his eyes in an instinctive knife-like malevolence when he answered.

"Because Calinescu remained undisciplined. He was under instructions to live a quiet, modest life in America. He was to be a gray little mouse, careful not to attract the attention of anyone. But what happened? He became a big capitalist, with a big villa, big cars, many women, notoriety. In recent years, from what I learned at the Center, he has attracted investigations of his fascist past. He has become a liability. True, he did many useful things for us and through him we have reached out in America to find venal politicians, manufacturers, people who can be useful in many ways to the Center. But always undisciplined."

His Russian words were slurring now, tripping over each other in rise and fall of slushy vowels.

"The Center has become quite concerned about him. They do not want him arrested. He may reveal embarrassing things which Moscow would not want revealed. So, one day they will release Radescu. And Radescu will do what I know he will do: he will hunt down Calinescu and kill him."

His eyes, now glassy and their lids fluttering, were raised to Matt.

"Too bad I left my service before that happened. How I would have liked to see that *sooki-sin*, that son of a bitch Calinescu get his one day. And how clever that we might turn Radescu loose to do it."

He made a wiping gesture with his hands.

"And no one could ever say that the KGB did it. It would be a simple matter of revenge."

Peter's glance was an imperative one: the conversation must stop here.

Matt looked at his watch and rose. It would take him a full hour to drive back to Headquarters and report to Wendell on this interview. He felt strangely both depressed and elated: he had learned what he had hoped to learn.

He muttered quickly in Peter's ear, "Remember, there's a strict Bigot List on this Browning business."

Rogov half sprawled in his chair, tough face now sagging into his chest. As Matt rose, he extended a large clammy hand.

"Thank you, Colonel Rogov," Matt said. "I appreciate your patience and your recollections. I hope we can work out a really good situation for you here in America once these . . . interviews are over."

Rogov struggled to open his eyes wide and to lift his heavy head.

"Yes," he answered in painful English, "yes, I also hope for good situation." But his lifeless tone belied his expressed hope.

Then, remembering, he pointed an unsteady *papiross* at Matt. Peter translated his swift words.

"You must move quickly to catch Calinescu. KGB knows that I have told you about him. He will run . . ."

Peter helped Rogov to his feet. He swayed uncertainly, taller than the two Americans, an ominous bulk of a man. He smiled a terrible smile, eyeteeth like gold fangs.

"He is useless now to KGB, to anyone. Besides, he is a swine."

He patted his massive chest in a gesture that was more a *mea culpa* than anything else.

"And what was I? A keeper of swine!"

Without a word of farewell, he shambled, with Peter's steadying hand on his arm, from the room.

CHAPTER EIGHTEEN

For an old street man, it had been child's play to uncover Calinescu's residential address although his name
was not listed in the Beverly Hills telephone book.
Three casual inquiries at the Beverly Hills real estate
tax office had elicited this information. It was equally easy for him
to purchase a map of Beverly Hills and to rent a tiny auto. Four
hours after he had given the slip to the FBI team at Los Angeles
International Airport, Steve Browning was driving slowly up the
high winding road to case Dimitriu Calinescu's home, under a
gloomy and rain-laden sky.

At the top of the canyon, a quarter of a mile above Calinescu's
property, he stopped the car, extracted himself with difficulty, and
walked through the open gate of a tiny modern house. There were
no signs of life; he crunched around the flank of the house and
found himself on a cement patio which cantilevered out over an
abyss.

A sweeping view of Los Angeles, under a lowering sky and
heavy-laden clouds sweeping in from the Pacific, held him en-
tranced for a moment. Then he looked down and grunted with
satisfaction: Dimmy's house sat on the top of a crag, a massive
square of masonry with a small open courtyard in its center. The
land dropped almost vertically down behind it on three sides.
Steve made out a heavy steel-mesh perimeter fence running along
the bottom of the ravine behind the house. Probably electrified.
Dimmy really had his flanks protected. Anyone standing on his
patios at the top had a clear view of anything or anyone in the ravine below.

Even before he had climbed back into his vehicle, his plan
began to evolve. The first angry streaks of rain slashed at his wind-

shield as he drove past the surveillance van and his mind, quickened with the challenge presented it, sifted through the bleak options, one by one. By the time he reached the bottom of the canyon, he had decided. The rain was the determinant. Pelting with increasing fury, it would drive everyone indoors. Everyone but Steve Browning. And so he had parked the rented car in the first side street he reached, and had begun the slow, long rain-drenched climb on foot up the road he had just driven down. And, to his good fortune, the surveillance van appeared unoccupied; its occupants were perhaps busy in its interior.

He turned, soaked but with assurance, off the road to follow that perimeter fence he had studied from above. It was his hunch that neither Calinescu nor any bodyguards would be peering over the retaining wall of the broad patios to watch for interlopers below, in this fury of a rainstorm.

He had been playing hunches all his life. Live by the hunch, die by the hunch—it was his credo. And it was now his hunch that Dimmy Calinescu was still up there in this well-protected citadel of a house. If he was wrong . . . well, at this juncture, that would be little worse than the situation he was already in.

But this perimeter fence was the immediate problem. Fully ten feet high, it was topped by a V of ugly barbed wire. He examined it closely at the first moment after turning off the road, careful not to touch it in any way. Then he burrowed tentatively at its concrete base with a jackknife. To his dismay, the base went down a full foot below the ground surface. The fence marched in an irregular semicircle at the bottom of the ravine, like a stretch of the infamous Berlin wall. It must have cost Dimmy a fortune.

Above him, where the slope disappeared in the tattered mist, Calinescu's house sat on the flat outcropping, now only fitfully seen.

At a crouch, he moved carefully through the driving rain, his eyes picking out a path through the tangled dripping underbrush parallel to the high fence which disappeared into swirls of mist. It was years since he had been in really good physical shape and, as the terrain tilted upward, he panted with the unaccustomed exertion.

Pausing for a moment to wipe his streaming forehead and eyes with a soggy sleeve, he grinned involuntarily at the unbidden memory of his infantry platoon on maneuvers through the piney woods of Georgia forty years ago. They had been caught in a cloudburst and, deliberately slogging through potholes of water, they had eventually dissolved in hysterical laughter. Here it was the same: from water-plastered head to squishy shoes, he was as wet as if he had flung himself into a swimming pool.

In this appalling wetness, he felt a brief, almost involuntary, surge of energy and purpose. For the first time in months, his mind was clicking with the precise incisive rhythm of his younger years. It was almost delicious to feel the juices flowing again, his body and mind melded into a single antenna sensitive to every sound, every raindrop, every swirl of mist rushing up the hill to the house above. Stevie boy, the rhythm in him said, you'll find a way into that fortress yet. Keep looking. Keep moving.

He touched the unyielding metal of the pistol stuck in his trouser belt. He had thought of wrapping it in a towel and keeping it dry, but that would have been awkward to carry and besides, a momentary dampness would do the weapon no harm. It would fire if and when he wanted to fire it.

His breath came easier now and he peered at the terrain ahead through squinted eyes. He had to find a way to get under or over this perimeter fence, make his way up the precipitous slope, thick and green with ground cover, clamber onto the terrace, and enter the house. All this without being seen. Once inside . . . well, he intended to move quickly once there. They could not stop him.

Taking one cautious step at a time, he continued his patrol of the fence, careful not to stumble or to step into the numerous rivulets now flowing downhill past him into a larger torrent rapidly forming a few feet below him on the floor of the canyon.

Through the indistinct wetness ahead, a sudden muffled periodic sound froze him in his tracks: chunk . . . chunk . . . chunk . . . Half a dozen soundless steps further, he made out the upper torso and head of a human figure half submerged as if hulking in a foxhole.

Step by step he eased up to the figure. Its head momentarily disappeared and again he heard the chunk-chunk-chunk sound. Clumps of wet dirt flew up out of the hole in a shallow arc and landed at Steve's feet. The digging had reached a point where a slightly built man might almost be able to wriggle through a hole tunneled under the concrete base of the fence.

Steve sank to a crouch and listened to the rasping sound of lungs gasping for air as the digger frantically went at his task. Occasionally the dull glint of the shovel, a small military-style entrenching tool, appeared with each fling of dirt. Finally he inched his way to the edge of the shallow hole, so close he could smell the sour sweat and the muddied sweaty shoulders of the digger.

"Mike, *um Gottes Willen*, what a place to dig for gold!" he whispered.

Out of the hole came a face that was an apparition. Mud-daubed, its only distinguishing feature was fierce staring eyes bulging out of sunken sockets and sunken cheeks.

"Captain Steve!" a strangled voice finally said. Both were motionless, as if two mortal foes met in no-man's-land of a battle, undecided whether to try to kill the other or to slink away in opposite directions. The eyes riveted him for moments on end and the haggard head shook with disbelief.

"Mike, for God's sake, Mike!" Steve whispered, reaching for the soaked mud-covered body of Radescu. Mike's hands apprehensively emerged from the hole and Steve literally pulled him out of it with the power of his embrace. In the pelting rain, he held Mike, almost cradled him. They clung to one another for a long minute without a sound.

Steve reluctantly released Radescu and shook his head in mock dismay at his appearance.

"They wouldn't ever let you into the Hotel Sacher looking like that," he informed Radescu, wiping the rain from his face with a soaked sleeve. "Now, I ask you, is this a nice way to spend an afternoon in Southern California?"

Mike, wiping the mud from his hands with an even muddier towel, was in no mood for jests.

"I have been here on hillside for two . . . no, three days now. I watch the gate and the wall of the house to see how I can enter."

He shook his head.

"It is too difficult. Gate is shut, too many guards. Out on road, too many police patrols. So I look for back door."

He pointed at the muddy hole he had been digging, the bottom of which was rapidly filling with water.

"I buy small shovel," he said shyly. "I am digging now"—he consulted a mud-daubed watch—"four hours now."

He held the trenching tool with a defiant fist and, emaciated chest heaving with his efforts, he added, "Very soon, I pass under concrete. Soon I go up hill."

He pointed a grimy finger where the Calinescu house appeared fitfully through the mist.

"And then?" Steve asked.

"And then, I meet again with my old Iron Guard acquaintance, Dimitriu Calinescu," Mike said, soft singsong voice speaking as if he were preparing to make a social call.

The muddied shirt clung to his wasted body like a soiled burial shroud. Long white hair, plastered flat to the sides of his head, the sunken eye sockets and flat glittering eyes made him an apparition. Yes, Steve recalled, like the skeleton-like Mircea Radescu they had picked up at the side of the road near Ebensee concentration camp so long ago.

"Mike," he whispered, "what happened to you? How did you disappear on that last meeting with Dimmy? I've got a thousand questions I want to ask. . . ."

But Mike shook his dripping head and touched Steve's jacket sleeve with an almost apologetic gesture.

"Not now, Captain Steve. Later, but not now. First I must dig hole, get under fence."

He looked up at the formidable wire appraisingly.

"Fence almost as good as the ones at Mauthausen. Much better than GULAG fence in Siberia," he said. "But another fifteen, twenty minutes and hole is finished."

Steve reached out and held Mike's bony body with both hands.

"Give me that shovel," he growled. "I've got to make a bigger hole if *I* am going to fit through it."

As Steve shed his sodden jacket, Mike caught sight of the pistol jammed in his belt and stared at it for a moment. Steve wrapped the gun in the ruins of his cotton jacket, heaved it over the fence to the other side, took the shovel from Mike's bony hands, and stepped into the shallow trench, grimacing as the cold muddy water lapped up to his ankles. Mike sat cross-legged beside him, leaning forward with fatigue, oblivious of the rain dripping off his muddy nose, chin, and cheeks. Grunting with each shovelful,

Steve worked at a rapid pace and the clods of wet mud flew out of the hole in a steady arc.

"I'm almost through, Mike," he finally gasped, head emerging from the hole. "A few minutes and we can wriggle through it, one at a time."

Both of them finally stood on the slope inside the fence, the pistol recovered and again wedged in Steve's belt. They were caked from head to foot with the wet ooze they had dug through. As if to celebrate their feat, the rain worsened and came down in solid sheets.

"Now listen, Mike," Steve panted. "I know why you're here. You can guess why I'm here. But if we're going to visit with our old friend Dimmy, I'm the captain. *I* lead the way."

Mike said, his voice a bleak monotone, "Captain Steve, give me the pistol and you stay here. Calinescu betrayed me to NKVD. I stay alive for years, years upon years, in Soviet GULAG, for only one reason: revenge. Do not deny me revenge."

Steve snorted with dark amusement.

"You're going to have to get in line."

He peered up at the rain slashing at them for a moment and clapped Radescu on his narrow shoulders.

"Well, what are we waiting for? Let's call on him together, shall we? I'm sure Dimmy will be absolutely delighted at seeing two old friends from Vienna, after all these years."

They laboriously climbed the steep ivy-covered slope at a tangent, bent almost double, Steve leading, finding foot- and hand-holds, and grasping Mike's cupped palms with his own. Once, Mike's tired fingers loosened and Steve barely caught him in time with a lunge at his wrist, else he would have hurtled all the way down to the perimeter fence. At that point, Steve sat carefully down onto the slanting hillside for a moment, feeling the cold wet earth on his bottom. Mike sat beside him, head hanging with fatigue. For a moment, he had the thought to leave Mike there and to struggle alone to the top. Mike was too far gone with exhaustion to clamber up there on his own. But he had let Mike down once before; he would not do so again.

Mike looked up, eyes glazed but determined, and nodded. They struggled to their feet and again, hands clinging to each other, plodded slowly upward.

Suddenly Steve stopped and pointed. Calinescu's mansard roof reared immediately above them. Within arm's reach was a waist-high retaining wall behind which lay the broad patios Steve had briefly glimpsed from above two hours before.

He bent down, voice barely audible above the slashing rain, and said in Mike's ear, "We're at the top. Now listen carefully. You must stay close to me when we go over that wall. We run a high risk of meeting bodyguards, dogs, electronic devices. Remember, *I've* got a gun. We've got to stay together."

Mike reached down and hoisted one sodden trouser leg. Just above his ankle he had taped a short ugly hunting knife in its sheath. He extracted the knife, tested its blade meaningfully with a forefinger, and tucked it back in its holder.

Steve shook his head vigorously, spattering raindrops as a dog shakes himself after emerging from a swim, and whispered savagely, "Look, Mike, you're not going to need that thing. We've got the firepower already. . . ."

Mike peered up at him, a slow bitter smile on his spattered, ravaged face.

"Captain Steve, I wait too many years for this moment."

Steve stared perplexedly down at him, then shrugged.

"All right, Mike. Now step on my hand: I'll boost you over the patio wall. Then you reach down and give me a hand. And be ready to move fast."

Within seconds, they lay on the glazed ceramic surface of the patio, their backs to the retaining wall, gasping for breath and intently watching the expanse of glass, now heavily draped, which formed the ground floor of the Calinescu mansion, for any hostile movement or sound. There was nothing to be heard except for the hiss of watery pockmarks as the driven rain riddled away at the gleaming patio surface.

Steve slipped off his ruined loafers and sodden socks and flung them over the wall. He motioned for Radescu to do the same and whispered, "We can move quicker and quieter in our bare feet."

Then at a crouch he moved to the shelter of a broad aluminum awning of alternate green and yellow slats which projected out from the house wall. He motioned Radescu to flatten himself against the house on one side of a door leading within, moving up to its other side. Then he awkwardly pulled the heavy pistol from his waistband, uncertainly flipped down the safety catch, and pumped a cartridge into the chamber. The dull snicker-click sound echoed around the patio but attracted no one. Steve jammed the gun again under his belt. It lay hard and cold against his belly. Damn, he muttered to himself, how I hate these things!

With excruciating slowness, he reached for the doorknob. If it's locked—he mouthed the words silently—we're going to be in some kind of soup. The patio had no other exits except this door leading into the house; they would have to tumble down that slope and start again . . .

He winked at Radescu and gave him a jocular thumbs-up gesture. Ah, Stevie boy, he exulted to himself, you and magic hunches!

He turned the doorknob as carefully as if he were working the combination on an erratic safe, and pulled it carefully. It swung open. Inside, a thickly carpeted corridor, unlighted and gloomy, led directly through a wing of the house to where there was light at the other end. That would be the inner courtyard he had seen from above, over an hour earlier. Beckoning Mike to follow, he slipped through the door and closed it quickly once they were inside.

Then both of them froze. At the other end of the corridor, less than twenty feet away, they made out a husky man clad in sports shirt and slacks, facing away from them on the threshold of a room whose door was obviously open. He wore a shoulder holster in which a snub-nosed revolver nestled.

As they stared at him, rivulets of water oozing from them onto the thick-piled carpeting, the sound of a harsh, old man's voice floated from the room.

"Get out there, in the garden, on the patio!" the voice commanded, clipped foreign accent somehow blurred. "Get out there and get wet, damn you! That's what I pay you for, no? To protect me! I'm leaving in half an hour and until then I want you and Basil and Ian to patrol outside. *Outside!* I don't want to see you inside and dry. . . ."

"All right, all right," the guard growled through the door. "I'm going."

He closed the door with an indignant thud and stood for a moment as if pondering whether to turn right or left. Steve moved

with a lightness he could scarcely believe of himself. The guard
half whirled as Steve charged him, holding the pistol by its butt,
and had but a moment to stare, stupefied, at the huge old potbel-
lied man before going down as Steve swung the pistol and struck
him once, hard, on the side of his head. He crashed to the carpeted floor and lay very still.

Behind him, Mike had closed up, eyes almost popping from his
head. He pulled open the heavy door through which that querulous voice had come, and hurtled through it with Steve close
behind. Together they slammed the door shut, secured it with a
huge old-fashioned key sticking in its lock, and turned to face the
room and its occupant.

It was a dark, heavy-paneled library, with books frowning from
floor to ceiling, an enormous globe of the world occupying an entire corner furnished in the elegance of a Renaissance chamber.
One entry wall was vertically covered with plaques, certificates and
scrolls of all kinds. Before a rococo desk, stood an old man, leaning
on a gleaming mahogany cane, already wearing an expensive epau-
leted white raincoat. An open attaché case on the desk behind him
was filled with neatly stacked U.S. currency. Fury and alarm completely distorted the old man's features.

"You damned robbers!" he shouted at them. "How did you get
in here? Don't you know that in two minutes my bodyguards will
be in here and will shoot you dead? How dare you invade my
house, you filthy . . ."

Pointing his pistol straight at the infuriated old man, Steve
reached with his other hand into his pants pocket, extracted a
soaked handkerchief, and wiped the mud from his face, before
passing it to Radescu, who did the same.

"How can you call us such names, make such threats?" Steve
spoke with injured innocence. "After we've come so far to visit
you in this difficult hour."

The old man straightened, puzzled, then leaned forward on his
cane to stare at the two faces intently, his lips turned down in a U
of incredulity.

"You prided yourself on your memory once, Colonel Calinescu," Steve jeered. "Surely you remember us. I am Captain Steven
Browning and this is Mircea Radescu, late of Mauthausen concentration camp and more recently . . ."

He turned inquiringly to Mike.

". . . of Norilsk forced-labor camp. Soviet GULAG." Mike spoke quietly.

"Aha!" Calinescu snorted. A gleam of recognition was followed by one of fear. "You, *Mister* Browning, with your brilliant intelligence career, and you, Radescu, his . . . his running dog. And you enter my house like sneak thieves. Why didn't you come to the front door like civilized men?"

"We would have preferred that," Steve replied, studying the drooping lip and lamed side of Calinescu, who stood nonetheless with the same arrogant bearing of the past. "But perhaps we might not have been welcomed. Besides, we're not here to socialize."

Calinescu licked pale lips.

"And what then? Are you here to rob? Here, there is much to steal. You are very lucky."

"No," Steve said equably, holding the pistol on Calinescu. "It's a moment, as the waiters say in Vienna, for *die Rechnung*, the payment of the bill."

CHAPTER NINETEEN

Even through the sheets of wind-driven rain, Silas could perceive how carefully Angelo Fusco and his colleagues had chosen the Place to administer Operation Scorpion's electronic bite. He sat on a raised platform within one of its now-vacant bedrooms, infrared binoculars in hand, peering at the scene below, seeing without being seen. Calinescu's mansion, of a peculiarly pretentious bastard design, lay gleaming whitely below him, a monster square of a building with mansard roofs, Moorish windows, and an open Italianate courtyard in its center containing a gushing fountain and a large religious statue of marble bearing a cross. (Fusco, ever a font of information, had identified it as one of the Archangel Michael, "but don't ask me why.")

The mansion was not only huge, it was virtually a fortress. He turned his binoculars to study the high meshed-wire fence. It meandered horizontally, halfway up those steep bushy slopes, as an outer defense, reinforced by what Fusco assured him were electrified strands along its top, guaranteed to jolt the bejesus out of any trespasser attempting to approach the mansion from below.

"What's the action down there?" Fusco had entered from the adjoining library, his command post, and stood looking warily at him, transcript sheets in one hand, holstered gun still strapped on over his shirt. "I don't think you'll spot any good-time bambinas with the big boobies cavorting around out there in the rain. Today is moving day for Jimmy C.—or so he thinks."

"Pretty damned quiet this last half hour. What's your audio coming up with?" Silas asked.

"Oh, Jimmy C.'s in there all right," Fusco said, "and he's having a fit. He's calling in those goons, his bodyguards, every ten minutes, asking them to check this, check that, pack this, pack that. And one of them does nothing but sit by the phone, says 'no comment,' and hangs up every time there's a call from the newspapers or the TV people."

"You'd think he'd be down at his offices on Wilshire Boulevard," Silas said, dropping his binoculars to his lap and wiping his sweated eyes. "How does he run his businesses from up here?"

"He does it very well." Fusco spoke with the flat assurance of one who really knows. "Since that damned congressional hearing on him four days ago, the press has been after him like wolves. He stopped going down to his office two days ago after a couple of people from some local Jewish group charged at him in the lobby and one old girl got a good swipe at him with her handbag. He's preferring assault charges against her but he doesn't like that to happen to him. So he's staying up here until . . ." He looked at Ruffing. "Until he shoves off. He's blowing town." He glanced at his watch. "Within the hour."

"For good?"

Fusco, with a cocky wag of his head, replied, "So *he* thinks. His secretary down at his office phoned him two hours ago and told him that his private jet is ready for takeoff. It's kept out at Ontario International, and the crew is standing by."

"You're all over him," Silas said, professional esteem permeating his words as he picked up the infrared glasses again.

"Listen to this." Fusco peered down at the roughly typed phone-tap transcripts. "He's leased a furnished villa down in Acapulco right on the water, fourteen rooms, six baths, belonging to some damned European aristocrat. And he's already paid advance rent for one month: ten thousand smackers."

"A lot of bread," Silas muttered.

"Ten thousand smackers! When I think how Betty and me have to scratch for a whole year to put aside five hundred bucks to spend a week down there in a one-room fleabag with the balcony facing away from the sea."

"The wages of sin," Silas said, studying the house and the slopes below it, "can be indecently high."

"Yeh, I know." Fusco nodded grimly. "But in this case, the wages are going to be paid in a different currency. We've got the goods on the bastard."

"Which means?"

"Which means that when Jimmy C. drives up to the airport in that chauffeur-driven silver Rolls, he'll be met by two of my pals from the LA Field Office with warrants for his arrest. Enough charges to put him away for years, even if he meets bail now. So maybe instead of Acapulco, he'll spend his future vacations in something without a view, like a cell at San Quentin. And at his age, it'll be a life sentence."

Silas, sitting on his improvised platform, lowered the glasses to meet Fusco's eyes, glittering with impending triumph.

"You've really got the goods? Nothing that can be quashed in court?"

Fusco tapped him confidently on his knee.

"Ruff, I've got enough TV film footage alone from what's been happening in that library down there to send him and about five of his political buddies into the slammer for years. And it's strictly legit, by the book. All the way down from the Attorney General in Washington."

He slammed one fist into the other.

"I got 'im, Ruff!" he exulted. "Fair and square, with every legal *t* crossed and *i* dotted. That Romanian son of a bitch is going to be in a jail cell by the end of this day."

"If nothing else happens," Silas said.

Fusco, fierce-eyed, pointed a vibrant finger at him.

"Nuthin's going to happen, Ruff! And that includes your sad-assed friend Browning out there somewhere, or the pathetic spook we spotted on the road yesterday. Look at that Fort Apache down there! Do you think anybody could get in there with anything less than a Sherman tank? Listen, every one of his cars, including the Rolls, has bulletproof glass."

Silas picked up the binoculars once again. The mist had thickened and, with a rush, a renewed sheet of rain thundered down, momentarily blotting the building below them from view.

"How many people are down in there right now?" he asked Fusco, panning the binoculars slowly. "I haven't seen a soul outside in all that wet."

"Hard to tell," Fusco replied, head lowered to read notes he had scratched on the top of the file in his hand. "Let's see; he's got six goons altogether on the payroll, usually two on and four off. Today, maybe four of them on duty, because they double as chauffeurs. Then there are three live-in servants, including a cook, all of them naturalized Americans from Europe; I've got cards on each of them in my safe. I'd say about ten people in all. There's sometimes a clown or two, somebody on the take, who stays overnight if he's taken on too much booze or if it's too late to go home. But no guests down there now: it's goodbye time."

An unbidden image of Mara von Kueppke in Vienna three decades ago swam unbidden into Silas' memory.

"Doesn't he keep any . . . ah . . . female live-in talent to warm his toes at night? He used to have quite a reputation as a swordsman, as I remember."

Fusco smiled bleakly.

"Listen, Ruff, Jimmy C. had a stroke some months ago that would have killed a horse, and that's the comment from the medics at Cedars-Sinai who treated him when they brought him in. He drags his left foot now, he can't move without a cane, and his whole left side droops. *That* took the lead out of his pencil, although, give him his due, he has had a babe up here every now and again, big friendly broad around forty. She's not in on the payoffs or even in the know. But she is sitting out there at Ontario International, waiting for Jimmy, her luggage already stowed away in his jet, they tell me."

A grin of pure malice split his lips.

"Jesus, I'd love to see her face when Jimmy drives up in his Rolls, one of the goons helps him out of the rear seat, and we hit Jimmy with the arrest warrant just as she puts her loving arms around him."

Silas said, "And they *pay* you for all this. I think you'd do it for nothing."

Fusco thought for a moment, then shook his head in mock protest.

"Naw, most of the time I earn the dizzying sums they pay me. But, yes, this one, Jimmy C., I'd do it for kicks. The guy's an acid; he corrodes everybody he touches. Taking him in is fun."

Clouds boiling out of the southwest hastened the end of the afternoon light. Silas proffered the binoculars to Fusco.

"Want a look? For just a minute, it's quite a view."

Fusco shook his head.

"I've seen it a million times, Ruff. Play with the glasses if you want. We're busy as hell in the Tank monitoring the closed-circuit TV in the library, and logging the in and out calls. We've got to be ready to move the minute the Rolls comes out of the garage. Then we send a radio signal to our guys at Ontario, we alert two tail vehicles, now parked down on Sunset, to pick up the Rolls—and Operation Scorpion starts to become Bureau history."

He winked at Silas and strutted from the room, a new cigarette dangling from his lips. It was very definitely Fusco's day, Silas thought, focusing the binoculars downward.

With surprising speed, the wind had shifted, and suddenly the Calinescu house loomed into view, its every detail clear and sharp in the fast-fading light. A string of chaste white bulbs abruptly came on in the inner courtyard, although every window in the house was dark, either shuttered or screened by heavy drapes. Jimmy C. apparently cherished his privacy.

Below, the plain of Los Angeles had turned to magic. Lights by the cluster sprang up as entire floors of high-rise buildings suddenly burst into parallel interstices of illumination floor by floor. A mesmeric fantasy of the mighty metropolis fighting off the gloom.

And here he sat, high above it, a middle-aged Peeping Tom, trying to penetrate the darkness—for what purpose? With all of his cunning, Steve would never have a chance of getting into Fort Apache. Would he even try? Weren't the odds better that he would simply disappear? As for his alleged remorse about Radescu, wasn't that quintessential Steve, putting Silas and everyone else off his trail? The chances were that Steve was in a dry place somewhere, not out in a driving rain. Maybe Mexico, by now.

Browning had always lived by taking outrageous risks, rolls of the operational dice. Win big, lose big; a riverboat gambler. Silas' own cautious soul was offended by such swagger; all right, he was envious. His own outlook was rational, pragmatic, tidy. One made reasonable assumptions, based on the best evidence, after patiently gathering and assembling endless bits of information. Silas loved mosaic patterns, complete with the predictably missing pieces. None of this brash, bold reaching for the jugular unless one knew exactly how vulnerable that jugular was. In all cases, one was ever ready with a fall-back plan.

His prudence, however, was of no help to him here. Steve Browning was gone, God knew where, and Mircea Radescu, seen only for a brief terrible moment in the glow of a tiny flashlight, was also gone.

For himself, there was nothing else to do but to return to Washington to face whatever music there was to face, and to retire. He had no idea where he would go or what he would do, once retired, but at Langley they were waiting there for him; the bureaucratic blade of the guillotine was already raised and waiting, and would drop on his head with precious little ceremony. And he did not deserve more.

Too damned bad, the whole thing: Steve's successes, his current disgrace, his own endless years of being an operational watchdog. Who would really give a damn in a few short years' time? Oh, in a couple of decades or so, the Agency's records on certain exploits would be declassified and turned over to research types, analysts who might well cluck or chuckle or write books mentioning Browning's gall or panache.

And what had Steve done? He'd gone sour, taken the other side's money. And not for that large a bowl of lentil soup either. His actions were beyond Silas' rationalization or forgiveness. Steve had let them all down and he knew he had and it was probably terrible for him to live with that.

Now, as Silas perched in this strange place, his thoughts gnawed again and again at the banality, the triviality of betrayal, and the ease with which principles and loyalties are bought. And in Steve's case, there was absolutely nothing redeeming about twenty thousand dollars.

Suddenly his binoculars caught movement just below the broad empty patio. Two dim forms, on hands and knees, were creeping painfully up the precipitous slope. He adjusted the binoculars for maximum clarity as one of them stood and gave a stirrup hand to boost the other over the wall, to be pulled up by the other in turn. For a moment, one of the figures stood up to discard what appeared to be his shoes; despite the slashing rain, that was unmistakably Steve Browning.

He jumped to his feet with an involuntary groan, glasses still pressed painfully to his eyes, when Fusco's voice, sharp with alarm, barked from the doorway of the adjoining room, "Come in here, Ruff, for Christ's sake! On the double!"

He jumped clumsily from the table and loped into the LP room. Fusco was huddled between two of the intercept operators, an auditor phone held to one ear, his dark face quivering with what he was hearing. As Silas entered, he reached for a toggle switch on the wall and the darkened TV screen on an adjoining table came to life. A single heavy figure leaned painfully over an enormous desk, securing stacks of currency notes into a large attaché case.

"Somebody's gotten into the house!" Fusco shouted. "The goons are calling the Beverly Hills Police. . . ."

He listened further on the auditor phone and his eyes burned into Silas' with a bitter flame.

"Goddamnit, Ruff, it's your two losers! How the hell could they have gotten in there without being detected . . . ?"

"I thought you said Jimmy's place was Fort Apache, impregnable," Silas said with a thin smile. "I've told you not to underestimate Steve if he really wanted to do something. Yes, he's in there, all right. And I'll bet your next paycheck that Mike Radescu is in there with him. I just spotted them with these glasses. They crawled straight up the cliff and just climbed onto that big patio. They must have gotten through that perimeter fence somehow. . . ."

The TV screen, green-tinged but with images clearly recognizable, now contained three figures in confrontational stances, and from a black circular amplifier beside the TV screen, the disembodied voice of Calinescu boomed out, "You damned robbers! How did you get in here . . . ?"

Fusco, face contorted with tension, listened and squeezed his eyes shut in a momentary spasm of rage.

"Dear Mother of God," he groaned, "they've got Jimmy C. in his library, alone."

He reached for his walkie-talkie lying on the workbench, pressed the talk button, and spoke with a tightly restrained urgency.

"Scorpion Ten. Scorpion Ten. This is Scorpion One. Listen carefully: Big trouble in the target house. Proceed as quickly as you can up there. They've already phoned for the police. The gates should be open. Enter the grounds. Identify yourselves to anybody you meet. You will probably be encountering armed guards. Do *not* fire. Repeat, do *not* fire unless deliberately fired on. I'm coming down right away. Don't let anyone in or out of that place. Hold everybody you meet in there. Do you read me?"

A crackled affirmative was heard. He barked, "Over and out."

To the younger of the two men sitting with headphones he jerked his head. "Stan, we need troops. Get your gun and come with me."

To the remaining operator, he called, "Tape everything, especially that video we're getting from the library. And notify the duty officer and the SAC by phone immediately that there's trouble up here. I need a backup squad right away. And get a couple of ambulances up here, quick!"

To Silas he shouted, "Come on, Ruff. We're going down there!"

Silas shook his head, and pointed at the closed-circuit TV screen.

"No, Angelo, I'm going to stay here and watch the Late Show."

Fusco, hastily donning his shoulder holster, said bitterly, "If that loser of yours commits . . . any kind of a felony in this case, nobody's going to lift a finger to save him. Hear me?"

"Shove it, Angelo," Silas cried at Fusco's disappearing back. "Get down there and try to stop what's going on first."

He slumped into a folding chair, his uncomprehending eyes following the scene unrolling on the small screen before him.

Steve took in the room—Calinescu leaning on his cane, the open attaché case stuffed with neat packets of paper money, the gloomy rows of books, and the ancient round bulk of the *mappamondo*—with an air of exhilaration. The hunch had paid off, the old *Fingerspitzengefühl* was still there. He had caught Calinescu poised for flight. A broad smile suffused his broad blubbery cheeks.

Beside him, Mike reached down to the knife sheath taped to his ankle and straightened, empty-handed, quivering with anger at Steve, who, without taking his eyes or gun from Calinescu, explained softly, "Don't get mad, Mike, but I lifted the knife when I boosted you up over the patio wall. I don't want anybody to find

you in here with a weapon in your hand. I've got a whole clip
in this one. That should be plenty for both of us."

He sensed Mike gathering his wasted body to hurl himself at
Calinescu and held out a restraining hand.

"Hold it, Mike, just a minute. We've got some matters to discuss with our old collaborator."

Calinescu, licking pale thin lips, spoke hoarsely.

"So, you have a score to settle? Now? Here? With me?"

Steve nodded.

"Yes, to all of the above."

The old man tapped his cane indignantly.

"Quite a hero, Captain Browning, sneaking in here with a gun
to threaten a seventy-three-year-old man who has survived a stroke,
an immigrant who has succeeded in the country of his adoption?
A man who has reached out to help hundreds of needy and
worthy?"

He lifted one pallid hand to the wall behind his desk, blanketed
with plaques, medallions, and testimonials immortalizing the grati-
tude of dozens of groups for his philanthropy.

Calinescu drew himself to an unnatural erectness. Contempt
now dripped from his every word.

"And *you* have a score to pay with *me!* You, Browning, venal
and corruptible from the first moment I met you. How eager you
were to take anything—a cigarette box, all manner of gifts,
money."

He pointed a palsied finger at Steve.

"Browning, people like you I have bought and sold all my life.
You're all the same whether you are politicians, merchants, spies
. . . you all have your price. My only problem was to determine
just what that price was; and pay it if I cared to."

Steve nodded, almost cheerfully.

"You've got me dead to rights, Dimmy. No question about it.
That was always a problem of mine: sticky fingers. And you
sensed that in me the first time we met, right? Well, I do want to
make a belated restitution."

He reached into a pocket of his soggy jacket, extracted a square
heavy metal object, and flung it at Calinescu. It landed with a
dull thump at his feet.

"That's the first corruption, remember? The silver cigarette case with the double eagle of the House of Habsburg embossed on it, the one you gave me at our first meeting to cement our friendship. God alone knows where you got it: probably looted from someone, somewhere. You know something? I've been ashamed to even carry the thing around, all these years. And I decided a long time ago to give it back to you one day. That day has come."

"And why did you wait so long, Browning?" The question was flung tauntingly at him. "I have been in America now almost thirty years."

Steve bobbed his head, a schoolboy eager to answer a hard one posed by teacher.

"Fair enough. For a long while, I honestly thought that I had put you behind me, a miserable and shameful little chapter in my life that I kept in a kind of a deep freeze mentally. I just didn't want to go near you. It's human, I think, to hate people who corrupt you. So I avoided you."

He waggled the pistol for emphasis.

"You know, Dimmy, the KGB made three separate passes at me. Each time I turned them away somehow: in New Delhi, Amman, and finally in Washington in a crummy suburban shopping mall. And you know, Dimmy, they have the same attitude as you do: that money can buy any American in sight. They offered me enormous sums to play ball with them—one hundred thousand, two hundred thousand dollars! How's that for putting temptation in old Browning's path? Of course, for them it would have been a real bargain. Imagine buying into a senior staff officer of the CIA! That would have been worth *millions!* Should I have held out for more?"

Faint shouts, a distant thump of racing feet, warned them that Calinescu's household was aroused and closing in on the library. Radescu glanced apprehensively at Steve, who talked on as if he heard nothing.

"I didn't realize until rather recently," Steve said softly, "that you, you cutthroat son of a bitch, had been working for the KGB all along. I guess I couldn't force myself to accept that fact although my old colleagues of long ago kept trying to tell me. But then I had to accept that it was you who had passed KGB money to me to give them the blackmail handle they used: that twenty-thousand-dollar check you sent me for supplying the affidavit I gave you for your immigration request. Now that put another light on it. You're not only a bastard, Mr. Calinescu, you're a KGB bastard."

"You took the money, whether it was KGB money or mine. You took it, greedily. You never questioned its origin!"

"That's right. I took it. And I've paid it back with interest: a ruined career. A destroyed marriage. But you and the KGB made a bad mistake, Dimmy. You confused corruptibility with treason. Whatever I am, there's no price tag on my loyalty. Can you understand *that?*"

Radescu, sunk to a near crouch, thrust his cadaverous face at Calinescu and rasped, "What about me? Wasn't it you, Calinescu, who betrayed me to the NKVD that day in the Sankt Pölten *Bahnhof?* And you, with ten thousand American dollars in your hand which I had passed to you. They didn't kill me, my Iron Guard commandant, as you thought they would. But they sent me into hell for over twenty-five years." He stamped a bare bony foot in rage, and his voice rose to a thin wail.

"Twenty-five years!"

Calinescu, scarred chin square and unrelenting, said to Radescu, in his crisp accentless German, *"Du hattest es verdient, Sau-Jude."*

As Radescu gathered his last strength to fling himself against his nemesis, Steve seized his arm in an iron vise. Behind them, the oaken library door was shaken by thunderous bangs and a shout of "Open up, or we shoot the lock off!"

Calinescu, shifting his weight on his cane, stared at the pistol pointed at him and spoke, his voice cajoling and reasonable.

"Look, you're both trapped in this room. My guards will break through that door in a moment. They will shoot to kill. Put down your gun and come and stand behind me. I will prefer no charges. I will let you walk out free."

He glanced at their bare feet, and with a thin smirk added, "I will even find shoes for you. I promise you."

Steve's voice rose above the growing hubbub outside the door.

"You've always said, haven't you, that everyone has his price. You found out mine and you paid it."

The babble of voices outside the door grew louder. An abrupt gunshot was followed by the sound of ripped wood. The library door was under attack.

Steve held out the pistol for a moment and tapped it with his other hand, his broad face briefly beaming as if something funny had been uttered.

"Do you remember the first time we met, Dimmy? You asked whether I was related to the Browning who made guns. I'm not, of course. But what do you know—this *is* a Browning automatic pistol! Maybe the other Browning was a relative after all!"

Two more shots echoed outside and the thud of human battering rams against the door made its collapse only a matter of moments.

"And now," Steve said, somber-faced, with the finality of a judge pronouncing sentence, "I'm repaying you what I owe you. For what Mike owes you. And for what the dead Jews of the Choral Synagogue in Bucharest over forty years ago owe you."

Behind him the door was splintering fast. Steve suddenly seized Radescu's arm, twisted it, and flung the frail old man to the floor in a tangled heap. Then, sighting the pistol at eye level and clenching it for steadiness with both hands, he fired at Calinescu, three shots in rapid succession, aiming for the heart. As the door burst open and the bodyguards with weapons in their hands hurled themselves at him, he whirled to face them, bare feet poised in a judo stance, and squeezed off a fourth shot directly at the ceiling.

The police later counted seven bullet holes in his body.

CHAPTER TWENTY

As Wendell had expected, with a sense of weary acceptance, the news of his impending retirement spread
through the Agency and beyond with the speed of
Brownian movements. He had immediately convened a
brief special meeting of all his senior Directorate officers and gave
it to them without fancy stitching: he intended to retire within
sixty days because his health had deteriorated to the point that it
was interfering with his ability to run the show in top form. He
urged them to carry on nobly in the interim. All of them, he
knew, were steeped in the devil's theory: something else had possibly gone badly wrong, and this was a convenient cover story.

But his announcement had caught his audience, filling every
seat in the conference room, like a jolt from an exposed wire.
After seconds of silence, Connors, whose naked barbs often signaled how the others felt, finally groaned, "There goes the neighborhood."

It had troubled him over the years how leaky the entire intelligence community had become, and he shook his head with secret
dismay when the following day, at a lunch for the visiting deputy
director of French intelligence, cozily and discreetly laid on by his
European Division people in a private dining room high in the
muted confines of the Cosmos Club, the guest of honor raised his
wineglass at Wendell with a secretive smile, and without referring
directly to his knowledge of Wendell's departure, asked for permission to toast him.

"Cher colleague Wendell," the Frenchman intoned, pronouncing it Wen-DELL in singsong Gallic, "may I compare you,
with only minimum hyperbole, to one of ours?" Then, with a
slight bow, he continued, "*Vous êtes vraiment un Bayard amér-*

icain, sans peur et sans reproche." To which Wendell, touching
the Frenchman's glass, responded that he could not accept comparison to a Bayard without fear or fault. The Chevalier had,
however, another trait: that of running first-class reconnaissance
and espionage networks against the enemies of France, which
made his victories possible. *That* evocation of Bayard he would accept. He also pointed out that Bayard had died on the battlefield,
in service. Would his guest please find a more comfortable paragon for him?

"*Formidable!*" exclaimed the Frenchman, not realizing that a
previous visitor from his service had also made reference to the
Seigneur Pierre Terrail Bayard and that Wendell, his curiosity
aroused, had done a little homework. It was a little conceit of his,
to try to stay one jump ahead of the others. Knowledge, even esoteric knowledge, in this town was power.

Maude, with whom he had long discussed the eventuality, was
openly delighted at his decision. At last, she said, she would no
longer have to share him with his exigent mistress, the office. At
last there would be no more ominous telephone calls in the middle of the night (telephone calls to him in the middle of the night
were usually bad news). The Thumper, the Beeper, and the cleverly hidden radio/telephone in his Mercedes, all could be removed forever from his life and hers.

But somehow his decision threw out of phase the delicately
adjusted and tested mechanism of his workday, the quarter-hour
coffins of time in which he voluntarily buried himself from the
moment he plumped into the swivel chair to the moment he left
it ten hours later. He now found himself for entire minutes peering vacantly at the abstract batik print on the far wall, bemused
that eight weeks hence he would no longer have to shovel his path
out of the daily blizzard of highly classified documents. Eight
weeks hence, the minutiae and trivia of the job would be affixed
onto someone else's shoulders.

Yet, after closely reading a particularly absorbing cable from the
field, he savored, almost in an olfactory sense, the fascination of
sitting here at the center of the delicately far-flung web where secret triumphs and problems reached him on an "Eyes Alone"
basis. Distant recruitments of spies and agents; precious nuggets
of documentary intelligence skillfully stolen from the depths of

somebody's Foreign Ministry files or simply from a sharp-eyed
reader of unclassified journals and research papers; the heady business of signing "Approve" or "Disapprove" on an operational ven-
ture which might, or might not, uncover the innermost military
secrets of western China or eastern Siberia—these were like
sniffing pure oxygen.

He did this job well, he knew this without false modesty. He
knew the limits of his authority, whether the Director would stick
or bounce on a specific topic or recommendation, whether his division chiefs could or could not find access to specific information
in their areas. He knew where the case officers were located with
specific aptitudes and talents when needed. After years at it, he
also knew where the elephant traps were located in this treacherous town and in this equally unpredictable business, and how
you skirted the traps, peering down at the bones of those who had
not the wit to avoid them. And he loved it, the unending, drudge-
clogged, occasionally exhilarating routine of it. One never knew
what was going to happen tomorrow, or for that matter by the
end of today, but whatever happened, he knew he could handle it,
deal with it, reach for the Secure Line to commence its resolution.
The flaps came flapping in to be solved, resolved. He had coped
with more flaps than an envelope company, he once told Clare,
and he could lick them as fast as they came in.

It was then that the swell of melancholy rolled over him.

Since this job was as much his life's blood as proteins or carbo-
hydrates, what sort of pill or drug was there, he thought, that
could come even close to substituting for the quiet sense of excitement that suffused him when his people (yes, *his* people) accom-
plished a mission or failed to accomplish one yet trying like hell
all the while?

"Telephone call from the Hill," Clare announced on the
"hold" line. "Representative Pfitzner returning your call."

He waited uneasily for the connection. Some things one could
learn from others, but this one he had to learn from the source.

His evening session with Jenny and the other events of that day
had left him drained. He had driven home in a blur, undressed,
and crawled under the cool sheets without wakening a softly
breathing Maudie in the next bed. Then he had spent half the
night with eyes wide open, reviewing what he had said, what she

had said, what he did, what he should have done. Nightmares then replaced sleeplessness: an image of Jenny's grandmother having her throat cut by an Iron Guard goon, succeeded by the half-forgotten visit to Mauthausen three days after the end of the war. It had been a very bad night. He did not associate Jenny Pfitzner with pleasant things.

He watched the winking eye of the "hold" button as if it were that of a weaving cobra. He need not have brought this on, but he had long ago learned that sooner or later all unpleasant prospects had to be faced. His own instinct was to face them sooner rather than later.

"Put her on, Clare."

And on she came, the deep rasping voice filling his ear.

"Jenny Pfitzner here. Is that you, George?"

This morning she was ostensibly as friendly as a neighbor ringing up for a cup of sugar. She could play social games as well as he. But he was not going to play games with her.

"Good morning, Madam Pfitzner," he answered. It was no longer to be "George" and "Jenny." "Excuse the disturbance of the phone call. I know you're busy."

"Sure, I'm busy," she retorted. "*You're* busy, too. I take it you didn't phone me to volunteer further testimony before my committee." The nasal New York drawl had no edge to it, no storm signals. She had apparently accepted his refusal to sleep with her; no hard feelings. But he knew Jenny better than that.

"I trust you and the other members of the committee have been briefed on what . . . happened out on the West Coast to your favorite Romanian," he said.

"I'm ecstatic!" she boomed into the phone. "I thought of phoning you to tell you how gratified I am that at least one son of a bitch war criminal is out of action, for good."

"All's well that ends badly, eh?" he said. "Now you're going to have to find another war criminal to beat on, I guess."

"The country's full of them," she retorted. "But, George, I did want to tell you how sorry I was to hear about what happened to your man out there. . . ."

"Oh, indeed!"

"Yes, *indeed*," she answered, nettled at the dryness of his tone. "Look, George, let's drop the icy-tone business. I told you I was

terribly sorry to hear about it. You guys have a bad apple every
now and again, but I've told you I trust you, George, and never
mind about what happened the other night. I still do."

He studied the bright batik print on the far wall before saying
to her, "You say you trust me. How about *me* trusting *you?*"

It was the clang of steel on steel.

"What do you mean by that, George?"

He drew a deep breath.

"Let me ask a quick question with an up-or-down answer: did
you have anything to do with that leak in the New York *Times,*
the Justice Department report on Calinescu and his bribery of an
Agency employee? The one who was killed out there?"

Her anger rasped in her reply. "What a hell of a question to
ask, just like that!"

"I'm asking it, Jenny, just like that. What's your answer?"

A curious silence at the other end. One thing he knew: Jenny
would not fib to him. Whatever else she was, she was no liar.

"George . . . it's not that simple to answer . . ."

"Mrs. Pfitzner," he said to her civilly, coldly. "Of the two people
involved in that story, both are now dead. That was a classified
document, stamped 'Secret,' from the Department of Justice to
us. It called for action within the executive branch of government.
I'm damned sure Justice didn't leak it, and *we* didn't leak it. Your
subcommittee, I understand, somehow got an information copy of
it. And from your answer, I sense that you were at least witting of
the fact that it was leaked to Barney Langer. True or not true?"

"Now look, George." The drawl of Jenny Pfitzner conveyed
acute embarrassment. "You know how I feel about Calinescu. I
wanted to put every bit of pressure on him and on the Administration to move on him. Barney was supposed to get a good background briefing on the Calinescu case. Nothing more. But he went
too far. . . ."

Wendell said, "Good morning, Mrs. Pfitzner. Maybe someday
we'll discuss the matter of mutual trust." He replaced the telephone thoughtfully on its cradle, cutting off her rush of words.

"Beautiful," Clare said from the doorway. "For once she got it,
instead of dishing it out."

"Miss Meehan," he said severely. "Telephone eavesdropping by

third parties is frowned upon in the federal government. Ever hear
of the Freedom of Privacy Act?"

"Eavesdropping, as you well know, is a way of life in the federal
government, not to mention in this Agency," she replied without
shame. "And you really gave it to her. Bravo."

"All right, all right," he answered unhappily. "Have you ordered
a car and driver from the motor pool? Now I'm going to perform
the rottenest chore of the year."

Clare said, keeping any reproach from her voice, "It's *your* idea,
Mr. Wendell. Personnel was ready to send Mr. DiBuono by himself to deliver the decorations to Mrs. Browning." She looked away
from him with embarrassment. "It isn't as if the DDO himself
has to be present. After all, Steve Browning . . ."

He nodded at the implicit reprimand.

". . . Steve Browning was a bad guy and doesn't deserve anything but minimal postmortem courtesies. Is that what you're trying to tell me, Clare?"

"It's what Personnel thinks, and in general what everybody's
saying, Mr. Wendell." She was not afraid of him in the slightest.

"Well, Clare," he responded with the heavy finality he used in
moments when he dug in his heels, "you know and I know that
the Soviet defector cleared Steve of the enormous suspicions we've
had about him. If there were any lingering doubts in my mind
about him, I would have Personnel send the decorations to his
family by mail. Or not send them at all. As it is, you can tell
everyone that George Wendell felt that Steve Browning, while a
flawed and tragic personality, still served his country and the
Agency well. And he's dead, and I intend to pay my respects to
his family. And I don't give a damn what anyone says about my
action."

Clare said, "The motor-pool vehicle with driver will be ready
at the front entrance at two-fifteen. It's a half hour's ride to Mrs.
Browning's house, and a half hour back. That pretty much takes
care of your afternoon."

They were a somber duo in the backseat of the government
car as the stolid Office of Security driver steered the vehicle
through the checkpoint at the gate, circled down a ramp onto the
sylvan glory of the George Washington Parkway, and headed west

to the Cabin John Bridge. DiBuono, sitting beside Wendell, opened his briefcase and extracted the leather-covered cases one by one.

"Appreciate you finding the time to do this, George," he said. "Steve had been awarded all these medals but of course the Agency retained them because Steve was under non-Agency cover at the time he won them."

Wendell held the decoration cases in both hands, peering down at the circular Agency medallions and the brightly striped lapel ribbons accompanying them.

"These are the hardest ones of all to win." He shook his head in admiration. "You had to stick out your neck a long way to earn one."

DiBuono nodded.

"You can say *that* again. You probably remember why he got them but I'll refresh your memory: These two are Intelligence Stars. This other one, the Career Intelligence Medal. Then these are the written citations. Now let's see: I've got to keep them all straight. This first star he got in 1948 for that Greek caper. This second one was presented to him in 1974. The commendation with it is attached but it's pretty vaguely written. Something about acquisition of information vital to the national interest. Do *you* recall the details?"

"I remember it well," Wendell said. "That was a hairy one. He recruited a little Yemeni Army procurement officer in France. When the officer returned to Yemen, Steve went into the country with two OTS photographers. The three of them, wearing Yemeni military uniforms, accompanied this procurement guy right into the central military depot, outside Sanaa. They spent the whole night photographing a Soviet SAM-3 ground-to-air missile system, *and* its instruction books. And got away clean as a whistle."

"Wow," DiBuono said, "talk about luck and gall."

Wendell grunted. "I remember that the Air Force people out at Wright-Patterson said that the information and photos of those SAMs were worth, conservatively, three million dollars. They learned exactly how good that SAM was in shooting down planes, and what its limitations were. And it cost us all of fifteen thousand dollars in a Zurich bank account."

He stared out at the green wall of the George Washington Parkway and said, half to himself, "The Yemenis are an unforgiving bunch. If they'd been caught . . ." He drew his finger across his throat.

Wendell closed the medal cases and handed them back to Di-Buono. When he spoke again, the bitterness in his voice could not be restrained.

"Do we also hand her the little memo of paper in his file? You know, the one that says, 'You are hereby notified that your employment has been determined to be surplus to the needs of the Service . . .' or however that damned thing goes. I'm sure Mrs. Browning would love to have that one, suitably framed, among these other mementos, medals, thirty-year pins, commendations . . ."

"Aw, come on, George," DiBuono rejoined. "You know damned well we wouldn't tell her that now. As for letting him go, you've heard of wartime heroes, Medal of Honor winners, who come home and hold up banks, can't cope, do badly in peacetime. Look at George Patton. . . ."

"Speaking of military heroes," Wendell rapped. "Steve Browning also got two Silver Stars from the U. S. Army in Italy in wartime. Do you happen to know where he got one of those?"

"No, I really don't, Goerge."

"Well, I'll tell you. He got it saving my rosy red ass, that's how."

They said nothing more to each other until the vehicle drew up at a conventional two-story residence sitting back from a ragged lawn, shaded by a pair of towering oak trees which antedated the house by half a century. Wendell recalled it dimly. He had come here at the housewarming twenty-five years earlier. Paint flaked from its upper clapboard exterior, and a rusted drainpipe hung unhappily from a corner of the roof. It was a house Steve Browning would live in; neglected, not of interest to him except as a base and a bed.

"This is it," the driver said. They got out awkwardly. Wendell, consciously pulling himself erect, marched up the walk, DiBuono behind him. As he reached the door, it was flung open and Joan Browning stood looking at them, pale fragile face making a palpable effort to smile. Her dress was appropriate for a very recent widow: a dark brown skirt and jacket, no jewelry, no cosmetics.

Wendell, in his best executive manner, boomed, "Hello, Joanie," and kissed her lightly on both cheeks. Her lips which brushed his were dry and cold.

"Do come in, please." She led the way into the living room, strikingly decorated with a woman's taste, in soft tints and colors. Nothing in the room reflected the fact that Steve Browning had ever lived here. No wedding photographs, artifacts, books, or souvenirs of his, although the woven rugs, wall tapestries, brass coffee tables, and a pair of African shields were evidence that this was a family which had lived in far corners of the world.

Three men sprang to their feet to greet them, two of them large, bearded, well-dressed adults, the third a husky adolescent with black-rimmed glasses and in unaccustomed jacket and tie, who bore an uncanny resemblance to Steve.

"You may remember my sons, George: Thomas, Edgar, and Timothy." Her voice was thin but steady as each of them shook hands firmly in turn with Wendell and then DiBuono. Only Timmy appeared under some strain, and the soft face, already taking on the heavy cheeks and the shrewd eyes of his father, mirrored a certain struggle to retain his equanimity.

Wendell had seen Joan Browning half a dozen times in recent years, always at large and confused receptions. She had never made any particular impression on him: a quiet mousy blonde with a soft Carolina accent and an indifferent way of dressing. That her eyes were so penetratingly blue he had not remembered, but the thick glasses magnified them now. She had aged very much since he had last seen her. It was true that she was at least fifty, but had this deterioration happened as a result of Steve's death or was it that he was not previously observant? She stood before her larger and taller sons with a smile that he could only describe as poignant.

All of them remained standing and the room seemed overcrowded with hulking males. The atmosphere was heavy, as at a wake. He faced Joan and her men almost formally, hands held behind his back, DiBuono similarly braced at his side. It was almost a confrontation.

"Joanie, Tom, Edgar, Timmy," he began, nodding at each of them in turn. "There's a little bit of unfinished business here today and I wanted personally to be present to complete it. The tragedy that has struck you, strikes us. Steve served his government for thirty-three years, all but one of them with the Agency and its predecessor organizations, and that includes OSS for four years. His death strikes *me* in particular, as you know, Joanie."

She knew. The first time he had met her, at a Sunday cookout, long after he and Steve had returned from Austria to Washington, he had told her how Steve had rescued him in wartime Italy. By that time, she had been married for three or four years, was heavily pregnant with one of the two older sons, and he recalled how she had looked up at him with an air of incredulity after he had finished his war story, as much as to say: had Steve Browning done *that?*

He briefly licked his upper lip, inexplicably dry, before moving on. "In this strange calling of ours, any decorations or material evidence of covert achievements by our employees must be retained by the Agency, at least until retirement. You can understand that for someone under diplomatic or military cover to be wearing an Agency medal or ribbon in public would hardly be the best security practice in the world. But Steve Browning did some incredible things in the service of his country, and he was awarded certain decorations for them. You have already heard the words of the citations which accompanied each of those feats. But today I want to hand the actual medals and commendations over to you, Joanie, and to your children, and I want you to be proud of what he did. I've come out with our Agency chief of awards and decorations, Mr. DiBuono, to read those citations again to you, all five of them. These decorations he earned; they're his, and now they're yours, forever." He wondered whether his fatal instinct for sonority had been excessive to the occasion but the Brownings nodded their individual appreciation.

DiBuono, uncertain and a bit unnerved by the silence in the crowded room, read the citations, one after the other, in his most orotund manner, each ending in the ritual phrase ". . . and reflects great personal credit on him and on the federal service." He then reached into his black briefcase and handed the medals, then the framed commendations, to Joan, one by one. She in turn handed them to Tom, her eldest, who passed them in turn to his brothers. Timmy, last to hold them, placed them on a nearby upright piano top in a neat line.

Joanie, pulling out a tiny handkerchief, briefly wiped her eyes, threw her head back, and firmly, if tremulously, said, "George, speaking for my children and myself, I thank you for your kindness in doing this. It means more to me than I can tell you and"—she gulped once—"even more for my children. Thank you. Thank you."

In the modest murmur that followed, she said, "Please join us in a brief cup of coffee. I know, George, how busy you are; but that's the story of your lives, all of you: how busy you all are." She spoke matter-of-factly, but Wendell did not miss the needle's point.

They chatted, still standing, holding coffee cups, in hushed tones. Yes, Steve would be buried in his hometown in Michigan, next to the graves of his parents and grandparents. Yes, Joanie would continue to live in this house; she really had no other place to go and she had her friends and her teaching job here. The house was hers, outright. No mortgage. Timmy would be leaving for his first year of college soon, but would be close at the nearby American University. Yes, she had been contacted by the Employees Assistance branch of the Agency, who had been most kind. . . .

Then Joanie said, "George, I'd like a quiet word alone with you in my workroom."

They sat on comfortable chairs in the plant-choked corner room streaming with afternoon sunshine, near the bridge table with its piles of student papers waiting to be corrected.

Here in this room where she clearly spent many of her home hours, Joan's soft passivity had vanished. Her voice rang with a tautness he had not expected of her.

"George." She looked at him with an owl-like attention. "I know how these things are, and I know that when you walk out of this house in a few minutes, the chances are that I won't cross your path again. After all, apart from the fact that Steve and you were colleagues for thirty years and more, you and I have really nothing in common." She paused, took off her thick glasses and polished them for a moment with the little linen handkerchief in her hand.

He knew exactly what she was going to say, and he had come to her house hoping that he could deliver his sad encomiums and depart without hearing her out. But another part of him said: This *is* really why you came, isn't it?

"George"—and she pronounced it as a mother or teacher would do in bringing an errant George-child to order—"I want to hear it from your lips, as the DDO: how did Steve die?"

When he had learned that the decorations were to be returned to Joan Browning and had insisted on being present, Wendell knew he must face the question. He was not at all certain how he would respond. He had been advised by the General Counsel and by Larry Chambers of Press Relations that he should leave any responses to them. Many delicate factors were at work here: the possibility of lawsuits by or against the widow Browning and the estate of James Callin and his bodyguards, the notoriety of further media publicity if Joan went public in the matter of Steve's death—all sorts of dicey possibilities best avoided. You, George Wendell, weren't there, so punt: tell her that any explanations will be given to her by our legal people already in touch with her, and simply stress that all her survivor benefits and pension are assured. . . .

Her brimming eyes were fixed on him as if his every word were life or death to her. What good would it do for him to blur or to deny the truth with her? Lawsuits? Negative publicity for the Agency? The Shop had already taken enough negative publicity in the past half-dozen years to last for a full generation to come.

Allen Dulles had insisted on taking the Agency's motto from John 8: ". . . and you will know the truth, and the truth will make you free . . ." It was gracefully, and, many said, cynically, carved into the polished marble on the wall of the main entrance of Headquarters. Wendell had spent a lifetime denying the truth to others for many operational reasons, and fudging on the truth for many more. But, as he looked at her, feeling the telltale pounding of his heart and temples, he knew that he was not about to withhold from her what she wanted to know.

"Joanie." He spoke with what he hoped was an even, dispassionate tone. "Steve left Washington to travel to California a deeply troubled man. His trip was completely unauthorized. He did it on his own, with his own funds. Steve knew before he left that he was one of a dozen GS-14 officers who were on a list to be involuntarily separated—fired, in plain terms—for low perfor-

mance. I don't know whether he told you that." He saw in her eyes
that Steve had not. "And, as a matter of fact, the list hadn't even
been finally approved by the Director. But you know how it is in
our shop." He made a deprecatory upward slash with one hand.
"Everybody stands around reading things they're not supposed to
read."

He sipped his coffee, by now barely lukewarm. Joan, intent and
motionless, held her eyes to his.

"Further, he had just learned that a former agent of his had
reappeared, a Romanian named Radescu, who had disappeared in
1947 in Austria and was thought, after all these years, to have died
in Soviet custody. As you know, Joanie, I was commanding officer
of that unit in Vienna at the time, and I know this case well.
Steve somehow found out that Radescu was in Los Angeles, bent
on revenge, and that's where Steve went, in deep depression, I am
certain. And the person who Steve probably thought was responsible for Radescu's arrest by the Soviets, a man Steve had recruited as a trusted agent in Austria, was also in Los Angeles.
You've seen the papers; it was a Romanian whose name was originally Calinescu, now changed to Callin."

Joan's smile was as bitter as he had ever seen on a woman's
face.

"And that was the man who corrupted Steve—twenty thousand
dollars' worth, according to the papers?"

Wendell nodded. "The same. Let me ask you, Joan: did you
know at the time that he had taken the money?"

The blue eyes drifted for a moment out of focus. She was examining the bits of her memory to determine their validity.

"I *knew* he had gotten the money from somewhere, but he
lied to me on just how he had obtained it. Like any new wife,
with a child on the way, I was deeply concerned about having a
house of our own. We were living in such a dreary little one-
bedroom apartment way out in Silver Spring and I was really after
him to get this place which was up for sale. I was a young teacher
out here in Maryland elementary schools and this looked like the
dream house I had always wanted." She bit her lip. "I should have
known that I was placing too much pressure on him. He was
proud. He wasn't going to admit that as a GS-12 he couldn't raise
that kind of money for a down payment. And one day he came in,

with a smile like a Cheshire cat, with this check from a California legal firm. He had invested in something really great on the West Coast after the war, he said, and had sold his investment at just the right moment. We had the house. How happy I was!"

The pale worn face illuminated with the bright memory and dimmed again.

"But from the outset, George, and God, I hate to admit it, the marriage was no good, at least for me. He was wrapped up in this clandestine business like a beagle taking up a scent. He went baying after agents, and recruitments, and big deals, and nervy stunts all over the place, and I came second. The kids came third. And we were a poor second and third. Half the time in the last thirty years I haven't known where he was or what he was doing."

Her lips curled with self-deprecation.

"Doesn't do much for a wife's ego to play that far back in the second fiddles."

"Joanie," Wendell said, bitterly amused at the familiar lament. "That's hardly a unique situation with Agency wives. I daresay my Maude could sing the same sad song."

"Yes, George, yes, I know." She nodded her head in emphatic agreement. "But there was something else there, George. You know it, and all of Steve's colleagues and friends, if indeed he had many real friends, they all knew it: he was basically a con artist. It pains me like a knife in my bosom to say, but it must be said. He had an ability to con even his own colleagues, and there are quite a few out there in Langley who should know one when they see one. But more terrible—he actually conned himself. He never really looked in the mirror to see what he really was."

She took a convulsive sip from her cup of coffee. "God knows, I didn't have a clue what it was I was marrying into. I was a young, naïve, happy elementary school teacher, fresh out of a North Carolina teaching college, with a brand-new position in a brand-new elementary school in Montgomery County. Meeting Captain Steve Browning, fresh from the war, from OSS, was a little bit like meeting a whirlwind. You know; with the uniform and the medals and all; he picked you up and he wouldn't put you down."

The thought thrummed in his mind that he had been sitting here entirely too long, and was hearing painful naked confessions he was not sure he needed to know. But as if she were reading his mind, she stopped her narrative and asked him severely, "What happened in that Beverly Hills house, George? Did Steve go in there to kill that man, Calla . . . ?"

"Call him Callin."

"Callin."

Wendell fingered the Phi Beta Kappa key. Harvard had been a happy time for him. When he retired and got into the tweedy jacket and baggy slacks routine, he would wear the key no longer chained to a vest, but he would carry it, perhaps in a little flap in his wallet. He lifted his eyes to hers.

"Joanie, Steve Browning never, to my knowledge, killed or wounded anybody in his entire life up to the moment he met Calinescu for the last time. He loathed guns. I'm sure you know that. But Callin was his nemesis, the man who corrupted him, a corruption that haunted him all his life. And therefore Calinescu had to be exorcised, destroyed."

Joan was no fool. She followed his lips as would a deaf-mute and he could see the sharp gleam of comprehension building in her eyes.

"Steve was in a box, a cul-de-sac. Not only did he know that he was on a list of those to be fired, he also knew that the Agency had received evidence that he had taken the twenty thousand dollars from Callin, that quite possibly he would be tried in a federal court. His world had closed exits. And his Agency career, which as you say was his obsession, his real life, was going to come to a swift and shameful end."

He paused and said dryly, "I'm convinced that he intended to kill Calinescu and then himself. How or in what circumstances, possibly even he didn't know. As it happened, he and Radescu entered Callin's house together (and I understand that Steve found Radescu skulking outside Callin's house, also waiting for a chance to get in at him). Steve and Radescu had words with Callin and Steve then killed him; executed him is perhaps a better word. Once that was done there was no need for Steve to have pointed his gun at the guards who rushed in. But he did, and then he deliberately fired one shot up at the ceiling, knowing that the guards, panicky and irrational, would fire back at him. And they did. They killed him, as he probably hoped they would."

Her reaction was amazing. He had thought she would burst

into troubled tears, bury her face in her hands. But, apart from trembling lips, she rose, walked to him, and said, "George, I thank you. From the bottom of my heart. Not because you told me this story, but because you told me the truth. I wanted this last act of truth from the Agency. I had hoped that for once I wouldn't get the sort of conning Steve used to give me. Your telling me all this openly, fully, means more to me than bringing over Steve's medals and citations."

Her farewell kiss on his cheek was warm and heartfelt as they stood on the doorstep, the black Agency car waiting at the curb with its engine running.

"How are you so sure I didn't leave anything out?" he asked with a twinkle, holding her hand in his for a last moment.

"Silas Ruffing came by late last night," she said. "He came straight from the airport and he told me the same story, the same facts. I wanted just this once to see how honest you all in the Shop could be."

CHAPTER TWENTY-ONE

Don Kobler, assigned on a tour of duty as Special Assistant to the Deputy Director for Operations, an officer genuinely "in the know," sat with the little cluster of his Agency peers who daily lunched together in his favorite corner (smoking permitted) of the vast, hangar-like Agency cafeteria. Although he was no higher in grade than the others, his Special Assistant status gave him a special aura. By their questions, deferential glances and gestures, the others made it clear to him: you're in the know, so tell us: what's cooking?

Indeed, Kobler knew to a large degree what was cooking. It was not for appearances' sake that he rose every weekday morning at 5:30 (somewhat later on Saturdays), sleepily performed his ablutions, and arrived an hour later at the Agency's telecommunications center, his third cigarette of the day already dangling from his mouth. There he picked up a half-foot stack of cables which constituted all of the Directorate's incoming and outgoing traffic for the night just ended. With this load, he trudged to the elevator, pressed the top button, tramped down the long corridor to the DDO executive office suite, and flipped on the garish fluorescent lights in that darkened area, thus opening it for business. Almost two hours later, steadily jotting his own observations on a lined yellow pad, he had winnowed out of that imposing stack about an inch of "Must Read" material for the DDO. And he read that inch more carefully a second time. With George Wendell, you did your homework or *he* drew blood. (There were many items he did not tell George Wendell, or flag for him, too trivial in nature for Wendell but of vast importance to Kobler, who had a reputation to maintain as a man "in the know.")

Floors below him, he knew, lesser Special Assistants were doing the same thing on a regional basis. But he, Don Kobler, had the full Oversight, the big picture: perched in his Directorate aerie, he knew what was going on all over the world. And by 8:45 A.M., so did George Wendell, the DDO.

Kobler, of course, did not advertise to the cafeteria luncheon hangers-on, or to anyone else, what he did *not* know, much of which they *thought* he knew. None of them, of course, asked him to speak of sensitive and risky operations going on inside the Soviet Union or elsewhere; they were all disciplined officers, steeped in the steely doctrine of need-to-know. Besides, each of them already knew enough operational secrets to last him a lifetime. What inordinately and understandably piqued their curiosity were Agency internal bubblings: who was getting the ax, who would be promoted, what games of musical chairs were going on in the hierarchy, to whom would the new juicy station-chief assignments be awarded? Rumors flew up and down the endless corridors like flocks of raucous gulls, but Don Kobler really *knew*; of that they were certain.

This day three cafeteria tables, pushed together in a T-shaped mass, permitted a half dozen of them to sprawl informally amidst the litter of bowls, plates, and plastic trays and to play their usual game of cat-and-mouse with Kobler, their blue-and-white identity badges serving as dangling credentials. It was a game which called for much elicitative skill, body English, and subtle circumlocutions. They were all very good at it, as indeed was he.

"So how long have *you* known that Wendell was going to pack it in?" one of his more knowing audience asked. "You can't tell me that you haven't known for months. Christ, how cozy can you get with us all the time, and we your little playmates from the CT class of '63?"

Since it would not do for him to admit, nor would they believe, that he had been as thunderstruck as they when the news of Wendell's impending retirement had been announced two days earlier, Kobler jiggled one large shoe under the cafeteria table, blew a cloud of cigarette smoke straight up at the ceiling, and made a gesture of embarrassment.

"Look, sitting Up There, a guy's got to be damned discreet. Suppose I had told you all in the strictest confidence, say, two months ago, that I knew that Wendell was going to quit, and when. That would really have given you a jolly, wouldn't it? And you, the pride of the clandestine service, would (in the strictest confidence, of course) tell only one or two of your closest buddies, and maybe your wife. I'd be willing to bet that within forty-eight hours of the time I leaked that news to you, some Agency wife would waltz up to Mrs. Wendell at some damned Georgetown klatsch and ask her why her husband was retiring. Or some goddamned newspaper columnist would get wind of it. Come on, men: a guy in my position has got to watch it and watch it carefully."

"And who's the new DDO going to be?" The bearded admin man for the East Asia Division was more than idly interested. His own division chief might be in the running, and if he were selected, all sorts of fortunate consequences might flow from that. "Who's in the running?"

Kobler's eyes gleamed and he held his forefinger along his nose with an appreciative grin.

"Good try, Paul, but nothing doing. Anything I said would make the pot boil more noisily." He peered at his watch and exclaimed, "Oh, Christ, I've got to brief the DDO and the ADDO together in fifteen minutes. The DDO is flying down tomorrow morning to the Farm to talk to the graduating CT class, and that means the ADDO has to mind the store over the weekend. Poor bastard just got back last night from Manila, mad as a wet hen about having his orientation trip cut short, I can tell you true."

That gave them a quick peek behind the opaque curtain of top Directorate management. That they were not as reverent as he would like was evident, however, in the cry of one of them to him as he sprang to his feet.

"If COS Buenos Aires opens up, remember, Don, I'm the guy who shook the hand of a guy who kissed the hand of Evita Perón."

"Did you say: her *hand?*" Kobler retorted, crushing his cigarette into an empty salad dish as he hastened away. "Boy, you've really got ironclad qualifications."

He carefully disposed of his tray and briskly walked the length of the cafeteria, aware of heads here and there moving close to each other, murmuring, "That's Don Kobler, in the DDO office." If there was one thing that gave him greater satisfaction than oversight into the complicated and compartmented workings of the clandestine service, it was internal recognition. He enjoyed this subtle perquisite of his job as much as he hated getting up at dawn to sift through five pounds of top-secret cables. There was, after all, nothing else *but* internal recognition one could achieve in this submerged career. Like virtue, however, it had its own reward.

Once seated in his windowless cubbyhole in the DDO suite, a room exactly ten feet square, barely large enough to contain his metal desk and chair, a visitor's chair, and a three-drawer combination-lock safe, he leaned back, new cigarette lit, to review the bidding. He had engaged in normal hyperbole with his cafeteria comrades-in-arms. Yes, the DDO and the ADDO would be talking about the major problems which had arisen since the ADDO departed on his orientation trip ten days earlier, and yes, Don Kobler would be present during much—but not all—of this discussion. But he would hardly be briefing either of them. He would take notes, handle some designated errands and hand-carries, nag a few delinquent division and staff chiefs on overdue memos. He was a glorified go-fer, goddamnit. But, modesty aside, he was a very good one. And if hard work, attention to details, and keeping his lines out were necessities to achieving further upward mobility, Don Kobler couldn't miss.

But, as he watched the curling cigarette smoke disappear into the blue-white fluorescent light over his head, he knew that something was quite out of phase, something that lay beyond his comprehension. A little bit like a dead skunk under the veranda back home: you couldn't see it but, by God, you knew it was there.

It was as perplexing a week as he had ever experienced in his Agency career. And much of his perplexity lay in the fact that he really didn't know precisely what was happening. It had been a week of frantic activity. These annual division operational reviews were enormous productions, with charts, endless briefings by officers in charge of projects, division budgets, planning and logistics. Sitting in judgment day after day on one of such reviews would tax the brain of any DDO. This was, additionally, an intensive period of regearing the Directorate for more audacious and aggressive penetrations into Soviet-controlled Europe, into Afghan-

istan, Central Asia, into the weird Russian toeholds in the
Yemen and Ethiopia, into Cuba. . . .

And yet, all week long who had been on the front burner?
Calinescu and Browning, Browning and Calinescu. And that sad
little creep Ruffing.

Precisely what had happened out in Beverly Hills was still not
clear to him. This was something that Wendell had played very
close to his chest together with Nordholm of Security and the
DCI. But yesterday, in the middle of one of the busiest days in a
long time, Wendell had simply canceled all appointments for two
hours and went off to deliver all of Browning's Agency decorations
to his widow. Now *that* took the cake. Even for an old war comrade, it was excessive. If he lived to be a hundred, he, Kobler,
would never understand George Wendell.

He looked at his consumed cigarette and stubbed it out, counting the dozen previous butts in the ashtray. It was scarcely after
midday; this curious level of tension was increasing his smoking
habit, he realized with a troubled frown.

Well, in the final analysis, he would be the survivor. Wendell
was leaving, somebody else arriving. With a new DDO on board,
Kobler's services would certainly be needed for continuity, perhaps for many months to come. And, in the meanwhile, he would
keep revolving his antennae in all directions. From this vantage
point, he could spot those overseas assignments opening up very
early on and position himself into a front-runner candidacy for a
good one. He had his priorities: Chief of Station in Singapore,
maybe Copenhagen or Stockholm, Lusaka or Dar. He wasn't senior enough to head a really big station yet, but he was ready for
his own show overseas, to be boss. And running a station could
end this high-level go-fer status. He was sick to death of Headquarters bureaucracy. He got things done; this was known and appreciated. Very well; they should let him do his thing out there,
on the front line.

As for Wendell, he had to admit, the man had taught him
much. For the first time in his career, he had collided with a senior officer who insisted on form together with the substance.
Wendell called it "style," and while he himself thought it was a
good deal of bullshit, it apparently mattered where it counted. If
it mattered, by God, he was going to develop "style," in dress,

manner, speaking, writing. Those little needlings about what were the plurals and the singulars in words of Latin or Greek origin; those arch little phrases flung at him. He would learn them, as he had learned everything else; they would become part of him and he would use them, as Wendell seemed to, to enormous advantage. . . .

The telephone buzzed; an internal call on the Secure Line.

"Alan, in Personnel," the other identified himself with the hushed tone of a discreet undertaker. "You remember, I owe you one?" Alan's voice was a half question mark.

"You owe me two, but who's counting?" he said joshingly, but something in him began to descend.

"All right, I'm paying you one out of two, OK? How would you like to know what your next assignment is going to be, starting 15 October?"

"I don't know what you're talking about," he exclaimed, shakily placing a fresh cigarette between his suddenly dry lips. "My tour in the DDO office doesn't end here for another six months."

"Well, you're wrong, old buddy," Alan informed him. "But I'm giving you this one strictly back-channel. There's nothing on paper yet, but your boss, the DDO, and *my* boss, Director of Personnel, had a couple of quick words on you earlier today. SueAnn, my boss's secretary, overheard what they agreed, and passed it on to me."

Kobler for a moment could not speak. Then, after a brief paroxysm brought about by swallowed smoke, he asked hoarsely, "Well?"

Alan said, "The DDO said you were a highly valuable aide. First-class. He remembered that you had bitterly complained several times about the Agency records and document retrieval system. Something about how difficult it was to find files quickly and efficiently. My boss immediately agreed and said there was not only a big problem over there but that a GS-15 supervisory slot would be open in the next three weeks. He said that would not only be a surefire way for you to get a promotion but that kind of support-staff experience under your belt would look real good down the road. . . ."

Kobler cried, "You're not shitting me, are you, Alan?"

Alan answered, much affronted, "Look, buddy, I'm only doing

you a favor. Giving you advance on something you wouldn't know about until your boss told you. If that's your goddamned attitude . . ."

"No, no, no," Don assured him. "No, I much appreciate the call."

Two years in Document Retrieval! He took up his black felt pen and commenced frantic doodlings on his yellow pad. Two years in the goddamned bowels of the building, peering at green video screens, computer printouts, supervising little old ladies and gum-chewing stenos, buried away from operations as thoroughly as if he had been temporarily entombed.

On a little three-by-five card, tucked under the leather-edged blotting pad, a dozen items were listed under the title "Wendellisms," one under the other. The last four read:

— *Zeitgeist*
— "none" always followed by singular, *not* plural, verb
— *Schadenfreude*
— criterion (sing.); criteria (pl.)

With a strangled howl of despair, he tore the card into many pieces.

CHAPTER TWENTY-TWO

"I've never seen you looking so . . . so *unpreoccupied* in years," Maude told him, looking at his profile from the passenger seat as he guided the Mercedes at very moderate speed across the granite dignity of the Memorial Bridge to the Virginia side. "You've already got that secret half smile of contentment, and you've still got sixty days to go."

"Fifty-eight, m'love," he said, turning an affectionate glance at her. "Fifty-eight days to go, and I can feel it all start to drain away. By the time I reach the last day, there won't be an ounce of adrenaline left in the whole system."

"Maybe you can find a substitute liquid," she retorted. "Like skimmed milk."

"Ugh," he grunted, making an exaggerated grimace. "You wives! You want me to live forever." He knew very well what she meant: his need to flatten that bay window unabashedly swelling under the tan sweater and ancient houndstooth jacket.

"Forever is a long time," Maude replied. "I'll settle for another twenty-five years."

"Done," he bayed, swinging the vehicle to the underpass leading to the airport, "but we've always been strong for quality, not quantity, haven't we?"

The clarity of the September morning sunshine and the glistening placidity of the wide Potomac filled him with exuberance. He sang in a rusty baritone, "Methuselah lived nine hundred years, Methuselah lived nine hundred years, but who calls that livin' when no gal will give in to a man what's got nine hundred years . . ."

"You *do* enjoy these trips to the Farm, don't you?" She smiled. "Getting away from that prison of an office does things for you."

He shook his head firmly.

"No, Maudie, it isn't just the Farm I like to go to. It's the CTs down there. Marvelous kids, most of them. Well, *I* call them kids. Their ages range from twenty-two to about thirty, and that sure as hell makes them young enough to be *my* kids. I've kept up the DDO tradition of visiting at the end of the long weeks of training and just before they're assigned to their first jobs. They're the new Agency blood, Maudie, fresh and brash, and it lifts the old spirits to see them sitting there with their engines running, ears laid back, ready to charge out and do the impossible for dear old CIA. You don't run into too many young patriots any more. Maybe that's why I love to see them."

Maude was silent and he sensed her troubled concern. He reached over, touched her soft chin, and patted the kilt creases at her knee.

"How on a Washington morning like this can you remain immune?" he teased her. "Do you realize how many hundreds of such superb days I've spent indoors in that office of mine, sitting in my damned swivel chair, looking out at the sun playing on the leaves, cursing myself for a fool that from dawn to dusk I never got a lungful of outdoor air. You're spoiled, Maudie; you're out in it all the time."

"I was wondering," she said after a pause, "what your last blood-pressure readings were. . . ."

He frowned. So like a woman to transform euphoria into unpleasant reality.

"Maudie," he said gently, choosing his words with care. "I deeply appreciate your concern but we're both old enough to be responsible for ourselves. I know my condition, Maudie, and I'm looking after it. I take these dreadful diuretics that make me trot to the boy's room ten times a day, plus two other kinds of pills, and there's precious little you can do for me. Worry is the most useless emotion in your marvelous repertoire. And reminding me of such things simply runs up the old irritation gauge."

"All right, all right." She raised her hands in resignation. "Not another word."

An organized confusion reigned at the entrance of the general aviation terminal of National Airport. Taxis and station wagons disgorged or swallowed baggage-laden passengers, and small children whooped in liberated glee between the vehicles. Wendell slid ponderously from behind the wheel and extracted a large carry-on bag from the trunk of his car.

"Great day to be bouncing through the sky," he said with satisfaction, looking up at the cloudless blue. Turning to her, he took in her slim, erect figure beside the Mercedes, red-checked tartan snugly hugging her narrow waist, and nodded his compliments. "The Campbells would be proud to see how you look in their colors," he said. "We'll have you dance a Highland fling in it tomorrow night when I get back. And I will sing outrageous Scottish barrack-room ballads which I learned during the war and which you inevitably will stop me from finishing."

Maude smiled tentatively and held out both her hands. He grasped them and pulled her toward him. He held her close, and she responded with an unaccustomed fierceness.

"We've got the entire family coming in for dinner tomorrow night," she said. "And that includes your only grandson. Don't you dare telephone up from the Farm and tell me that either the weather or those question-and-answer sessions have delayed you until the next day."

He kissed her briefly but fully on her lips.

"The family's one thing, luv, and seeing George Sheridan Wendell III will be a joy," he said with a wink, "but wild horses couldn't keep me away from your world-famous *risotto alla milanese*. Like MacArthur, I shall return."

"You had bloody well better," a familiar voice assured him.

"Well, for God's sake, the master pill-roller of Langley," Wendell exclaimed. Dr. Angus Hocker, in a disreputable sweater, corduroy slacks, scuffed yellow hiking shoes, and a knockabout Irish hat, stood at their side, a bright red airlines bag slung over one shoulder.

"Before you ask the inevitable question, George, no: I'm not following you around. I'm on the griddle to go down to the Farm and tell these estimable young DDOs of tomorrow a few unpleasant things about the effects of drugs, alcoholism, and excessive sexual activity on their youthful systems, not to mention their careers."

Maude beamed at him. "Angus, it's so good to see you—and to know you'll be with George."

Wendell, shaking his head, exclaimed, "I begin to see the pattern here. Dear old George is going to get thirty-six hours of weekend medical surveillance. From Maude to Angus and back to Maude."

"It's a good put-up plot," Angus laughed. "Even if it isn't true. But the CTs at least listen to an old worn-out doc. DDOs don't."

A bald mustached young man emerged from inside the terminal building with a swift gait and a worried look. He spotted Wendell and Hocker with a smile of relief and hastened to them.

"Mr. Wendell, sir; Dr. Hocker. The gooney is leaving in five minutes. Will you follow me, please!" He picked up Wendell's and Hocker's bags and headed back to the terminal.

"Goodbye, Maude," Hocker said. "I can't tell this man much. But I will sit in silent reproach if he so much as reaches for a salt shaker or a slice of pie."

Wedged in the tiny seats at the front of the twin-engine Agency plane, Wendell and Hocker were silent as its propellers howled to life. It waddled slowly off the ground into the clear pale blue Virginia sky and lumbered in a tight half-circle to set its course. Wendell, exhilarated, leaned to Hocker and half shouted in his ear, "Would you believe? This is the first time I've gone down to the Farm in the last two years without a thick batch of briefings to read. I used to have a briefcase full of 'must' clippings from the press on the Agency, congressional legislation. Couldn't waste a minute. Today, behold!" He held open his hands, palms upward. "Nothing! Free! Lord Almighty. Just a nice commuter ride in the sunshine, together with the Senior Spook of Medicine."

Hocker leaned back at him, shouting in his ear over the roaring engines. "That's the spirit! And incidentally, thanks for getting me off the hook with your announcement to retire. I was really over a barrel, you know; your condition was such that I should have told the DCI long ago but you wouldn't let me. Couldn't have held out much longer."

"Did the Director ring you up to ask about my condition?" Wendell asked into one of Hocker's hairy ears.

"Did he ever!" Hocker exclaimed. "Ten minutes after you told him you wanted out, he was on the horn. Asked if this was some sort of put-up job, whether it was an excuse or the real thing. I told him what I told you: that George Wendell is not well even if he looks like the Rock of Gibraltar. He listened, thanked me, and hung up."

He peered at Wendell's freshly shaven and scented face so close to his own.

"How's it going this morning, George?"

Wendell's eyes caught his.

"I'm A-OK this morning, sir," Wendell said. Hocker nodded meaningfully. It was Wendell's graceful way of lying.

Behind them, a half-dozen young Agency men and women sat in cramped discomfort, buzzing to one another about the presence on board of the DDO Himself *and* the Director of Medical Services. The close-shaven heads of pilot and copilot, each clad in light jackets and slacks, looked reassuringly steady through the open door to the cockpit as the horizon bobbed up and down when the little workhorse of a plane droned through bumpy patches of air.

"I'm involved in the paper part of an autopsy on Steve Browning's body," Hocker's voice suddenly blurted in Wendell's ear. "Routine business, but very sad. They're bringing the body to Washington first and then it gets shipped to Michigan for burial."

He noted an intense muscular twitch in Wendell's cheek and added hastily, "Sorry if this bothers you, George. I know that he served with you in wartime."

Wendell peered grimly out the tiny window at the rolling green-patched Virginia landscape and the shimmer of a dozen rural ponds below. His encounter with Silas Ruffing yesterday at the day's end rose like an unbidden ghost.

It had been Ruffing who had phoned asking to see him. Wendell had sought to solicit Kobler's assistance to find out what Ruffing wanted to say, but his ubiquitous Special Assistant had inexplicably gone home in midafternoon, telling Clare that he didn't feel well. That, in itself, was strange. But Ruffing had said that it was his last workday in the Agency before retirement and he left Wendell no choice. At 5:45 P.M., Clare appeared at the door, her pug face set in a somber cast, and said, "Silas Ruffing is here."

The slight shaggy figure standing in the doorway of his office seemed shrunken, buffeted by harsh winds. Wendell noted that he already wore on a chain the telltale indicator of his retirement status: his blue-and-white staff badge with photo had been replaced with a yellow plastic square with a large *T*, Temporary. For *T* badge wearers, there was no tomorrow in the Agency.

Silas was clearly in no mood for auld lang syne. After a brief shake of the hand across Wendell's desk, he retreated behind a chair to stand at a kind of loose attention, declining an offer to sit down.

Wendell sat back in his chair, prepared to let Silas get it all out of his system, dismayed at the intense unspoken sorrow that seemed to engulf the man. In previous months, he had personally heard out the farewell comments of a dozen departing Agency warriors, although he might well have turned this chore over to his Deputy or to Personnel. He owed them that final courtesy, he reasoned, and, on a less exalted level, if it achieved catharsis for them, they would be less likely to spill their guts to some sensation-mongering columnist or to the Barney Langers of this world.

It took Silas two or three deep breaths before he managed to say, "They got to him, do you know that?"

He studied Silas for a moment with fingers touching on the desk before him. How much did Silas know? Perhaps Rogov had not told everything. "If you're referring to the KGB, we're quite aware of all that," he said, trying to communicate sympathy and regret at the same time. "But maybe *you* know something we don't already understand?"

Silas had shut his eyes for a moment as if summoning courage to say more.

"All I know," he finally said, his words hoarse and half strangled with emotion, "is what I saw two nights ago in Dimmy Calinescu's library: Steve Browning, lying in his bare feet, flat on his back, mud-caked and drenched to the skin, with seven slugs in him. God, whatever he had done, he didn't deserve that!"

He held up his hands to hide both eyes in a paroxysm of grief.

Wendell leaned across his desk, deep-set eyes peering over his reading glasses at Silas.

"I think we're both agreed that he wanted it that way, Ruff." He tried to inject gentleness and finality into his words. "You might say he literally committed suicide—after committing a cold-blooded murder."

Silas' eyes flashed with momentary rage.

"How about 'justifiable execution'?"

Wendell said, "It won't wash. That's not the way *we* do things, Ruff, and I'm damned disappointed to hear you say that. Yes, Calinescu was probably a cutthroat and a criminal but that's what we've got this whole complicated system of due process for."

He tapped his own chest.

"I don't know what happened in places like Vietnam, Ruff, but *I've* never countenanced, requested, or even hinted at anyone being rubbed out for any reason." He paused. "For *any* reason," he repeated.

Silas studied the beige carpeting for some moments before he spoke. His thin voice was contrite.

"Forget what I said. It's just that when I think about Calinescu, the quality of my mercy gets pretty strained."

He stood like a penitent petitioner before a stern judge.

"George, when I walk out of here tonight, the chances are that I'll never set foot in this Agency again. No complaints, understand; if I were in your shoes or the Director's, I'd really tie the can to old Silas Ruffing's tail. But I have a last favor to ask you. Did the Sovs make it with Steve? Did he really sell us out and pass them the family jewels? I've really got to know, George, or it'll trouble me every remaining day of my life."

Wendell folded his plump hands. In the "in" box at his right elbow lay a dozen vital cables and memoranda which had to be read carefully and released or bucked back to their originators before he could go home this autumn evening. He would be very late again for dinner. Maude would be cross. The food would have to be reheated.

But at this moment, nothing was more important to him than telling Silas Ruffing what he knew.

"I'm putting you on the Bigot List for this case, Ruff, the last one you'll probably ever be on. I'm making you witting about what we know about Steve and the KGB connection. Understood?"

Silas placed one hand pseudo-seriously over his right breast.

"Cross my heart and hope to die."

"All right, then. We've turned this Agency upside down these last weeks to uncover everything we can. This is the best we can figure out what happened."

He gathered his breath as would a diver on the high board.

"Three times in the last nine years, the Soviets approached Steve and tried to recruit him. The first occasion was an assessment sort of pitch in New Delhi, an offer of lots of money, with only a vague hint of blackmail. But you know old Steve. He apparently tried to turn it around. He reported to the station chief that he had attracted a live KGB-nik who might be hooked if the station let him pass the guy some 'smoke' to keep him nibbling. Headquarters agreed and Steve gave the Sovs some innocuous stuff: an unclassified embassy telephone directory, a couple of unclassified CIA economic assessments. Nobody in the station dreamed that it was *Steve* who was on the hook, although your CI crowd sent out the usual caveats. Then he was transferred out of Delhi and he apparently hoped that was the end of it."

The corners of Silas' mouth had drooped in an involuntary gesture of contempt for Browning's naïveté.

"Of course that wasn't the end of it," Wendell went on. "But a lot of time went by and with Steve in Washington, nothing more happened. Then he was assigned to Amman three years later and the Sovs buttonholed him again in a very cozy 'accidental' tourist encounter at the ruins of Jarash. On that occasion, the Sov politely told him that they would blow the whistle on him if he didn't produce. Nothing specific in the way of blackmail, but this time they didn't want chicken feed. Mind you, it was during this tour that Steve pulled off that incredible Yemeni caper, the one that got him one of his Intelligence Stars."

"Incredible," Silas muttered, arms folded before him.

"Steve knew what was happening to him." Wendell spoke in a fatigued monotone. "He knew that someone here at Headquarters, like yourself, would smell a rat if he asked to be transferred home scarcely six months into his tour there. But his pride or his panic, we don't know which, wasn't going to let him admit to anyone that he was on a KGB sing-or-sink list. So he did an outrageous thing: he deliberately and blatantly tried to recruit a Jordanian general who indignantly reported the pitch back to the Jordanian service. They promptly PNGed Steve, which was exactly what he knew they would do. He got a stiff written reprimand from my predecessor DDO for doing that. But he was out of Amman, running away from them, except that they weren't about to let go."

Silas said, "That poor, sad-ass son of a bitch."

"Seven months ago," Wendell continued, with a glint of irritation at the expletive, "right in the middle of the parking lot at Tyson's Corner shopping mall, they arranged to bump into and to put the heat on him again. Was he or was he not going to play? And Steve knew they had him. What he didn't know was that the FBI had been tailing the KGB man for months and had him blanketed as Steve grabbed the guy by the lapels and told him to shove it sideways and that he wasn't going to play with them any more. The KGB man told him that was too damn bad. We know precisely what was said because the FBI has a motion-picture film of the encounter, taken with a telephoto lens. They got the dialogue by using a lipreading expert to transcribe what Steve and the KGB man said to each other."

Silas absorbed the information with an expression of involuntary professional satisfaction.

"That's first-class," he blurted. Then, with an appraising glance, he asked Wendell, "How did he ever cover up this KGB business on his polygraphs?"

"*You* know Steve," Wendell answered with a snort of dark amusement. "He took a routine flutter sometime after he got back from Delhi and managed to screw it up so that the operator didn't know what to make of the readout. After all, Steve had reported the name of his Soviet contact in Delhi as well as the other details, and Security thought that any equivocations in the squiggles should be attributed to Steve's long career in clandestine ops that makes it hard to give a clear yes or no to any questions concerning unauthorized contacts. And he hasn't taken a poly since that one."

"And so when this Calinescu thing came up in Congress and the IG people started grilling him, he knew that it was only a matter of time before he'd have to take another one. Everything started converging on him."

Wendell nodded.

"You've got it. So he went to a northern Virginia gun shop one weekend and bought a used handgun. We've traced it by the manufacturer's number on it. It was a nine-millimeter automatic pistol."

"Wait a minute!" Silas shouted. "Where did you get the details on these KGB contacts? None of that stuff is in the files. . . ."

Wendell rose very slowly to his feet and walked around to Silas. He stood half a foot taller than the round-shouldered little man, and he stared down into Silas' quick, keen eyes before speaking almost conspiratorially.

"He wrote it down himself, Ruff, all of it. It was in an envelope he gave to his secretary just before he flew out to Los Angeles, addressed to me and with the words 'In the Event of My Death.' And it all checks out, Ruff. He was a bad boy but he didn't sell us out."

Ruffing reached out with his right hand and Wendell shook it firmly and repeatedly.

"And *you* were a bad boy, Ruff, to hide that damned memo on him from the Justice Department. I won't even try to tell you the grief you've caused me by your action."

Silas gnawed his mustache and bit his lip remorsefully before replying.

"George, I've given specific statements to the IG and the Director, taking full responsibility . . ."

Wendell shook his heavy head.

"You can't do that, Ruff. *I'm* the only one who takes full responsibility around here."

But Silas, clenching his hands into fists, asserted, "You can accept bureaucratic responsibility, George, but if you had gotten that Justice memo and had acted on it, Steve might be retired today, and he might also be alive, and so might Calinescu. *I've* got to live with that."

Silence hovered in Wendell's brightly lit office like an uninvited shadow. Wendell finally said, with an effort, "Sorry it had to end this way, Ruff. I wish you well."

Silas, glancing around the large airy room as if to remember all its details, said, half to himself, "You know, when I reached Steve, he was still alive but just barely. He seemed to want to say something. I bent down with my ear close to his mouth and he whispered, 'Tell Timmy I'm sorry I missed his birthday again.' Then he died."

He paused and shrugged his narrow shoulders.

"I passed that on to Joan. I shouldn't have. It really broke her up."

Silas moved uncertainly toward the closed door, and peered back at Wendell standing motionless. With one hand on the doorknob, he said, words trembling a bit as they tumbled out, "God, he was an incredible operator! He had some terrible flaws but he was the best street man in this Agency. It was his whole life."

"*And* his death," George Wendell added.

CHAPTER TWENTY-THREE

Yawing slightly to the right and left, bouncing with the air currents, the Agency plane swooped ever lower, now skimming the placid surface of Chesapeake Bay. Dead ahead lay a single forlorn airstrip, its runway lying like a straight gray matchstick from the water's edge into the exuberant green forest. With one bump, then another, the plane landed and rolled off the runway to a modest landing apron where a handful of station wagons, a fuel truck, and a fire engine and crew awaited them. The daily arrival of the gooney from Washington was very much a routine event but the size and caliber of the reception committee varied with the rank and importance of those arriving. From the plane window, Wendell noted, with a half smile, the presence of the chief of the training center, his deputy, and the Farm's security officer. He was happy not to overhear their private comments to each other on what they thought of weekend arrivals of VIPs.

Wendell, first out of the plane, clambered cautiously down the short ladder to the ground, sniffing the fresh scent of the forest air and gazing around at the hushed mass of pine woods on all sides. On such a September day, the boondocks were not hard to take.

As always, much was made of him by the training cadre officers gathered at the airstrip, as befit a Deputy Director. A thin aluminum chain, to which a temporary visitor's badge had been affixed, was ceremoniously draped around his neck, and he underwent much informal slapping of his back and what-the-hell-is-going-on-at-Headquarters banter.

But the chief instructor at the Farm, a rugged-looking man with snow-white hair, elegant ascot brimming out of his open-collar shirt, with the ramrod erectness of the West Pointer he once was, took him by the elbow and steered him to a quiet corner of the landing apron. There he fixed Wendell with a hawk's eye and in the deceptively soft speech of the Deep South asked, "George, what in the living hell's really going on? Without so much as an advance blip, you suddenly pack it in. They tell me you're using a medical reason, but I just don't goddamn believe it. And then there's this crazy business of Steve Browning. Shot to death in some goddamned Beverly Hills pad? Do these two things have anything to do with each other?"

Hank had served on the old German Branch with him twenty years ago and what he lacked in Machiavellian brilliance, he fulfilled in shrewdness. With this man there was no middle ground: either you told him everything or you looked straight back at him and said: I just can't talk.

Wendell, gazing past him at the soothing shaded mass of scrub pine, said, "Now's not the time to discuss it, Hank. Maybe over lunch, a few weeks after my retirement. But I'll tell you this much now: no, it wasn't entirely my health, although everybody, including Hocker over there, tells me my blood pressure is breaking new world records. As for Browning . . ." It was hard to look into those unblinking eyes. "I can only say this about it: it was an appalling tragedy. I take my own share of blame for it. It started way back in Vienna, thirty years ago, and I simply wasn't quick enough, intuitive enough, to have sensed what was wrong there."

Hank, seamed face creased in a solidarity grin, squeezed Wendell's upper arm in a momentary vise.

"It can wait. And I'll take you up on that post-retirement lunch. But you're going to find some edgy, worried CTs at the Q&A session this afternoon. These kids have developed some sharp antennas. And they're getting mighty nervous about who is running the Shop in Langley and why you're suddenly quitting. They don't like the smell of it."

He gave Wendell's arm three light taps with his fist, to emphasize his words.

"You're a kind of security blanket, George, do you know that? And when that blanket disappears suddenly, there are a lot of people who feel a cold chill."

Wendell lightly punched him once in return.

"I've been called a lot of rotten names in my time, Hank, but a security blanket is something new. Am I a hundred percent pure wool?"

"Only between your ears," Hank said. He could say these things to Wendell and make them sound like endearments. But as they turned back to the others, Hank murmured to him, "But do me a favor and zero in on the kids' concerns, won't you? They're really waiting to hear from you on why you're leaving and how you feel about leaving. You'll touch on that?"

Wendell nodded. "Will do."

Rank had its privileges. He and Hocker were immediately loaded into the shiniest and newest of the Farm's official station wagons. Within five minutes of their arrival, they rolled out of the tiny airstrip area toward the VIP billet.

"I never cease to be astonished," Hocker told him as mile after flat mile of the Farm's area rolled past, "at just what sort of an inner society you DDO fellows live in. You fall on each other's shoulders like long-lost relatives. It's really a kind of . . . I don't know, extended family."

"Haven't you heard?" Wendell's eyes narrowed conspiratorially. "We're actually an invisible government. Ask any investigative journalist worth his salt, or any congressman. Or even, God bless them, the members of my class at Harvard. We goddamned spooks are always up to something that's illegal, immoral, or fattening. It's not too difficult to develop a siege mentality, us against the world."

"That's exactly what I mean," Hocker retorted. "You just gave me the kind of programmed response that illustrates this inner-group mentality I'm talking about."

"You're probably right, Angus," he said with a wink, but his tone belied the lighthearted signal. "It *is* a sort of us-against-them attitude on our part. And damned if I can see how it can ever really change. We're almost a different caste even inside CIA. In India, the Brahmins stick with Brahmins, untouchables with untouchables, right? Thirty years ago, when I started in the old DDP, I thought we were *all* honest-to-God Brahmins. We had the arrogance of youth, the brains, the energy. And we had marvelous motivation: a first-class enemy to square off against. We were the Can Do crowd. Now, after the public barrage against the

Agency over the past seven or eight years, we've become the un-touchables. Hard for an old Brahmin to accept that."

"The Director says we're all supposed to be one happy family," Hocker chided him, studying the bitter frown on the face of his fellow passenger. "All these Chinese walls between directorates have got to start tumbling down. . . ."

"Oh, indeed!" Wendell interrupted. "Look, Angus. I don't buy the theory that somehow we're all interchangeable parts in the vast assembly line called Intelligence. Trying to make an opera-tions officer out of a research scholar, or vice versa, won't work ninety-nine percent of the time. Exceptions may prove my rule, but it's apples and oranges all over again."

"Then what you're preaching is elitism, pure and simple. The clandestine services officer is a separate, superior species, and smells better than . . ."

". . . Smells *different from*, Angus." Wendell grinned. "If that makes me an elitist, guilty as charged. But there's a deep respon-sibility involved when you adopt an attitude that *your* people, DDO people, *are* the brightest and the best. And I can tell you with a heavy heart that our people have failed the standards, at least *my* standards, not once but many times." He paused and half to himself said, "Take Steve Browning, for example . . ."

Hocker, alert button eyes above the thin long nose, turned to-ward him.

"It's bothering the hell out of you, isn't it?"

"Yes," Wendell admitted, peering ahead at the narrow, empty high-crowned road. "Yes, it is, Angus, among many other things."

From the front seat, the officious young administrative officer stationed at the Farm turned to face them, sun goggles obscuring most of his youthful face. He cleared his throat and read from a clipboard.

"Sir! May I read your schedule for today? Arrival at VIP Lodge, 1150 hours. Lunch will be served at the VIP Lodge starting at 1200 hours, buffet style."

He looked up apologetically at them.

"The VIP Lodge is filled just now with a group of NFAC ana-lysts down here from Headquarters for some kind of brain-storming session, but they're departing when lunch is over. We've reserved for you, Mr. Wendell, the nice room at the end, the big one with the private bathroom, the one you liked last time, sir."

"Appreciate that," Wendell murmured.

"Dr. Hocker has the next one to yours." Hocker nodded.

The clipboard crept back into view.

"At 1400 hours, the DDO addresses the CT class in the small auditorium, followed by a Q&A period. We've left that open-end, by your request, sir. Free time, approximately 1600 to 1800 hours. Then we have a happy hour from 1800 to 1900 hours at the VIP Lodge. Dinner, again buffet style, is served 1900 to 2000 hours. The CTs have been invited to come over from their billets after dinner and sit around the fire with you. Bar will be open on the honor system from 2000 hours to midnight."

He looked up, as an excellent retriever would after depositing the dead mallard at his master's feet.

"How does that sound, sir?"

"First-class. You run a very tight show down here. That will be fine," Wendell assured him, and the worried young goggled face relaxed in relief.

Evening around the fireplace at the VIP Lodge. *That* was a moment he looked forward to very much. The warmth of the flames, crackling logs, and the drinks would relax the sense of deference of the CTs and they would gradually pitch into him on a number of issues that gnawed at them. No holds barred. The last time down, they had really taken him on concerning the Agency's support of the Shah of Iran in 1953.

"We couldn't *ever* do anything like *that* today," one hirsute young CT had flung at him, with a worried tug at his neat dark beard.

"You're damned right we couldn't," Wendell had retorted. "Because today is a different world. The *Zeitgeist* has changed. What was quite permissible and condoned twenty-seven years ago is totally impermissible now. But you can't damn us for doing what we did then. There were no ground rules then. There are now."

But, the worried young bearded one had continued, suppose they asked him to go out tomorrow and try to put the Shah's son back on the Peacock Throne again, and he didn't want to try. What then?

"I guess *I* would be part of the 'they' you speak of," Wendell told him. "But the top rung of that 'they' ladder would be the President. If you can't stomach what *he* tells us to do, be prepared to have the courage of your convictions and resign. Because if you didn't follow my instructions *or* resign, I'd fire you on the spot."

"How about my blowing the whistle to the press?"

"I hope"—Wendell's avuncular rumble took on a cutting edge —"that by the time you reach any such point, we'll have some federal legislation on the books that will put you in jail for blabbing secrets to the press. That's a kind of moral arrogance that could lead to disaster."

They had listened carefully, the young ones, and they frequently didn't agree, but these open, occasionally brutal exchanges had been good for his spirit and theirs. These quick clever young people who were fed to the teeth with some of the Shop's indoctrination bullshit wanted to hear clear signals, even if disagreeable ones. . . .

"We're at the Lodge, sir," the official young man announced. He sprang out of the vehicle and hurried to open the rear door on Wendell's side.

"Better enjoy every little perk that's left," Hocker whispered to him as he exited, unassisted, from his side of the station wagon. "Nobody opens doors for retirees."

"And retirees don't have to leave their homes to give inspirational sermons on Saturday afternoons," Wendell grumbled as they followed the young administrative officer, bearing their baggage, up a winding cement path to the motel-like Lodge.

"Ah, come on, George, you love every minute of it," Hocker hooted at him. And it was true. But a strange giddy sensation swept over him for a fearful second and he was thankful that Hocker was striding ahead of him on the narrow pavement and did not see him falter and pause.

CHAPTER TWENTY-FOUR

Wendell had initially hesitated about visiting the Farm on Saturdays. The working-week schedule of the Career Trainees was, after all, a tough and unremitting one, with much supplemental reading and writing up of operational problems on Saturdays and Sundays. The conventional thinking of the Training faculty was to turn them loose and give them whatever free time they could on weekends. But to Wendell's pleased surprise, most of the previous classes had without grumbling forgone the free time to sit and jaw with him. As Hank said, the opportunity for them to zing some uninhibited questions at the DDO was simply too good to pass up.

At 1400 hours, precisely on schedule, and stuffed with the Farm's buffet lunch, he perched on the edge of a modest table in the well of the well-illuminated but windowless lecture hall. Facing him were two dozen youthful Career Trainees, lounging and chatting around him in a semicircle.

They were a far cry from the white-male exclusivity of years past. He counted five women, three black and two Asian males. The Agency's Equal Employment people must be busting their britches with pride, he thought wryly. (Locked in a Neanderthal recess of his heart, never to be uttered, was his deep reservation about using women as clandestine-service case officers.)

All of the CTs were clad in what he derisively termed "shipwreck casual," from jogging suits to threadbare T-shirts and jeans. At the Farm, on weekends at least, the dress code excluded only nudity. Here too their garb did not fill his traditional soul with pleasure. ("You want them in uniform?" Hank had joshed him. "Each one wearing his little CIA beanie, cloak and dagger?") But heartening him, as always, were their faces: alert, reflecting intense and skeptical curiosity, an impatience with cant, a yearning to be talked to honestly. And today he could read it in their eyes: why was he, the quintessential Old Boy of the Service, packing it in?

They all were painfully aware of the buffeting the Shop had taken these past half-dozen years in the media and the Congress, and they knew that a large number of the Agency veterans, many of them bearing esoteric skills and irreplaceable know-how, either had retired early or had more or less ceremoniously been booted out. Was a new purge in the making? Anything that happened in the Puzzle Palace was of grave concern to them.

He waited until the babble died and the chief instructor had intoned the ritual introduction.

". . . and the floor is yours, George."

He stood motionless, erect, stern-eyed (the way DDOs and DCIs were supposed to stand), and intoned in what Maudie called his Churchill voice, "There's a mind-set in Washington that the Agency is filled with old school ties. And indeed it used to be that way. But would you please give me a show of hands: how many of you are graduates of Harvard, Yale, Dartmouth, Cornell, Princeton, Amherst, Brown, Smith, or Wellesley?"

Six hands went up, four male and two female.

"I thought so," he rumbled. "So much for the future of the Old Boy or Old Girl network in the Agency. The rest of you may consider yourselves from this moment on as members of a permanent persecuted majority in CIA."

The ripple of laughter was friendly enough. He had addressed six previous CT graduating classes at the Farm, as DDO. Usually he would lob to them an introductory irony or two ("Kipling relates a saying in the old Indian Army that in battle it was best to leave the butchery to blackguards led by gentlemen. That more or less describes our agent operations abroad . . ."), then a homily or two on the trials, tribulations, richness of experiences, and future friendships that lay ahead. Then Welcome Aboard . . .

But Hank had sensed the mood of his charges well. His soft-shoe graduation speech would not do.

Above him, in the last row of the semicircular seats, sat Angus Hocker, one heavy yellow hiking shoe conspicuously crossed over the other, a half-smile on his thin lips. He had every right to be present if he chose (after all, the health and well-being of these young staffers was his concern) but it somehow disturbed Wendell to see him there. With his wispy hair and long scrawny neck, he seemed a bespectacled vulture waiting . . . waiting for what? Then he remembered with a sudden rush of embarrassment that Angus had asked him during lunch if he could sit in on what Angus called the "preaching of the Gospel according to St. George," and that he had offhandedly assented.

Straight before him, and sitting slightly above his eye level, sat a slim attractive woman student in her mid or late twenties, hands folded on the table before her, blond hair parted in the middle and falling in smooth, straight lines like a golden waterfall. Her attractive brown eyes reflected an indefinable sadness. She was also the best-dressed woman in the room, with a stylish forest-green woolen dress. Her Agency badge dangled from her neck like a medallion. She wore no rings on her soft fingers. And for some reason, she looked familiar.

Wendell always sought to talk to one particular face in any audience. Hers appealed to him. It would be she he would watch today for evidence of boredom, credulousness, hostility, and, he hoped, some approbation. Her eyes held his unwaveringly as if to establish a private communication between him and her. Did he note a liquid nuance in those eyes, one of private concern or perturbation?

The throb-throb-throb of his pulse suddenly accelerated, exactly like the two previous occasions in his office, and a slow, almost exquisite squeeze behind his rib cage in the center of his chest intensified as if turned up by some internal rheostat. This time there would be no help; his medications lay in his room at the VIP Lodge a mile away. It was good to have the corner of the table solid and supporting under his haunch.

Feeling this way, he reluctantly abandoned any lengthy exhortations. These could wait until evening around the fire. And the Q&A would also have to be cut short. But, at that moment, the rheostat reversed itself; the chest squeeze ebbed.

"I don't know about you," he said, looking at one intent face after another, "but with a glorious autumn day like the one outside, it's almost a sin not to be out enjoying it. I hope to see at least some of you out at the Lodge tonight and we can have our usual gloves-off exchanges. So save your sharpest arrows for then. I want to make a couple of personal observations, followed by a few questions, and then we'll all get out in the sun."

A pleased murmur. An extra hour of Saturday-afternoon tennis or loafing was just fine with them. From the top row, Hank gave him a discreet thumbs-up gesture and handed a folded note to the student nearest him. Hand over hand the note was passed into the well and Wendell leaned forward to claim it. It had been carefully stapled, and the hastily written message read: "Forgot to tell you but one of these woman CTs, Maryanne Wolcott, is a niece of Steve Browning, on his wife's side. The one in the green dress. But no one in the class knows this, at her specific request. FYI."

He tucked the note thoughtfully into a trouser pocket, and looked up to find the unwavering russet dark eyes fixed on him. It was she! Of course she looked familiar: the pale blond features of Joanie Browning, minus the thick-lensed glasses, were etched on that composed, if somber, face. He could now understand more of that expression of half-submerged distress that had struck him when he looked at her the first time. She had learned what had happened to Steve.

"The news of my impending professional demise," he began, hoisting himself to a half-sitting position on the small table, "is unfortunately *not* greatly exaggerated. I will retire, with a total of thirty-five years of government service, within sixty days."

Almost defiantly he looked around at them, arms folded, noting with a wry satisfaction the expressions of consternation and concern.

"I think," he went on, "that thirty-five years is quite enough time to devote to any single government, and while there are some who never want to retire, I'm definitely not one of those."

He pushed himself away from the table and paced slowly to one side of the raised platform.

"I also think I'm right when I say that old CIA officers never die, and never fade away—they just become think-tank consultants somewhere—or come right back to work under contract." He waited for the amused ripple to die down.

"I know how disconcerting such things sound—all of a sudden, the DDO is quitting. Why? Is there a new RIF in the works? Is an outsider going to be appointed as DDO with as much knowledge about clandestine operations as I know about quantum electrodynamics? The answer to those, my dear colleagues, is: none of the above."

They were all looking at one another, eyebrows raised, and he sensed that this was what they wanted to hear.

"Before I go on," he said, now standing at the precise center of the narrow platform, "does anybody here know what a Bigot List is?"

A long moment of exchanged blank looks. The attractive young blonde in the forest-green dress slowly raised her hand.

"Miss . . . ah . . ."

"Wolcott, Maryanne Wolcott."

"Yes, Miss Wolcott."

Her voice was a firm, throaty, indefinably southern-accented contralto. Had he held his eyes shut, it would be the voice of Joan, holding the medals of her dead husband in her hands.

"I remember hearing that it was a World War II British intelligence expression for what we call Personal and Limited operations. It was a kind of a special clearance."

"Brava, Miss Wolcott. Entirely correct," he called to her. To the others, he said, "Very well, I'm putting you all on a special Bigot List, so that you must keep silent about what we talk about here . . ." He smiled at their discomfiture. "Until Monday morning."

He resumed his short-step pacing of the platform, grasping at the lapels of his worn jacket like a front-bench orator in Parliament.

"My departure is hardly the end of the world. Someone else will take my place. True, much cannot be passed along by me. The new DDO will have to rediscover where the old minefields are in Washington, as well as the new ones, whom to trust, whom not to trust, how treacherous it is to cut corners. He may also learn, as I have, that any Agency clandestine operation involving more than perhaps ten people isn't clandestine any more and gets printed with all due speed in the Washington *Post* or the New York *Times*. Which brings us to the classic dilemma of how an American clandestine intelligence service can function within an increasingly open American society. The answer to that one is: with enormous difficulty. But we have no choice."

Was he laying it on too heavily? They certainly all seemed to be listening.

"New ground rules have been laid down. And however restrictive those ground rules are, at least we have them. In the past, we had nothing in the way of rules, and we did things we've bitterly learned to regret."

Aha, the vise had tightened again, a great broad suffocating band, tightening with each step. And in his temples, a deliberate slow drumbeat, almost audible, preoccupying. He quickly anchored his body again on one edge of the table, jaws tight with his determination to continue.

"Another point: in our service, there's a kind of Gresham's law that goes to work: bad officers drive out good ones. And when you leave here, get assigned, and see a colleague doing unacceptable things by the current regs or by our own laws and you do nothing, you are as guilty as he. West Point has such a rule and it honestly ought to be adopted by us: one of mutual responsibility."

With enormous effort, he straightened his shoulders and looked around him, deliberately avoiding the stare from Hocker, who was leaning intently forward at him, hands on knees. He pointed an admonitory finger at the class.

"If you sense that your fellow employee, be he (or she) your closest buddy, is moving to some outer rim of psychological pressure for whatever reason, for God's sake, do something to save him! Tell Doc Hocker, sitting up there! Tell me! Tell somebody who can help! To know and to do nothing is . . . inexcusable, unforgivable."

Maryanne Wolcott lowered her eyes. There, she knew he had spoken directly to her.

He stopped. They were puzzled, all of them, a sort of stunned silence of expectation. Was that all?

"Let's have some questions," he heard himself say, as if from some distance. He mopped his brow, heavily beaded with sweat, until a student rose, a compact, cocky student, his bright red sports shirt open at the collar. Wendell nodded in his direction.

"Sir, we've heard some strange stories about the death of a senior staff officer . . ."

"You refer to Steve Browning, who was killed in a tragic encounter out in Los Angeles earlier this week."

His tone was brisk and businesslike, as if answering a familiar question under oath before a congressional committee.

"I served with Steve Browning in Italy and Austria in OSS. Incidentally, I am alive and standing before you because of his quick-wittedness and courage under enemy fire. So what I say about him is hopelessly subjective. But I may pre-empt another question by saying that he was *not* out there on Agency business: it was a . . . a personal matter."

Miss Wolcott's marvelously contained face, he noted, could not restrain unbidden tears from blurring the corners of her eyes. But something more had to be said, if he was to be as honest with the class as he had urged them to be with each other.

"Nonetheless," he intoned, too late aware that he had deepened again into his Churchill voice, "the case of Steve Browning is one that touches me deeply."

It was interesting to watch the faces of the instructors seated in the rear row, high above him. They were leaning forward in their chairs, waiting for him to explain.

"When I arrived with my OSS team in Austria in the last days of World War II, I quickly learned something that depressed me inordinately; that the Soviet Union considered itself at war with the United States, ideologically, politically, economically."

He was leaning into his pain now, speaking slowly and carefully. He hoped he could say it all and get back to his room without attracting any suspicions of these lynx-eyed young people that he felt ill.

"From the moment this Agency was created, its principal target quite rightly was the Soviet Union. And so it is today, over a third of a century later. And you all well know that the KGB and the Soviet leadership feel exactly the same way about us. For them, we are the Main Enemy. It's part of their doctrine, their training. Their goal, simply put, is to weaken, undermine, and if possible, without sustaining unacceptable damage, to destroy the United States' power and leadership of the free world."

He smiled grimly at the young CT with the red sports shirt.

"And what, you may ask, has that got to do with the price of potatoes? Just this: Steve Browning was a soldier in this silent war between us and the Soviets. He fell in that war as surely as if he had been cut down at the top of a disputed barricade. He fought well; his two Intelligence Stars and other commendations speak to that. But over thirty years is a long time to remain a participant in a war and the cumulative pressures, tensions, all exerted their toll on him."

For a moment, he faced them, head lowered, weighing the limits to which he could go. Their expressions seemed to reflect his inner turmoil. Just what was he trying to tell them? He caught the eyes of Maryanne Wolcott. Tell us everything you can, her defiant glance challenged him; Steve Browning is dead and you alone can speak up and explain his death. Otherwise, it had no meaning.

He carefully poured a half glass of water and sipped it in an absolutely silent room. Yes, there was something more to be said, for them to hear and for him to admit.

"In retrospect, there were many symptoms," he said, his eyes flickering from one of them to the other. "Things we should have been watching for in Steve's career, many indicators denoting accumulated stress and strain on him that we missed. In this I must bear my own share of the blame because I knew him well from our OSS days together. But, like other senior Agency people, I became absorbed in my successive jobs, immured in the endlessly busy bureaucracy of clandestine-service management. So did his other immediate supervisors over the years."

He glanced up at Doc Hocker, who pursed his lips, raised his eyebrows, and wriggled uncomfortably in his chair. Angus needed no pointing finger; he was part of the *mea culpa*, and he knew it.

"What emerges from this tragic business?" He spoke directly at Maryanne now to the exclusion of all others. "I said it a few minutes ago and I say it once again: in this strange and arcane calling of ours, in which we're all on one enormous Bigot List, unable to talk to others outside our service about so many things, the biblical admonition applies to us tenfold: we are our colleague's keeper and . . ."

And an enormous pang paralyzed his speech, tightened around his throat, and squeezed the breath from his lungs. He reached up with both hands as if to tear loose a leaden choker around his neck and he peered, swaying, at the hushed class through a thickening filter.

It was fascinating, he thought, how the floor rose up to meet him. For a split second, Miss Wolcott was in his vision. He wondered why both her slim hands reached out for him across the endless space between them. Angus Hocker's thin voice, now for some reason abrasively piercing, called to him, "George, for God's sake, George!"

He was surprised and embarrassed to find himself lying on his back, Miss Wolcott's face very close to his own, her hands cradling his head. Her image vanished and there was only the sound of that peremptory shout of Angus': "Hank, get the oxygen tank, quick!" Then: "Stand back, stand back! I need room for CPR!"

Maryanne Wolcott's face reappeared, blurred, just above him, and the touch of her fingers on his forehead was cool and dry and loving. Why did women want to get into this veiled, unloved calling? But Maudie always responded to that question with a derisive "There you go, the last of the male chauvinist spooks."

Too bad about this latest fainting spell. But with a few hours' rest, he could sit with them tonight. They'd all sit, drinks in hand, by the blazing fire at the Lodge and try to reach each other across the enormous space of age and experiences and make an effort to bridge the chasm of different times, different imperatives. The past needed so much explanation.

And tomorrow, Maudie, waiting in the Mercedes at the airport, would look at him with loving reproach as Angus and he approached. That wretch Angus would whisper in her ear and she would quietly drive him home, prepare a cup of hot bouillon, and tuck him into bed.

Then Monday would come, with Clare bustling to organize his desk and his papers and Kobler leaning in the doorway of his office, bursting to brief him on the flaps and recondite successes from all over the world. A good man, Kobler, and with more polish, more seasoning, he'd probably go far. Not his cup of tea, Kobler, with that raw ambition, but there were many pluses. . . .

He wondered at the distant thumps on his chest, the hoarse panting of Angus' breath as he straddled over him and blew his hot foul air into his mouth.

But there it was, suddenly, in a marvelously blinding golden light: the waving, undulating line of treetops beyond his office window, the high green wall swaying, beckoning. It was so easy to reach over to his Doomsday Book, with its quarter hours neatly blocked in for days ahead, close it, and step into the fresh clean air of the outdoors.

CHAPTER TWENTY-FIVE

Silas Ruffing watched the BMW sedan with diplomatic plates emerge from the Connecticut Avenue traffic flow and pull into a parallel service lane, where it halted. A uniformed black chauffeur alighted, courteously opened the rear door, and the sole passenger, a woman, emerged into the warm Saturday sunshine. She spoke a few words to him; he nodded, took his place behind the wheel, and drove off. Until the vehicle disappeared from sight, Silas did not move from his position under the awning of a boutique. Surveillance techniques cannot readily be shed, once well learned.

The woman waited for the traffic signal and walked sedately across the avenue. As she reached the sidewalk near him, he emerged from the awning's shade and approached her. For a moment, she stopped, frozen, as one would when encountering a ghost from another time, another world.

"For God's sake, Silas," she exclaimed with her soft Germanic inflection, pronouncing his name "See-las," "it's actually you! And just like Silas of old times—coming out of the shadows!"

"Mara," he said, looking at the soft, still-youthful cheeks and chin and the deep-seated eyes. "Why is it that time simply stops dead in its tracks for some people and ravages the hell out of others?"

She kissed him on both cheeks, firm busses given only to real friends. Mara smelled of expensive cologne, radiant health, and the good life. She was, he noted, wearing a chic form-fitting knitted suit of dark blue with a necklace of pearls and a pert little blue hat which deepened the color in her near-violet eyes.

"Thirty-three years later, Silas, and you still talk the same old *Quatsch*," she chided him, but she was clearly flattered.

"All right," he rejoined, "but don't you come up with the same old *Quatsch* and tell me how great *I* look."

He knew exactly how he looked. A mirror in the boutique window told him the unmerciful truth.

All this her alert eyes took in as she said with a smile, "We make a deal, Silas: today, nobody tells lies. Either we tell the truth or we say nothing? *Abgemacht?*"

And she held out her gloved hand in mock seriousness.

"*Abgemacht.* A deal!" He nodded and shook her hand in agreement. Pointing up the street, he said, "*Ein kleiner Spaziergang.* The restaurant is one block up."

He took her left arm, crooked it around his right elbow, and they moved slowly up the broad sidewalk. Thus they had strolled, more than thirty years before, arm in arm through the green parks of the Ring in Vienna. For a brief moment back then he had dared to hope that he could succeed Steve, become Mara's lover, to bask in the sunlight of those eyes and the approval of those youthful curled lips.

But the chemistry was wrong. He had taken Mara to bed two weeks after Steve had decamped from Vienna, in a musty room under the eaves of a rustic gasthaus in Grinzing. God knows she had dutifully performed the act of love to please him, and he remembered the warm sweet smell of her body to this very hour. But immediately he and she knew that it was no good. And the following morning, as they mournfully chewed through their breakfast in the *Speisezimmer*, both of them with eyes downcast, she finally had reached across the table, an ageless woman of sixteen years, and had touched his cheek with a smile.

"See-las"—he remembered her every word—"you are too much a brother to me. I can't . . . go to bed with you. Do you understand?"

He had nodded miserably and a sadness infiltrated his life which had continued from that moment to this. Yes, he understood.

And so, for the remainder of his tour in Vienna, they had walked and talked and eaten and laughed together, and had touched one another as two orphans from the same family. But never again did he feel that sweet yielding body next to his.

When he was ordered home, they had clung to each other on

the train platform of the Westbahnhof, oblivious to the outrageous comments and catcalls from the American military men hanging out of the train windows, and she had walked away without once looking back.

Now to his side glance, her once slim body was that of a svelte matron mindful of her weight. But the tilt and animation of her oval face was that of the sixteen-year-old Mara von Kueppke. That she was pleased to see him again was unmistakable, and the trill of her laughter, coming deep in her throat, was genuine. But then Mara never could feign anything. What she had experienced early in her life had burned all of that away.

"I hope your husband doesn't mind you having lunchtime trysts with strange men," he said to her, eyes gleaming slyly at her.

"He certainly would mind, Silas, if he knew," she answered in the same jocular vein. "But he's been away in New York City on embassy business with our Austrian Mission to the UN."

She caught his quizzical expression.

"Certainly you must know that I've been an Austrian citizen for over twenty years, Silas, and married to a dear and thoughtful man for much of that time. My Ernst has had a very good diplomatic career and there is much to come."

She peered sidewise at him with a puzzled expression.

"Your friend Steve Browning must have told you all this. We met a few days ago, as you probably know."

He patted her gloved hand on his arm and nodded soberly.

"Yes, I know, Mara. He told me, of course. He also told me you weren't that happy to see him."

Her wide lips curved in an ironic smile.

"We agreed we wouldn't tell lies to each other, Silas. No, I wasn't at all happy to see him. Although I must say that his—how do you say—his disposition, his outlook was very sad. All of those marvelous high spirits drained out of him. Life has not gone well with him, I think."

"You're right. Not well at all." He bit his lips to keep his tidings to himself. They could wait.

Sauntering up the tree-lined avenue with the dappled sunshine flickering at them through the leaves, she became expansive.

"But I *am* glad to see you, dear Silas! I remember with such pleasure how like an older brother you were to me. So kind you were, so . . . so *liebenswürdig!* Why haven't you called me sooner?"

"I honestly didn't know you were here until Steve told me. When did you arrive in Washington?"

"About three months ago. We have a very nice house in Bethesda off River Road. At last I got to America! How I dreamed of it back in Vienna! And you know, Silas, those things about America you used to talk to me about, most of them are true! It used to sound like paradise back in that miserable Vienna of cold apartments, little food, much fear . . ."

They reached the end of the block and Silas turned right for a dozen paces down the side street, to the entrance of the Eagle restaurant.

"I've never even noticed this place before," she observed as he held the heavy door open for her. "But then there must be a thousand *Spelunkes* like this one in Washington."

"The owners of this place would be deeply wounded if they heard you referring to it as a *Spelunke.*" His chuckle was genuine. "They would refer to it as the poor man's Rive Gauche."

It was a thin lunch crowd. They had arrived somewhat late and the outer room of the restaurant was three-quarters empty. Silas led her to a corner table as Mac-I appeared, white shirt open at the throat, dead cigar, as always, wedged in his mouth. His shrewd eyes narrowed with a conspiratorial recognition and he had the grace to extract the cigar from his mouth as he approached and spoke to them.

"Well, look who the tide has cast back on our shores!" he exclaimed to Silas with a wink. "And bringing in the beauty of the year." He turned a roguish eye on Mara, who smiled uncertainly back.

"How's everything in the back room?" Silas busied himself with a battered menu, not trusting himself to look up. "Everything OK back there?"

"Everything's OK back there," Mac said. "Maybe you'll say hello to the boys for a minute."

"Maybe for a minute, Mac."

He gnawed his mustache and peered up at the rotund figure.

"And what's for lunch in this gastronomic orgy?"

"The trout," Mac said, still appraising Mara with professional approval. "*Au meunière,* if you want to sound like a snob."

Mara nodded hesitantly. Mac was something new to her in the way of maître d's.

"Two trout *au meunière,*" Silas told him. "Bring a carafe of your best bathtub Chablis, some French bread, and a lot of thundering silence."

"We're beginning to get a picky kind of clientele in here lately," Mac muttered as he withdrew.

Mara watched his broad retreating back with an incredulous stare.

"Where on earth did you find this place?" she asked. "That fat little waiter is insulting, untidy! Is this the best you can afford?"

Silas said, eyes cast down sheepishly, "I rather like to come here. It's a . . . a sentimental thing. I should explain that this little restaurant is owned by people who have retired from the Agency. The inner room has a couple of *Stammtische* where my Agency colleagues eat and drink in a kind of private atmosphere."

Her eyes gleamed with malicious humor.

"So, that means that each table out here is . . . how do you say it . . . bugged?"

He patted her hand with an answering grin. "Only if the patrons are speaking Russian or Chinese."

He studied the ruby ring on her finger, a superb oval gem surrounded by a dozen tiny diamonds. The stone seemed to encapsulate a crystallized drop of blood. She followed his glance.

"I haven't worn this in years," she said with a sad sigh. "This ring is the only heirloom of the von Kueppkes that I still have. Everything else was stolen from me."

The ruby, he thought, was identical in color to those spreading stains on the shirt and slacks of Steve Browning as he lay dead on the library floor. . . .

Mac deposited the carafe of wine on their table with a growled "Courtesy of the management."

"What goes on here?" she asked, face and voice quizzical. "Free wine?"

"I'm an old customer," he said. "When they see me sad, they want to make me happy here."

She shook her head perplexedly.

"Just like the Silas of old: always talking in ironies."

"That's about all there is left of the Silas of old," he said. "Just like the smile of a Cheshire cat."

She peered at him intently. Something was quite odd.

It was hard, devilishly difficult for him to know where to begin. He deeply wished that this meeting had been what she imagined it was: a chance reunion, a *Wiedersehen*, after three decades, with the onetime American lieutenant who had been kind and fraternal to her, together with Mike Radescu, from the time she had moved in with Steve. Both had become her watchful Januses. And after Mike disappeared and Steve had departed, for a year longer he had made certain, in the military Sodom that was postwar Vienna, that Mara had sufficient food to eat, clothes to wear, and enough vitamin tablets to last her a decade.

It would have been marvelous simply to celebrate all that, and the fact that she had survived, married well, and had children. The thought that he had helped, that he had never exploited her (except for her work as a paid member of the excellent surveillance team he and Radescu had created), gave him a brief glow of warmth and gratification. But it chilled quickly. He had to get on with it, and damned if he could find the precise moment to do so.

He reached out distractedly and touched her short smooth fingers. They were warm to his touch and she moved them to touch his in return.

"Dear Silas," she said, as one says to a beloved relative long not seen.

He withdrew his hand, poured a glass of wine for each of them, and clinked her glass to his.

"*Servus, Schatzie*," he said.

"It's a long time since I heard that toast, Silas." She smiled. "*Servus, Herr General.*"

"I thought I was only promoted up to *Herr Oberst*," he said.

"You're old enough now to be promoted to general," she announced, eyes twinkling at him. "In Austria, age is important, you know. But that's the last promotion. You're never going to make *Feldmarschall*."

For just a moment they were not sitting in a tacky little restaurant off Connecticut Avenue in northwest Washington, but in an equally seedy gasthaus in Grinzing, near the porcelain stove. But two were missing: Steve Browning, attired in his best loden jacket with one huge paw around the sparkling-eyed woman-child named Mara, and the warmth exuding from the silent liquid-eyed Mircea Radescu, who sat puffing a small black pipe and took in the three persons who had become family for him.

Silas drank deeply from his glass. The wine was chilled and dry and had a decent bouquet, much like the table wine of Grinzing; less fruity, perhaps. Looking up at her from under his shaggy brows, he found her taking him in with an expression of pity she could not screen.

He tapped his glass with his fork, a fragile tinkling sound, in a wave of impatience to be done with this, to get out of here and be alone.

"Bad news, Mara."

"I see it in your face, Silas," she said, looking down into her wineglass.

"Steve is dead." He did not trust himself to look at her, the eyes widening, the wide mouth open in a silent gasp.

"It happened less than forty-eight hours ago," he said. "Out in California. It's not been made public yet but you'll be reading about it in all the papers or seeing it on TV, maybe by this evening."

For a moment he thought she would cry. She did not but reached hastily for a paper tissue in her handbag and mopped at her nose.

"What do you know of this, Silas?"

"I was there, Mara. Now listen, I can't tell you much for a variety of reasons, but he died in the home of Dimmy Calinescu. Dimmy's guards killed him."

She said, voice tremulous, "If he is dead, Silas, I am responsible. It was I who told him . . ."

". . . I know all that," he broke in, his words drowning hers. It was going to be hard enough to speak his piece without her self-incriminations. "But you didn't ask him to go to Dimmy Calinescu's place. He did that on his own. It was something that he felt he had to do. He was there with Mike all right but you have no responsibility at all."

Her eyes were now as they looked when she described decades

before what had happened to her in East Prussia when the Red Army came: dulled and filled with horror.

"Did Mike succeed? Did he kill Calinescu?"

"No." He let out the word like a whistle. "No, Mike didn't. But Steve did, just before Dimmy's guards killed him."

She sat stock-still, her eyes widening with disbelief. Silas stroked his shaggy mustache and looked away.

"And what has happened to Mike, that poor dear man?" Her eyes flashed with sudden animation and concern.

"He's all right," Silas said. "If you call 'all right' anybody who's spent three years in a Nazi concentration camp and over twenty-five more in Soviet labor camps."

She hid her face in her hands briefly, as if in secret prayer. When she revealed her face again, it was composed.

"And so you arranged all this to tell me these terrible things."

"Not entirely," he replied. "There were a couple of other reasons. Not the least was an irresistible wish to see you just once again. And because . . ." He looked helplessly around him, his words stuck in his throat.

". . . Because Steve asked you to?"

He nodded, gratified at her prescience.

"Yes, he did. And don't be upset when I tell you that he told me what to tell you while he lay dying. I have not told anyone else this, for apparent reasons." He licked his lips. "He said that if there was one thing he intended to do, it was to 'pay back Dimmy for that black eye he gave you, the one you had when he first saw you.'"

She twisted the ruby ring on her finger, eyes cast down at her plate.

The clatter of flatware and murmur of conversation floated to them from diners in the far corner of the room, and when Mara's head came up, Silas saw something he had never seen before: tears in her eyes. Her voice was tremulous.

"And what are they going to do with that sweet, kind Mike Radescu?"

"Well, he happens to have an Austrian passport. But it's a fake. So there's a technical charge of illegal entry. Then they've got to sort out his story and his background. Fortunately, it doesn't look as if he will be charged with anything involving Calinescu's death. It's just that he's in sad shape."

"*Mein Gott!*" she breathed. "Who will look after him?"

He smiled as does a golfer who looks down a difficult fairway at the distant green.

"Well, since I'll be a *Pensioniste* after the first of next month, I thought I might start a new career as career counselor for illegal Romanian immigrants," he said, looking over her shoulder at the U. S. Government heraldic symbols affixed in a double row to the wall. "And don't look at me like that, Mara: two losers deserve each other."

"I feel there's much you haven't told me about this dreadful business, Silas," she said. "Perhaps there's much you can't say."

"I told you what was important," he said. "Except for one thing . . ."

Mac approached them with heavy tread, and removed his cigar from the corner of his mouth long enough to say, with a jerk of his thumb, "Lunch is ready, Ruff. We're serving it in the back room."

To Mara, he made a deferential nod.

"Follow me, please."

Mara, startled, looked inquiringly at Silas. He shrugged and beckoned her to follow the stubby proprietor. They pushed through the saloon door one behind the other. The back room this day was empty of customers except for one person sitting at one of the round oak tables, a gaunt, almost cadaverous figure with carefully combed dead-white hair and sunken eyes that glinted moistly at them. Mara stopped and stared at the figure who rose just in time to receive the impact of her rush to him and her enveloping arms.

"Easy on him," Silas said as the two figures in close embrace rocked back and forth as one. "I've got to bring Mike back to Los Angeles next week in one piece. I've given the District Attorney my word."

Radescu bent his ravaged face, wet with his own tears and Mara's, to kiss her hand, murmuring, "Gräfin Marushka," when Mac intoned, "Now, will yez all sit down? Sort it all out while you eat. The trout is getting cold."